ENTITY

MERE JOYCE

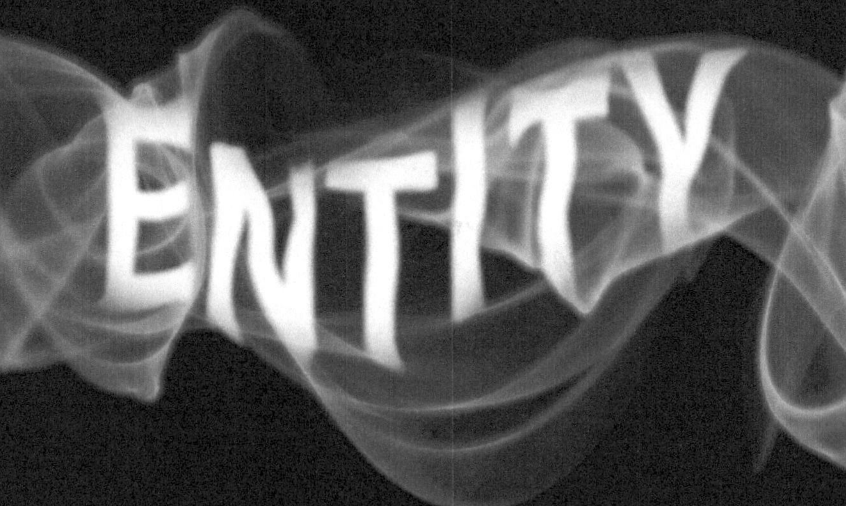

ORACLE OF SENDERS

Entity
Oracle of Senders Book Four

www.merejoyce.com

FOR EVERYONE WHO MADE IT BACK TO CAMP WANAGI ONE FINAL TIME.

WITH THE DARK INTENSITY OF TCHAIKOVSKY'S "HAMLET OVERTURE" streaming through my earbuds, I close my eyes and muse about how often beauty is inspired by death.

A profound line of thought, until it's cut short by my little sister pounding on my door.

Starting from my reverie, I pause the overture and glare across the room. "Rose, if you're here to bring me another club mix to listen to, I swear you're going to bear witness to the slow and torturous demise of my eardrums."

Rose pushes open the door and stands on the threshold of my room, her hands behind her back and an unimpressed expression gracing her features.

"You're the one who asked for music suggestions," she says.

"That's not music," I complain. "That's… noise. With a bit of heart-thumping anxiety thrown in."

She rolls her eyes. "Whatever, Beethoven."

I sigh, rubbing a hand over my face as I place my earbuds on the desk. "For the last time, Beethoven didn't have poliosis."

She doesn't miss a beat. "Whatever, Pavarotti."

I press my lips to keep from cracking a smile. "That's not even a composer."

Rose tilts her head to one side. "Whatever, Redenbacher," she continues.

"Rose…" I try to groan, but I wind up laughing instead. My sister stares at me for another few seconds. Then she starts laughing too.

When I catch onto a rhythm of normal breath again, I lean back in my chair and give her an exasperated look. "What do you want?"

Rose pulls her arm from behind her back and holds up a brown envelope. "Mail came. Package for you."

I stare at the package, my eyes growing wide and the hairs on my arms prickling. Before my brain's even formulated a response, I spring from my chair and lunge across the room to snatch the delivery from her hands.

"Why didn't you tell me?" I ask. I rip into the package, discarding the outer envelope and pulling out the smaller envelope within—this one shaded a deep, metallic blue.

"What do you think I'm doing right now?" she replies.

I spare her an irritated glance, waving the envelope in one hand while I fish out my phone with the other.

"You could have been quicker," I say. I study the envelope, then use it to make shooing motions towards the door. "You can go now."

"Thanks for the dismissal, Your Highness," Rose

mutters. She turns and starts to head out of the room.

"Rose," I say, halting her movement. She glances back at me, and I wave the envelope again. "Thank you."

She grins, then pulls the door shut behind her.

As soon as I'm alone, I open my phone messages and send a text.

It came.

The reply is immediate.

Meet me in five.

Scooting my chair closer to my desk, I close out of my music library and open a new video chat. My foot taps the overture's rhythm as I wait until, after considerably less than five minutes, the call is joined. A few seconds after his name appears, the video clicks on and Meander Rhoades comes into view, his cup of tea still steeping as he drops into his chair.

"It's about time," he says as soon as he sees me. "Does it always take so long for your post to arrive?"

"It's only the afternoon," I laugh, before realizing the implication of his annoyance. "Wait. Did yours already get there?"

"Yes," he says. "This morning."

I balk. "Why didn't you tell me?"

Meander shrugs as he reaches over to pull the tea bag from his mug. "I was waiting for yours to arrive."

I smile. "Did you open it?"

"No, not yet," he says. He takes a cautious sip before placing the mug back on his desk. "You?"

"Nope." I glance down at the envelope, my foot's tapping growing more intense. "Should we do it now?"

Meander stands and crosses his small room to grab the envelope from his school bag. He raises a questioning eyebrow, and at the signal of my nod, we open the envelopes at the same time.

For the past three years, I've received invitations to Camp Wanagi in April or May. But this year, those months went by with no word about whether camp would be occurring at all. Now, one week into June, my fingers trace the card's lettering, the invitation almost as surreal as the first time I received one when I was fourteen. That time, I couldn't believe such a thing as Camp Wanagi actually existed. This time, I can't believe it's almost at an end. This isn't my first trip to Camp Wanagi. It's my last. My final year as a member of the Shade sector. My final chance to work with the Oracle of Senders before I have to decide how ghosts are going to affect the rest of my life.

I read over the invitation, overwhelmed by the reality of the summer I'd honestly started to believe wasn't going to happen.

"Looks like we're going to Chile," I say, re-reading the description of our locale before glancing at the itinerary I've been provided. After our early dismissal last summer, I'm surprised there's not a note of caution tucked into the envelope with everything else—a threat of punishment should I do something crazy like sneak off on an international trip to perform an exorcism.

"My flight leaves June fifteenth," Meander mumbles as he reads over his own itinerary. "That's only a week from now. Not giving us much time, are they? My boss isn't going to be happy. He thinks I'll be graveside all summer."

My flight leaves on the day before Meander's, though I can't imagine our travel paths would have aligned even if we'd left our homes at the same time. Still, we're only traveling one day apart from each other. And we're both traveling within the next week. My head is already full of all the things I'll need to pack—not to mention the violin recitals I'll be dropping out of. I don't have a boss to annoy. But there will be angry instructors who were counting on my participation over the next few months.

Not that it matters. Not that any of that is even remotely important now. We're going. Camp Wanagi is running, and we get to have our final summer with the Oracle.

Together.

I look at the screen and see that Meander's head is bent as he reads over his documents. I watch him in silence, my smile growing along with my excitement until the latter can no longer be subdued.

"Meander?" He glances up at me, and through the screen our gazes lock. I bite the inside of my cheek to try and keep from grinning like an idiot, but it's no use. It's never any use with him. "One week until we're together," I say in a quiet voice.

Meander slumps back in his chair. He lets my words sink in, then breathes out a huff of disbelief before sitting forward with a beaming smile.

"One week," he repeats. He gives a breathy laugh. "Only one more bloody week."

I nod, gripping the invitation tight and trying to calm my leg, which has gone from toe-tapping to knee bouncing with the giddiness I can't seem to contain.

I am more than ready for this summer to begin. One week is not a lot of time. But it's long enough. Two years ago, I looked forward to attending Camp Wanagi. Yet even then, the final days of preparation were laced with nervousness of what I would find—of how the relationship Meander and I had built over our time at home would translate when we connected face-to-face. I don't have those fears anymore, nor do I fear whatever spirits might be waiting when I land in South America. I don't have any reservations about accepting the Oracle's invitation and joining my sector for another year of camp.

I'm not going to miss out on my final year as a Sender-in-Training. And never in my life have I been so happy to head for the dead.

THE NEXT WEEK EXISTS IN A PARADOX OF TIME, THE HOURS SPEEDING AND
dragging in equal measure. I pack, cancel recitals, and
listen to endless lectures from teachers and parents
both about how I am compromising my future chances
of success in favor of a few weeks of summer fun. The
days are frustrating, tiring, and overwhelming as I get
everything ready for the last-minute trip. But after six
days, two flights, and a two-hour car ride from the city
of Santiago, the busy rush is swept into the past as I
finally arrive at Camp Wanagi.

The black car pulls up to our destination, and my
brows furrow as its wheels slow to a stop. Climbing
from my seat, I step outside and wait for Dylan
Benowitz to exit the car after me, both of us staring
ahead as he slams the door shut before crossing his
arms over his chest.

"This is… What the hell is this?" he asks as we
survey our surroundings.

Dylan and I met up in New York, traveling overnight before sharing a car with two of the Wraith campers. The other kids stand a little away from us, their expressions as confused as ours. After three years of vastly different locales, I'm not surprised to find myself somewhere peculiar. But the Oracle has still managed to surprise me with where we've ended up.

"It's an unfinished eco-resort," the driver says as she unloads our bags from the trunk. "It'll be opening for business in October. You get a free trial."

June may be summer to Dylan and me, but it's winter in Chile now, which means we're not here during the peak tourist season. The temperatures are, thankfully, not too frigid, and my Wanagi sweater and fall coat are warm enough as we grab our luggage. Stepping onto a wooden boardwalk, we head along a path that stretches through a sea of grass and greenery. Far off to the right, the plain we're on rises, the hill gentle and probably sloping down into further fields of green on its other side. Ahead of us, the resort stands in the middle of the quiet landscape, a maze of boardwalks that wind among the grasses and plants. Closer to the resort's center, the earth between the wooden paths has been landscaped with gravel stone, flowered gardens, and benches for resting. Then the paths veer off again, traveling between large, bulbous domes I assume are the buildings we'll be staying in.

"Nice scenery, at least," I say.

"No water in sight," Dylan mutters beneath his breath. "Good start."

I nod in silent agreement, hitching my backpack higher on my shoulder and letting my violin case swing slightly as I walk. The Wraith campers managed to get their bags first, and they walk at a faster pace, eager to reach the biggest dome in the middle of the resort. But Dylan and I amble more slowly, taking in the landscape, each of us lost in our own thoughts.

"It's weird, being back," Dylan says after a moment.

"Yep," I agree. "It always is, isn't it?"

"Uh-huh." Dylan scratches his head, ruffling the dark hair that has gone from shaggy to unruly. I wonder when it was he last dragged a comb through it.

"You glad to be here?" I ask.

He lets out a quiet laugh and flashes me a grin. "Yeah. You?"

"Yes," I say with my own smile. Dylan nods, and we fall back into silence as we make our way up the path.

We enter camp through the main dome, a huge circular space that will eventually serve as the eco-resort's lobby. I'm surprised by the decadence of the dome's interior. The decor is awesome, everything carved from grainy wood and accented with tall plants of lush green. In the middle of the dome, a huge mural of deep blue-green mosaics tile the lobby floor. The outside of this resort was nice, if a bit rustic. But the interior of the dome is like a luxury hotel.

We check in at the desk with an Oracle worker who hands us each a key to the same dome. She points us in its direction, but when we turn from the desk, we veer instead to where Sabeena Kriti and Naasir Ereng are sitting at one of the huge wood tables set out in the back half of the lobby.

"We'll show you our rooms," Sabeena says after we've made our hellos. "We're all together in one of the…" she glances up at the dome's ceiling. "Whatever you call these things."

She finishes the glass of water she's been drinking and drops it in a dish bin before beckoning us to follow her. She looks small as she moves between the other campers, her petite size now accented by hair cut to shoulder length. She looks especially tiny with Naasir trailing a few steps behind her, his tall, broad form a dark tower next to her short, lithe frame.

"Each sector has their own place," Sabeena explains while we walk. We exit the lobby via a side door, stepping onto another wooden pathway leading straight out to a smaller dome. My arm comes up, and I instinctively swat the air as something flies by my face, until Naasir gives me a silent, reprimanding look. He reaches his hand out, and the insect lands on his finger as I force my arm meekly to my side. "Each one of these things has a common room, space for cooking, a bathroom, and two bedrooms," Sabeena continues with a smile. "The leads will bunk out in the staffing quarters in the main building. Everyone is close. Each sector is within walking distance to one another, and there's a pavilion ten minutes from here for the classes."

When we reach the dome, Sabeena uses her key to unlock the door, and I get my first glimpse of our new, temporary home. The dome is set up in similar fashion to the lobby, with one notable difference. My delight turns to panic as I look up at the ceiling—which is made of nothing but a mesh screen propped up with a series of metal poles.

"We have no roof?" I ask in disbelief. "Doesn't it get cold here at night?"

"The temperature drops to around freezing," Naasir says. He studies the ceiling with neutral contemplation. "Better cold than rain. It takes a long time to get the furniture dry."

I look between him and Sabeena, horrified by the prospect of sleeping in a glorified tent all summer.

Sabeena sees my look and laughs. "Don't worry," she says. "The roofs are still under construction. But the bedrooms and bathrooms are finished."

"Just don't leave your violin out here," Dylan mumbles. He glances around the rest of the room before giving Sabeena a skeptical look. "And what happens in the event of a sudden storm while we're having some quality lounge time?" he asks.

"There are tarps," Sabeena says. "I'm not really sure how it works. Alex told me there are protections, but they probably take a while to put up. In the case of an unexpected pour, your best course of action would be to… get out of the way."

Dylan nods. "*Wonderful.* So much for our good start."

"Your room is there, to the right," Sabeena says with a shrug. "Bathroom in the middle, and our room to the left."

My eyes veer to Naasir, expecting him to take over the tour. But he doesn't say anything—or even move from his spot by the dome's door—so Dylan and I head to the bedroom alone.

"This is preposterous," Dylan says. He ruffles his hair and lets out a laugh. "Just like it should be."

I smile, shaking my head as I push open the bedroom door. But once I've taken a step inside, my smile freezes in place—then falls altogether. The room is decorated as it always is, with black bunks and dressers. But this year, there are only two sets of bunks—only four beds in total. Last summer, one member of the Shade sector died. But that left five guys to share a room this year. Which means we're one bed short.

"What the—" Dylan drops his bag to the floor and eyes me sideways. "I take it by your surprise that it's not Meander who's bailed."

"No, not him," I say. My last text from Meander was on my phone as soon as we landed in Chile. He won't arrive here until this evening, but he messaged me from the airport just before he boarded his flight from the UK.

"Sefa?" Dylan says. "I don't believe it. I thought he was a lifer, for sure. Unless—" he looks at me. "You don't think anything happened, do you?"

I shake my head. "Sabeena and Naasir didn't seem too weird. But they have to know. If he was hurt or… worse, they'd be acting different." I wonder why they didn't say anything, although I guess it's not their job to explain. Sefa's their friend, not their responsibility. Still, the lack of preparation for this discovery makes it sting a little more.

"Well, at least I still have my trusty bunk," Dylan says. He picks up his bag and drops it on his usual bed, while I falter, not knowing if I should do the same. It feels stupid to be overwhelmed by a change in the furniture. And while I suppose it's not really the *furniture* that's making me a tad short of breath, regardless of the underlying cause, I'll be damned if I'm going to have an anxiety attack because I don't know which bunk to claim.

Luckily, I have no cause for freaking out. When I walk farther into the room, I notice Naasir's camp sweater tossed on the bunk Sefa usually used. It might be strange for him, sleeping on the top bunk after three years of being closer to the ground. But it means I can reclaim my usual spot across from Dylan.

I drop my stuff on the bunk, then take a moment to sit and catch my breath. My eyes stray to the far side of the room, to the wood-paneled wall that feels too empty without the third set of beds. I didn't think about what the room would look like without a bunk for Reed. But I never questioned that there would be five beds in the room. The empty wall makes me uncomfortable, and I force my eyes away from it to sweep my gaze up to Meander's bed instead. I know he's on his way. But I have to admit I'd feel a hell of a lot better if he were here now.

Dylan starts to unpack his belongings, rambling on about something he did a few weeks ago at home. He's trying to cover the stillness of the room, the sense of loss that has unexpectedly followed us from Greenland. For a minute, I ignore him as I work to keep my breathing steady. But when I realize what it is he's doing, I join in the conversation, making small talk until the room feels a little less dead.

We finish unpacking, then return to the resort's main dome. Alex appears through the bustle of campers, and we follow our lead for a tour of the campgrounds before she's roped into other duties by an impatient Sender carrying a huge sack of laundry.

Finished or not, the place certainly feels like a resort in full swing. Campers come and go, some of them people I recognize from courses, few of them people I really know by name. It's sort of like returning to the same place for a yearly vacation. The company is largely comprised of strangers. But there's an undercurrent of familiarity each time someone hurries past in a hoodie similar to my own.

"We're the oldest campers," I say after the tour, as we snack on chips in the lobby and watch a couple of Wraiths hugging each other by the front desk. "It's kind of weird."

"No weirder than just about everything else this year," Dylan says. He shrugs, but his eyes are uneasy as he watches the two younger campers laughing through their embrace. "Come on," he says when he finishes his chips. He crumples the bag and tosses it into the bin. "Let's go back to our rooms. The girls should be getting here soon."

No one is present when we return to the dome. Sabeena and Naasir both arrived yesterday, which apparently means they've had time to find other places to spend their leisurely hours. So, with only the quiet of Dylan's company and the breeze filtering in through our rudimentary ceiling, I lounge on one of the sofas and fall into a doze, sleepy from travel and the emotional toll of arriving to camp.

When I wake, it's to the sound of footsteps coming from the path outside, and Robbie's gleeful voice carrying over and down through the mesh roof.

"...get you sorted." He opens the door to the dome, and my eyes are drawn not to him, but to the girl at his side. A girl I haven't seen in almost a year—a girl I haven't spoken with in almost two.

I expect Dylan to bounce out of his seat as soon as our company appears. But he stays rooted to his chair, staring wide-eyed as Mim Castillo steps into the room.

She looks different than either of the last two times I saw her. She's gained weight since her stay in the hospital, and she no longer looks gaunt. But her hair is still longer, and although there is a pink streak of color to the right of her face, it's shaded a pale pastel rather than the vibrant hot pink of the past. More than any of those things, however, is the simple fact that Mim just looks older. I haven't properly seen her in two years. With everything we've all gone through, it feels more like it's been a lifetime.

"Hello," she says when she sees us. Her voice is calm and soft, no crackling energy or nervous strain edging the word. She sounds as she looks—mild and still.

"Mim." I stand up and move forward stiffly, unsure if I should hug her or just stay back where I am. I end up lingering by the arm of the sofa until, after a pause, she moves farther into the room. Her suitcase rolls over the dome's tiled floor as she shortens the distance between us. She looks me over, smiling at my hair as she points to her own.

"We match. Sort of," she says. I smile too, and she leaves her suitcase behind as she moves in so we can share a brief hug.

"It's good to see you," I say.

Mim's eye lock with mine, a moment of contact I'm not used to with her. "It's good to be here," she says. "Thank you."

I know what she's thanking me for, though it's not really me she should be thanking. Nevertheless, I nod, and she steps back as her eyes travel over to Dylan. He looks like a scared puppy staring up at her from his spot on the sofa. For a moment, the room is tense with expectation. But then Dylan sighs, pulls himself up, and rounds the sofa to throw his arms haphazardly around Mim's shoulders. She laughs, hugging him back. Then his grip tightens, and he whispers something in her ear while her eyes start to shine.

I avert my gaze to give them a moment of privacy and focus instead on Robbie. "Nice hair," I say, admiring his overly ambitious mohawk dyed in about five different shades of purple.

Robbie grins. "I thought it'd be nice and mellow. I see you're still sporting your updated look."

"Easy maintenance," I say, as if I've decided that keeping the white in my hair, eyebrow, and eyelashes falls under the same category as simplifying my haircut.

"Nothing easy about it," Robbie says as he studies my head. I'm not sure if he's referring to the short pompadour style of my hair—which is slightly more dramatic than I used to bother with but which makes me feel particularly grandiose whenever I'm dressed in my recital suit—or if he means the reality of losing pigmentation because of an encounter with a ghost. Either way, I give him a nod as Mim and Dylan stop embracing. She turns away to discreetly wipe her eyes, and Robbie thwarts any potential for an awkward pause by showing her to her room.

CAMPERS FILTER INTO WANAGI AT DIFFERENT TIMES, ALTHOUGH THIS year, it seems like everyone in Shade is arriving early. Meander's flight doesn't land until late afternoon, which means he won't reach the resort until the evening hours. But at the very time his plane is rolling to a stop on the Santiago runway, Kornelía arrives at the dome.

Dylan notices first. After Mim has settled, and Sabeena and Naasir have returned, we talk about our time at home until Dylan's nose suddenly lifts. His eyes veer to the mesh of our roof, then his head whips around in the few seconds before the door unlatches. His senses are both impressive and slightly disturbing. But it's not actually Kornelía's presence that he's picked up on—it's someone else's.

When the door swings open, a snout appears and, for a second, I wonder if a wild animal has wandered into our tent. But as the dog walks into the room, I spot the harness with a handle on its back, one I soon realize is being gripped by a familiar hand.

Back in December, Kornelía Tumisdottir lost whatever remained of her sight. I knew my friend was now blind. But I didn't realize she had acquired canine assistance, and my guess is that no one else did, either. A quiet hush falls over the room as Kornelía and her guide dog enter the Shade dome. We all remain silent until Dylan gets up and crosses the room.

"Who's this?" he asks with innocent curiosity as he goes to the young German Shepard and straight away begins to scratch behind its ears.

"Dylan, you're not supposed to pet a guide dog while they're working," Kornelía replies in a stern voice. She stands tall and straight-backed, though even her serious expression and rigid stance can't hide the fluid grace of her figure.

Dylan's hand snakes back to his side with her reprimand. "Oh, right," he says. He gives her a sheepish smile. "Sorry."

Kornelía's mouth remains a tight line for about half a second before it breaks into a grin, and her shoulders relax into a more comfortable pose. "It's all right. I knew you wouldn't be able to resist."

Dylan grins too, immediately forgetting the reminder as he returns to petting the dog. "It's a he, right? What's his name?"

"It's Dylan," she replies at once.

Dylan looks up at her, his expression caught between flattery and mortification. "R-Really?"

Kornelía laughs. "No," she says. "I didn't get to name him. But we are well-matched. His name is Draugur. It's the Icelandic word for ghost."

Her eyes are still the same tawny shade, but they are unfocused as she twists her head to one side. Even so, she seems to know what—who—she's searching for. Her neck turns with confidence, the movement stopping only when her face is directed at Mim.

The other girl stands, gliding over as softly as Kornelía herself might. The two come face to face, both of them looking surreal in their altered ways. Dylan gives Draugur a final pat. Then he steps back while the girls embrace.

Kornelía may not be able to see anymore. But nothing about *her* has changed. If anything, it feels already as though Kornelía is more herself now than she was last summer when she was forced to wear the myodiscs. She hugs Mim, Dylan, and me with as much light warmth as ever. Her smile is bright, and her whole manner radiates ease. Even when she surveys the room, her unseeing eyes take everything in with a serene sort of grace.

"Sefa's not here," she says after a few seconds, her words simple and solid as fact.

"Robbie said he'd explain tonight," Sabeena says. Her voice is sad, though she perks up in a rush to add, "you don't have to worry, though. It's nothing to be concerned about."

I'm relieved Kornelía doesn't mention Meander's absence, even if I don't need to be. I know he's on his way. But he's the only one missing now—at least for those of us coming back. Kornelía's intuitive understanding of this year's Shade roster is a comfort, and her silence confirms to everyone else that he will, indeed, arrive.

Yet even so, I'm mildly anxious as we eat dinner

and take another walk around the campgrounds. Our group is incomplete, and in my mind, the most important member has yet to arrive. I try to hide my nervous anticipation, asking the others about their homelife and talking a little about the last violin recital I had in the spring. But my mood is not truly lightened until sometime after seven, when Kornelía shifts in her spot on the sofa next to me, her arm reaching out to give my knee a pat.

"He's here," she says.

I don't even question how she knows. I only squeeze her hand where it still rests on my leg, then stand and cross the dome as the door opens and Meander steps inside.

His eyes find mine immediately, though I'm distracted from locking gazes with him when I notice the small cut on his cheek—a cut that wasn't there when I talked to him yesterday. I step closer, eyeing the cut until I catch his expression and know he doesn't want to talk about it in front of everyone else. And that simple knowledge—that this is not a private conversation shared over a computer, that we are, in fact, together in this room full of people—makes the always surreal moment of seeing him in person settle firmly into fact. My smile spreads, and I rush forward to tackle him in a hug. Meander breathes out a laugh, dropping his bag and clutching me tight. His lips press softly against my neck, and a small tremor vibrates down my body from the point where our skin touches.

I offer to show him to our room, proving myself a terrible host as I ignore everyone else and lead him away with every intention of grabbing his sweater and pulling him into a proper kiss as soon as we're alone. But when the door is shut behind me, Meander again lets his bag drop to the floor, before he turns around and pins me to the wall instead. I grin as he pushes closer. Then my arms encircle his neck, and my chin tilts up so our lips can finally meet.

This isn't the first time I've seen Meander since last summer. In December, he came to Canada for Christmas break. And in March, my parents surprised me with tickets to London—a guilt present because they wanted to take Rose to Disney World and worried how I might scar her for life if I came along and saw someone unexpectedly dead. Knowing they didn't want me on the trip hurt. But when I realized their compromise was to let me visit Meander, a weird, tangled part of me was thrilled with their decision to appease their guilt by sending me overseas.

December and March were brilliant. But it's been three months since Meander and I have touched, kissed, or been close enough for our breaths to mingle as we stand face to face. We talk every day, so this moment is all about making up for the physicality we've missed. Hands roaming and throats mewling with desperate noises that make both of us laugh, we kiss fierce and deep until we're breathless. Then we stand so close our lips hover, both of us beaming as we stare into each other's eyes.

"Hey," I say. My fingers twist in his hair, while his thumb strokes the edge of my ear.

"Hey," he repeats. He kisses me again, a soft, chaste kiss that makes me hum in approval.

"How was your flight?" I ask, returning the movement.

"Long," Meander replies. He kisses me and presses

our bodies a little closer. "Yours?"

"Long," I agree. I push back against him, and soon we're once more lost in a fog of happy oblivion.

Only when we hear Robbie's voice out in the main room do we force our mouths apart. We take a quiet moment to stand together. Then I gently grasp his jaw so I can look more closely at the cut on his face.

"What happened?" I ask in a cautious voice. My finger traces the air above the cut, careful not to touch it. I have two suspects for who may have committed this small atrocity. Well—one subject, and a whole host of possible dead people.

When Meander's eyes fall to the floor, however, I know this wasn't the work of a ghost.

"Mum threw a plate," he mumbles. My hand stills, my suspicion hardening into disgust. Things have always been bad at Meander's home. But lately his mother's job hasn't been going so well, and when Meander refused to tell her where he kept his earnings from his work—earnings he used to travel to Canada in the winter and London in the spring— things became considerably worse. She didn't want him to attend camp this summer. In the past, she was happy for him to disappear for a couple of months. Now, she wants him to share the misery of being stuck at home with her.

"Meander…" I don't have any profound wisdom to bestow. I can't offer any practical help, and he already knows how I feel about this horrible situation. So, I don't say anything else. I only lower my hand to his shoulder and pull him against me until he drops his head and wraps his arms tight around my back. He sniffs once. Then he pulls back and composes himself with a breath before turning around and, for the first time, noticing our new bedroom set-up.

"Who's missing?" he asks.

Despite the morose topic, I can't help smiling at his question as I direct him to the empty dresser drawer that'll be his for the summer. He was in the room with everyone a moment ago. Yet he appears not to have noticed the collection of other Shades.

"Sefa," I tell him. "Although I don't know why. Robbie said he'd tell us tonight. Which means he's probably waiting for us now."

Meander glances over his shoulder with a smirk. "How long do you think it will take before we piss everyone off with our continued absence?"

"At least a few more minutes," I say. I step forward and kiss the back of his neck. Then I help him unpack his things.

When we finally force ourselves out of hiding, we find that Alex
has also joined our group. She and Robbie have raided
the snack bar, and the coffee table before the sofas is
full of drinks, chips, and a few leftover fruit bowls
from the dining hall. I retake my seat next to Kornelía,
while Meander drops onto my other side, his leg
pressed to mine and our hands resting close.

"Welcome back, everyone," Robbie says as soon as
we're seated. "It's good to see everybody again."

"Except that we're not all here," Sabeena replies at
once.

"No, we're not," Robbie says. He glances at Alex,
then steeples his fingers together under his chin.
"You're probably all aware by now that Sefa won't be
joining us this summer."

"We are," Kornelía says. "But we don't all
understand why."

"Then it's a good thing I'm such a deep well of

information," Robbie says with a grin. "Sefa wanted to return to camp this year. But, something happened at home. His grandfather passed away."

A slight pang strikes in my chest at the mention of a dying grandfather, and I think of my own long-deceased—but only recently gone—relative. Sefa sees the ghosts of the elderly, and he's always held a special place of honor for the grandparents that raised him. This must have been a horrible tragedy for him. I'm sorry for his grief.

"How is he doing?" Mim asks.

"He's okay," Sabeena answers in Robbie's place. She tucks her shortened hair behind her ears. "We talk every couple of weeks. He's sad, but his grandfather was sick and in a lot of pain before he died. Sefa knows he's at rest now. So, it's okay."

"But he has his grandmother to take care of," Robbie continues. "He couldn't leave her alone, which is why he won't be joining us here in Chile."

"We wanted to let you know," Alex says, "that he's still working with the Oracle. He's doing some course work—something the rest of you don't have to worry about now that you're final year campers—and he might even manage one or two case files closer to home. He's still a part of Shade. He always will be, even if he's not here."

"We're all still part of Shade," Robbie agrees. "No matter who is no longer here."

The dome we are in this year is large, and with the mesh ceiling overhead, it feels a little endless. The nine of us—seven Shades and two leads—are tiny in its fold. To think we started as twelve Senders makes my stomach hurt, and I shift my hand so I can twist a finger around Meander's. We are only nine, but we could easily be eight. Or seven. Hell, if the whole of last summer had gone as disastrously as some of it did, this year could have seen only six Shades remaining in all.

Robbie and Sabeena talk more about what Sefa will be doing in Samoa while the rest of us listen. After a moment, Meander's gaze casts about the room, silently taking in our dome and the sector mates within it. Unlike everyone else, he didn't have a big reunion greeting, mostly because I ambushed him the moment he entered the dome. I don't think he minds, though. He's not one for attention, and he looks content to size up the differences in our camp mates for himself—knowing full well I'll fill him in on any details he's missing later.

I watch him survey the room, his fingers stroking the side of my leg as he examines his surroundings. His stare lingers on Mim for a fraction longer than the others, but aside from that, he's completely calm in the face of everyone's changes. He doesn't even seem surprised by the sight of Kornelía or Draugur, whom Dylan still sits next to, his hand on the dog's back. Meander observes the others. Then he relaxes into his seat as Robbie explains more about the course work Sefa will be partaking in at home.

The sector stays together until Kornelía announces that she needs to take Draugur outside. Sabeena and Naasir stay in the dome to have a longer chat with our leads, but the rest of us—the five of us who have not all been together for two years—head out for a walk along the wooden paths.

"It's strange, being here," Mim says after a little while. She hugs her arms close to her chest as she walks, her whole body swaying as if she's wading through gentle water. "We're all strange now, aren't we?"

Not many would argue that statement. Dylan, with his gray skin and wild hair, walks with one hand close to Draugur's snout. Kornelía holds the guide's handle, her eyes staring into an endless nothing as she glides along the boardwalk. Meander still wears his collar high, always careful to hide the scars on his neck, though the one on his jaw remains ever visible. And I suppose I've got the white of my hair to remind everyone that something in me has changed too.

"We were always strange," Dylan remarks in a low voice. "It's just getting harder to hide it."

Mim tilts her head and studies him, her stolid look eventually breaking into a soft snort of laughter. Dylan catches her gaze in the corner of his eye, and the two smile at each other from opposite sides the boardwalk, while Kornelía stands between them—lost in her own dreamy world as she walks, content and serene, with her dog.

At the back of the group, Meander's hand finds mine, and we share a private smile of our own as our fingers lace together.

Being here is strange. Being here for the last time is even stranger. But here tonight, walking the paths with these particular people—it's not really strange at all. Everything is different. Everything is always different at Camp Wanagi. But our differences have brought us here. And, despite whatever hell we're thrown into over the next ten weeks, in this instance, *here* is a very good place to be.

WE STAY UP LATE OUR FIRST NIGHT AT CAMP, TALKING OUT IN THE MAIN room until, one by one, everyone trickles to bed. I'm as tired as I always am after travel and reacquainting myself with camp. But Meander and I stay up the latest, waiting for the others to disappear before snuggling closer to resume our earlier catch up. I want to stay on the sofa all night, talking and kissing until I fall asleep curled against his chest. But when the sun disappears the temperature drops, and eventually it's too cold for us to keep looking up at the stars through the mesh of our ceiling.

When we step into the bedroom, the hum of the heater and the humidifier for my violin make me wonder how long it will be until someone complains about the noise. But then my stomach twists, and I remember that Shade's most vocal complainers are not here anymore. For a moment, I linger in the doorway, staring at the empty wall where the last set of bunks should be. At some point this altered sight might settle into normalcy. But as I push myself beyond the threshold, my skin still skitters with the oddness of our new arrangement.

Entering the room makes me vaguely uneasy. But once I climb into bed, the humming dark is quick to pull me into a heavy sleep. In the morning, I'm the last one to wake—a feat that would make me feel lazy, if I wasn't rewarded for my sleepiness by waking to the soft comfort of Meander stroking my hair.

"Morning," I mumble when I open my eyes to see him sitting on the edge of the bunk.

Meander smiles, his fingers trailing along the patch of white on the right side of my head. "If you want to keep sleeping, you can," he says. "But everyone else is going to the lobby for breakfast. They thought you might want to come along."

I stretch my arms over my head, then prop onto my elbows. "Are you going?"

"I don't know." He shrugs. "I don't fancy a busy dining hall. But I am in dire need of tea."

"We have a kitchen in here," I remind him as I sit up more fully.

"It doesn't have a kettle," Meander complains. He swipes disheveled hair from my eyes before leaning in to plant a quick kiss to my lips. "What sort of kitchen doesn't have a bloody kettle?"

"You should have smuggled one in your bag," I say, smiling with the sleepy warmth of this utterly casual—and remarkably tactile—conversation. "Lesson learned for next time. From now on, you don't go anywhere without an emergency tea kit."

If we had a kettle close at hand, the temptation to

decline breakfast in favor of spending the morning together might be too hard to resist. But perhaps the lack of a ready excuse is for the best. This is, after all, the last summer I'll have with the only other people I can truly call my friends. The reality of our post-Sender futures is creeping in like a soft current leading to the sea, and if I wasn't already aware that everyone is together for only a short time more, Sefa's unexpected no-show has made it abundantly clear. One way or another, I intend to be with Meander again after our time as Shades has come to its end. But the others? I have no idea when—if—I'll ever see them again.

I want proper alone time with Meander. But I don't want to feel guilty while I have it. So, as much as it pains me to push away the possibility of a few extra private moments, I make myself get up so we can be social.

Meander joins the rest of the sector in the main room while I grab the quickest shower I can manage so I don't make everyone wait too long for food. My hair takes more time to style these days, and it's the one place I won't rush. But I hurry everything else to make room for it, and I'm quick enough that, when I make it out of the bathroom, only Dylan is at the point of commenting.

"About time," he says when I step into the main room. "I'm freaking starving!"

"Sorry," I say, smiling at the sight of him sitting cross-legged on the floor, Draugur's head in his lap. He scrambles up from under the dog, while on the other side of the room Sabeena 'tsks'.

"You shouldn't be doing that," she says. "Guide dogs aren't pets. Kornelía, you should tell him off before he causes problems."

Kornelía stands, and Draugur follows. The two of them move in tandem as she leads the way out of the dome.

"It's fine," she says with a gentle laugh. "If it were anyone else, I'd tell them to stop. But Dylan's... different with dogs."

No one can argue that, and Draugur doesn't seem at all perturbed by the spoiling. He is on full alert as he walks by Kornelía's side, guiding her along while the others follow her lead. Meander's eyes stay stuck on the pages of a book until I run a hand a through his curls to remind him of his surroundings. He's startled by the touch, and I smile at the familiar sight of his post-reading confusion as he blinks out of his haze. Then he drops the book as he stands, grabbing my hand so we can make our way to breakfast.

The lobby dome is packed, which has the effect of making our small camp appear much larger than it probably is. The noise is overwhelming, voices echoing in the rounded space and bodies crowding together as everyone tries to find a seat at the long benches set out for our meals.

"I take it back," Meander mutters as we survey the lobby, his voice mostly lost amidst the clatter. "Tea can wait."

I've never been as averse to crowds as he is, but the sight of the bustling campers makes me regret this decision too. The room is chaos, and it's not even full. The newest campers—the fresh batch of Revenants— won't be here until tomorrow night. I can't imagine how ridiculous mealtimes will be then.

Kornelía's presence attracts attention, and some of

the younger kids clear seats so that the seven of us can sit together. It's a peculiar reaction, but I suppose to the others we're a peculiar bunch. Everyone is affected by spirits differently. But our sector is out of the ordinary, even for Camp Wanagi. Most groups don't have coma victims—or deaths. Most campers don't have such obvious physical damage from the spirits they see, either. I remember our very first night in France three years ago, when Robbie saw a ghost and bled from his ears, while Alex's eyes rolled back a little in her head. I remember how strange those sights seemed then. Now, I don't think I'd blink at such a response to the dead.

I tug Meander's hand to keep him close as we make our way to the table. The others look as confounded by the crowds as we do, at least, and we all share bewildered glances as we take our seats.

"This is, like, a proper camp or something," Dylan says.

"Awesome, isn't it?" Robbie asks as he appears from nowhere to slide in alongside Dylan. He's got a plate loaded with French toast and scrambled eggs, and the sight of it makes my stomach pinch with hunger.

"Awesome's not the word I'd choose," Meander grumbles.

Robbie grins. "It's not so bad." He attacks his eggs with a fork, spearing a heap and holding it up towards the ceiling. "The shape of the roof makes it echoey. But the food's great."

The food does look great, so I push back from the table, eyeing the line to the counter and the separate line for the beverage station. Apparently, every single camper came for breakfast at the same time. There can't be more than about thirty of us in total. But the cramped back half of the lobby where they've placed the tables and the breakfast stations makes the wait feel like it's going to be endless.

"Come on," I say to Meander. "You get us tea. I'll get us breakfast. If we survive the hoard, we'll reconvene here."

Meander smirks, standing to follow me while Dylan slumps in his chair with a huff. "Tag-teaming meals is cheating," he says.

"I'll get you a juice," Mim says with a roll of her eyes. "You grab the biggest plate you can find. Just make sure to bring me some toast, okay?"

Dylan sits up and flashes Mim a grin. "Deal," he says. He pops up from his chair and brushes the top of Draugur's head. Then he bolts for the line.

I'm surprised by how easy Mim and Dylan are together—how easy they both are with Kornelía as well. As far as I know, nothing has ever been officially resolved in terms of Dylan and his dating switch from one girl to another. But so far, neither Kornelía nor Mim has been out of sorts in his or each other's company. Of course, neither girl has given Dylan any seemingly romantic attention, either. I don't know what's played out between them, if anything. But I'm happy they're all on speaking terms.

I join Dylan in the wait for breakfast, which takes considerably longer than the beverage line. By the time I make it back to the table, Meander's already three-quarters of the way through his tea.

"If yours has gone lukewarm, I'll drink it and get you a hot one," he says with a nod towards my mug.

"Is that genuine concern for the quality of my

beverage, or a secret hint that you want another cup?" I ask.

Meander takes the plate I've made for him, smirking as he starts in on a small bite of French toast. "Probably a little of both."

I take my seat and dig into my own toast, while further down the table, Sabeena folds her arms on the wood top.

"Do we really not have any courses this summer?" she asks.

"Mhnnn," Robbie says, incoherent through a mouthful of egg. He shakes his head and swallows before answering in proper English. "That's right. No courses."

"But why?" Sabeena presses. "Courses are important. This is our last summer here. Our last chance to learn."

"You'll be too busy for coursework," Robbie says.

"Doing what?" I ask. Honestly, I haven't given my schedule a single thought. Up until yesterday, my mind was totally preoccupied with getting here—not with plans for what Sender activities I'll be partaking in for the next ten weeks.

"You'll be doing lots of things," Robbie says with a shrug. "Starting today with scouting out a spot for Sunday's initiation."

"We get to see ghosts today?" Kornelía asks. Her voice contains a note of excitement, and I remember what she told me about her blindness—that she's only blind around the living. Kornelía exists in a world of what she describes as 'white nothingness', except when she's near ghosts. I'm sad her choice has become the invisibility of life or the solid sight of death. I'm also horrified by the fact that she must look forward to visiting haunted places just so she has something to see.

But of course, Kornelía's not me. She, like Sabeena—who continues to badger Robbie about the importance of structured lesson plans—has always been genuine in her eagerness to help spirits. Given how unpleasant seeing ghosts is, it's a continual surprise to be reminded of how differently my sector mates feel about their Sender abilities. After three years, I've learned that releasing a spirit can be profoundly good, and I get why what we do is important. But I don't like it. I never will. And it's strange that no one else seems to share that opinion.

Well, almost no one else.

"Line's short," Meander says, his gaze back on the beverage station. His arm brushes against mine as he pushes back from the table. "I'm going to grab another tea. I'll get you some orange juice." He stands and looks down at me. "The bloke ahead of me was complaining that it's all pulp. So it should be right to your tastes—you freak."

"There's no point in drinking orange juice if you don't get any orange in it," I say in total seriousness.

"Right," he says. "Unless, of course, you aren't a fan of chewing your beverages?"

I give him a stern stare. "It adds texture," I argue.

Meander breathes out a laugh, and for a moment, his eyes linger on mine. Then he gives my neck a gentle flick as he turns to rejoin the line.

I watch him go. Then I shift to listen to Sabeena's continued diatribe, all the while understanding exactly why it is I'm not disappointed to be missing out on courses this summer. I don't really care what my schedule looks like. Because I didn't come back to Camp Wanagi to study the Sender craft. And while I'll make the effort to spend time with my fellow Shades, they're not the reason I'm in Chile, either. Almost no one understands why I dislike being a Sender. But three years ago, I found someone who does. Somebody who gets my feelings about the dead and gets my feelings on just about every other topic too. Someone who gets *me*. Completely, and perfectly, whether we're facing down ghosts or running away from them—whether we're dealing with the dead or sticking solely to the joys and frustrations of life.

6

"SO, HOW ARE WE SUPPOSED TO KNOW WHAT KIND OF GHOST THE NEW KIDS see?" Sabeena asks as we wait for a van near the front of the resort.

"We have a list," Robbie says. He flashes his clipboard, then ducks as a wasp flies by his head on route to Naasir. Shade's most stoic member lets the wasp dart in and around his fingers, like it's performing in an obstacle course.

"Any new Revenants who can see dogs?" Dylan asks after we've all paused to take in the insect's mystifying flight.

"No…" Robbie begins as he slowly turns his head away from Naasir. "You're still the one and only."

"Damn straight," Dylan replies, although his quiet tone fails to cover his disappointment.

Mim gives him a consolatory pat on the shoulder. "What are the new abilities?" she asks.

"They range," Alex says. Our other lead pushes hair

behind her shoulders and lets her sunglasses drop down over her eyes. "They always do. We'll let the campers themselves tell you the details. We don't want you forming ideas before you've had a chance to meet them in person. But today we have three locations to scout—three places that should align with the campers' experiences."

It's nice the Oracle is respecting the Revenants' rights to tell their own stories. But normal camps wouldn't lead an expedition without crucial know-how like being acquainted with everyone's medical info. Sometimes, ghosts are a cause of physical pain. It'd be nice to know beforehand if we're likely to need a first-aid kit at the initiation—or a stretcher to roll someone away.

When the hired van arrives, we pile in and spend forty-five minutes driving through the brilliant Chilean countryside. Hills, valleys, and blue pools of shallow lake pass by the window, while I listen to Mendelssohn's "Symphony No. 4", my shoulder pressed into Meander's as he reads a thick paperback with a spine so cracked some of the pages are coming loose from the binding.

The first location we stop at is a restaurant at the edge of a town. I'm not sure if the building is still in operation, but the dining room is closed when the van approaches.

"There've been a few reports of unusual activity here," Robbie explains as we climb out of the van and begin wandering around the building's exterior. Alex retrieves a key for the lock, and Naasir follows her inside to look around.

"If we end up here," Meander says, peering through

the windows at the cramped kitchen with its stove tops and ovens, "I'm not going in."

"We won't end up here," Kornelía replies. Her head moves gently from side to side, as if she's trying to spot someone in a moving crowd. "There aren't any spirits here."

"Not sure why the rest of us were even invited back this year," Dylan says, one hand already sliding to Draugur's head. "You can do the job just fine on your own, Korni."

Kornelía smiles. "Just because I can see them doesn't mean I can communicate with them." She tilts her face towards him. "And besides, I only see humans. What would we do without our dead dog whisperer?"

Dylan grins, but as he studies her face, his own falls into a more solemn expression. His hand continues to scratch at the guide dog's head, while his eyes search Kornelía's until she sighs.

"Stop staring," she says.

Dylan starts, looking embarrassed to have been caught—and spooked that she knew what he was doing. I smile at his sheepish expression, then amble off to continue exploring the restaurant's exterior until the others return to the van, ready to move on.

The second place we arrive at is more promising. As soon as we climb out of the car, Kornelía begins to nod.

"There's a spirit here," she says.

"Draugur doesn't seem bothered," Dylan remarks.

Kornelía smiles. "He never is. It's one of the reasons we bonded so well."

As we walk towards the house, I feel the shift in the air, a slight chill that hints at the ghost but suggests it's probably not one I'll be able to see. Still, I head up the walkway with everyone else, prepared to go inside. But before we've reached the front door, Meander clears his throat, a quiet, strangled sound that rings alarm bells in my head.

"We'll stay outside," I say, trailing back to his side.

"You don't have to," he mumbles. "If you want to go in—"

"You know I don't want to go in," I tell him.

He smiles, stepping a little closer to let the others pass around us. I'm happy for the excuse to get a few minutes alone with him, but my hopes are disappointed when Mim stays outside as well.

"It's not easy," she says by way of explanation as she steps over to where we stand. "Being near them."

"You decided to come back," I say. "I wasn't sure you would."

She smiles, a soft smile I've only seen on her a few times. "Neither was I," she admits. "But I know I need to face what happened, so I can learn how to make the most of my talent going forward. It's not easy, but... I needed to come back. I need to prepare."

"Prepare for what?" I ask.

"My final project," she says.

I give her a dubious look. "You already know what you're doing for your final project?" I haven't thought about what I'll do, though I suppose maybe it was stupid not to plan ahead. Campers travel all over the world to face their last Wanagi ghost. And this time, no one is going to select the spirit for me.

I grip Meander's hand, bothered by the notion of having to prepare for our departure from Chile—not to mention the reality of either one of us having to face a ghost. Soon, we'll be tasked with choosing our own case and trying to release a spirit all by ourselves. And while I'm hopeful Meander and I can find ghosts located in areas close to one another so we won't be totally apart for the second half of our summer, given our past exploits, there's a chance the Oracle will make us plan for releases in different regions.

That's not a possibility I'm yet ready to entertain.

"I've had a lot of time to think about it," Mim replies in response to my question. She stares into the distance as she contemplates her own upcoming trial, her fingers twisting in the beads of the rosary I've noticed she no longer keeps hidden under her shirt.

Above us, something smashes against one of the upstairs windows. The three of us jump as the glass breaks, and soon Robbie's head appears in the pane.

"Shit," he says next to the hole in the glass. His head turns away, but his words continue to filter down. "This place is uninhabited, right? No one's going to come after us for the window?"

"Was that from the ghost?" Mim calls up.

Robbie's head peers down at the three of us still outside. "Nah," he grins. "Alex's just trying to kill me."

"All I did was toss you the keys," Alex says from inside the house.

"Chucked the keys," Robbie argues. "Right at my head."

Mim smiles, then lowers her eyes. "It must be weird for them too," she says, distracting us from their bickering. "It's their last summer as well."

I hadn't considered that, but of course she's right. And unlike the rest of us—most of the rest of us—Robbie and Alex have been attending Camp Wanagi in one form or another for eight years. I have no interest in returning to camp as a lead for the next generation of Shades. Two of us will, and I'd make a guess as to who, if I could. But I don't know my friends as well as I sometimes think I do. It's one thing to assume that Dylan will befriend any dog that comes his way, or that Kornelía will know who's about to enter a room a beat before everyone else. But I have no idea who would like to return to camp, or who might think they've got something valuable to pass on to the next group of campers.

After the others have returned outdoors, Kornelía and Alex discuss the haunted house for a solid fifteen minutes. Then we get into the van and head to the final spot on our list. The third place is not a dwelling at all but a boggy plain next to a small lake. I'm a little uneasy as we step out of the van, my eyes drawn to the lake's edge. But before I've even noticed her sidling up beside me, Kornelía places a hand on my shoulder.

"The spirit didn't drown," she says in a calm, quiet voice. "She's behind us, out in the field."

I smile, putting my hand on hers and giving it a little squeeze. "You are wonderfully eerie," I say. "Thank you."

Kornelía gives me a tinkling laugh. Then she drops her arm as Robbie calls her name.

"We've heard it said that this ghost was left here, abandoned after a fight with some friends," Robbie says to her. "Can you tell if that's true? Any of it?"

Kornelía starts towards the spirit's location, her steps more cautious than usual over the unfamiliar terrain. She lets Draugur guide her, the dog's walk easy and sure as he pads across the field. It's a spectacularly surreal sight to see her in her white dress, the dog before her and Robbie's mohawk bobbing along to her left. I watch them move a little ways into the distance. Then I lean against the side of the van and let my gaze shift to Meander.

"Do you feel anything?" I ask.

He shakes his head as he comes closer, one shoulder dropping against the van door. "Nope. Might be too far away. Might be too weak or too… neutral for me."

I smirk. "If only there were more neutral ghosts."

"Ones just vaguely bored of the whole 'being a ghost' thing?" he asks. "I suppose those wouldn't be too bad. How much boredom can you pull out of someone?"

"I wonder if anyone's ever *actually* died of boredom," I muse.

Meander laughs. "You're such an idiot."

"I'm serious! Like, what if someone just… couldn't make themselves care anymore? Not because they were depressed or suffering or anything. Just because they were, you know, *bored* of the living experience?"

Meander shakes his head, amusement dancing in his hazel eyes. "Maybe somewhere there's a Sender with a talent for that," he says.

"Maybe," I say with a frown. "What a crappy talent to have, though. It'd be rather *boring*, wouldn't it?"

He breathes out another laugh and reaches a hand to my waist. Before I can make any further stupid remarks, he stops me with his lips. I smile into the kiss, resisting the urge to tangle my fingers in his hair by more discreetly pressing a hand to his chest as he pulls back far enough to meet my eyes.

"Bloody hell, I've missed you," he murmurs. And even though we've talked every day for the better part of the last year, I know exactly what he means.

"Yeah," Robbie yells from across the field, interrupting our moment, "I think this one will work!"

He walks back with Kornelía, the two discussing something among themselves. Closer to us, Alex makes notes on the clipboard, while Naasir stands amidst a visible cloud of insects—the remaining three Shades watching him in awed dismay.

"So, if this spirit isn't, you know, bored enough not to care about my presence," Meander says close to my ear, "I'll have to stay back here during the initiation. Out of harm's way."

"*We'll* stay back," I say, swiping at an errant curl dangling near his eye. "Out of harm's way... Out of everyone else's too."

"My thoughts precisely," he says.

I think of tomorrow night, the rows of campers watching whatever show happens with the ghost while, in the dark quiet of the shadows, the two of us stay out of the spirit's range. Where it's safe. Where we're alone.

My smile spreads and I lean back into Meander just as Robbie claps his hands startlingly close to my ear.

"Time to pack up!" he says in an overly cheerful tone. He eyes the two of us with a knowing smirk, and my cheeks flush as I try to remember that the Oracle didn't pay my expenses so I could spend the entire summer wrapped in Meander's arms.

Even if that would be a totally valid use of Sender funds.

7

Sunday is overcast and chilly. Workers on the resort make a racket putting the tarp over our dome in anticipation of rain, so we spend the day spreading out and exploring the campgrounds and surrounding foothills. I don't see the new campers. But by the time Meander and I get back to our dome late in the afternoon, Sabeena and Mim fill us in on their arrival.

"They looked bewildered," Sabeena says as we sit on the sofas.

"I certainly was our first year," I say.

"Part of me wanted to warn them off," Mim admits. "They have no idea what they're in for."

"But they're in for it, no matter if they're here or not," Meander says.

Mim sighs. "I know. But it makes you wonder how bad it would have gotten, if we hadn't ever come."

"Maybe not as bad for some people," he acquiesces. He opens a hardcover he checked out from the camp library, his attention already shifting to the pages. "But probably worse for others."

"I wouldn't ever warn them away," Sabeena says. "We need this place. I can't imagine going through this stuff alone."

"Me neither," I say. I think about the days before Camp Wanagi, the days when I went to therapy and learned to keep everything ghost-related to myself. The possibility that there might be others like me was a hope I never dreamed I'd be given—actually *meeting* others like me was a dream I could never have hoped would come true. Things haven't been easy here, and there are several incidents I wish could have played out differently. Some people might have fared better without the Oracle in their lives. Maybe people like Mim. Almost assuredly people like Reed. But I found what I never thought I would here. I wouldn't give that up, no matter how hard it was to reach this point.

The dome's outer door swings open, and I blink out of my thoughts as Dylan walks in from the path, a bag of chips held up to his lips and Naasir trailing behind him.

"Isn't that, like, your fourth bag today?" Mim asks, her face wary with distaste as she eyes Dylan's snack.

"I have no idea," Dylan says with a shrug. He empties the bag and wipes his mouth before looking around at the rest of us. "What's up?"

"We were talking about the new campers," Sabeena says. She drops her legs from the sofa to make room.

"Right," he says as he drops onto the sofa's far end. "Initiation's tonight. So... Are we going to be drill sergeants like the Entities were our first night here?"

Mim snorts. "I can just see you demanding everyone

stand at attention."

"I can be commanding," Dylan says through an extremely unconvincing whine.

"I'm sure you can," Mim replies.

Sabeena props an elbow on the armrest and rests her head in her palm. "I guess we're supposed to dress up."

"We don't have to," Mim says. "It isn't a game."

"It kind of is, though," Sabeena says. "The costumes, the midnight waking… It's meant to be a show."

"And look where it got us," Mim says. "If I recall, we were all almost killed by a falling building during our initiation."

Meander looks up from his book, at least halfway still listening to the conversation at hand. "I'll stay out of the way tonight," he says. He glances at Dylan. "Besides, we're doing this in an open field. Last time we tried that, we were attacked by dogs."

"Not *attacked*," Dylan says. "And it wasn't my fault the dogs came. I didn't draw them."

"Based on your track record, I'm not so sure about that," I say.

Dylan glares at me like I've double-crossed him. "Excuse me, murder boy. You were involved in that collapsing building too. At least my dogs didn't try to crush everyone."

"No, they only tried to tear our flesh apart," Sabeena chimes in.

"Who's tearing flesh apart now?" Robbie asks.

I look over as he, Kornelía, and Alex enter the dome together, the trio back from some meeting with one of the camp's instructors. Kornelía's the only Shade who's done any work so far this summer. She's been talking with instructors and the new Revenant leads, preparing for tonight's event.

"No one," Mim says. "We were just reliving old initiations. Do we really need to dress up and all that tonight?"

Robbie shrugs. "Don't have to, I guess. But it's much more fun if you do."

"The new campers are always unsettled," Alex agrees. "It helps to make a bit of a production."

"I'm not sure the weird outfits and late-night mystery helped me feel any easier," I say, remembering how bizarre the whole of our first night in France was.

"Ah, but you remember it, don't you?" Robbie says.

Meander scoffs. "We almost died. I think we'd remember it with or without the fancy dress."

Robbie waves a dismissive hand. "Don't be so dramatic. You didn't almost die." Meander fixes him with an unimpressed stare, and after a moment Robbie relents. "Okay. You *may* have almost died. But really, that's life, isn't it? A series of events where you almost die, until one happens where you actually do."

"Very inspirational," Meander deadpans, while I laugh.

Despite my own lack of conviction, when Sunday's midnight hour approaches, I don't hesitate to change into my ghost-seeing outfit. The gray suit I wear to violin recitals fits overtop the ridiculously perfect regency-era shirt Meander gave me as a long-belated birthday present last year. The lacy cuffs flow down to cover half of my hands, while the ruffled cravat sits neatly between the modern suit's lapels. I button the jacket and place the green square of fabric from Reed Vodden's sweater into the breast pocket. Then I chain the outfit's newest addition—my grandfather's watch, which my grandmother had repaired and given to me after Christmas—to the belt before tucking it into my pocket.

I stare in the bathroom mirror, touching up my hair and knowing I look absolutely ludicrous. But I can't help smiling at my reflection, anyway. Day-to-day, I dislike being noticed by onlookers curious about my hair. But dressing like this invites the attention. I *know* I'll draw stares in this outfit, and people will *definitely* think I'm strange.

It's weirdly comforting. And perhaps Robbie is a little bit right. It's kind of fun too.

When I get back to our room to put away my regular clothes, Meander is sitting on my bunk. He grins when I walk through the door, and I still find myself blushing under his interested gaze as he stands to greet me.

"Think I will appropriately weird out the newbies?" I ask as he crosses the room.

"They're not going to forget you in a hurry," Meander replies.

He steps close and traces one finger along my jaw. When his arm lifts, I realize he's got something wrapped around his wrist. I reach up to take his hand and step back to see the same thing wrapped around his other wrist too. Turning over his palm, I study the tartan pattern tightly wound around each arm as my eyebrows raise in curious amusement.

"Is that my scarf?" I ask.

Meander glances at his arms, his cheeks flooding with pink. "Sorry," he mumbles. "I sort of unintentionally nicked it from you at Christmas. I didn't realize I was still wearing it until I was halfway across the ocean."

I feel along the fringe of the scarf I gave Meander to wear when he visited me in December, my lips spreading into a smirk. "You thief," I tease.

"I may also be guilty of property damage," he admits. He holds up both hands. "Thought if I cut it in two, I could use it to protect my wrists. Make them, I don't know… less vulnerable to attack."

My eyes widen as I realize what he's suggesting. "Meander, is my scarf your first collection?"

He laughs when he sees the excitement in my face. "If that's what this is, then… yeah. Suppose so." He gives my foot a kick, his smile turning slightly shy. "Sorry I stole your scarf. And, um…. ruined it."

I take his hands in mine and bring him to my lips. "It's yours," I murmur against his mouth. "I'm glad you've found some means of protection. They also look pretty great on you."

"You won't even be able to see them under my jacket," he says. "And they're more for practicality than aesthetics. I'm not going to be tromping around in the dark, pretending I'm a hipster or some such nonsense. I'm not—"

His rambling complaint is cut off by a knock on the door, and I give him another amused smile before I turn to answer it. Mim is on its other side, her arms encircling a big heap of cream-colored yarn. She doesn't even take in my unusual appearance. She glances right behind me, to where Meander still stands between the bunk beds.

"Can I see you for a minute?" she asks. Meander's expression seems as confused by her request as I am, but he shrugs, while I make an awkward motion to tell them I'll leave. Mim, however, shakes her head, patting my arm as she walks through the doorway. "You can stay. This won't take long. I just… I wanted to give Meander something."

She pads across the room and holds out her bundle. When Meander lifts it from her grip, I see that it's not a pile of yarn but a cable-knit cardigan crocheted—I'm sure—by her hand.

"This is… what's this?" Meander asks, clearly unsure what to do with Mim giving him a present. I smile, having a better idea than he apparently does of what this might be for.

"It's a way of saying…" Mim sighs, her eyes rising to the ceiling. "I don't know. 'Thank you' seems stupid. But… It's for what you did. Last year. For being willing to do it, no matter the risks." She looks back down at him and smiles, before her look hardens into a more familiar fierceness. "Anyway, it's for you. And you'd better appreciate it, because I didn't make anything for anyone else." She throws me an apologetic glance. "Sorry, Cal."

My smile widens into a laugh. "I didn't do anything. He's the one who deserves the gift."

Meander examines the cardigan, the cream yarn adorned with wooden buttons and a higher-than-average collar. He eyes the neck, then gives Mim a curious glance.

"Oh…" she makes a vague motion towards her own neck. "That was Kornelía. She… told me. Not just about that. She… She told me about a lot of the things I missed." She glances at me again, discomfort etching her features. She looks like she's going to say something else, possibly about what happened in the cave in Tonga. But before she can amp up the awkwardness of this situation, Meander cuts in.

"Thank you," he says in a bit of a rush. "It's very nice." He rolls his eyes at his own words as he drapes the sweater over his arm. "Honest. It's… I'm not used to getting gifts, so… thank you."

Mim smiles, looking relieved at the change in subject. "You're welcome," she says. "I'll go now." She turns to leave the room, stopping on her way by to give me a proper once-over. "Of all the people I would have expected to dress in something like this, it wouldn't have been you."

I nod. "Mmm. Dylan, right?"

Mim laughs. "Right." Her gaze sweeps over my suit, her eyes resting a moment on the green fabric in my breast pocket. "I like it," she says at last. "You're a lot different than the last time I saw you, Cal. But I think that's good?"

"It is," I say.

She nods. Then she leaves the room, while I turn back to Meander.

"What were you saying about not being a hipster?"

He shakes his head, staring at the cardigan for a long moment before putting it on. The garment is bulky, but it still fits tight to his lean frame. The cream looks soft and inviting next to the vibrant red and green pattern of the scarf, and when he does up the buttons, the collar comes high enough to cover most of the scar on his neck—though a small portion still peaks out in the front.

"I guess I'll do my part to freak out the new campers too," he says, glancing in the mirror and touching his fingers to the faded mark of the garrote rope.

I stand behind him and wrap one arm around his

waist. "You're not a freak," I remind him.

He meets my eyes in the mirror, and I rest my chin on his shoulder as he leans his head back.

"We're completely normal," he says. "*And* we're total freaks. I suppose it's all a wash, in the end. Either way—" He lifts his head and turns around to face me properly, "—we're here. Together. Which I suppose means it doesn't matter what we look like to everyone else."

I reach up and let my fingers glide along the scar on his neck. Then I raise them to his chin and bring him into another kiss.

When we make it out to join the others, I'm unsurprised to find Kornelía in her white dress, her bare feet and the new addition of Draugur giving her an even more otherworldly appearance than in previous years. Sabeena wears her sari, and while Mim seemed dubious about the whole idea of dressing up, she has her rosary and a pink shawl knotted over her collarbone. Naasir is wearing his usual clothes, but he has the ring he was given during our first year at camp, along with a metal arm band that coils around his forearm and ends in twists that look like an insect's wings.

The six of us all appraise one another, before everyone turns as the bathroom door opens and the last member of Shade steps out into the room.

"Well, what do you think?" Dylan asks.

I don't even manage a double take at his appearance. One glance is enough to make me—and half of the sector—burst out laughing.

"What the hell are you wearing?" I ask.

Dylan is dressed in what can only be described as a mustard yellow, pin-striped gangster suit—complete with matching fedora.

"What?" Kornelía asks, her chin turned and her grin wide. "What is he wearing?"

"A unique yet stylish ensemble perfect for a night on the town," Dylan says.

"You look like Dick Tracy," I reply through my laughter. "From the movie, not the comic."

"Dylan, you *can't* wear that," Mim chimes in.

"And why not?" Dylan asks. "Everyone else gets to wear costumes. I decided I would too."

"You'd never actually wear that if you were looking for a ghost," I say.

"Of course I wouldn't," Dylan replies. "Because I seem to be the only sensible one who doesn't need to play dress-up to get shit done."

"That Dick Tracy's official motto?" Meander asks.

Dylan glares at Meander, though it's hard to take the expression seriously with his hands on the hips of the outrageous suit. "Shut it, Scarface."

My neck bristles at the name, and I open my mouth to warn Dylan to shut up. Before I can, however, Meander leans into my side, his expression thoughtful.

"I'm not up on popular film," he says to me. "But Scarface is cooler than Dick Tracy, yeah?"

I grin, nerves settling with relief. "Definitely."

"Whatever," Dylan says. He wipes imaginary dirt off his shoulders and tugs his fedora down over his eyes. "I didn't don this beauty for you sorry bunch. We've got a show to put on. It's go time."

"Is it out of your system yet, or are you going to be saying action movie dialogue all night?" I ask.

Dylan considers the question, then shrugs one yellow-mustard shoulder. "Haven't decided yet. We'll see where the night takes us."

"Well, that's as true a statement as we're going to get," Mim says. She stands, readjusting her shawl before heading for the door. "Let's get this initiation started."

As we cross the wooden boardwalks at five minutes to midnight, Naasir veers off into the shadowed greenery. When he rejoins us, he's picked up some kind of beetle that probably shouldn't even be active in the winter and yet lively skitters over his arm. Meander gives me a sidelong glance, and I smirk as we fall back a step to stay well out of the insect's path.

The Revenant dome is on the opposite side of the lobby, and when we enter the sector's living quarters, we find the main room empty. The new Revenant leads—Ralli and Anna—are already at the initiation spot waiting for the arrival of the campers. Our chosen location is too far away to walk, so there are two vans waiting out front to take the rest of us over once the new kids are ready to leave.

"Which way do we go?" Dylan asks when we're inside the main room.

His uncertainty almost makes me laugh. I remember

when we were collected our first night by campers who seemed confident and cocky. Maybe we're just a particularly uncool bunch, but none of us looks like we have a clue how we're actually supposed to accomplish rousing the new recruits.

"You go that way," Kornelía says, pointing a finger to the right. "The girls are on the other side."

Or maybe I'm wrong. At least one of us knows what she's doing.

Dylan glances behind him, then motions for Naasir, Meander, and I to follow. At the door to the new campers' room, he hesitates to cast another gaze our way. He nods, as if it's a signal we worked out beforehand. Then he throws open the door and barges into the space like he's totally used to waking strangers in the middle of the night.

A chorus of groggy, confused complaints greet my ears as five boys are addled from their sleep. They do, indeed, look bewildered as Dylan claps his hands and flicks on the lights, giving them a full view of his gray and mustard glory. They also look young. Way younger than a few years our junior. I remember when I started at camp and first met my mentor, Daniel. I thought he seemed so much older—and wiser—than me. Now, I understand why. It's not just the fact these kids are younger than we are. It's that they haven't yet experienced the full effects of being a Sender.

"Let's go, kiddies," Dylan says, taking charge while the other three of us stand back in looming silence. I don't have the energy to command the Revenants to line up and march out of the room. It's weird enough seeing my past reflected back at me—weirder still when the boys start heading out of the room, each of them staring at us with a grotesque sort of awe.

"Who are you?" one of them asks as he walks by. He wears all black, and his dark hair is so long it completely covers his eyes.

"No time for questions!" Dylan calls, evidently reveling in his newfound power. "Move it!"

"You should have worn a drill sergeant's get-up," I tell him as he files out behind the last kid.

Dylan grins. "Maybe I should have gone in with some speak-easy. Probably would have freaked them out even more."

"I think you've done a good enough job of that already," Naasir says. "Let's go. The girls will be waiting."

Whatever effect we had on the campers is nothing next to their dumbfounded state upon seeing Kornelía. She stands before the group in the main room, her arms raised wide in what I suspect is an unnecessary show of theatrics. I'm relieved to see her playing up her vision loss. What happened to her was life-changing and, one could easily argue, devastating. But tonight, Kornelía is having fun with it. After everything that's happened, I'm glad she's able to do so.

"Tonight," she says, her voice higher and more lilting than normal, "we are going to see a girl. I don't have to tell you that she's not exactly what you would call… living."

She grabs onto Draugur's handle, and the dog lets out a low, loud bark that startles half of the campers. Kornelía takes a moment to let the sound fade until the quiet of our surroundings settles creepily over the uneasy Revenants. Then, without another word, she turns and leads the way.

We walk outside and load into the vans, letting the new campers travel together so they can speculate among themselves about what they're going to face. When we arrive at the edge of the boggy field, the vans stop a little way back from where the rest of camp waits, and we wait for the Revenants to unload before guiding them on. The whole process feels a little ridiculous from our angle, but I can tell the new kids are as bothered and confused as we were our first night at camp. I've never been convinced the Oracle's penchant for secrecy is necessary. But it is effective to lead the campers out on a midnight stroll in a foreign country. Effective, if not a little cruel.

I'm glad when we reach the other sectors, the group parting to let the new Senders into the middle of the semi-circle they've formed. Kornelía walks directly into the clearing to pass off the Revenants to their leads, while the rest of us hang back, filling in the spaces at the edge of the group and keeping a respectful distance from the spot of paranormal activity—lest we interfere with the new campers' chance to shine.

"We still don't know anything about these kids, though, do we?" Dylan asks as Ralli and Anna welcome the new recruits. "We don't even know what their talents are."

"Someone must be able to communicate with this ghost," Sabeena whispers. "Otherwise, we wouldn't have picked it as the spot."

"Yeah, but we didn't pick it, did we?" Dylan asks. "Korni did. And Robbie. We had no say."

Sabeena shrugs one shoulder. "True."

In the middle of the circle, Anna holds her hands out. Her long hair is braided down her back and, when a non-ghost related sweep of wind washes over the field where we stand, I'm reminded of the afternoon in Greenland when that same hair twisted around her neck at the hands of a spirit. I swallow, the memory of my panic causing me to reflexively grab for Meander's hand. He eyes my sudden movement but doesn't hesitate to lace his fingers with mine, pulling me a little closer to his side.

One of the Revenants—a boy named Hien—stands between Anna and Ralli, his eyes wide and uneasy as he stares at the group of watching campers. I pity him, especially when he begins to shake, and a nauseous expression crosses his face. He turns to look behind him and begins to raise his arm as if he's going to point at something further out in the field. But before he has time to interact with the spirit in any way, the Revenant boy with the long, dark hair grabs his ears and crouches low with a whine.

"Jonah, do you hear her?" Anna asks, while the boy hunches into a ball. I can barely see him through the crowd, but I do see Anna approaching, while Ralli puts a hand on Hien's shoulder. I don't know what these campers' abilities amount to. Some Senders can see ghosts, others communicate or sense their presence differently, and a few even manipulate certain aspects of the dead's existence. At a best guess, I can surmise that Jonah hears something, while Hien seems to be seeing. But I really have no idea what's going on. Which means I have no idea why Jonah begins to cry, while Hien goes into what looks like convulsions, and one of the girls from the new group steps forward, brushing past Hien on her way out into the darkness.

"Desta," Ralli calls, while the rest of the Revenant

sector steps back as Jonah suddenly lashes out. He smacks Anna in the face, and she staggers back, clutching her cheek. Ralli lets go of Hien and rushes forward to help, while one of the other Revenants snaps at Jonah.

"What the hell is your problem?" a gaunt boy with sleep-messed, platinum-frosted hair says, and the cleared space allows me a partial view of Jonah raising his head and glaring, his face red and streaked with tears.

"Get away from me," he growls when the other boy approaches, and when the boy doesn't stop, Jonah stands and pushes him away. The other kid curses, spits on the ground, and rushes forward. Ralli and Anna both start yelling, and it takes Naasir stepping in to pull the other boy back before the Revenant leads are able to start trying to talk Jonah down.

"They've gone," Meander says from beside me, and I glance at him before following his gaze to see that, in the turmoil of the fight, Hien and Desta have both disappeared.

"Where did they go?" Sabeena asks. She raises her voice to be heard over the commotion. "The other two. Where did they go?"

"They're with the ghost," Kornelía says. She points into the night, then motions Draugur to head forward.

"Korni, you can't go," Mim says. "It's too dark."

"We're fine," Kornelía assures her. She starts off with her dog. After a beat of hesitation, Mim and Anna rush to follow.

The girls disappear into the dark night, while Jonah pushes roughly past the others in the semi-circle, making his way towards the vans. He sniffs as he passes us, and when Dylan tries to grab his arm, Jonah swings out and clocks him in the jaw.

"What the hell?" Dylan says, grabbing his chin and spinning in a circle as he mutters a string of other curses. "What is wrong with that kid?"

"He has trouble processing what he hears," Ralli says. The new Revenant lead puts his hands behind his head as he stares after Jonah. "He's... he hears ghosts. But he can't see them. And he doesn't hear them clearly. What he does hear... It disturbs him. And he's spent years being told it's not ghosts, you know? I think it's really messed with his head."

I look off into the distance, thinking about the years of therapy I attended when a well-meaning doctor tried to figure out why it was I insisted I saw the dead. I can only imagine what it would have been like if I heard static and painful wails without having a ghostly body to attach the noises to.

"Should we go after him?" I ask.

Meander steps behind me, his arms wrapping around my front. "No," he says next to my ear. "Leave him alone for a bit. Let him get far enough away. If it were me, I wouldn't want anyone else around just now."

"He's right," Ralli says. "We were told to give him space if he needed it. But no one said he'd be so violent. He was warned about tonight. We usually don't tell the new campers, but we took him aside and warned him what was coming. He said he could handle it."

"Great handling," Dylan mutters, still clasping his jaw. He looks around at the confused group of chattering campers. "So, where the hell did the girls go, anyway?"

"Shit, I don't know," Ralli says. "They must have gone to the ghost. We were going to take Hien over. Let everyone else follow. Anna was going to make the ghost play with her hair a bit…"

"And get herself strangled again?" I ask in annoyed surprise.

Ralli glances at me, probably wondering for a moment who the hell I even am. We've attended camp together for years, but we've never conversed outside of a classroom.

"She doesn't usually have a nasty response from ghosts," he says. Meander scoffs at that, and I lean back against him, glad I have someone who shares my belief that letting a spirit mess with your physical being is not something to do for fun.

"I hate to break it to you," Dylan says. "But so far your night hasn't exactly gone to plan. Who knows what else might go wrong?"

Ralli mutters something beneath his breath as he turns back to face the campers. He surveys the crowd, then starts to head towards the remainder of his sector. When he's halfway to the uneasy Revenants, Draugur's bark echoes through the air. Everyone stops, listening. For a few seconds, there is silence. Then, in the darkness of the black field, someone screams.

"What now?" Ralli mutters. He rushes through the crowd, pushing past the stunned Revenants on route to the field beyond. Dylan is right on his heels, and with the exception of Naasir, who stays by the edge of the group, watching for Jonah's return, the rest of Shade follows. Hurrying forward, we run through the dark, tripping over ruts and stones until we spot the missing campers standing behind Kornelía—while the girl's guide dog barks and snarls at a low-hunched puma prowling in the shadows.

"Fan-freaking-tastic," Dylan says when we all stop short at the sight of the cat.

"You sure your talent hasn't expanded to include feline connections?" I ask. "This would be the perfect time to test it out."

"As much as I would love to throw myself in front of a puma to try my hand at wildlife mediation, I'm afraid I definitely don't do cats," he replies.

"How do we fend off a puma attack?" Ralli asks.

"Get the vans," Sabeena says. "Get all the kids who are back there in the vans. Then get the drivers to come here and scare the puma off."

"And if the drivers aren't quick enough?" Meander asks.

Sabeena scowls. "It's better than nothing!"

"You're right," I say. "You go. Tell the others."

Sabeena glances at the puma, then nods her head and jogs back to the rest of the group. An excited chatter breaks out behind us, but soon the sounds fade as the remaining campers rush to the vans.

"Why isn't the ghost affecting it?" Meander asks. "Cats and dogs are usually bothered by paranormal activity."

"Not that dog," Ralli says.

"No," I agree. "But *he*'s unusual."

"It's a weak ghost," Ralli says. "If that has any bearing on the situation. I-I can't see it or anything. But I've heard. Desta—that's what she sees. Ghosts dealing with weakness in some form."

"How does the ghost feel?" Meander asks. I glance

at him to find his eyes trained on the puma, watching as it paces in front of the dog.

"What do you mean?" Ralli asks. "When she was alive?"

"No, now," Meander corrects. "How does she feel. Is she peaceful? Frustrated? Afraid?"

"Afraid," Ralli answers. "I think… I don't know. I haven't seen her. But Anna said she was terrified in the days that led to her death."

"Okay," Meander mumbles. He rakes in a breath, then turns to Ralli. "Go help the others get back to the vans. When you're there, tell the drivers to blare their horns. Loud noises go a long way to scaring off predators."

Ralli nods and bolts back the way we came, while Meander turns his gaze to me.

"What are you planning?" I ask. "It's a ghost. She's not going to materialize into some kind of mystical bodyguard."

"No, but she might get stronger with me nearby," he says. "And if the ghost is stronger, the cat might pick up on it. It could at least buy us time until the vans arrive."

I sigh, looking at the group of campers still standing behind Kornelía. Everyone is frozen, no one quite sure what to do. I'd suggest they run for it, if I didn't worry about how well Kornelía can make it over the field at a fast speed.

"Fine," I say at last. "Hopefully the vans won't take long, anyway."

"You should go and check," Meander says. "Make sure everyone gets on board."

"Are you trying to get rid of me?" I ask.

He smirks. "Of course I am. I don't want you getting eaten by a puma."

"It's not high on my priority list, either," I say.

"Then you should head back," Meander says more seriously.

I roll my eyes. "You know I'm not heading back."

His teeth scrape along his bottom lip as he considers me. "Yeah, I know," he says at last. He grabs my hand as we start for the group. "All right. I've got to get the puma's attention on the ghost. But I'm not sure I can even do that with the dog in such a state."

"Dylan—" I call.

Dylan nods, already listening to the plan. "I'm on it."

He heads towards Kornelía, sneaking up behind her so he can try to calm Draugur down. While he does so, Meander and I approach the back of the group. When his breath starts to hitch, we venture a little farther, then stop. He coughs, closes his eyes, and squeezes my hand tight. I rub his arm, watching the puma and feeling for the moment Meander's grip on me loosens—the moment his strength starts to leave him.

"What are you…" Anna trails off as the edges of her sweater flutter and the stray hairs by her face blow back. She sucks in a breath, feeling the change in the air. I can feel it too, even though I can't see the spirit. As my strength as a Sender has grown, I've gained the ability to sense pretty much any human ghost. The temperature is dropping, and there's a charge in the air as the ghost's fear ramps up. I've seen spirits interact with physical objects enough time to understand the shifts in our environment.

I keep rubbing Meander's arm, my gaze flicking between him and the cat. Dylan whispers calming words to Draugur, and the dog's barks lessen, fading to growling whines as he softens under Dylan's stroking pets. Kornelía joins in the act, hushing him with a soothing hand on his head. The puma, on the other hand, grows more agitated as the dog calms down. It mewls and hisses, pacing frantically as its attention shifts from the dog to a spot next to the group. Its large paws swipe through the air, while Meander's grip starts to lose its intensity, and his breath comes so shallow I know he's not taking in enough oxygen.

"What's happening?" the girl named Desta says in a hushed tone.

"He's doing something to the spirit," Anna replies.

"He can't keep it up," I say. I know he wants to help, but I'm not going to sacrifice Meander to uphold this stand-off. "We might have to make a run for it."

"It'll attack if we do that," Anna says.

"It'll attack if we stay still too," I argue.

"Not while he's distracting it," Mim says. "But… you said he can't keep doing that?"

I'm surprised by her lack of knowledge, until I remember she hasn't been around Meander since he was strangled just after his sixteenth birthday. Maybe someday the wounds on his neck will be old and faded enough that ghosts will no longer be able to choke him. But more than a year after the incident, he's still susceptible to passing out if he's in a spirit's presence for too long. And when he has a hand in releasing a ghost, all of his wounds—even the oldest, most faded of the bunch—still cause him pain.

He's been in the spirit's presence for too long now. He's losing his grounding, and I can't keep up a fast enough pace if I have to carry him unconscious away from this scene.

"We have to go," I tell him, tugging his arm so he staggers back a step.

"The ghost," Anna says, looking between the spirit and Meander. "If he stops…"

"He *has* to stop," I snap. "He bought us time. Now we have to run."

"Run?" Hien whispers.

I nod. "Yes. Run. Kornelía?"

"I'm ready," Kornelía says. She grips Draugur's handle with one hand, and Dylan's hand with the other.

"Okay," I say. I pull Meander back another step, ready to bolt away at a faster speed. "All of us, stick together as best you can. Ready? Three, two, one. Go!"

We stagger back, all of us rushing at once, while the Puma crouches low to attack. It hisses at the ghost at the same time Meander takes a gulping breath. He grips my hand and pushes his legs to move faster as the growling cat bounds forward.

The puma hisses again as it rushes towards us, paw swatting through the air and catching the back of Kornelía's flowing dress. She shrieks, and with her cry Draugur turns so fast he nearly knocks both Kornelía and Dylan off their feet. The dog begins a snarling, snapping growl, while Dylan grabs Kornelía by the shoulders and pushes her roughly to the side. Draugur cuts into the puma's path. Then he jumps forward, while the cat crouches to make another strike.

Distant lights shine, and a blaring horn wails into the night as Kornelía calls Draugur's name. The dog snaps again at the puma, and the cat starts in for a second running swat. The van bounces wildly over the field, racing through the uneven grasses. Its headlights catch on the puma, and the cat arches back, retreating three steps before turning tail and pouncing away. It runs directly where the group had been standing—where the ghost must still be. With a deafening yowl, it trips over its own feet in an effort to dodge the spirit's energy, rolling in a clumsy show of startled fear before it regains its footing and disappears into the night.

We stop running as the cat vanishes and the van pulls to a stop. Kornelía assures us she's fine, and Meander half-collapses against me, breath ragged and limbs shaking. I drop my head against his. Then I laugh with relief as the van doors open and Ralli ushers us inside.

9

"Look at it this way," Robbie says as we relate the events of the initiation on Monday morning. "This time, you didn't cause the trouble. You fixed it. That's growth."

"I'm not sure that's how it works," Mim says.

Robbie sits on one of our two sofas, a half-eaten kiwifruit in his hand. "Oh, come on. You never let me give sage advice."

"Because you clearly don't understand the definition of 'advice'," Alex teases. She sits on the floor with her computer on the coffee table, the screen open to an online course she's taking for school. Watching her work is a curious reminder that normal life exists alongside our days of camp. This is our last summer at Wanagi, and in September I'll be starting my final year of high school. I don't know what my future holds in terms of ghosts and the Oracle. But I've already started collecting university pamphlets in my search for schools with the best music programs. It's interesting to see how other people balance their non-Sender existence with their supernatural pursuits. I don't know what Alex is studying. But I doubt she's earning her degree from an Oracle-funded program.

"You didn't let me get to the advice part," Robbie argues. Alex sweeps an arm out, motioning for him to continue with whatever inspirational spiel he's got planned. Our other lead pauses, considering his words. Then he shrugs. "Okay, so it's not advice, per se," he admits after a moment, while Alex hangs her head in exasperation. "I'll just say this. You worked as a team. That's the important part. You figured it out together. And you survived."

"Add another 'almost death' to the list of our achievements," Meander mumbles.

I smirk, peeling an orange and popping a slice into my mouth while Robbie nods.

"Exactly," he agrees.

"None of it would have happened if that kid hadn't freaked out," Dylan says. He rubs lightly at the bruise on his cheek. "Everything was under control until then."

"That kid wasn't either of the ones who ran off to find the spirit," Kornelía replies.

"Yeah, what was with that?" he asks. "Why would they just bolt off after some ghost?"

Robbie takes a bite of his kiwi and speaks with his mouth full. "You can ask them on Friday," he says. "When you start your mentoring."

"Oh right," Dylan says. "I forgot about that."

Something vibrates against the right side of my thigh, and I look beside me as Meander digs his phone from his pocket. With an inaudible sigh, he switches on the screen and checks his notifications, eyes skimming a message that makes his jaw clench tight—a sight that makes my own jaw harden as well. I know full well who the text is from. Since his arrival in Chile, Meander's been bombarded with messages from his mother, spiteful texts written in such abhorrent fashion they are both hardly decipherable and unquestionably hostile. Day and night, she sends him complaints, claiming he left chores unfinished and errands incomplete. Whenever the horrendous mood strikes her, she sends him lies, ones meant solely to keep him from relaxing at camp.

Her behavior makes me sick, and I can't fathom what Meander will do when he returns home to England at the end of the summer. But for right now, I can at least take a sliver of solace in the fact she's not able to throw any more plates his way.

"There are eight new Revenants," Sabeena says as Meander's teeth scrape his lip while he tries to decide how to reply. I force myself to look away from him, focusing on Sabeena's comment and giving him time to respond without my interfering stare. "Only seven of us. Who gets the extra camper?"

"And who works with the boy who hears the ghosts?" Kornelía adds.

While the others talk, Meander shuts off the screen and starts to put his phone back in his pocket. When he stops, raising his arm and switching the screen on again, I look over to see if yet another message has come through. But instead of the stream of texts, Meander's phone is open to his mother's contact information. For a few seconds, his finger hovers as he stares at the screen. Then, with a sharp intake of breath, he swipes and presses to block her number from his phone.

He glances at me, and I give him a sad smile as he switches off the screen again and tucks the phone back in his pocket.

"You can choose who you work with for yourselves," Robbie says. "Or we can draw straws."

"And what do we do if we don't want to be paired off at all?" Meander asks in an annoyed sulk.

I wait for Robbie to explain why the fourth year to first year mentoring sessions are a critical part of the camp ecosystem. But before he has a chance to ward off Meander's complaint, Sabeena comes to his surprising aid.

"He's right," she says. She leans back in her seat and taps her chin in thought. "Why do we have to mentor one-by-one? We all have something to offer the new campers. Why can't we speak to all of them?"

"There's not enough time for that many mentoring sessions," Robbie says with a shake of his head.

"But what if there didn't have to be," Mim reasons. "What if, instead of us each breaking off for a weekly meeting, we have a single weekly meeting—all of us, with all of them."

"A group session?" Robbie looks at Alex, and she glances uncertainly around at the rest of us.

"Why not?" Naasir asks.

I eat the last of my orange and crumple the rinds in my fist. "You said it yourself," I say after I've swallowed. "It's important when we work as a team."

"And we've had… problems, in the past," Kornelía says. "Because we didn't work together."

"Because we didn't share enough of what we'd

learned," Sabeena agrees.

"I…" Robbie's eyes return to Alex.

"I don't know if there are any rules," she says with a shrug. She glances around the room again. "But they *are* right."

"Yeah," Robbie says. "They are." He stares at his kiwi for a moment before nodding. "All right. I'll talk to Buxley, see if we can come to an arrangement. If everyone is in agreement?"

We all nod our assent, although it takes a nudge from my elbow before Meander joins in. Robbie nods again too. Then he spends a quiet moment finishing his fruit before going off in search of the woman who will decide our mentoring fate.

"Well, you got your wish," I say after Robbie is gone and we've ventured outside.

"That's not exactly what I had in mind," Meander mutters. He pulls out his phone again as we walk along the path towards the lobby. Switching it on, he makes another check of the screen.

"Any new messages?" I ask.

He shakes his head. "No. I can't see her bothering to text me from another number. That's too much work. She should be quiet now."

He gives the phone a tired sigh as he puts it away once more. Then he steps a little closer to me, and I let my arm brush his as we continue up the path.

"At least this mentoring will be better than one-on-one," I say, drawing him away from the exhaustive thoughts of his mother. "You won't have to do nearly as much talking."

"Nearly? I don't intend to do any talking at all," he says.

"We'll see how that goes," I say. "If Sabeena doesn't put you on the spot, Mim will. Or Dylan will throw some insult your way so you're forced to defend yourself."

Meander frowns. "Yeah, you're probably right."

"If it gets too dire, I'll rescue you," I promise.

He glances at me with a smile. "You'll be good in the session."

"No, I won't," I scoff. "I'm terrible at giving advice." I'm not a natural leader like some of our sector mates. I don't volunteer to take charge of projects, nor do I go out of my way to check in on the progress of my fellows. I'm persistent, when I need to be. And I'll take part when I think I can assist. But I'm no wise mage. No one's ever going to come to me for help planning their future.

"You're not terrible," Meander says. "And I don't mean you should give advice, anyway. Not specifically. It's just that… You listen. You help. And in the general scheme of things, you're… you know—*good*."

My cheeks warm, flattered by his assertion—even if I'm not convinced it's completely true. Although perhaps I'm being too hard on myself. I'm no leader, but I do like to help. I can't offer the new campers— or anyone else—the answers to the questions that so often plague people with abilities like ours. But I've gone through a lot in the past three years. Maybe that means I can offer *something*.

We enter the lobby, the dome dim after the brightness of the day and full of the sounds of clattering dishes and chattering campers. Meander surveys the crowds before us. Then he glances at me with another sigh.

"It's too noisy here," he says. "Too many people.

Why does it have to be all talking or course work or squaring off with dead people, anyway? Why can't there just be some time to—"

"Pretend you're not at a summer camp for ghost-hunters?" I ask.

He smiles. "Precisely."

"Well, you're not in class now," I say. "No ghosts around. I can shut up so you don't have to talk, if you want?"

Meander leans his shoulder against mine. "You don't count," he mumbles, and even the pouty way he says it makes my stomach take flight. He may not like people, and he might have no interest in mentoring anyone new. But Meander is remarkably good at saying the right thing—at making even the most mundane of moments extraordinary.

He takes a few steps through the lobby, and I watch him move until he turns back to give me a questioning gaze. Then I smile and step forward to grab his hand.

"I'm not sure I'm mentor material," I say. "But I guess I do have some experiences to share. So do you. And, for the record? You're *good* too, Meander. Better than I think you realize."

He rolls his eyes with a scoff, though I know him well enough to catch the true emotion behind the dismissive gesture. My thumb strokes the back of his hand, and I watch the pink spread in his cheeks before he offers me a half-shy smile and tugs me along so we can continue on our way.

ROBBIE TALKS WITH MRS. BUXLEY, AND OUR SECTOR IS GIVEN PERMISSION to do group mentoring instead of one-on-one meets.

On Friday, a week after arriving at camp, we travel as a group to the Revenant's dome for our first session. I'm nervous about walking into the room to find eight pairs of expectant eyes turned our way. But when we reach the dome, only five campers are actually present—and only two seem to even remember we're having a mentoring session. Kornelía and Sabeena take charge of locating the missing campers. By the time everyone is finally compiled, we've spread out in more or less a circle, the Revenants sitting on their dome's sofas while the Shades rest on the coffee table or sit on the hard, tiled floor.

"We'd have more room in the lobby," Desta says. Her dark eyes watch us warily, though she looks more at ease with Kornelía than with the rest of us.

"We couldn't speak privately there," Sabeena says.

She perches on the edge of the coffee table, elbows on knees and chin in her hands. "We thought this might be more comfortable."

"We're here to help you," Kornelía says, the same thing we usually say when we're facing a ghost for the first time. The situation here is vastly different, but the approach makes sense. We don't know how to solve these kids' problems. We're not professionals, and we certainly don't have all the answers—or even know what the questions will be. But the role of a mentor is not to be an expert guru. We're here to help and, like when we work with a ghost, part of that process includes figuring things out for ourselves. And, perhaps, improvising a solution that hopefully won't do more harm than good.

"How are you going to help us?" one of the girls asks. She flips thick dreadlocks behind her shoulder, her long earrings tinkling as the hair pushes them aside.

"We're in our final year at camp," Kornelía says. "We've gone through the same things you have—or will."

"I doubt it," Jonah mutters.

"Why do you look like that?" the boy with the platinum hair cuts in, looking not at Jonah but at Kornelía. His gaze is trained on her unfocused eyes, yet I don't think it's her sight that he's commenting on so much as her generally, ethereal presence.

"We've gone through changes," Sabeena says. She looks at the boy. "What's your name?"

"Trick," the boy answers, his chest puffing as if he's used to defending the name. "And what changes? I thought people saw ghosts here. Like, normal people. No offense. But you don't look normal. None of you looked normal that night."

I can only imagine what was said about our appearances the night of the initiation when the Revenants drove to the field or hung out in this very dome after the near puma attack.

Kornelía smiles. "We're normal enough. And we do see ghosts. Or interact with the spirit realm in some way. Not everyone has the same abilities. You know that already."

"Ghosts aren't real," Jonah says from the end of one sofa.

My anger flares at his scoffing tone. "Then why are you here?" I ask. I've heard too many people claim ghosts aren't real. In the past, I never spoke out against their mocking accusations. But I'm not as silent as I used to be.

His eyes are still almost completely obscured by his hair, but his expression is tough when he turns to me. "I don't see ghosts."

"No," Kornelía says. "You hear them."

He bristles, his arms folding across his chest. "I hear *things*," he mutters. His English is good, but I don't think he speaks it natively. I wonder where all of these campers are from. I wonder if any of them share a homeland with any of us.

"If the Oracle found you, it means that what you hear is paranormal," Kornelía says.

"How would they know?" Jonah asks. He shakes the hair from his eyes and stares at Kornelía with a hard, yet almost pleading sort of disbelief. "I don't understand what it is I hear. Why would they?"

"Tell us what you hear," Mim says. "Explain it as well as you're able to."

For a moment, Jonah looks like he's not going to speak. But eventually, he opens his mouth as his eyes drift to the corner of the room.

"I hear noises," he says in a low voice. "Sounds like… like cries. Wailing, or groans. Sometimes… words. Or parts of words. Sometimes…" His eyes move back to Mim. "It's stupid. Doctor says it's my brain. Not ghosts."

"But you're here," Mim says. "Which tells me you don't quite believe what the doctor says."

"I did believe it," Jonah says. "But then… the words started to make sense. Some of them. I went to a house and heard 'cat'. Over and over. Cat. Cat. Cat. Then I found out. A woman had died there. She fell from a loft. Because she was looking for her cat. I got mad. Yelled out that the cat was dead. I don't remember what happened after that. I… I passed out. When I woke up, the sound was gone."

"You released her," Mim says with a smile.

But Jonah only scowls. "I don't want to hear ghosts," he says. "I don't want to be a freak like all of you. I just want to stop the noises. That's why I'm here. To make the noises stop."

"They won't stop," Meander says. "Unless you get rid of the ghosts and clear a space for silence. You can't run away from it. You don't get that option. None of us do."

"Why would you want to stop?" one of the Revenant girls asks. She has about ten piercings that I can see, and she speaks English with ease. "You help the dead. That's incredible."

"Not to me," Jonah says.

"Well, you're stupid, then," the girl replies.

"No," Sabeena cuts in. "He's not stupid for wanting to stop. You're not stupid for liking whatever ability you have. That's what we're here to tell you. See, there's a lot of secrecy in this camp. Because everyone experiences the paranormal world differently, and everyone's feelings towards their talents is different as well. Some of us cherish our abilities. Some of us fear them, or hate them, or think they are a nuisance. But you can't fight with each other because your beliefs are different."

"That's how we can help you," Mim agrees. "We can't teach you about your own talents—you have to figure that part out for yourselves. But we can teach you how to share. And how to work together. Because if you don't—"

"What, we'll fail camp?" Jonah says. "So what?"

"You'll die," Mim replies, her voice so sharp everyone in the room takes note.

The eight Revenants sit up straighter, their eyes wide as they survey us anew.

"We won't really," the girl who was arguing with Jonah says. "They're just ghosts. They can't harm us."

"Tell that to Meander," Mim says. The Revenants look confused, and for a few seconds Meander stares at the ground, resisting the invitation to put himself in the spotlight. I give his hand a squeeze, and he swallows before lifting his chin and pulling down the neck of his collar so the younger kids can see his scar.

"A ghost did that?" the girl asks. Meander nods. Then he looks at Mim.

"Ask Mim what a ghost did to her," he says. The Revenants look back at Mim, and she tells them about her coma. Then she tosses the conversation to

Kornelía, who shares what happened to her sight.

"If you really want a good idea of what a ghost can do," Kornelía says when she's finished relating her tale, "you should ask Reed."

The Revenants look around, waiting for another person to talk. When no one speaks, the boy named Trick shrugs his shoulders.

"Which one of you is Reed?" he asks.

"None of us," Naasir says in his deep and somber voice. "Reed is dead."

The silence lingers for a long moment. Then Trick lets out a shaky breath and flops back against the sofa.

"And here I thought it was the cancer that would kill me," he says.

"Cancer?" Dylan asks.

Trick nods. "Diagnosed when I was three. In and out of the hospital until I was twelve. It's been a couple of years now. But… there's always the chance for relapse. That's where I started seeing ghosts. The hospital. It's the *only* place I see ghosts. You can imagine what the nurses thought of me. I was the cute kid with the imaginary friends—until they realized all my friends were dead patients."

"They think you were crazy?" Jonah asks.

Trick shakes his head. "No. Not really. Most of them thought it was a game. A few thought it was guardians watching over me. My parents believed that. My mother… it scared her, at first. She thought it was someone come to take me away, you know? But in time, she decided I was being protected."

Mim's smile is fond as she nods. "It's hard for those who don't see."

"Harder still when you don't yet understand," one

of the girls says. "My father runs a tour company in New Orleans. Takes visitors to graves and tells them morbid stories of the people who supposedly haunt them. He spent years laughing at me, thinking it was all part of an elaborate show where I pretended his tours were real. I idolized him as a kid. Thought we had a special gift, both of us. But when the Oracle came to him, he was shaken. Turns out, he never believed. Not for a moment. All those tours, all those stories… lies. He never once believed ghosts exist." She tucks her palms under her legs. "Are they really that dangerous? The ghosts?"

"Not always," Kornelía says. "But sometimes. And not everyone sees them or hears them." She tilts her head in Naasir's direction, and he takes over the narrative as he explains his ability to know when someone nearing their end will have unfinished business after they die.

We all explain. One by one, we go over our talents, talking about what they used to be and how they've changed in the years since we started attending camp. Then the new campers tell us about their abilities too. Jonah with his voices, Trick with his hospital. Celiste— the girl with the dreadlocks—sees ghosts who exist within the same family, while Hien describes his experiences as ghosts concerned with betrayal. Desta sees weak spirits, and the girl with the piercings, Ines, senses when objects were of particular importance to someone dead. An Australian girl named Evie admits that she doesn't yet understand the connection between the ghosts she's seen, and—to our surprise— the last camper, a boy named Zahur, says he sees ghosts who have died on open water.

"Reed saw ghosts who drowned," Sabeena says with a quiet nod. "You would have been a good match for him."

The boy looks horrified to know he shares a similar talent to the dead camper. "What happened?" he asks.

We tell him. Then we talk about the other things that have happened, and a bit about our own first year at camp. The Revenants don't say much, but I suspect they'll have more questions in our next session. I'm glad I didn't have to attempt this kind of mentoring alone. And, as much as he didn't intend for it to unfold this way, I'm happy Meander made the suggestion he did. It makes a lot of sense to do this as a group. We have a lot of adventures to relate, and a lot of mistakes to confess. If we stop these kids from repeating the tragedies we've faced, it will have been time well-spent.

We talk for two hours. Then we leave the Revenants and have dinner together in our dome. It feels empty without ten of us here, even after all this time. But it feels comfortable too. We're all different people, and many of us don't even talk when camp is not in session. But we're a family, of sorts. We understand things no one else does. I hope the new campers have that too, eventually. Because if anyone wanted to know what wisdom I could share, it's that being a Sender is a hell of a lot easier when you have support.

 quickly fractured, the sector splitting off into ever-changing groups as each Shade attended lessons or worked on ghostly assignments. But without any classroom time to force us apart, our movements in Chile are different. Every day, Robbie and Alex hand out task sheets for us to complete, which mostly consists of odd jobs around the camp like helping with meal prep and shelving books in the library. When our daily chores are finished, Meander and I spend whatever time we can manage alone, and I have no idea what the others are up to while we're off wandering around the outskirts of camp in search of somewhere private to spend our afternoons. But when we're in the lobby for mealtimes or at the dome in the evening hours, more often than not the whole of Shade is together.

Two weeks into camp, in the dusky light of the

winter evening after the end of our second mentoring session, the seven of us lounge in the dome's main room. But by five o'clock, our new routine is interrupted when Robbie trudges in hefting a collection of hiking backpacks.

"All right, y'all ready?" he asks as he drops the pile onto the sofa, nearly spilling Kornelía's coffee in the process.

Dylan reaches for the cup, grabbing it just before it tips and falls out of her hand. "Ready for what?" he asks as she gives him an appreciative smile while he places the cup on the table.

"Ready for your trip," Robbie says. He rounds the sofa and sits, propping his legs up on the heap of bags.

Dylan watches him settle into place. Then he glances around and catches my eye. "You know anything about a trip?"

"Not a clue," I say with a shrug.

Robbie sighs. "Your final year trip," he clarifies, though it's not much of a clarification to any of us.

"We need more to go on," Sabeena says after checking to see if everyone else is as stumped as she is. "We haven't heard anything about a final year trip."

"Unless this is for our final projects," Naasir suggests.

I haven't picked a final project yet. In fact, beyond my initial surprise at learning that Mim is already planning for the event, I still haven't given it the slightest consideration. The first two weeks of camp have been remarkably ghost light. Outside of scouting for and participating in the initiation, no one in the sector has seen any spirits here in Chile. And, since we don't have any courses this summer, we haven't even been learning about the dead. All in all, the start of our final year has been easy—almost carefree. I'm not sure I'm ready for it to change quite yet.

"It's not your final project," Robbie says, alleviating the whispers of my panic. "This is a precursor. Every year, the oldest campers are given some tasks. It's kind of like a scavenger hunt. The idea is, you work together to solve… problems. Problems that speak to your specific talents as Senders."

"Are you saying the *problems* are ghosts?" Mim asks. Her cheeks flush and a bit of her old temper sparks in her words. "The dead are not playthings."

"No one said they were," Robbie replies. He shakes his head and raises his palms in surrender. "There are ghosts. And they will help you with your tasks. But you can also help them along the way. You might be able to release them yourselves. And if you can't, I promise the Oracle won't abandon them after the hunt is finished."

"We *might* release them… but that's not the aim of the trip?" Meander asks.

"That's right," Robbie says.

Meander's eyes flash with annoyance. "Then what's the point? If the purpose isn't to get rid of the spirits, then what's the point of putting us through the hell of being near them?"

"To see how you handle it," Robbie says without missing a beat. "To see what you're capable of."

Meander's jaw tightens, and I know he's holding back a further remark about how we've already provided enough proof of that. The Oracle knows how we're affected by ghosts. Which suggests there's more to this trip than simply seeing how we deal with the dead.

"Sometimes this final mission only takes a few days," Robbie continues when he's satisfied that Meander won't argue his point more. He drops his legs to the ground and sits up straighter. "But this one's going to require a bit of extra time. You'll be gone for a couple of weeks."

"Weeks?" Mim asks. "What about our mentoring?"

"You'll skip a session," Robbie says with a shrug. "You'll meet again when you're back." He stands and looks at the backpacks before giving us a grin. "For now, though, I suggest you pack your bags. We leave tonight."

"Tonight?" Mim asks. She sounds incredulous, but I can't say I'm surprised by the sudden announcement. The Oracle might have wanted the fun of keeping this a secret. But given the delay of camp this summer, there's a good chance they only finalized the details of the hunt in the past twenty-four hours.

Robbie gives us a time to be packed for, then leaves us to question each other about the trip we didn't even know we were going to be taking.

"They really want to send us on a ghost scavenger hunt?" Dylan asks.

"Maybe it's meant to be fun," Kornelía offers.

"Doesn't sound fun," Naasir replies.

"It's not for fun," Meander says. He turns to me. "They want to test us. See how useful we are."

"Useful to what?" Dylan asks.

"To the Oracle," Meander says. "That's what this whole camp is about, isn't it? Getting new recruits."

"The Oracle's not headhunting." Dylan says.

"Maybe not totally," Kornelía replies. "But he's

right. They aren't giving us free trips just for the sake of it. We've always known that."

"Yeah, but… isn't it our choice?" I ask. "We don't *have* to work for them. We haven't signed any contracts." A fresh swell of panic rises in my chest at the thought of letting the Oracle decide my future.

Meander raises one arm onto the back of the sofa, crooking his elbow so he can gently rub my neck. "No, they can't make you work for them," he assures me.

I nod, breathing slow to ward off the coil starting in my gut, while on the other sofa, Mim tilts her head.

"But you think they'll try to convince us to?" she asks.

"Only if they think we're a good fit," Sabeena says. "Otherwise, testing us is pointless. They won't want to give us jobs if we're no good."

"But if we are good, do we even want the job they're going to offer?" Dylan asks. He looks around at the rest of us. "I don't know about you all, but ghost hunting has never been my future plan."

"You want to work with dogs," Mim says with a smile, before her face falls and her expression turns uncertain. "Is that still true?"

"Sure is," Dylan smiles. "I want to be a vet. I'll be damn good at it too. At least whenever a dog comes in."

"Things have changed for me," Mim reflects. "But I think… if they want me, I'll work for the Oracle."

"The Oracle is the only place I'm understood," Kornelía says. "I don't think I'd fare well in the living world. Not yet anyway. I have a lot still to learn about the dead. I hope they allow me to learn it with their help."

I'm glad Mim and Kornelía know what they want

out of their future, but their responses make me a little cold with unease. Unease, or perhaps jealousy that they've got it all figured out.

"What about you two?" Mim asks. She looks between Meander and me before settling her gaze on him. "What do you think you'll do? After you've left the Oracle?"

No one needs to ask Meander if he'll work for the Oracle when camp is done. He has a nastier relationship to the dead than any of us. Everyone knows he wants nothing to do with being a Sender.

"I don't really fancy working at the cemetery for the rest of my life," he says. His finger trails lazy circles on the back of my neck, the movement as bored as his tone as he answers the question. "When I was little, I used to watch a show about a postman in a village. I thought that would make a nice job. Maybe not in a village—too many busybodies—but it'd let me work on my own, outside, on the same route every day. That could be doable."

He's told me all of this before, along with two or three variant job descriptions that amount to pretty much the same thing. Meander is one of the smartest people I know, and I hate that he doesn't intend to complete higher studies or work his way into a profession that will utilize his skills. There's nothing wrong with being a post officer, if that's really what he wants to do. But it's not. Meander isn't planning for passionate work or any sort of fulfilling career. He's planning for something *doable*—because he thinks that's the only option available to him.

"What about you, Cal?" Kornelía asks.

"I..." Faltering, I swallow my frustrations and

feel my way back to the present to try and imagine what my own future might be like. "I don't know," I admit after a flustered pause. "I don't really have any plans…"

"Who are you kidding?" Meander says as he goes back to rubbing my neck. "You're going to study music. You'll either wind up a famous violinist, or a frustrated grade school teacher."

My ill-mood cracks as I laugh. "The only two possibilities."

Meander eyes me with a smile that is fond—and maybe even a little proud. Which takes me by surprise. Meander's always happy to listen to me make music. But I never imagined he'd be proud of my playing. No one's ever been proud of me just because I know the notes of a violin.

I can feel my face flushing with heat, part with pleasure and part with the teetering tension of not wanting to disappoint him—while knowing full well that what he's suggested will never come true. I fully plan on studying music. But I don't see myself ever playing in an orchestra—or teaching students how to advance their technical skills.

Which of course leaves me to wonder what I *will* do. I don't need a complete answer to that question yet. But an idea would be nice. A direction, however vague, would give me purpose and make me feel like I have some small measure of control. But what direction could my future even take? Music helps me make sense of the world. It helps me make sense of spirits too. But what does that mean for my future? If I took those truths and tried to set them at the center of my goals, what kind of life would I even be preparing for?

Impossible questions of a future I can't even begin to envision flutter through my head, crowding in and suffocating my thoughts until Kornelía throws me a lifeline by guiding the conversation elsewhere in the room.

"Naasir, do you think you'll work for the Oracle?" she asks, shifting the group's focus and allowing me a moment of peace to wade in the wash of my quiet confusion.

"I can't see how I would," Naasir says in response to Kornelía's question. "I am glad to help. But I don't see ghosts. And I have obligations at home."

"I'll work for the Oracle," Sabeena says. "I don't have anything exciting waiting for me at home. Just the same day-to-day. I love my family. But I'm so bored when I'm away from here."

"So, the girls will stay, and the guys will leave," Dylan muses.

"Sefa's staying," Sabeena corrects. "He's not here, but he's still working for the Oracle. Once his grandmother dies, he'll have no reason not to be a Sender."

"And Lu left," Kornelía adds, referring to the first member of Shade who did not return after her second summer. "She didn't have a choice, but she *did* leave. I don't know if she wanted to work for the Oracle or not."

"This is, of course, assuming the Oracle wants us to work for them, anyway," Dylan muses.

"Why wouldn't they want us?" Mim asks. "They've paid for us to come here. They've given us the chance to be together while our talents develop."

"Yeah, but maybe they've been watching those developments to see how they played out," Dylan says with a shrug. "If I was gung ho to be a part of the Oracle, would they want to pay me for hunting for ghost dogs? Most people don't even know they exist. No one's bothered by the lingering spirit of their dachshund."

"Do they pay us at all?" I ask. I've never given it much thought. But the truth is, I have no idea what the world of the Oracle looks like outside of camp. "It could be volunteer-based, for all we know."

"I doubt so many people would run these programs and disrupt their daily lives for free," Kornelía says. She presses her lips together in thought. "But it could be that Senders are paid case-by-case, instead of on a regular basis."

"Like freelance work?" Dylan asks. He looks contemplative. "I suppose, if they did want me, freelancing could be a possibility. It would be a great way to pick up some extra cash now and then."

"*If* that's how it works," I say. "No one's ever told us."

"No one tells us anything," Meander agrees.

"Well, I guess we'll find out soon enough," Mim says. "We've only got eight weeks left. Then our time at camp is done."

The thought makes me a little sick, though it's less to do with leaving the Oracle than with leaving a particular Shade. We just arrived. But already, there are only eight weeks left until Meander and I are separated again. And this time, there won't be another camp session in the works to keep us placated.

Kornelía seems to sense the change in my emotions. Unless someone else—maybe everyone else—is as stunned by the closeness of our end here as I am. With a gentle smile, she reaches a hand beside her and feels for the pile of backpacks. "We'd better get packing," she says.

Her ability to alter the course of our conversation based on what she senses is disturbing, prying, and probably—from her end—ceaselessly exhausting. I can't imagine being constantly bombarded with the emotions of other people. I have a hard enough time dealing with my own.

"Robbie said we leave tonight," I say, helping her in whatever small way I can—hurrying the conversation so she can maybe find somewhere quiet while the rest of us escape her ever-knowing mind. "Whatever we're doing for the next two weeks, it starts soon."

OUR SHADE SECTOR SCAVENGER HUNT STARTS WITH A THREE-AND-A-half-hour van ride before we arrive at—to everyone's surprise—a ski resort.

"This is where they're sending us?" Dylan asks with a grin. "Hell yes. I'll take staying here over a mesh-covered pod any day."

"We don't know that we're staying here," Mim says.

"*We* don't. But *you* have the power to find out," Dylan says, eyeing the envelope in her hands.

I expected that our leads would accompany us on this trip, but they haven't. Robbie and Alex escorted us to the front of the resort and waved us off like doting parents sending their children away to school. They offered us no hints of where we were going, nor did they provide any instruction for what to do when we arrived. The ride was longer than I expected, but the destination is pleasant. And suspicious. Dylan's right—we don't actually know what's in store for us now that we've stopped.

But Mim does have the answer. Or at least the next step. When we arrived at the hotel, the van driver spoke to Mim in Spanish and handed her an envelope before she disembarked. Now, she cracks its seal and pulls out a sheet of paper.

"It says to check in," she relates. "Our first clue is here. We need to solve it before we can move on. And…" she peeks into the envelope before tipping it upside down over her hand. A small coin-shaped piece of wood falls into her palm. "We have this."

Naasir takes the coin from her hand and looks it over. Then he hands it to Sabeena, who in turn hands it to Meander. On one side of the coin is the outlined shape of a cartoon ghost. On the other is a set of numbers.

"Coordinates?" Meander asks. He hands the coin to me, and I in turn give it to Dylan, who nods.

"Looks like it," he says. "What's it called? Geocaching, right? GPS coordinates leading to a specific place. Must be where we're supposed to go."

"The sheet says we should start in the morning," Mim explains. "For now, we're supposed to check in and…" She glances up at us with a smile. "Relax."

"Yesss," Dylan says. He grabs his bag and hurries for the resort's main entrance.

"What do you think we're going to face when we figure out where those coordinates lead?" I ask as the others start to follow him.

"Hopefully not a full-fledged ghost encounter right off the bat," Meander says. He sighs, bending down to grab both his bag and mine. "But I wouldn't be surprised if it was."

"If it is a ghost," I say as I try to grab my bag from

him but am thwarted as he moves his arm out of reach, "I suppose we don't *have* to face it."

"No," he agrees, "I suppose we don't." He gives me a little smirk. "But we probably will, won't we? We've always been foolishly well-behaved when it comes to camp."

"Well-behaved?" I tease. "We did flee the country last summer."

Meander grips the bags and steps forward. "Yes, there was that *one* incident."

"And the cave in Tonga," I add. "Not to mention sneaking off in Paris."

"All right, you've made your point." He laughs, stepping to my side and letting his fingers trail over mine as we head into the resort.

At some point during this hunt, we're going to face things we don't want to. But the first evening feels like we've unexpectedly struck it rich. After checking into our rooms, we have a late-night dinner at the resort's restaurant, stuffing our faces and watching the distant specks of people gliding down the snow-covered slopes. Afterward, Dylan badgers us until we all agree to join him outside on the main pavilion, where a huge patio is outfitted with a hot tub that's so large it'd more accurately be called a pool. None of us brought bathing suits on this trip, but we all sit at the tub's edges, dangling our feet in the water as we watch the skiers. After Mim insists we go back to our rooms so we're ready for tomorrow's early start, Dylan uses his own funds to order room service dessert and a movie rental on the room's tv.

In the morning, we meet the girls and enjoy a hot breakfast in the quiet dining room before loading into the waiting van. When we pull out of the resort's parking lot, Mim gives the driver the coordinates and is instructed to open the glove compartment in order to retrieve the directions for our first task.

"We're supposed to discover a name," Mim says. She reads over the printed sheet. "Find the name and bring it back to the resort. There, we'll find the next clue."

It takes about forty-five minutes to reach the coordinates etched onto the coin, enough time to leave the resort and all semblance of civilization behind. When we pull to a stop, the area around us is empty aside from some overgrown train tracks running parallel to the road and, on their far side, a small, boarded up railway station.

"Who wants to take bets on whether it's haunted?" Dylan asks as we peer at the squat building with its rusted steel roof and crumbling stone walls. The station would have been quaint when it was in use, its white-wood doors and twin bench seats giving it the impression of a peaceful country stop. It makes me feel like we're visiting one of the old heritage buildings we have in Canada from the days of steam trains and horse carriages—or it would, if it weren't for the massive dusty-brown mountains looming behind the station's exterior to remind me I'm nowhere close to home.

"We should all take that bet and not tell you when we actually see the ghost," Mim says with a snort.

"Like you could hide it from me," Dylan replies with a grin.

"Like we could hide it from anybody," Sabeena says as she pulls open the van's door.

We wait until everyone has exited the vehicle before

Mim takes the lead in picking her way over the tracks on route to the railway station. A funny side effect of being at camp is our total lack of caution when entering places like this. Under normal circumstances, I would never approach an abandoned building in a foreign country—or, hell, even in my own city back at home. But here, no one seems concerned about the safety of the structure, or the possibility of anyone residing inside. I wonder if that will change for those who stay working with the Oracle after camp is done. Would Mim be so ready to walk into the shell of a station on her own? Or is there safety in knowing the Oracle has made its mark on this address?

Mim pushes against one of the white doors, rattling the old wood but unable to loosen it from its frame. Dylan tries the middle door with the same result, but when Naasir gives a forceful push to the farthest door on the left, it falls open and slams against an interior wall.

We join Naasir at the open door, peering into the dim corridor of the railway station. Mim sneezes, muttering a curse about the abundance of dust. She pauses long enough to rub her nose and make a futile attempt to wave the dust away. Then she steps over the threshold.

As soon as I've entered the building, I make a preliminary sweep of the rectangular room, feeling for changes in the air. Then I focus on Meander as he does the same. He stays close to the door, ready to bolt if the ghost makes itself known, and the sight of his caution is a painful reminder of how he is always on edge, constantly prepared to flee. It's not just here, where we know a ghost is likely to exist. It's everywhere. At camp. At the resort. At every store or restaurant or house we've ever been to together. He can't go anywhere without planning for the worst, and although I know he'd never wish his talent on anyone, I would take every one of his scars and all of the pain that came with them if it would mean he could walk around without always waiting for an attack from the dead.

"So how do we look for the name?" Dylan asks while I tense in anticipation of what Meander will feel.

"It's not a big space," Mim says. "We can walk around together. Or split up. Try to find something with a name written on it—the name of the station, maybe."

Meander gives me a nod to let me know he's okay. When I see the drop as his shoulders relax, I face the station's interior and take another step inside.

We all venture in, wandering more or less as a group as we explore the station. The space is small and dark. The doors must have once acted as the station's main source of light, and we spend a moment working the other two free from their warped frames so we can clear the air and see more of what's around us. There are a few rotted benches, what I think could have at one point been a luggage rack, and a gated counter where the station workers would have sold passenger tickets.

The dust is heavy, and mildew permeates the building's interior. When the third door is opened, we go outside and round the building, getting fresh air as we search for something stating the station's name. Two broken sticks that were probably once the bottom part of a signpost poke from the ground on the station's left side. But the upper half has long-since disappeared— cracked off by bad weather or, more likely, stolen by someone interested in a unique souvenir.

The outside of the building is uninteresting, so we head back in, Mim sneezing again as we make our way across to the ticket counter. Meander tries to open the rusted latch to get behind the counter. When it doesn't budge, he climbs over the waist-high gate instead. I follow, along with everyone except for Kornelía and Naasir, who wait in the main part of the station near a set of disused benches.

Behind the counter we find a long desk and two cubbies where clerks must have sat to do work. The desk and the first cubby are empty. In the second, a cupboard opens to reveal an old ledger book shoved against the side of a shelf. Meander grabs the book, looking at its cover before cracking it open. When he does, a folded slip of paper flutters to the floor.

Dylan bends down to pick up the paper, reading over its contents before looking at us with a shrug.

"Well, we've got a name," he says. He turns the paper around to show the picture of a man, along with a list of text that's laid out like a fact sheet of his life. "Good thing you picked up the book," he adds with a glance at Meander.

"They knew you wouldn't be able to resist," I say with a smile.

"It can't be that easy," Sabeena says. She takes the paper and reads it over.

"We're supposed to find a name," Dylan says as he stands at her side. "And there one is. Martin Diaz. Perfectly good name, if you ask me."

"Yes, but how do we know it's the *right* name?" Sabeena asks.

Dylan shrugs at Sabeena's comment, while beyond

the ticket counter, Kornelía—the member of Shade most likely to sense if we're on the right track—lingers with Draugur near the benches. Her expression is calm, but unfocused, like she's not an active participant in our conversation. Like she's not fully occupying the same space as us at all.

"She's being awfully quiet," I say as I lean my elbows on the counter. The dog raises his head, considering me as if he knows who I'm talking about. Then he moves towards us as Kornelía returns to the far side of the counter.

"Don't want to spoil the fun," she says when she's close.

"Fun?" I look at her face, at the eyes that can no longer look back at mine. "There's a ghost, isn't there?"

She nods, while everyone else looks her way.

"Why didn't you say anything?" Mim asks. She stands against the frame of one cubby, taking the paper from Sabeena and reading over Martin's details.

"Because that would give it away too soon," Kornelía replies.

"Well, we kind of figured there would be a ghost," Dylan says. "That doesn't change the task, though, does it? We still need to find the name. Why would this paper be here if we weren't supposed to..." He glances at Kornelía, one eyebrow raised. "Is *Martin* the ghost?"

Kornelía doesn't reply, at first. For a moment she stands completely still. Then she shakes her head. "It's not Martin."

"Do you know who it is?" I ask.

She shakes her head again before raising her unseeing eyes to the ceiling. "I don't. But I know the question you haven't thought to ask. The question that solves our task for real."

"Which is?" Dylan asks.

"What's the *ghost's* name," Meander answers in Kornelía's place.

I look over to find him watching the ceiling, though he's unperturbed enough I know he doesn't sense whatever spirit she's referring to.

"So, we have to ask the ghost their name?" Mim asks. She sounds annoyed again. "That's a cheap way to unravel a clue."

"Let's make sure it's the right way to unravel it before we jump to conclusions," Sabeena says. "We don't know what the ghost will say. We don't even know if any of us—Korni notwithstanding—can see it." She looks at Kornelía. "Is it a child?"

"No," Kornelía says.

Sabeena shrugs. "That means it's not me. Or Dylan. Or Naasir."

"Can you sense anything else about the ghost, Kornelía?" I ask.

"She's up there," she says. "But I can't get a sense of where—or why. I do get a... cramped sensation. There's not much room. She doesn't like it."

"If they sent us here, it means one of us can see her," Mim says. She pushes off the doorframe, dropping the paper as she looks between Meander and me. "We're the only three left."

Meander swallows before opening his mouth. Pink spots bloom on his cheeks, embarrassment at the fear he's about to admit to.

"I'll go up first," I tell him before he can speak. "If we can even figure out where we're supposed to go.

Mim can come too. If neither of us sees her, we'll let you know. But there's no sense getting her riled up without cause. This place doesn't seem stable enough for that. I'd rather not risk that roof crashing down if she gets pissed off."

"Neither would I," Mim says.

She glances around the ticketing office, then crosses to a small alcove at its right side. I keep on her heels, and together we turn into a shallow entryway dotted with two doors. One leads back outside, to the rear of the station. The other presumably leads upstairs.

We push and pull at the second door several times before I manage to throw my weight against it hard enough to get it unstuck. When it flies open, I stumble forward, muttering my own curses as I grip the grime-smudged stairs to keep from smacking my face. Meander helps me get back to my feet. But even as we stand, I can see the change overcoming his features, the open door enough to allow the ghost's presence to filter down to him. With a soft smile, I push him away from me, trying to keep him out of range. He gives me a last look—one of co-mingled disappointment and gratitude—before I turn to head up the stairs.

The station's upper floor consists of two small storerooms, the second of which contains a pull-down door to an attic. No ghost makes itself known in the rooms, so I open the door to let down the attic's ladder. It creaks and clanks until it thuds to the floor, and I take a shaky breath as I prepare myself for the inevitable confrontation to come. But when we ascend the ladder to the station's tiny, uppermost floor, it's Mim who sucks in a breath and winces as she looks into the center of the sloped room.

"You see her?" I ask, even though I don't need to. It's easy to tell when a fellow Sender sees ghosts. Even Kornelía seems to behave differently when the dead are nearby.

Mim nods, stepping forward and speaking to the spirit in Spanish. She says a few words and then asks the question we're supposed to, waiting a moment before turning back to me.

"Her name is Constanza," she says. "Constanza Diaz."

I nod, wondering if that truly is all we were supposed to get from this meeting.

"She must be related to Martin," I muse. "I wonder why his information's downstairs."

"I don't know," Mim says. She turns away from me, studying the ghost I can't see before asking her another question.

"She was a mother," Mim says. "She worked here and got stuck—trapped under something that fell. Her child was only two." She faces me again, and I'm startled to see unshed tears glistening in her eyes. "I'm going to stay with her, for a little. See if I can help."

"I..." I don't know what to say, or what to do. The attic is stale, cold, and confined. It makes me uncomfortable, especially when I imagine a mother lying trapped in the small space, her life dwindling while her toddler was probably at home wondering when she would come back. I'm thankful I don't see the spirit, and I want to get out of the dusty attic's hold. But it doesn't feel right to leave Mim alone, so I take a slow breath and nod. "I'll stay too," I say. "Unless you don't want me to."

"You can stay," Mim says. She smiles, looking a

little relieved that I'm not abandoning her. I nod again, then sit on the floor near the ladder's opening.

For the next several minutes, the air swirls cold around me as Mim and the ghost converse. The others are likely wondering where we are, and I'm tempted to sneak downstairs or at least send Meander a quick text. But I trust that Kornelía can sense all is calm here. Because it is. Honestly, I've never seen a spirit encounter so calm before. Mim stays standing at first, but eventually she sits as well, tucking her legs under her and pushing her hair behind her ears. Her fingers rub at the rosary around her neck while she speaks in a roll of soft, foreign words that sound like they're full of peace.

I haven't seen Mim around many spirits before. But her reaction to this one is surprisingly placid. She's not shivering or retching, passing out, sweating, or crying in pain. She seems, if anything, less affected by this ghost than the times I saw her spirit interactions in the past. At least, she seems that way until I realize she's crying. I hear her sniffing, and her words take on a tremor as she continues to talk through her tears. I've never known Mim to get particularly emotional around spirits. But then again, the two ghosts I've seen her with were both from before the coma that stole a year of her life.

When her head tilts back, her eyes closing as she nods, she takes a bigger breath and smiles.

"Martin was her son," she explains to me. "That's what we needed to know. That's what *she* needed to know. That he was okay. I told her he wouldn't want her to stay here. I told her he'd want her to be at peace."

Her words fade in time with the change in the air, and the room fills with a shimmer of white that my development as a Sender has allowed me to glimpse even when I can't see the spirit myself. The ghost's release approaches so suddenly that when music skims through my head, it makes me start. I sit upright, glancing at the shimmer before shifting to watch Mim. Tears streak her face, but she smiles as the wavering light grows, and I'm close enough to her that the ghost still manages to suck away my energy as it leaves.

THE OTHERS ARE FAR ENOUGH FROM THE SCENE THEY DON'T PASS OUT with the spirit's release. But they must give some share of strength, spreading the depletion between us. When Meander climbs up into the attic, I'm still semi-conscious, with it enough to hear him call my name—even if I can't get my eyes to open or my mouth to form any sort of response.

It's not an easy feat to get us down from the attic. After I've slept in the van, waking in time to disembark at the resort, I laugh as Meander apologizes for half-dropping me down the ladder before my dead weight collapsed against Naasir.

"I'm sorry you had to do that," I say as he holds my arm to steady my shaky steps. Mim is still asleep, though Naasir has an easier time carrying her cradled in his arms. "And I'm glad the ladder wasn't very tall."

Meander walks with me up to the hotel room,

where I sprawl out on the bed while he sits by my side, stroking my ear as a serious expression settles over his features.

"I should have come with you," he says.

"No, you shouldn't have," I reply with a sigh. "Mim had it under control. With you… it would have gotten out of control." His jaw tightens at my words, and I utter a sleepy groan. "Which isn't your fault. But… she didn't need help."

"I can see that," he says. His finger moves along my chin and down my neck before he lets his hand drop away. "You should get some sleep."

"Stay with me," I mumble as my eyes slip closed.

Meander shifts, sitting back against the headboard. After a few seconds, I hear the first rifling pages of a book, and the soft, familiar noise is enough to send me drifting into another comfortable doze.

By the time I wake again, it's evening. I could easily sleep for the whole night. But Dylan wants to know if we had any luck with our clue and, since Mim was drained more completely than me, I'm the one to offer him an answer.

"Her name was…" I struggle to sit up, stifling a yawn as I work to remember what Mim told me. "Con… Constantine? No, *Constanza*. Constanza Diaz. Martin's mother."

Dylan looks around at the group, which currently consists of everyone except for Mim. "Constanza. Ring any bells?" he asks.

For a moment, everyone is silent. But then Sabeena jumps up from her spot.

"Yes!" she exclaims. "I've seen the name somewhere… in the bar downstairs?" She looks around for confirmation, but no one has any to offer. So instead, she huffs and heads for the door.

"I guess we're going downstairs," I say as I drag myself off the bed.

"Are you up to it?" Meander asks.

I stand up and stretch my arms over my head with a smile. "If I pass out in the elevator, you'll know why." He looks me over like he's trying to work out the likelihood of that scenario actually playing out, and I laugh. "I'm fine. And if I get winded before we've found the name, I'll let you know. You just might have to carry me back upstairs."

He presses his lips together, probably to stop from making a suggestive comment the rest of our sector wouldn't like to hear. I give him a little smirk, then fix my bed-messed hair so we can join the others in the search.

We take the elevator down and wade through two groups of skiers on route to the bar. It's an open area, full of tables set against a wall of glass that looks out over the hot tub and the far slopes. About half of the tables are full, people eating their dinners or sipping on drinks as they listen to music streaming from the house speakers out across the pavilion. The aroma of hot food full of warm spice makes my stomach growl in anticipation of a gourmet meal. But before I can suggest a dinner break, Sabeena tugs on Naasir's arm, her face alight with excitement.

"There!" She points to an ornate display of lush greenery set along one part of the wall across from the bar. In the middle of the display is a plaque. The text is not written in English, but when I am close enough, I can still decipher the name along the plaque's bottom edge. *Constanza.*

"Okay, so we found the name," Dylan says. He stares at the plaque and then glances at me. "Did the ghost say anything else?"

"I didn't see the ghost," I remind him. "Mim was speaking Spanish, so I don't know… but we were just told to find the name, right? We found it."

"Yeah, but what do we do next?" Dylan asks.

"Look for another envelope," Kornelía replies. "Or at least another coin."

"Right…" Dylan considers the greenery before us. "Like, in there?"

Naasir steps up beside him, looking at the plants and then down at the soil bed laid out just behind the plaque. "Try here."

"We can't just dig in the dirt," Dylan says.

"Sure you can," Kornelía says with a smile. "We'll cover for you."

"I said *we can't* dig," Dylan balks. "Not sure how you took that to mean *I can.*"

Kornelía doesn't say anything else, and after staring at her for a moment, Dylan grumbles about us making the dog boy dig up the buried bone. I laugh as he turns to the dirt, throwing furtive glances over each shoulder while we try to crowd in and block him from view. I'm sure we look way more suspicious this way. But luckily, it doesn't take him long to push dirt aside and pull out the plastic folder containing our next clue.

Dylan opens the folder and retrieves the envelope. Inside, there's another coin, and a piece of paper with a number to text to let someone known we've completed the first task. Dylan does so, and we get a response saying a van will be waiting at three in the morning.

"Three AM?" Dylan says. "Guess that means an early night." He rifles a hand through his hair, frowning when he remembers his fingers are covered in dirt.

"Fine by me," I say through another yawn. "But can we eat first?"

We have dinner, then return upstairs for an uneventful evening. Dylan goes with Kornelía to check on Mim, while Sabeena and Naasir sit out on the balcony of our room while I change into pajamas and crawl back onto the bed. I try to fight with the clock to make sure our alarm is set for the middle of the night, but I'm too tired to make sense of it. Eventually, Meander laughs and pushes me away, and I watch him set the time before he settles beside me to resume his book.

When the alarm blares in the middle of the night, we make groggy work of showering and brushing our teeth before meeting the girls in the lobby. The French onion soup I ate for dinner sloshes uneasily in my stomach, my waking and sleeping pattern too erratic to deal with the dark, snowy sky as we head outside. I groan as the van starts over unsteady terrain, wishing I had something to ease my gut. Meander rubs my leg, and I lean against his shoulder to try and sleep off the worst of the sickening pain.

It's still dark when we reach our next destination. I expect another hotel, but this time we're left at a functioning house in the middle of a neighborhood. The thin, tall building with its stark white exterior is plain next to the ski resort. But it's not an abandoned, half-rotted shell. We even see a family eating breakfast through a lit window in the next house over, a simple sight to suggest this place isn't wholly preoccupied with death.

No one is in our house, but there are furnishings and a letter in the kitchen welcoming us for our stay. We drop our bags on the kitchen table, and Dylan raids the cupboards while Meander reads over the letter.

"Our next task is to locate a toy," he reads. He looks up from the sheet. "So just about as useful a directive as last time."

"Could be worse," I say. "At least it doesn't tell us to *'locate something red'* or *'you'll know the clue when you see it'*."

"Way to be an optimist, Cal," he mutters.

"Okay, we've got to find a toy," Dylan says while his head is still stuck in the fridge. "Any ideas *where*?"

"Likely not in there," Mim replies.

Meander glances up from the sheet of paper. "It doesn't give any hints," he says.

"Next door," Kornelía says. She nods, then tilts her chin towards the home's left side. "There's a spirit one house over."

"There's a family next door," I say. Even now, I can hear the kids outside, probably getting ready to start their morning at school. Kornelía nods again, but she doesn't elaborate any further. Which is explanation enough for all of us.

"Damn," Dylan says. "They're not going to make this easy on us after all, huh?"

"Do we know for certain we have to speak to the ghost?" Sabeena asks. "It could be a trick. We don't want to focus on breaking into someone's house, while the toy we're looking for is here all the time."

"That's a fair point," Meander says. "It'd be hypocritical of them to force us to trespass."

Dylan closes the fridge and unscrews the bottle of soda of he's retrieved, despite the early hour of the day. "So, we're looking for the toy here first?"

"It's a good place to start," Mim says from her spot at the table. "If we don't find anything, we'll know where to look next."

We can't go next door while it's morning and the family is at home. So, we spread out around the house and spend a leisurely hour scouring each floor in search of a hidden toy. Meander is right in that it doesn't make sense for the Oracle to have us breaking and entering. But I also can't imagine we've been dropped at this random house only to find a doll stuck in some closet. The two of us tackle the second floor, hunting through the bedrooms and the bathroom. But once we've gone over each room twice, we stare around one of the plainly furnished bedrooms, unenthusiastic about our odds of success.

"We could knock out some walls," Meander jokes.

I let out a huff as I drop onto the edge of the bed. "Let someone else do it. I've got no desire to look for hidden boxes or secret rooms."

Footsteps creak above us as Naasir and Dylan explore the attic. We raise our eyes, watching the ceiling for a moment. Then Meander sighs.

"This is pointless," he says. He sits next to me, one hand running through his curls as he shakes his head. "This whole trip. I get it. They want to know they'll have a strong return on investment from us. But shouldn't they bloody well ask if we even want to be considered for a Sender's job? I know we came back to camp, but..." he glances at me. "There are other reasons for that. Reasons not involved with interning for the sodding Oracle."

"Maybe that never occurred to them," I say with a frown. "You and I are the odd ones out. Most campers see the possibility of working for the Oracle as a good thing. Or at least an indifferent one."

"Yeah, perhaps," Meander says. "Or maybe they know we can't escape it, so they figure we'll wind up with them one way or the other."

The statement strikes at something in my chest, and I turn to him, concern creasing my brows.

"We have a choice," I say, my voice unconvincingly weak.

"We do," Meander agrees as he shifts closer to me. "They can't force anything on us. No one's going to make you face ghosts for the rest of your life, yeah?"

My worry grows as I study him. "But I *will* face ghosts for the rest of my life," I say. "We both will. We may not have to work for the Oracle. But we don't have a choice in what we see. In what we experience."

Meander opens his mouth to respond, then closes it as uncertainty clouds his features. Uncertainty that barely covers a ripple of fear, the same kind of fear that keeps him from planning for a happier future. There's no dream-scenario in which a magic potion or some voodoo spell takes our abilities away. We're stuck like this. The only question is, are we stuck doing it as a job—or avoiding it as we try to keep our days mundane?

We sink into silence as we both consider the unimpressive possibilities of what our Post-Wanagi lives will hold, until footsteps creak above us again, followed by the clunk of our sector mates descending the attic into the nearby hall. Meander eyes the ceiling, then looks back at me. For a moment, our gazes linger, both of sharing in the misery of all our unanswerable questions. Then we stand from the bed, our fingers laced as we join the others in the hall.

"Find anything?" I ask, my voice probably too falsely cheerful as everyone reconvenes on the main floor.

"Nothing," Sabeena says. "Unless we've missed a secret spot, there aren't any toys hidden in this house."

"Well then," Dylan says with a shrug. "I guess that means we've got to talk to the ghost."

"Maybe," Sabeena says. She brushes hair from her face and stares out the front window. "But I have another idea first."

SABEENA'S OTHER IDEA IS TO TALK TO THE KIDS NEXT DOOR.

"You can't just talk to some strange kids," Dylan says. "That's way creepy."

Sabeena rolls her eyes. "It doesn't have to be," she says. "Kids like me. I can talk to them, see if they know something we don't about the toy."

"You don't even speak Spanish," Mim reasons. "How are you going to speak to them? They probably don't know much English. And I'd be shocked if they know any Hindi."

"You can come with me," Sabeena says. "To translate."

"Then why doesn't Mim just do the talking?" Dylan asks.

Sabeena shakes her head. "*Trust me.* You know dogs. I know children. I'll talk to them. They'll talk to me."

Dylan raises his hands in surrender, while Mim sighs and waits for Sabeena to lead the way outside.

At some point in the hour or so we've been indoors,

the two boys ventured outside. I thought they were getting ready for their day at school, but they don't appear to be in any hurry. They lounge on the front stoop, a ball between them as they sip juice from glass bottles. Sabeena doesn't check for adults or even ease herself in with a far-off wave. She bounds over to the boys with as much energy as the kids themselves probably display during their play. Mim hurries after her, surprised at her quick movements. The rest of us stay near the door of the other house.

"Okay, this feels even creepier," Dylan says after a minute of watching the scene.

"Should we go inside?" I ask.

"I don't want to leave them alone," Naasir says.

"So…" I start, "…should we join them?"

"Beats standing here like we're waiting for her to lure them over," Dylan says.

Sabeena is already well into her conversation with the boys by the time we cross the distance between the houses. The kids must be brothers, both of them sharing the same dark, curly hair and lopsided grins. When we reach them, it's apparent that Mim is only there to translate the actual words, not to participate in the discussion. Even if she weren't present, I'm still pretty sure Sabeena would find a means of communication. The boys flank her sides on the doorstep, talking—from Mim's snippets—about football, which in my personal vocabulary means they're discussing soccer. The conversation flies fast between the four of them, Mim barely able to keep up with the translation, although I'm not sure Sabeena's listening to half of what she says, anyway.

"Is your ball your favorite toy?" Sabeena asks. The

boys nod enthusiastically, bouncing the ball between them to show off their skills. Sabeena gives them a delighted clap, then settles with a more contemplative expression. "Are there any other toys around here?"

One of the boys starts speaking in a rush, and Mim translates a list of the toys they have inside. Sabeena listens for a moment before putting a hand on his arm to quiet him. Then she smiles and taps the side of her nose.

"I mean a special toy," she says. The words are vague, but her manner is so conspiratorial it's like she knows exactly what she's talking about. "Something out of the ordinary."

The two boys pause, staring at each other from her either side. When Sabeena sees their expressions, she smiles as if she's just revealed a secret. "Ah. You know what I mean, don't you?" she asks.

The boys look at each other for confirmation, before one of them shrugs.

"Over there," he says, pointing to a hill a little ways off from the street.

"Are you here about the ghost?" the other one—the younger one—says in a hushed voice. As soon as he says it, his brother smacks his knee hard. The younger boy flinches back, but even still it's easy to catch the fear in his eyes.

Sabeena catches it too. "Is there a ghost in your house?" she asks the boy. He looks at her, his eyes widening as he takes in her concern, until his brother stands up and grabs the ball.

"We've got to go," Mim translates for him as he hauls up his brother, leaving the glass bottles on the stoop as they head inside the house.

Sabeena watches them go. Then she looks at the hill.

"Over there," she repeats. She stands from the step, brushing herself off and sparing the house a final glance. Then she trudges across the road.

At the top of the hill, a few trees and bushes dot the landscape. We walk around the hill for about five minutes before Kornelía stops by one of the trees.

"There's something about this one," she says. Her hand reaches out to gently stroke the tree's bark, her fingers a little clumsy as they feel along the uneven texture. I watch her movements—still awed and saddened by the way her eyes stare off to the side of the tree, unseeing the actual mass in front of her— until Sabeena steps between us, obscuring my view.

"There's a hollow," she says. She hesitates for half a second before dipping her hand into the darkened space inside the tree. She feels around and squeaks, her arm angling up so she can pull at something lodged within. When she retracts her hand, I don't think any of us are surprised to see the little wooden bear clutched in her grip, its front engraved with two dates: *1963-1970.*

"I think it's safe to say we've found the toy," Dylan says. "But what about the clue?"

Sabeena stares at the bear, one finger running over the etched dates. Her expression is pained, and for a moment she doesn't seem to hear Dylan's words. Then she blinks and looks back at the tree. With the bear clenched in one fist, she puts her other arm into the hollow and feels around again until she fishes out the envelope meant for us.

As soon as the envelope makes its appearance, Dylan whips out his phone, ready to text. But Sabeena grabs his arm before he can even unlock the screen.

"Don't," she says in a quiet rush. She presses her lips together, looking at the house across the street.

"What do you mean?" Dylan asks. "We found the clue. Now it's time to get out of here."

"Not yet," Sabeena replies. She glances at Kornelía, her eyes shining. "The ghost—it's this child, isn't it?" She holds up the bear as if Kornelía can see it, and the tall girl nods as if she does.

"So young," Sabeena says. She closes her eyes and squeezes the bear. "Those boys are afraid. No ghost should make people afraid. It means at least three are suffering in place of one." She opens her eyes and looks between us. "I have to help the child."

"Hey, I'm all for helping ghosts," Dylan says. "But that house is occupied, remember?"

"He's right, Sabeena," Mim says. "The boys talked to you. But do you think their parents will be so happy to let you inside their home?"

"No," Sabeena admits. She wipes at her eyes and shakes her head. "But I need to get in there all the same."

"You don't mean—" I stare at Sabeena, remembering all too well the children we helped in Tonga. The house we broke into more than once.

Sabeena nods. "If I can catch the boys again, I can get them to talk. Ask them where the ghost is. I can… I can have them leave a window open for me."

"And if you don't get to talk to them again?" Mim asks.

"Then we'll find another way inside," Sabeena snaps. She fixes her gaze on Mim, holding the other girl's stare. "You helped the last one. I need to help this one. I don't care if I get in trouble doing it."

"Yeah, but what if you get all of us in trouble doing

it," Meander says.

"I…" Sabeena sighs and looks down at the bear. "You can all stay in the house. I won't need a translator for the ghost. You can stay out of sight. I'll take the blame myself."

The rest of us look between ourselves, everyone knowing this is a bad idea but all of us unwilling to throw Sabeena to the wild without backup.

"We'll stand watch for you," Naasir says after a moment.

Sabeena smiles at him, nodding as she lifts the bear. She kisses the wood's top, then replaces it in the hollow of the tree. For a few seconds, she rests her palm against the tree's bark. Then she turns around and heads back for the houses.

Sabeena spends the better part of the next eight hours sitting on the front porch. The boys do go to school—or disappear somewhere else throughout the day—but only one parent leaves with them, while the other one remains stationed in the house. The day is boring, the rest of us watching movies on Dylan's laptop, hanging out in the house's back garden, and falling into the silence of our own pursuits. When the boys finally return home in the afternoon, I'm the first one of us still inside to notice them. Pausing Beethoven's "Ghost Trio", I pull out my earbuds and tap Meander's shoulder, and the rest of us gather to watch the exchange through the sitting room window.

The boys seem wary when Sabeena and Mim first approach. But it doesn't take long before the kids are pointing at the house. Sabeena nods as they convey their information. Then she folds the two boys into a hug.

When the girls return, Sabeena's plans have begun.

"They said the ghost is in the back room on the second floor," she relates. "Their grandmother's sewing room. No one will be inside tonight. They'll leave the window open for me."

"Let's just hope they don't mention all this to their parents," Dylan says.

"They won't," Sabeena replies. "They know this is a secret."

The ease with which she has convinced the children is unsettling, and I'm glad I know Sabeena well enough to be certain that her motives are pure. I would hate for the wrong person to get an ability like hers. The side effect of her talent seems to be that—like Dylan and his dogs—Sabeena has an affinity for gaining the trust and confidence of the young. A useful talent, ghosts or no. But one that could be horrifically abused if bestowed to the wrong person.

The house we are in is stocked with food, so we forage for dinner and spend the evening spreading out and claiming rooms for our inevitable overnight stay. We're not in the haunted location. But the unfamiliar house still feels strange, and the knowledge of what Sabeena is going to do makes the evening tense. Meander and I try to steal away for a while. But after far too short a time, Sabeena calls up the stairs asking us to come down for our turn at keeping watch in the back garden to wait for the lights to turn off next door. We do, switching back and forth with the others as we sit out in the freezing night until the house finally grows dark around eleven.

Once the lights have turned off, Sabeena paces the living room until nearly midnight before deciding it's safe enough for us to venture next door.

"Hold up a minute," Dylan says before we leave. He crosses to the coffee table in the front room, snatching up the folder and fishing out our instructions for what to do next. He skims through the note and programs something into his phone. "If the shit hits the fan, I'll text the powers that be," he explains when he's done.

We take the back way out of the house, glad there are no fences between this property and the one next door. The night is overcast, no moon or stars to give us light. It's also cold. Snow threatens to fall, and after my earlier stint keeping watch, all I want is to get back inside. I hunch my shoulders, glad I brought my heaviest fall coat and hoping Meander is warm enough in his thinner jacket.

The neighbor's house is dark. But without hesitation, Kornelía glides to the correct window and stops, Draugur staring up as he sits by her side.

"And how do you propose getting up there?" Dylan asks in a whisper once we are all standing underneath the window.

Sabeena smiles, probably remembering doing something just like this in Tonga. At least this abode is not as tall as that beachfront treehouse had been. She looks at Naasir and, without waiting for a command, he steps forward and lowers to his knees so she can climb onto his back. Without a sound, he lifts her high enough she can grab the edge of the sill and shimmy the window up to start pulling herself inside.

"We are so going to jail for this," Dylan mutters once we all hear the thud of her landing.

"Just keep that phone close," Naasir says with an unusual note of worry in his tone.

Dylan waves the phone, clutching it tight, while above us Sabeena's back presses against the half-opened window.

"If she's not careful, she's going to fall right out," Meander says.

"Anyone know how to call for medical assistance here?" Dylan asks.

"The Oracle will," Kornelía says. "But don't worry about it yet. She's okay. She's with the ghost."

"What do you see, Kornelía?" I ask.

She tilts her head up, and I'm surprised to see her close her eyes as if she's working to concentrate. Kornelía has always seen the dead in her mind's eye, but it used to be easier when her eyes were closed. I wonder if doing it now is a force of habit, or if she still finds the small separation from the world an extra aid in discerning spirits.

"It's a boy," she says. "We know his age from the bear. He's six or seven, and he's scared."

Meander doesn't seem able to feel the ghost, but as Kornelía explains the spirit's emotions, he takes an involuntary step further away from the window.

"He was sick," Kornelía continues. "I think maybe he was always sick. Or he was for a long time. And it scared him."

"Do you know what he needs?" Mim asks.

Kornelía shakes her head. "I can't communicate with him," she says. "I know he's scared, and I can sense he was sick when he died. But those aren't very useful—especially since Sabeena could tell you the same without me here."

Her voice takes on a wilting, almost apologetic tone, as if the extraordinary ability she's gained is still something she considers weak. She can't speak with ghosts, which I suppose means she doesn't have much chance of ever being the direct cause of a spirit crossing. But I would have hoped that, by this point, she'd come to some understanding of how great her new type of vision is.

"Do you think she'll be successful?" Mim asks as she stares at the window. Sabeena has moved away now, but we can't hear anything from inside. She must be keeping her voice low so as not to disturb the rest of the house. At least, I hope that's what accounts for the lack of noise drifting out from the windowpane.

"Yes," Kornelía says. "If the spirit was complicated, the Oracle probably wouldn't have sent us here."

"We weren't explicitly told to release every ghost we see," Dylan says.

"No, but Robbie did say we might be able to help them," Mim says. "And releasing them makes this feel like less of a game."

"Was it ever a game?" Meander asks.

"No," Mim agrees. "It's a test, remember? If we don't want to release the spirits, that's fine. But it says a lot about us if we do."

"We can't free every single ghost we see, though," I say. "None of us can. It doesn't work like that."

"Which is why we've been sent to these specific ghosts," Kornelía reasons. "Because we *can* release them."

"Or, alternatively," Meander says, "these are the spirits in close enough range to camp."

"He's got a point," Dylan says. "You might be grasping for a purpose, Korni. I can't believe the Oracle would ever want Sabeena doing this."

"I think they would," Mim says.

Dylan sighs. "And that's why you're a lifer, and I'm not."

Mim rolls her eyes, then glances back up at the window. "It's cold. I hope it doesn't take too long."

It does take too long. For the better part of the next hour, we stand under the window, shivering and chattering until we finally hear a cry from above us. Then we still, waiting for more noise—either from Sabeena or the rest of the house. After a terse moment of silence, a low sob breaks into the snowy quiet, and Sabeena appears at the window, her face wet with tears and a furious look in her eyes.

"He's going!" she calls down with a hiccup of breath. "Help me out before he does."

We scramble to action, Naasir standing below the window as the rest of us crowd behind him in a crescent of waiting arms. Sabeena climbs over the windowsill, her legs dangling as her top half stares at something in the room. I can just make out the impression of light through the window before my focus shifts as Sabeena slumps into unconsciousness. For another tense second, we all wait, wondering what to do. Then her body slips, sliding at a painful angle until she drops from the second story window.

We fumble forward, all of us crowding closer. Naasir catches her by the hips, and Mim dives to stop Sabeena's head from slamming against the ground.

15

"I HAD TO TRICK HIM," SABEENA SAYS THE FOLLOWING AFTERNOON when we're on route to our next location. She leans sluggishly against the van's window, her eyes closed and an ice pack held against her ribs. "He wanted his parents. That's all he cared about. I didn't know what else to do. I couldn't come back after I'd found information. So, I… I lied. I told him his parents were dead. I have no idea if they are dead or not. They're probably not. They're probably still alive, but I told that boy they were dead so that he could go and see them. He was so excited. He was so excited to leave when he thought his mother was waiting on the other side of the light."

She sobs, and tears leak from her shut eyes. Naasir grips her shoulder, but he doesn't offer her any soothing words. It'd be hypocritical if he did, I guess. If any of us did. I once made a ghost angry by calling him a coward, an insult he took so seriously he crossed over just to spite me. But that's a bit different from tricking a child for the sake of completing a release.

"I've never done that before," Sabeena says with a sniff. "At the time, it felt necessary. But now…"

"Now, you're sleep-deprived," Mim says. "Don't let that cloud your reflection."

Sabeena wipes her face and nods. Then she sniffs again and opens her eyes. "So, where are we going now?" she asks.

"No clue," Dylan says. "Driver here won't tell us anything."

The driver has indeed been tight-lipped, but as soon as the accusation about him is made, the man turns in his seat and says something to Mim. She nods, then shifts around to face us from her seat up front. "He says we'll be there in two hours."

"Good," Sabeena says. She closes her eyes again. "That means I can get some more sleep."

The evening hour is upon us when we arrive at stop number three, which this time proves to be a rugged hostel at the foot of a mountain. We're led into the building, where we find our lockers and put away our stuff while other travelers mingle in their own groups, passing us by on their way to the lodging rooms. After we've unloaded our bags, we connect to the hostel's Wi-Fi to check our contacts from home. My inbox is empty. But Meander has an email from his half-brother Liam. He opens the message with an easy air. Yet as soon as he begins skimming the lines, frustrated exhaustion falls over his features. By the time he's finished the email, he shifts his weight from one foot to the other as he struggles to type out a reply.

"You okay?" I ask in a quiet voice while we linger at

the edge of the lobby.

He pauses, one hand rising from his phone to run through his curls.

"She's lost her job," he says, referring to his mother. "Shit." He looks up at me, and his eyes are so troubled my chest constricts. "She's going to be impossible now."

"I'm sorry," I say. He drops onto a wide window ledge, and I squat next to him, wishing we were not in a busy hostel. "Is there any chance she'll find something new by the time camp's over?"

"Doubt it," Meander says. He sighs, his jaw tightening as he stares at the phone. "We can hope."

I wish I could do more than hope. Meander's mother is already brutal. But if she's still unemployed when he comes home from camp, she'll be more abrasive— and possibly more violent. He doesn't deserve that. He doesn't deserve any of what she puts him through.

I place my hand on his knee, and he releases a breath as his fingers start moving over the keyboard of his phone. He writes a fast reply to his brother. Then he shuts off the screen and clutches the phone hard in one hand.

"Do you need space?" I ask. "I can make up an excuse for you. Not sure how private the rooms will be, but there's probably somewhere outside that you could be alone."

Meander smiles, his free hand reaching down to where mine still rests on his leg.

"I'm fine," he says. And I know he doesn't totally mean it. But I also know we're in a crappy situation that's not at all cut out for trying to deal with big news like this.

"You let me know the moment you aren't," I tell

him. He nods and squeezes my hand. Then he stuffs his phone in his pocket, and we both get up to join the rest of our sector.

"Apparently, we have to order a coffee," Dylan says, filling us in when we meet with the group. "They have a restaurant here? We can order a coffee and skip this leg altogether."

"We've said it before… I doubt it will be that easy," Mim says.

"The first clue was to find a name," he reminds her. "That was easy."

"And who supplied the name?" she says.

Dylan laughs. "You think we need to order coffee from a ghost? Maybe there's a barista haunting the coffee bar."

"We might not have to order directly from the dead," I say in a low voice as a group of people look our way. "But Mim's right. I'm sure the clue will have something to do with a ghost."

"There's no restaurant on the premises, at any rate," Meander says.

"There aren't any ghosts here, either," Kornelía adds.

"And there's more to the instructions," Mim says. She snatches the paper from Dylan's grasp. "It's an address. Look."

"Which means we'll have to go out for a night on the town," Dylan grins.

"What town?" Mim asks. "We're in the middle of nowhere."

She isn't entirely correct, though certainly Dylan's fantasy of a big night out isn't likely to come true. The hostel is situated in a little village, with three restaurants and a street cart clearly targeting backpackers stopping on route to the mountainside.

"Whatever," Dylan says. "As long as we find somewhere to eat first before looking for the ghost. I'm starving."

"Let's get some food," Mim agrees. "Then we'll find someone to ask about this address. It should be dark by then."

"Nobody thinks we should find the place *before* it's dark?" I ask.

"Of course not," Meander mutters. "That would be far too sensible."

"Yeah," I say. "How foolish of me."

"Mmm." He nudges my shoulder and offers me a smirk—his amusement almost covering the turmoil I know he's storing out of sight.

We leave the hostel and walk a block to the nearest restaurant. Mim orders for the group, and we make it through the entire meal before she decides to ask one of the waiting staff if they know where we can find the address. She flags a server on his way by. When she shows him the paper, he nods and, with a bored expression, gestures out the window.

"Up the mountain," Mim translates for him.

"Up the mountain?" Dylan asks. He stares out the window that mostly just reflects the restaurant's interior. "We can't get that far tonight."

"Tonight?" the man answers in rough English. "No, no. Takes three days."

"Three days?" Dylan repeats.

Mim asks the waiter a question, and he responds while pointing out the window again.

"He says we'll need a guide," she tells us. "It's a hiking trip."

"That explains the backpacks, then," Meander says. He sits back in his chair, a brooding displeasure settling over his features. I give him a questioning glance, and he sighs. "I hate hiking," he grumbles, and I smile as I give his knee a squeeze under the table.

After we've finished our meals, we make our way to the guide station, only to discover that our arrival has been expected. The older woman running the station gives us a meeting time for the next morning. Then, with a plan for the day ahead, we trudge back to the hostel.

While the others head in for some rest, Meander and I stay outside, braving the cold so we can talk more about his brother's email and what it might mean for Meander's return home. The conversation is not an overly productive one—neither of us has any real idea of what he's going to face, or what he can do about it when he does—but Meander seems to feel better after talking it through. We sit together on the edge of a large stone garden planter until the cold is too much. Then we go inside for a night of tossing and turning in the unfamiliar—and totally un-private—space.

The next morning, we meet our hiking guide, a guy named Cristobal who has a scruffy face and a grin so flashy it rivals Dylan's.

"The ghost kids, yes?" he asks with amusement as we approach.

"Great," Meander mumbles. "Something to talk about on the hike."

We crowd in to collect the extra supplies we're bringing with us—food, proper winter gear, reflective ponchos, and some safety equipment in case we wander off track. I don't like the warnings Cristobal gives us about the dangers of our upcoming quest. But at least we're prepared in case disaster strikes.

While we load up our things, our guide explains where we'll be heading. Our first two days will be with another group of tourist hikers, before we veer off for our own purposes on day three. Cristobal speaks English pretty well, which means Mim won't have to act as translator again. But before we leave, the guide tilts his head, speaking to her in a low Spanish as he utters something that makes her eyes flash with annoyance.

"Ask her yourself," she snaps as soon as the words have escaped his mouth.

Cristobal's hands fly up in surrender, but when she doesn't relent, he turns sheepishly towards Kornelía.

"The hike is meant for beginners," he says. "But there are still a few spots…"

"I'm fine," Kornelía says, cutting him off. "You have our waivers from camp. I have all the permissions I need to be on this trek." Before he can offer any further comment, she turns away, placing a gentle hand on Mim's arm and asking her to help with the jacket and snow pants. Cristobal watches her, an uneasy expression on his face. But then he resigns himself to her presence and moves on to make sure everyone else has the equipment they require.

We get our things on, then wait for the tourist hikers to arrive before setting off in a large group. The trek starts with a walk through snow-dusted foothills, before we wind around to a well-trod path at the base of a mountain. I'm curious to know how far up our three-day trip will lead. We're not experienced hikers, so I doubt we'll go far. I wonder how long it would take someone to actually reach the top of the summit.

"Last night you said you hated hiking," I say to Meander after the first hour of walking. "When have you ever been hiking?"

Meander gives me a disgruntled frown. "Year nine. Stupid hiking trip for school. We had to tromp through a forest for three hours. It rained the whole time. Half the ground was mud." He waves his arms, his voice raising with irritation. "I walked right through a nettle plant. And then, as if all of that wasn't enough—" His voice lowers to a clenched whisper, "—in the middle of the bloody woods was a ghost."

His arms drop dramatically to his sides, and when I see his dark glower, I start to laugh.

He looks my way, his expression shifting into one of incredulity. "Are you laughing at me?"

"No," I say through another laugh. His glower comes back with harder intensity, and I laugh more, covering my mouth to try and stifle it. "I'm not. It's not funny."

"No, it's not," Meander says, his lips cracking into a smile even as he continues to scowl.

I bite the inside of my cheek and clear my throat, trying to stop from laughing. But when I glance back at him, we both crack up. He shoves my arm, then grabs my sleeve and pulls me close against his side as we continue along the path.

The hike is beautiful. The footpaths curve around a rocky stream before we start a gentle incline up the mountain. At this level, the landscape alternates between pockets of sloping green hills and flat sections covered with sprinklings of snow. Ahead and above us, the higher points of the mountain are white-capped as they stretch into the fog-hazed sky.

The other travelers talk among themselves, a few of them asking us questions while the rest look vaguely annoyed having to share their tour with a bunch of teens. Everyone finds Kornelía and Dylan anomalies, though. Even in this unfamiliar landscape, Kornelía walks confidently as she steps alongside Draugur, while Dylan trails at the dog's other side, so attuned to his movements the two step in synced patterns, making slight curves or pauses at the same time. I don't think Dylan has a clue what he's doing. But his lack of awareness makes the whole thing an even more peculiar sight to behold.

When we stop for a picnic lunch overlooking a meadow complete with a babbling brook, both groups eat together, admiring the scenery and stretching our legs while Cristobal muses about the abundance of insects given the winter season. Then, late into the day after another few hours' walk, we reach the small building that will provide our overnight accommodation. The place is something between a hotel and hostel, a clean lobby and breakfast area leading to a few wide rooms full of sleeping cots. The seven of us are roomed together, while the other group shares their own space.

We unload our supplies and, after a bit of rest, gather on the wide garden patio built behind the hotel. We cook dinner over an open grill, everyone hanging out like we're having some kind of weird party. It's a unique experience, the night cold but the fire hot, and it's nice to relax in the fresh, mountain air. The mood is easy, until late into the evening when Draugur's ears perk, and Dylan nearly trips over a stone ledge as the wind is knocked from his lungs.

"Dylan?" Mim asks. She reaches forward to help him up from his knees, while the older hikers watch on with curious glances.

"Is he okay?" one of the adults ask.

Dylan's face grows sicklier in the shadows thrown by the dancing flames, his expression pinched with pain. "I'm okay," he croaks.

Mim gets him to his feet, and we gather close, half-blocking him from the others' view. He glances at us, then looks into the wilderness beyond the patio, his lips turned in a weak smile. "Someone's here. Only I can't…"

He keeps his sights ahead and takes a few cautious steps. He makes it to the edge of the hotel's property before he staggers back into Mim.

"Oh, man!" he mutters to himself.

"What is it?" Kornelía asks. She faces him, her head swaying slightly from side to side as if she's trying to read his emotions. "Is something wrong?"

"No," Dylan says. He runs a hand through his hair and moves forward again. "No. It's just… it's not a dog."

"What do you mean?" I ask. "What are you seeing?"

"It's a fox," Dylan says. He looks at me and grins. "I've never seen something other than a dog before."

He takes a few further steps beyond the patio before he kneels and holds out his hand. For a minute, he stays like that, still as stone as he waits for something the rest of us can't see. Then he groans, his hand lifting carefully to touch the dead fox that must have come his way. He swipes his hand through the air a few times. Then, with a suck of breath, he drops his arm and looks far off in the distance. He stays kneeling for another minute. Then he returns to the patio with a sigh.

"He darted away," he says. His tone is strange, a bit of disappointment mixed with a bigger dose of intrigue. "He's too wild—doesn't have the patience I need to understand why he's still around." He stares into the night, his mood dampening. "I wish I could help him. But I didn't get even an inkling from that encounter. Maybe I can't communicate with the wild ones."

"Or maybe you just need more practice," Mim says.

"Maybe," Dylan agrees as he continues to stare into the dark. His expression grows melancholy, and Mim takes his arm.

"Come on," she says. She tugs him in the opposite direction from where the fox went. "Let's go for a walk before we head inside."

She holds his arm, and he nods, casting a final glance after the ghostly fox before the two of them venture off for a quiet conversation of their own.

16

THE SECOND DAY OF OUR HIKE IS MORE INTENSE THAN THE FIRST. WHAT started as a gentle walk along well-defined paths quickly turns into a cold, snowy, steep-hilled climb complete with treacherous ridges. I'm not, strictly speaking, afraid of heights, but I am nervous on the narrow pathways that give me flashbacks to a time when I worried about ghosts sneaking in with the wind and knocking me over a ledge. I keep my eyes focused ahead when we reach the narrowest point rounding one portion of the mountainside. When I step on a loose rock, wobbling off-balance in my panic, Meander holds out his arm for me to clutch until we make it to the far side.

Once we are back on wider ground and my pulse has returned to a normal rate, the breathless endeavor is rewarded with the sight of a tall, thin waterfall in view across an expanse of grassland below us. I've visited Niagara Falls on more than one occasion back at home.

But that waterfall is surrounded by roads, attractions, and mass crowds of people. I've never seen a waterfall in a natural setting before. The stunning sight almost makes the precarious trek worth it.

The afternoon portion of the hike is easier than the morning, and when evening falls we spend the night in another hostel that feels more like a cabin. On the third day, the other tourists continue on with a new guide, while we follow Cristobal down into a plain further across the mountainside.

"Where are we going?" Sabeena asks our guide once the campsite and the other hikers are no longer in sight.

"The Smiling House," Cristobal replies.

"Smiling House?" Sabeena asks. "What kind of place is that?"

"A house," Cristobal says, unhelpfully. "It's said to be haunted. But you know about that, huh, ghost kids?"

Sabeena rolls her eyes behind his back, and a collective smirk is shared among the rest of us. I'm used to people making stupid or mocking comments about ghosts. But it's a lot easier to bear the skepticism of non-Senders when I'm surrounded by those who understand the truth.

The morning of our third day is uneventful. But in the afternoon, Dylan discovers that the ghost fox from our first night has been trailing him. He's ecstatic when he catches sight of it again, lying to Cristobal and saying he caught sight of a living fox instead. Our guide is amused by his enthusiasm at what, to him, is probably an ordinary sight. But Cristobal's amusement fades when Dylan outright bolts off the path, trying to catch up with the ghost before it darts out of sight again. The fox disappears, and Cristobal loses his cool as he lectures us all on the dangers of straying from the path—and the horrors awaiting us should we get lost or injured in the wilds.

After his berating, Dylan doesn't leave the path again. But he keeps his eyes and his other senses trained, constantly peering over hills and around bends in hopes he'll spot the ghost.

It's nearly four in the afternoon when we finally reach our destination. A camp has been constructed for us, where two other tour guides are ready with fires and winter-approved camping tents. I'm not looking forward to a night of sleeping outdoors. But for now, I've got other things on my mind.

"This is the Smiling House," Cristobal says as he leads us up a private path to a surprisingly modern—and obviously affluent—glass, steel, and wood-beam house. Nothing about the home's design suggests smiling. Its construction is interesting, but the whole house is comprised of sharp-cornered squares and rectangles, giving an impression that, if anything, is arrogant and stern.

"What is a house like this doing all the way up here?" Sabeena asks.

"It's a summer residence for the family who owns it," Cristobal says. "They don't use it during the winter months."

"It doesn't look very old," Meander says.

"It was built fifteen years ago," Cristobal explains. "The same family has lived in this area for, oh... hundreds of years, I imagine. They own much of this land."

"Do they know we're here?" Mim asks.

"Yes," Cristobal says. "The Smiling House has always been a curiosity for certain tourists. The family allows visits, with their permission. You have that permission."

"Should we go in now?" Sabeena asks.

The hour is not late, but the winter season means it's already dark. I'd rather enter the Smiling House during the day. But if we have to do this at night, I want to get it over with as early as possible. Mim and Sabeena have already seen ghosts. Dylan and Naasir can't interact with the dead in the way most haunted houses will allow. Which means there's a decent chance this ghost will be seen by me. Or Meander. I don't like either of those scenarios. But I'd prefer to find out which of us will suffer while our tour guides are still awake—should medical intervention prove necessary.

"Let's go now," I say as I survey the home's cold exterior.

"You can eat first, if you like," Cristobal begins.

"We'll eat after," Meander mumbles. "If we're not unconscious."

Cristobal looks at him, a question shining in his eyes that he doesn't bother to ask. Instead, he shrugs his shoulders and points back towards the camp.

"I'll be there, waiting with food." He holds up a set of keys. "I've been instructed to let you go alone. But—" He pulls the keys against him while he gives us a stern stare. "You are not here for fun, ghost kids. Be mindful of the space. Treat it well. The family is gracious in letting you into their home. Do not betray their kindness by disrespecting their property."

I resist the urge to roll my eyes, or to give Meander a furtive glance. I don't want Cristobal thinking we won't take his warning seriously. And, if he somehow has insider knowledge that one of us might cause a bit of destruction, I don't want him to make any guesses as to who the culprit will be.

"We'll respect the space," Mim says. She holds out her hand and waits for Cristobal to drop the keys into her palm. He does so, hesitantly. But Mim shows no hesitation as she turns away from him and stalks up to the house.

I'm glad our guide is not trying to tag along. The seven of us leave him on the path, where he lingers until we've reached the house's front door. Mim turns on her heel, waving him off and waiting for him to take the hint. Cristobal pauses for another beat, seeing if we'll continue inside. When we don't, he hunches his shoulders and stalks off in the direction of the camp.

"Okay," I say with a sigh once he's out of sight. "How are we handling this?"

"We go in, look around, figure out if there's really a ghost," Dylan says. "Or a coffee bar. Who the hell are we going to order coffee from up here?"

Meander stares at the house, teeth running over his bottom lip as he contemplates what to do. For our first two tasks, we walked right into the places we were sent. But the Smiling House is different. It's easy to see that Cristobal doesn't totally trust us. If Meander walks inside and sets off a volatile spirit, the Oracle could be looking at some hefty fines for property damage.

Which is, of course, the Oracle's prerogative. If they want to risk it by sending Meander here, then fine. But explaining that to our hiking guide while we're three days away from our getaway van might be difficult.

"We can go in one by one," I suggest with a casual

look at the others. "Feel it out."

"That's stupid," Dylan says while, to his either side, Mim and Kornelía sigh—the breaths so in sync it'd make me laugh if this weren't a more serious moment. "What?" Dylan asks, until Mim gives him a pointed glance, and the reason for our hesitance slowly dawns on him. His head turns in Meander's direction, his expression a weird mix of lingering dislike and newfound pity. An expression that makes Meander's jaw immediately tighten in frustration.

"We'll all go in," he says, and this time it's me giving him a pointed glance because I don't want him getting hurt or in trouble just so he can save face with Dylan. But when he catches my gaze, the fear in his eyes sweeps away my annoyance. He doesn't want to go inside. But neither does he want to be anyone's burden, and right now, that's probably exactly what he feels like.

I nod my head in silent agreement of his plan. But I make sure everyone else goes inside first before I grab his arm and spin him to face me. "You don't—"

He cuts me off with a kiss, my stomach swooping as he wraps a hand around my neck to hold me close.

"I know," he murmurs against my lips. He smiles, rubbing the tip of his nose against mine. "I'll be fine. I've got you."

The casual remark sends a tingling spark cascading from where our noses touch. It doesn't make me want to go inside. Rather, it makes me want to grab him and haul him off somewhere safe. But I nod again and let him walk into the house, keeping close to his back and watching his every move for the first signal of a disturbance.

We enter the front foyer, walking beneath high ceilings and sidestepping the wide, steel staircase as we make our way to the sunken living room. I'm surprised to see that the space is empty. The family must clear out their belongings when the house is not in use—or the Oracle warned them about who would be entering their home. It hardly seems efficient to move furniture up and down the foothills of the mountain. There must be storage nearby to keep everything protected in the winter months. At least, I hope the Oracle didn't force such a drastic move in preparation for whatever we're going to face here.

The rest of our sector wanders around the empty room, their expressions puzzled by the lack of furniture. But the confusion turns to awe when they check out the valley views offered by the large front windows. They are all fine, and I'm fine too, no static or smells assaulting my senses. Which means I don't feel fine as I survey the group before looking back at Meander.

His gaze is fixed not on the windows but on the staircase. He swallows several times as he draws in slow, careful breaths.

"Meander?" I touch his arm, but as soon as I do he shakes his head.

"I don't..." he pauses, glancing at me before looking across the room to Kornelía. "Is there someone here?"

"I'm... not sure," Kornelía admits. The uncertainty makes everyone take notice. The rest of the sector stops whatever they were doing to focus on where Kornelía stands, her chin raised towards the house's second floor. "I mean, I think... It feels like... I don't see anyone, but..."

"I feel weird," Meander cuts in. His eyes snake back to me. "I feel like there's maybe a ghost, somewhere far off. But not close. Not exactly *here*."

"What the hell does that mean?" Dylan asks. "Do we need to go hunting around the mountain?"

"No," Kornelía says. "There's dead energy. But Meander is correct. It's not really here. Not right now."

"So… how does that impact us?" Sabeena asks.

"It means we keep looking for a clue," Mim says. "Let's explore the rest of the house."

Unlike the last house we stayed in, this time we don't split up. The ghost—or whatever it is—makes us nervous, and we all stay together as we move from room to empty room. There's nothing in the three main floor rooms, nor is there anything in the kitchen or the expansive dining area beyond. We go out to the back balcony, taking a moment to appreciate the night-shadowed scenery before heading up to the second floor. There, we enter another three empty bedrooms and a bathroom with nothing but the fixtures still in place before we reach the biggest room on the second story—the only room that proves to have something within it.

"Um…" Dylan says when he opens the door. "Anyone else find this just a little bit creepy?"

Inside the otherwise bare room, a round, black wood table has been erected in the middle of the space. Unlit candles line the table's outer edge, and a single, long match sits on the table's middle. Seven chairs rest pulled back, awaiting someone to sit in them.

"Bloody hell," Meander mutters as soon as he takes in the sight. "They can't be serious."

"What is all this?" Naasir asks.

"It's a séance," Meander says. He takes a shaky breath. "We seem to be reliving all our greatest hits."

I rub his back as I survey the table, remembering what happened the last—and only—time we were a part of a séance in Greenland. I don't know if the Oracle has chosen these tasks on purpose to mimic our previous experiences, or if it's only coincidence that this is how the Smiling House has to play out. But I'm not smiling. So far, the location is not at all living up to its name.

"WHY WOULD THE ORACLE HAVE US DO A SÉANCE?" DYLAN ASKS.

We enter the room, moving around the table until we're each standing behind one of the chairs. Mim reaches forward to grab the match, twisting the stick between her fingertips as she studies the unlit pillars of wax.

"It means the spirit's not really here," Meander says. His voice is quiet and flat, the emotionless tone speaking volumes of the emotion he's actually feeling. It's bad enough he'll likely face a ghost on this trip. But doing so in a setting like this, in front of everyone, probably makes the situation ten times worse.

"We have to call it forward," I say to Dylan. "The séance can… help. It, uh, focuses our energy and draws the ghost to us. Or something like that. I can't remember—last year it didn't go so well."

Meander's lips twitch at my rambling response. He gives me a quick look before taking another deep breath and sliding into his chair.

"Might as well get this over with, yeah?" He motions for us to join him so we can light the candles. We do, everyone sitting and Mim striking the match. She lights her and Kornelía's candles. Then she passes the match around until, one by one, all the pillars are lit.

"Now what?" Dylan asks. His tone is remarkably perplexed for someone who watches as many horror movies as he does. I would have expected he'd jump all over this task. Instead, he seems confounded by the concept of it.

"We all hold hands, close our eyes, and call on the spirit like a bunch of barmy idiots," Meander huffs.

I smile, shaking my head as I look his way. "Eloquently put."

He smirks, then holds his palm out for me to take. The rest of the sector follows our lead until we've all formed a circle of hands. Then, Meander provides further instruction as to what we're supposed to say to bring the spirit forth.

"Despite popular belief," he explains as his eyes scan the table before settling on Naasir, "séances work best when they are led by someone who believes in the afterlife—but doesn't necessarily have direct contact with it."

I didn't know this, but I'm not surprised that Meander does. He likely read up on séances after last year's incident to be better prepared should he be forced around the table a second time. And now that we're here, I'm glad to know the Oracle has supplied us with the correct Senders to achieve our task. Last summer, the séance in Greenland was led by a local woman who was not a Sender herself. This time, the task is apparently falling to the only remaining member of Shade who does not see ghosts.

"Why would that make a difference?" Sabeena asks from Naasir's right side. She glances at her friend and then stares back at Meander. "Is he going to be in any danger?"

"No," Meander says. "But if someone else makes contact, they might get distracted. Especially if it's a ghost they can communicate with. Naasir won't be distracted."

Naasir looks hesitant to take charge of this venture. But after looking around the table and staring at the flame of his candle, he offers Meander a slow nod. He raises his eyes until they stare eerily at the empty space above the table. When his eyes drift closed, the rest of us follow suit so we can wait for his words to have an effect.

Last year, I thought the idea of a séance was fairly gimmicky in its nature. And while that hasn't exactly changed, I don't feel stupid sitting in the self-created dark of my closed eyes and bowed head. Mostly, I'm just nervous, fretting about what's to come and waiting for the moment Meander's hand clenches my own as the ghost makes its painful appearance.

"Tonight, we call on the spirits of the Smiling House," Naasir says. The words are hokey, but his voice is so deep and serious it's hard to make light of the situation we're in. "We come in peace, with friendly intentions. We would like to talk, if you are willing. We would like to help."

A slight chill descends over me, while to my right Meander sucks in a breath. I open my eyes as the candles around the table start to flicker. But while

Meander's breathing is labored, he stares first at the table and then around the rest of the room, his expression more confused than tormented.

"It's here," he says, catching my questioning gaze. "But it's… it's not?"

"She's here," Kornelía says from the other side of the table. The tall girl smiles. "But she didn't show up where she was supposed to."

"Where is she?" Dylan asks. One by one, the others open their eyes, until we're all sitting around the table holding hands and staring at each other.

"Close," Meander says. He studies the flickering candlelight. "But not so close she's bothering us."

"Two doors over," Kornelía says with a nod. "She's waiting for someone to talk to, now that we've brought her here."

A quick glance around the table makes it obvious no one else is experiencing the ghost. Which means Meander is still in trouble. He swallows, then drops his hands, breaking the circle. We all let our hands fall as he pushes away from the table, standing and staring uncertainly at the door.

"I'll go," he says. "If… If the candles start shaking, blow them out."

"Do you want—" I hesitate, trying to find the best way to phrase my words. I don't want him to go alone, but I also don't want to insist on tagging along if he wants to tackle this by himself. "Back up? You know, in case you need to raise the alarm?"

To my relief, Meander nods. "Yeah," he says in a quiet voice. "That might be a good idea." I stand and cross the room, while he takes a final look at the group. "Get back to the séance," he says. "Don't talk to the ghost, just… stay focused. If anything goes awry, blow out the candles and make a concentrated effort to dismiss the spirit. It probably won't work, now that she's here. But it wouldn't hurt to try."

"We'll keep the circle," Naasir says. "Until you are done."

The rest of the sector rejoin their hands and close their eyes, a weird sight to see us off. Once we are out in the hallway, however, the unnerving turn of events feels a little more normal as Meander takes my hand while we make a slow approach towards the room.

"Thank you for coming," he says, his face etched with familiar wary discomfort.

"Want me to go in first? See if I can speak with the ghost so you don't have to?" I ask.

Meander smiles, shaking his head. "You don't feel anything."

"You do," I reply.

He nods. Then he pivots to face me, his brows furrowing as he talks. "It's weird, though. I can feel the tightening of my throat. The stinging of the scars on my neck and my arm. But… they don't *hurt*. Not yet."

"Maybe the ghost isn't very strong?" I offer.

"Let's hope that's the case," Meander says, though he sounds unconvinced.

We walk the length of the hall and stop in front of the room Kornelía told us about. Meander finds a steady rhythm in his breathing, and I wait for his nod before opening the door.

The room is large, a bedroom complete with panoramic views of the wilds outside. I don't feel the presence of any spirit, not any more than I did when the small chill misted over us during the séance. In fact, as I walk into the room, the view and the setting make me feel somehow warmer—not like the temperature is rising but like my mood is growing lighter. I was expecting the worst, I suppose. But this room doesn't feel full of malicious energy. Honestly, it feels a bit like the opposite.

I turn to Meander, checking to gauge his reaction and thinking perhaps we've got the room wrong—that we misinterpreted Kornelía's instructions or that the spirit has since moved of her own accord. But one look shows me he is unmistakably affected. He stands in the doorway, staring at a very specific point in the room near the far corner of the windows. His breathing is erratic, and when he loosens his coat to itch at his neck, I can see the telltale bruising that appears when he's in close proximity to a ghost. But he's still upright. And his eyes continue to show more confusion than pain.

"What do you see?" I ask as I walk back to his side.

He shakes his head, curls swaying as he steps fully into the room. "It's a woman. Old. She… She's been here for a long time. Longer than this house." His voice is raspy, but he manages the words without having to stop for air. His hand continues to scratch lightly at his neck, but even that speaks more to irritation than hurt.

"You're doing okay," I say, more of an observation than any useful statement of fact. I'm confused too, and since I can't see the ghost, I don't have any dead clues to help me understand what's going on.

"Yeah…" Meander blinks, his eyes clouded with doubt as he turns to me. "I don't feel… I don't feel *great*. But it's not like it usually is."

"Could this be a change?" I ask. "In your talent?"

The hope is unmistakable, even to my own ears. But Meander's smile is sad when he looks back at the ghost.

"I wish it were," he says. "But I don't think so. It's her. She's..." He takes a step back, his eyes drifting as he follows the movement of the ghost. She must be getting closer. He steps back a second time, and his gaze inches slightly downward, probably to see her face. "Who are you?" he asks, and even the question is unusual. He's not asking how he can help or what it is the ghost needs. "Your family? Did they..."

He pauses, nods, then winces and closes his eyes. When I touch his arm, he shakes his head and gently clutches at the hem of my coat.

"She can't remember the name, but... it's here..." He winces again, squeezing his eyes shut as he tries to work through the many books he's read to pull out something to connect this woman with her family. I watch him struggling to sort through information, his own unique hellish version of what it's like when I hear music in my head. Then he gasps, coughs, and clutches my coat tighter as he opens his eyes. "A composer," he says in a rush. "Um... shit. Where did I read that... He lived in the... eighteenth century? He was friends with someone... Haydn, I think." With a frustrated sigh, he turns to me. "Absolutely ridiculous name. D something. Did, or Ditt. Yeah, Ditt. Ditter..."

My brain does its own scan of composers, until one appears in my mind alongside a few phantom notes of music.

"Dittersdorf?" I ask with a laugh as the name unfolds.

"Yes!" He snaps his fingers as he tries to catch onto

his own thoughts. "What was his first name?"

I have to think about it myself for a moment before I can answer. "Oh, uh—Carl!" I blurt at last.

"Carl!" He faces the empty space where the dead woman presumably stands and takes a moment to regain his breath. "Carl?" he asks in a softer voice. "Um… Carlos?" He listens to her response, uncomfortable but functioning as he nods at whatever she says. "There was a café with that name, back down the mountain. Abuela? Yes, I—"

He takes another, sudden step back, his expression bewildered as his eyes trace something through the air.

"What's happening?" I ask, frustrated that I can't see this, that I can't anticipate what's coming or understand the conversation now taking place.

Meander's breath is more unsettled as he coughs a second time. "She's… *oh*." He winces, letting out a quiet groan of pain—that twists partway through into a little laugh.

"Are you… Is everything okay?" I ask.

Meander stares wide-eyed at the ghost until he blinks away to study me.

"She doesn't need my help," he murmurs, his soft words part short of breath—and part full of surprised awe.

"She… doesn't?" I ask.

"No." Meander shakes his head. Then he lets out a choked—but genuine—laugh as his bloodshot eyes lock with mine. "She's not miserable. That's why she's not so intense. She's…" He takes a wheezing breath, shivering as he sways on his feet. I slide a hand around his back, and he leans his weight against me as he looks back at the ghost. "She's happy," he whispers.

"I'm… drawing out her happiness."

"Happy?" I stare at his profile, studying the slight smile on his lips until a similar expression forms on my own face.

"There was another house before this one," he explains. "Same family. Different house. She's been here for centuries. She knows she's dead. She knows she can leave. But she's happy watching the generations. She doesn't need my help. She's a… She's a happy ghost."

"The Smiling House," I say. "She's exudes happiness, not fear or pain."

Meander stares at the ghost for another few seconds. Then he drops his head onto my shoulder. "We should leave now," he says. His hand slides down to mine. "I'm starting to feel lightheaded."

I don't need any more convincing. Pulling him alongside me, we walk out of the room and shut the door behind us. Down the hall, Meander stops before we reach the room with the others. Leaning against the wall across from the door, he pulls me over so I'm standing against him, lightly pinning him in place.

"She touched me," he says. "Touched my cheek. Reminded me of my gran… only, you know, dead." He reaches up and strokes the side of my ear, the movement he always makes to ensure he avoids messing up my hair. "Her touch hurt. But it was also oddly comforting? I've never experienced anything like that before."

"Your talent has changed," I say. "You don't just deal with anger anymore. There are a lot of emotions in the world." I smile, giddy with the joy of knowing he got this experience. "It's about time something pleasant popped up."

He laughs. "I'm glad you were with me."

"I am too," I say.

He strokes my ear again, then draws me into a soft, languid kiss. When I pull back, his eyes remain closed, a beautifully content smile on his lips. For a moment, I continue to watch him, every bit as content as he is.

Then I swipe a curl away from his eye with a smirk.

"Dittersdorf?" I say. "*That* was the best way you could get to Carlos?"

Meander opens his eyes, blinking out of his haze before he shoves me with a soft laugh.

"Shut up. You were there... You shifted my thinking."

"So, in other words, you couldn't get me out of your mind?" I grin.

"You've got a permanent installation in my brain, Cal," he says, and my grin goes swoony as he pulls me back to him.

"Do I hear voices?" Mim calls from inside the séance room. "Are you okay?"

"Yeah, we're fine," I call back. I grab Meander's hand as we make our way into the room. "We can end the séance now."

We join the others at the table, retaking our spots while Meander instructs Naasir how to send the spirit away.

"We thank you for your time," Naasir recites with a solemn bow of his head. "And we ask that you now leave us in peace. We are going to close our channel of communication. We will now bid you farewell."

No one closes their eyes for the final portion of the ritual, but when Naasir stops talking, we take turns blowing out our candles before Meander breaks from the table to flick on the room's light. He spends a few seconds ensuring the spirit has gone—or is at least staying out of our way. Then he nods, flicks the light back off, and leads the way out into the hall.

"So, does that mean we're done here?" Dylan asks.

"Yes," Meander says. "I got the answer to our clue. I know where to go. And what to order. Abuela. Sonrisa. That's what she said."

"Grandmother's smile?" Mim asks.

Meander nods. "That sounds right."

"Well, look at that," Dylan says. "No crumbling buildings. No falling out of windows. I'd call that a win. Now we can get back to camp and eat. I'm starving."

"You're always starving," Kornelía says.

"Fast metabolism," he says. "Got to keep fueling this wonder machine."

Kornelía shakes her head and steps alongside Draugur on route to the stairs. Meander and I stay back, waiting until the others are halfway down before following at a slower pace.

"Carlos Chávez, Wendy Carlos, Carlos Simon…" I list as we amble down the steps.

"Are these all composers?" Meander asks.

"Just filling you in," I tease. "You clearly need more musical literature in your life. I know what I'm getting you for your next birthday."

"An encyclopedia of musicians named Carlos?" he asks.

"I think it would prove very useful," I say.

"Agreed," Meander says. "Especially if it's big enough I can smack you with it."

"That doesn't sound like a good use for your present," I chide.

Meander smirks. "I guess that depends on where I'm smacking."

My cheeks flood with heat, and I'm not sure what's better—the implications of his statement, or the fact that, after seeing a ghost, he's able to make such innuendos at all. I catch his gaze, amusement and desire dancing in the starburst of jade in his eyes. I let his stare wash over me until my whole body feels joyfully off-kilter.

Then I do my best to rope in all thoughts of *smacking* as we meet the others downstairs.

18

WHEN WE RETURN FROM OUR HIKE AND LOCATE THE CARLOS COFFEE SHOP, we discover that it's run by the family that owns the Smiling House. Mim completes our task by ordering the Grandmother's Smile special at the bar. But instead of returning with a porcelain cup, the woman who took the order arrives with an envelope on a tray. She slides the instructions onto the table and asks if we'd all like a drink to go. We give our new orders and wait until the beverages are made before heading outside to read the instructions in the privacy of a nearby field.

"It says we have to look for the scene of a crime," Mim reads.

Everyone's gazes turn in my direction. "Guess that means we know who'll see the next ghost," I sigh.

"Could not be a non-murdery crime," Dylan offers.

"Maybe," I say. "But given the trajectory of this hunt, I doubt it."

Dylan offers me a pitying nod of agreement before he

gets his phone out of his pocket. Texting the number, he tells whoever is on the other end of the line that we're ready to go, and we're instructed to meet the van outside of the hostel in thirty minutes.

As we pull onto the road and leave the mountainside behind, Mim puts a hand on Dylan's shoulder.

"Are you all right?" she asks. "You never got to find out about the fox."

Dylan shrugs as he stares out the window. "Can't free them all," he says. He turns to her with a grin. "But maybe someday I'll come back. I know where he is. I can practice at home, try to find some foxes near where I live."

"Don't go wandering through the woods at night, looking for dead foxes," I say from the back row. "You're liable to run into a wolf."

"*Dude.*" Dylan's eyes widen as he turns in his seat. "You think I could see a wolf?"

"You saw a fox," I say. "Wolves seem like a logical addition to your repertoire."

"Yeah," he says, mulling it over. Mim pats his shoulder, and he goes back to staring out the window as she turns in her seat to look at Meander and me.

"You didn't release the ghost in that house," she says. "I still don't understand why."

Meander explained what happened before we left the Smiling House. But he's not the only one who's never experienced a happy spirit before.

"She didn't need releasing," Meander says for the second time. "She's not suffering. She's content."

"Content to be a ghost?" Mim asks. She sounds skeptical, even though she's had days of hiking back down the mountainside to think through the concept.

"For now," Meander says. He sighs, running a hand through his curls as he leans back against the seat. "I suspect she'll leave someday. When her family stops living on that land. Until then, though, she's happy. And they seem happy too."

"Do you think they know she's there?" I ask.

"It's called the Smiling House," Meander muses. "They probably know there's something."

"What if you *had* released her, then?" I ask. "I wonder if they'd have been pissed. Or do you think they want her gone?"

He shrugs. "She wasn't threatening. Or depressing. Her presence was comforting."

I nod, thinking about what I felt in the room. "It was. There wasn't anything bad about that place. Maybe that's why they keep living in such a secluded area. Because it's so nice." I smile. "I never thought I'd say that about a haunted house."

Meander shakes his head. "Me neither."

Mim shifts back in her seat, and the van falls into silence as we head away from the mountain. After a while, I take out my phone and scroll through my vast library of classical music. Over the past ten months, I've dedicated time to studying music from as many genres and eras as I can. But classical pieces are still the only things I listen to for pleasure.

I scroll for long enough Meander looks over my shoulder, wondering what I'm searching for. When I stop on "Le Prise de la Bastille" by Carl Ditters von Dittersdorf, he chuckles, taking the earbud I offer him so we can listen to the symphony together.

We spend an entire day in the car, stopping twice for a travel weary Sabeena to be sick at the side of the road. By the time we reach our next destination, it's so dark I think, for a moment, that the domes before us means we've arrived back at camp.

"Same idea, different place," Mim says as we unload our bags. "But I think this resort caters to the winter crowd. It should be warmer. And have rooms with roofs."

We check into our roof-covered suite, only to discover a spread of replica newspapers left on the kitchenette's counter. The papers span nine decades, reprints in English that detail an assortment of criminal activity in the surrounding areas. Headlines like *Accident on the Rail Claims Twelve*, *Armed Robber Takes Bank*, *Delantero Strikes Again*, *Gomez Twins Wanted for Assault*, and *Mysterious Figure in Black Kills Couple* decorate the newsprint, a fascinating—if not grotesque—recollection of the area's greatest crime hits.

"Do you think this is meant to be helpful?" I muse as I read over each headline, "or are they, you know…"

"Taking the piss?" Meander finishes, head bent over one of the papers as he reads the entirety of every article printed. "Time will tell, I suppose. One of these might be the crime scene we need. But we won't rightly know until the ghost makes its appearance."

"I'm too exhausted to look at all this now," Sabeena says. She holds her stomach, her face drawn with sickness. "I'm going to bed."

"Without dinner?" Dylan asks.

At the mention of food, Sabeena groans. She rubs her stomach and pivots away from us, staggering as she leaves the room.

"I'll bring her water after we eat," Mim says. "Let's have our meal, then go to bed. We'll read up on these crimes tomorrow."

After a quick dinner at the resort's grill, Meander and I wind up being the only ones invested enough to look at the newspapers before heading to bed. But despite reading through all of the accounts, nothing stands out as a probable connection to our current locale. So, when the sector reconvenes the next morning, it's not the papers we focus on. It's the area—and the resort—that we need to figure out so we can tackle our next task.

"Why don't we ask one of the clerks?" Mim suggests. "See if anyone knows of any major crimes in the area."

"Always a great way to introduce yourself," Dylan says. He gives her a sarcastic thumbs up.

"As much information as we can get on our own is better," Kornelía says. "If it's something no one wants to talk about, they'll shut down as soon as we ask direct questions."

"We don't know that they won't want to talk about it, though," Sabeena says. "For all we know, they're the ones that left the newspapers."

"Not likely," Meander says. "And we're probably talking about a murder. That's not a topic hotel staff love to natter on about. Especially not if it happened nearby."

"But we don't know *anything*," Sabeena counters. "We need facts before we can assume it *was* a murder, or that it *did* happen close to here."

"We do," I agree. "And talking to the hotel desk might be the best way to get those facts. But I've also seen people clam up around the subject of murder before. We should sleuth out what we can first. Then we'll talk to the locals, if we still need information."

We break off in groups, wandering around the

resort to try and get a clue to the crime scene we're after. Meander and I head around the grounds, feeling for the presence of a haunted spot. Near the front pavilion, I overhear a group talking about their upcoming day-tour of the area—which one woman in the group complains is the only activity available during the winter months.

Nudging Meander's elbow, I shift our path and go back into the lobby, where I ask one of the clerks about the tour and learn it's a five-hour sightseeing trip with a local guide. Meander groans when I ask if there's room for our group to join, and I give the clerk my most enthusiastic smile to cover his displeasure. The clerk calls the tour guide to ask about availability. When she hangs up, she informs me that instead of joining the others, she can secure us our own, private trip.

"Five hours?" Meander asks as we look for the rest of the sector so I can tell them what I've arranged. "Five bloody hours on a sightseeing tour. This is going to be worse than the hiking. Do you know what we could do with five hours?"

I smirk. "Don't tempt me with thoughts like that. We're supposed to be doing this, remember? If we don't find the crime scene, we'll be stuck here. As nice as this resort is, I would like to retrieve my violin one of these days." I frown, thinking of my instrument abandoned in the empty dome. "I hope it's all right at camp."

"It's fine," Meander assures me, the snark in his voice dropping as he rubs the small of my back. "Robbie said he'd look after it. And he knows you're high-strung enough to give him ample shit if he doesn't."

I turn to him with a huff. "I'm not high-strung."

Meander laughs. "You are about your violin. But it's okay. I'm ready to bite someone's head off whenever they interrupt my reading. You're allowed to be protective of your instrument."

Despite his assurance, I continue to grumble about my perceived fussiness until we find Kornelía and I tell her the new plan. Her expression is thoughtful as she listens to me talk. After a few beats of silence, she nods.

"I'll stay here," she says. I'm surprised by her decision, which of course she senses. She smiles and pats the top of Draugur's head. "Too complicated a transportation system," she adds. I have no idea what she's talking about, but she continues on even while she starts to turn away from us. "I'll stay here and see what I can find. Although I suspect you'll do fine without me."

"Are you sure?" I ask, although I don't need to. Kornelía seems to almost always be sure these days. The meek girl I used to know has faded, and in her place is the surreal, unearthly woman I caught glimpses of near the end of our first summer in France.

"Yes," she says. She raises her hand in a gentle wave, then continues outside to wander along one of the hotel's stone walkways.

"She's a bit creepy, isn't she?" Meander asks once she's gone. "I wonder how much she actually knows— how much she doesn't tell us."

"I try not to think about it too much." I give him a look. "Or think about you too much when I'm close to her. I think we were her biggest source of aggravation last year."

His lips curve upwards, while his eyes catch onto

mine with a softer expression. He wraps an arm around my waist, and I lean into his side as we head in the opposite direction from Kornelía and her dog.

It's not until the rest of us are outside for the tour that we realize what Kornelía meant by complicated transportation. With wide eyes and a slightly gaping mouth, I watch as our tour guide Ben leads a group of pack horses out for us to ride on.

"Horses?" Dylan asks. "We're riding horses?"

"Best way to see the area," Ben says. "I don't like the Jeep. It's too noisy. And too crowded for a tour of six." He's a younger guide, probably in his late twenties, with a pudgy, cheerful face. "Beauties, aren't they? They'll take us anywhere we want to go."

I can feel Meander's eyes on me, but I try to ignore his stare until I'm sure he's going to burn a hole in my face. When I twist slowly on my heel to meet his look, his gaze is so stony I have to work hard not to laugh.

"I'm annoying but adorable?" I try in my most innocuous tone.

For a second he continues to glare at me. Then he shakes his head, smiling begrudgingly as he shoves me on route to approach the horses.

"We'll take the pack through the valley," Ben explains as he helps us get situated. I've ridden a horse exactly once in my life, on a one-hour riding tour when I was eleven. I have to push myself up three times before I get enough traction to get over and settle into the saddle. Then the horse starts wandering off on its own, and I grab the reins in a panic until Meander tells me how to ease the horse to a stop.

"You've never been on a horse before," I say as my horse finally halts. "You're not supposed to be a master-rider already."

"I'm not a master," Meander says. "I've just read enough books to understand the basic commands."

"Yeah, yeah," I grumble. "You and your *reading*."

He grins, and I'm happy enough he's no longer glaring at me that I don't even mind when the damn horse starts walking away again.

I certainly didn't expect to spend a day riding horses through the Chilean wilds. But Camp Wanagi never fails to surprise me. We travel down into the valley, the day cool but not as cold as our hike in the mountain's foothills. Ben talks about the area for a while, then lets us ride in silence before taking us on a tour of a vineyard. I wonder what it would be like to see these sights in January, when Chile is warm and alive. The scenery is pretty, but everything feels a little stilted, like things are trying to sleep while we insist on keeping them awake.

After the tour of the vineyard, Mim tries to engage Ben in a discussion of local mysteries, but he doesn't take the bait. Avoiding any push into murdery territory, he takes us to a secluded lagoon and—to my further surprise—stops to teach us how to fly fish.

"We stock the lagoon even in the winter," he explains at our collective confusion. "It's not as good a time to fish as the summer. But we work with what we have."

"Unless someone was fed mercilessly to these fishes," Meander mumbles close to my ear, "I don't think this plan is going to work."

"Give it time," I say, although I don't really disagree with his assessment. "People talk while they fish, don't they?"

"I wouldn't know," Meander says. "I've never fished."

"Well, it's time to learn something new," I say.

"I already rode a horse today," he says. "Isn't that sufficient?"

"Apparently not," I reply. I nod my head at the stuff Ben is unloading from his pack horse. "Besides, I want to see you in those."

Meander takes in the sight of the wide, rubber coveralls we'll have to don to stand in the water. He blinks a few times, then cuts his gaze to me.

"You do realize you have to wear them too," he says.

"Then we can look like idiots together," I sigh.

Meander smirks. "We spent all morning bouncing around on horses. I think we've already managed that feat."

I've gone fishing a couple of times, once with some distant cousins of mine and one or two times with my dad when I was little. But I've never done anything like fly fishing before. Luckily for me, none of us has, and we're all awkward as we venture into the lagoon. Dylan and Sabeena get their fishing wire tangled together, and Dylan almost takes out Naasir's eye with a rogue flick of his line. Meander falls waist-high in the lagoon, and in helping to catch him before he's submerged, I get a face full of water that messes up my hair. Naasir catches the first fish but has to get Mim to help take it off his line. She does—and winds up dropping her rod in the process.

Ben watches us, instructing from the shore and laughing at our many mishaps in the water. Mim proves to be the best fisher among us, though I don't think any of us would count ourselves passionate about the hobby. I only manage to hook one fish, but I'm happy enough with the outcome to tramp out of the water, calling it quits. Meander is quick to follow my lead, and soon Sabeena gives up as well. The three of us take off our fishing gear and sit at the edge of the lagoon, watching the other three as they attempt to catch more.

"What will we do after the fishing is over?" Sabeena asks. It's early afternoon, three hours into our five-hour tour. I suspect we'll need about an hour to get back to camp. But that still leaves another hour for more touring.

"There's a beautiful ridge just at the base of the mountain," Ben says. "We'll take the horses up. Watch the skies and see the distant waterfalls. If it were warmer, we'd go farther up. But we'll keep close to ground level today."

"Are there any places of local interest around here?" I ask, trying for another stab at getting something ghost-related out of this tour. "Any local legends people like to explore?"

Ben shakes his head with a laugh. "No legends," he says. "Just the beauty of the natural world."

Sabeena gives me a concerned look, and I frown as I lean back against my hands.

When the others finish up, Ben packs the fish we caught to take back to the hotel, claiming the resort staff will cook them for dinner. Then we mount our horses and return to the trails. I slump forward in my saddle, tired and wishing I'd never suggested this plan. As unique an experience as the day has been, it's gotten us nowhere closer to solving the next clue.

We traverse the foothills, taking in the sights and

then trotting along a different path back to the hotel. When we're about forty minutes from the resort, Ben kicks the horses into a canter. Ten minutes later, when he starts talking about how the landscape flourishes in the summer seasons, my ears begin to sting. For a few seconds, I think it must be sunburn, a twinge of ache in promise of further pain tomorrow. But then the sting grows, pooling inside my ear until it swarms like a small hive of bees—pinching and humming and swirling into static.

I sit up in my saddle and look around, trying to spot where the noise is coming from. On all sides we are surrounded by nature. There are no houses, no railway stations, no hiding places where a ghost might be. I scan the horizon, but I can't find anything to explain the sudden noise in my ears.

"Cal?" Meander brings his horse as close as he can and eyes me with concern. I open my mouth to tell him what I'm hearing, until Ben shifts his weight so he can half-turn to check on me. My mouth shuts, and I point to my ear instead, a motion Meander understands well. He scans the area and then looks back at me, his expression confused as he mouths 'ghost?'

I shrug, and mouth back a 'maybe'. We both look around again, but as we keep on, the static starts to fade. When it disappears completely, I cast a final look over my shoulder, wondering what the hell was trying to make contact.

19

I DON'T SAY ANYTHING ABOUT WHAT I HEARD UNTIL WE'RE BACK AT THE hotel and have located Kornelía. Then I tell everyone what happened in the wilds.

"Are you sure it was way out there?" Dylan asks. "Couldn't the noise have been from here and carried in on the wind or something?"

"Carried on the wind thirty minutes from civilization?" Meander asks.

"Makes about as much sense as a murder victim in the middle of nowhere," Dylan grumbles.

"It's not necessarily a victim," I say. "It could be anyone who has murder on their mind."

"And we were on a traveled path," Sabeena adds. "Lots of people have passed that way."

"We don't know how long ago the person died, either," Kornelía says. "It might not have always been the middle of nowhere."

"Are you sure you heard a ghost?" Mim asks. She

seems as skeptical as Dylan. "You said yourself you didn't see anything."

"I don't hear static when there's no ghosts around," I sigh.

She glances at Meander, her expression still dubious. "But you didn't see anything, either."

"No," Meander says. "But if Cal said he heard something, he heard something." He sits back against the sofa with a disgruntled frown that makes me smile. "Just because I didn't see it doesn't mean there was nothing to be seen."

"Okay, okay," Dylan says. "So you heard a ghost, about thirty minutes away from here."

"Thirty minutes on horseback," Mim reminds him.

"Yeah, right. Great. Okay, so what are we supposed to do about it?"

"We're supposed to find the scene of a crime," I say. "If it *is* a murder victim, well then… that's the scene of the crime."

"We have to go back," Naasir says.

I nod. "I think so. But when?"

"We're not under surveillance," Mim says. "We can go whenever."

"On foot?" Dylan asks.

"Horses aren't that fast," Kornelía says. "Not when they're walking."

"Yes, but they weren't walking," Dylan says. "Not at the time."

"That's true," I say. "It'd probably take us about an hour to get back there on foot."

"I can't go an hour on foot right now," Sabeena says. "I'm exhausted."

"I don't think we should go right now, anyway," I

say. "We'll attract attention. It'd be better to slip away when no one's likely to notice."

"You mean at night?" Mim asks.

"It'd be less conspicuous," I say.

"And less likely someone will find us if we all fall off a ridge," Dylan adds.

"Bring your phone," Meander says. "You can text for help if someone falls. Unless all seven of us manage to fall off at the same sodding time. In which case, we probably deserve it."

"All right," Mim says. "So, we rest. Eat. Sleep. Wake up at what, midnight? Go out then."

"I can come with you, if we're going on foot," Kornelía says. "The dark won't matter to Draugur." She smiles. "Or me."

"We'll have to go on foot," I say. "Unless anyone fancies stealing some horses."

"So we can run them off the ridge too?" Dylan asks. "Nah. Let's stick to our feet. I trust my legs more than I trust a horse who's been pulled out of the stable at bedtime."

We all agree to the plan. But when midnight arrives and we finally set out, the land around the hotel is much darker—and more intimidating—than we expected.

"I can't see a thing out here," Dylan complains. He ruffles his hair. "Maybe we should reconsider the horses."

"I'm not sure how well horses would even do out here," Mim says. "Does anyone know if horses can see at night?"

Nobody offers an insight into equestrian vision facts, but it doesn't matter. Before we have time to debate the logistics or morality of stealing some horses, Meander comes up with a different plan.

"If we're going to steal something, why don't we make it the Jeep?" he asks.

I stare at him, my expression blank as I take in his serious and far too casual manner.

"You want us to steal a car?" Sabeena asks.

Meander shrugs. "We were talking about taking the horses. The car would be easier. The keys are probably kept in the lobby. And we'd be safer in a Jeep than walking on foot in the wilderness.

"Yeah, sure," Dylan says. "Safe. Safe until we *drive* over the ridge, all together, crashing and exploding into a fiery inferno."

Meander rolls his eyes. "We'll wear seat belts. And drive exceedingly slow." He glances at me. "The car's got headlights, and a horn... you know, if any more bloody pumas attack."

"Draugur *would* be safer," Kornelía adds.

I glance around the group, crossing my arms with a sigh. "I can't believe I'm about to say this," I mutter. "But sure, let's go steal a car." Meander starts to pivot on his heel to head for the lobby, but I grab his arm and hold in place. "Just one thing," I add as he turns back to me. "Does anyone even know how to drive?"

I'm old enough to get behind the wheel, but my parents haven't offered to enroll me in driving lessons, and I haven't bugged them to take me to any parking lots for vehicular practice. I don't really care about driving, at least not yet. Maybe someday I will. But the drives to and from my violin lessons and recitals are about the only one-on-one time I have with my parents these days. And if I could drive, I'd be stuck chauffeuring Rose around too.

I can't drive. And I know Meander can't, either—even if he probably could muddle through in a pinch. Kornelía is unable to take the wheel. Which leaves only four possibilities. I look between the others, everyone silent and waiting until Dylan kicks absently at the ground.

"I can drive," he says. His shoulders slump in resignation. "I'm not any good at it, but I *can*."

"Just… take it slow, all right?" Mim says.

Dylan scoffs. "I'm against the whole fiery inferno plan, remember? I'll get us there alive. Might take us as long as walking would, but I'll do it."

It doesn't take us long. Meander sneaks into the hotel and finds the key from the empty front desk. Then we creep into the shed where the maintenance tools and Jeep are located. All of us load into the car before Dylan chances turning on the ignition. The sound is horrendously loud to our ears, and I hope the hotel staff are heavy sleepers. No one comes rushing out of the resort to see what's happening, at least. The night remains otherwise quiet, and Dylan mumbles a private thanks for Jeep's automatic transmission as he eases us out of the shed.

I sit wedged in the backseat, half in Meander's lap because Ben was right when he said there wasn't enough room for such a large group. Despite the promise, we don't have enough seats or belts to cover us, so Kornelía sits up front with Draugur by her feet while the rest of us strap in as best we can. We keep up a crawling pace, and my heart stays in my throat as I wait for us to be apprehended by hotel staff, lose control of the car and go careening down a wild hill, or be attacked by some monstrous beast living mountainside. But the car is faster than the canter of our horses, which means I don't have to suffer for long. Five minutes into the drive, I close my eyes, focusing on the sounds around me and trying to pick up on any slivers of static. When the first burble of supernatural sound rakes through my brain, I sit forward in the seat and grab Dylan's shoulder.

"Stop!" I say, probably a little too loudly. Dylan starts, and the car lurches forward as he steps hard on the gas.

"Freaking A, Cal," Dylan says. He puts a hand to his chest and eases off the gas, pressing the break and bringing the car to a clunky stop.

I don't apologize for my outburst. As soon as he shifts into park, I climb over Meander and stumble out of the Jeep.

"Cal, hold on!" Meander calls after me. I force my legs to slow until he can catch up. "Did you forget it's dark out here?" he says. "Don't go falling off ledges without me, you idiot."

I smile, grabbing his hand and pulling him forward. "I heard something. I don't want to miss it."

Meander lets out an amused breath. "It's dead. I don't think it's going anywhere."

"I know," I say. "But still. Over here. I... Yeah. Here."

I close my eyes again, listening as a steadier stream of static fuzzes into existence. I can't hear any music, and I don't feel particularly cold apart from the natural chill of the night. There aren't any detectable smells, either, nothing making me cover my nose in disgust. But the static is unmistakable. It pinches and curls, pressing my eardrums until my whole head feels tight with the beginnings of an ache.

I listen until I'm sure no music or voice will break through the fuzz. Then I open my eyes to find Meander watching me, a soft smile on his lips that makes me blush—until Dylan catches up and barrels in to break our stare.

"All right, so where's the ghost?" he asks.

"I don't know," I say with a sigh, trying not to make it obvious I was so easily distracted from my task. "The static is here, but there's nothing else. The ghost is close, but I can't see anything."

Circling the area, I listen to the static and try in vain to spot any ghostly apparition. Then I look at the ground under my feet, thinking of our first year at camp and the ghost whose body was buried in the woods. The Oracle has been putting us in similar situations throughout this hunt. Given our current location, a trapped corpse six feet under would make sense. Yet as soon as the memory of the French forest appears in my mind, Kornelía steps up beside me.

"He's not buried," she says. Her chin points towards the earth. "But he is below."

"Below where?" Dylan asks. He shines a flashlight at the earth around us. "We're on solid ground."

"I-I'm not sure," Kornelía falters. "He's here. I mean, he's close. But I can't tell…"

"Does anyone hear that?" Naasir asks, cutting into her trailing speech.

"I hear static," I say. "What do you hear?"

"Not static," Naasir replies. "Something else." He pauses, waiting and listening to whatever noise he's picked up on. Then he looks at his feet before kneeling down and pressing his ear to the ground. Dylan shines the light down as the rest of us grow silent. I close my eyes again, searching the static to try and sense what direction it's coming from, while Naasir listens to something under the grass.

"What do you hear, Naasir?" Kornelía asks after a pause.

"Wings," Naasir says. I open my eyes to see him climbing to his feet, one finger pointed ahead. "That way."

"What do you mean, *wings*?" Dylan asks. Naasir doesn't answer, and Dylan looks at me with bewilderment dancing in his eyes. "What the hell does he mean by *wings*?"

"I have no idea," I say. I look at where Naasir is already walking. "But we'll probably find out soon."

Naasir leads us so far into the wild that the still-running car is a distant speck. Just when I think we're going to lose its light, the ground starts to slope. For the first few feet, the downward turn feels like we've crested a small hillside. But then Naasir steps too fast, and he falls, one leg dropping over the edge of a hidden ledge.

"See?" Dylan grunts as we all clamber to grab hold of Naasir before he drops completely. "Dark. Ridge. Fiery inferno. I was right!"

"Be quiet and pull," Mim says.

Naasir scrambles at the side of the hill, trying to gain purchase. But then he stops, and my grip on his arm slides with the heaviness of his full weight.

"Let me go," he calls up.

"You're not sacrificing yourself for the sake of a scavenger hunt!" Dylan calls through gritted teeth.

"I'll be fine," Naasir says. "It's not far. Shine the light."

Mim grabs the flashlight with one hand and shines it over the ledge. When the beam illuminates the drop, we see that it's only actually a few feet.

"Let me fall," Naasir says again.

I glance at Meander, Dylan, and Sabeena. Then, with a shrug, I give up my hold along with everyone else. Naasir drops onto his knees and bounces up to his legs, backing a few paces before he looks up at us. "This is where we need to go. Come."

The rest of us line up along the edge, staring into the shallow dip.

"So much for your inferno," Mim says with a snort.

"Be quiet and jump," Dylan replies, though his irritated words are sliced through with the relief of his smile.

We climb down, all except Kornelía who decides to stay up with the car. I feel bad that she's missing out again, but while we could struggle to help her with the ascent when we leave, I don't know how her dog would climb back up the ridge once he was down it. Mim stays at the base of the ledge, talking with Kornelía while the rest of us walk on. Naasir leads the way back in the direction we came from, and soon we realize that it wasn't a ridge we were climbing over— it was an earth-covered building.

The static grows as we approach the crooked door that's still snug in its casing.

"This is it," I say with a hard swallow.

"Why is there a house here?" Dylan asks. "It makes even less sense than the one by the mountain."

"I don't think this is a summer getaway," I say.

"There must have been a landslide or something," Sabeena adds. "This was probably above-ground, once. Or at least… it wasn't crushed like this."

"How trusting are we that there won't be another landslide while we're inside?" Dylan asks.

We all glance at each other nervously before I sigh.

"No slamming doors," I say. "Try to keep vibrations at a minimum."

Meander lets out a heavy breath and grabs my hand as we approach the house. Naasir pauses at the door, listening. But this time, he's not the only one to hear the noise. It flutters at the edge of the static in my head, making me tingly with anxious anticipation. Naasir grabs the doorknob, twisting it roughly from side to side before tugging at the stuck wood. He pulls again, harder, and the door squeaks open a fraction. When he pulls a third time, the crooked wood flies open.

Releasing a fluttering hoard of huge, white-winged creatures.

"What the hell!" Dylan calls, while I'm immediately transported back in time to the night when Naasir's swarm of mosquitos flooded our room in Greenland. Apparently, I'm more traumatized by that event than I realized. My eyes go wide, my stomach flips, and with a throaty yelp of panic I curl into Meander, burying my face in the crook of his shoulder. He raises the hood of his coat and lowers his head on top of mine, wrapping his arms around me to keep us burrowed together while the wings assault our arms and backs.

Dylan curses until Sabeena yells at him to turn off his flashlight. My skin crawls, the sound of the wings loud and solid close to my head. My vision is blocked by Meander's coat, but Dylan must eventually listen to Sabeena's command. The fluttering does not stop, but the wings do start to move. When we're no longer being flown at, I chance a peek out into the dark. There is no flashlight on, but the moon is bright enough I can see a mass of moths the size of my fist circling Naasir, their wings bone-white and almost glowing next to his incredibly dark skin. He watches them without fear, his expression awed as they circle him. They swirl in tandem, curving around his body several times before finally flying up and dispersing into the air.

"Is everyone okay?" Mim calls from away at the base of the ledge.

"We're fine," Dylan yells back. He doesn't even offer a quip. He only kneels down, one hand raking through his hair as he catches his breath.

I pull back and look at Meander, vaguely embarrassed by my freak out—but feeling much better when he caresses the side of my face, smiling as he asks if I'm all right.

"Yeah, I'm fine," I say. I point to my ear. "Except for the static. How are you?"

"I'm fine," he echoes. He points to his own head. "No static."

I smile and lean back against him with a groan.

"Those were ghosts," Naasir says when the last of the winged creatures are out of sight.

I shift my head to look at him. "The moths were ghosts?" I ask.

He nods, then offers me a rare, warm laugh. "Not like that. They were ghost moths. I never expected to encounter one. Certainly not so many. They're rare."

"They're freaking huge," Dylan says. "And I swear, if we get in that house and see *anything* resembling a skin suit, I'm out."

I groan again, closing my eyes for a few seconds of

relief from the chaos of this trip. Then I step back from Meander so we can approach the ruined house.

"The moths are all gone, right?" I ask when I reach Naasir's side. He nods, and I don't let myself think about what other horrors might be waiting beyond the door. Moving forward, I step through the dark, crooked doorway. As soon as I cross the abandoned threshold, the static swoops in with more force.

I hold onto the doorframe, dizzy from the static's press.

"Okay?" Meander asks, hovering at my side.

I swallow against the swell of sickness in my stomach, trying to ignore the pressure in my head. "Y-Yeah," I stammer. I regain my footing, then push on into the house.

The room we walk through is small, with an empty half-tiled wall on one side that probably once housed a kitchen. I'm curious to know how old this place is, and how it got to be in such a disastrous state. I don't think this was ever a mansion like the Smiling House. But I can't tell from the buried wreck if it was once a nice little cottage, or if it was only ever a crude shelter for someone in desperate need of a place to stay. It's empty, which at least suggests a family didn't suffocate under a landslide. But there *is* a ghost. Which means that someone definitely died here.

The questions of our surroundings and the people who may have once lived within it fade when I venture beyond the first space and into a shadowed inner room. Halfway through what may have once been some sort of kitchen, I'm assaulted by the sudden onset of music. The notes are from a song I don't know, but one which my year of study tells me is probably from the forties or fifties. The melody is slow, each note drawn out like the languid sharpening of a huge knife. No voice cuts through the instrumentation, though I suspect in reality the song would include a vocal track. All I hear, however, is music, loud and scraping against every nerve in my brain.

I grab my ears and lower my head until I feel something tugging at my arms. Forcing my eyes open, I drop my hands and lift my chin before Meander grasps my face. His breath is labored, and I can see the pain in his expression while he studies the pain in mine. He says something to me, but I don't hear the words over the music and can't make out what he's trying to convey.

"You have to yell!" I shout, causing him to flinch back before he gives me a pain-laced smirk.

"Okay!" he shouts back. "But *you* don't!"

"I—Oh." My smile is sheepish, and he laughs quietly enough I can't hear it before he leans in and plants a soft kiss to my lips. When I feel the shallow suck of his breath, I push him gently away from me. "Get outside," I say under the noise of the melody. "I'm fine."

Meander hesitates, until a spike of music makes me wince, and he mimics the movement as one hand reaches up to his neck.

"Go," I tell him in what I hope is a stern voice. I don't like seeing ghosts. But they don't make it so I can't even breathe. Meander already had his spirit encounter this week. This time, it's up to me.

He opens his mouth, but at my pointed look he sighs and nods. He says or mouths something I think is 'be careful', and I nod as well before he reluctantly moves out of the room. I follow his movement with my eyes, disappointed he's gone but relieved when his distance settles the music in my head. I haven't seen the ghost yet. But it must be close, and it must have emotion strong enough for Meander to exacerbate.

When he is gone, I realize I'm the only one in the room. I thought the others would have followed, but apparently, they're happy to leave this task to me too. I wouldn't want to enter this house by myself. But I don't mind being the only one in the room with the ghost. I've never been particularly suave, and when I'm around spirits, I'm an absolute mess. Right now, I don't even have my suit to give me a powerful edge. If history has taught me anything, it's that this ghost will send me falling to my knees or crashing haphazardly into some old furniture. It's nice not to have to worry about looking like a blundering idiot around the rest of the sector.

I just hope I'm not so spectacularly clumsy that I knock myself out while I'm here on my own.

20

Bracing myself against the coming storm, I cross to the kitchen's far side. The door leading from this space is crunched, and the handle sticks. I twist and push with as much caution as I can until I finally get the jam to release. When I'm fairly sure the house is not about to cave in on top of me, I enter a crooked, narrow space that was probably once a hallway. Two steps down the corridor, music flares in my head as the temperature plummets. One step more, and the ghost finally makes his appearance.

I hug my arms to my stomach, biting back the queasy swell and the awful throb of pain. My ears pound with the grating, low rhythm of a strumming guitar, and I take shaky breaths as I'm consumed with a longing to run away.

"Useless."

The ghost's first word slides through the static, and I force myself to look at him. If I were to hazard a guess, I'd say he was in his mid-to-late forties when he died. His shape is thin, small, almost wiry. But I get the impression he was anything but weak. He watches me, small pockets of mist forming eyes that are trained my way. His mouth is not visible, but I can make out a pointed chin as he tilts his head. *"Can't stomach it,"* he says.

"Me, or you?" I ask. I'm sure my voice is cracked, but I know that doesn't matter when it comes to ghosts. The man retreats, his short, blue-white fog legs moving back until they are at the far end of the hall. The motion is one of surprise, perhaps because he didn't expect me to talk with him. It's not likely he's had much contact here—although if the Oracle knows about him, it suggests there have been others who have proof of his existence.

"I'm not useless," the ghost says after a pause. *"I'm the best. One more day. All I need. One more day."*

"One more day for what?" I ask.

The ghost comes closer, and I get the distinct impression he's sizing me up. The music flows like a torturous river through my head, and I shiver as I lean back against the wall.

"Can't stomach it," he says again. *"Leave him to me."*

"Leave who to you?" I snap. I hate the way ghosts are always so cryptic. It's like dying erases not only a full memory, but also a full sense of vocabulary too. A few words, some phrases, some ideas. They get stuck on a loop inside what's left of the brain, and it's hard to get the dead to focus on creating anything new.

I expect a similar repetition now, but the ghost again comes closer, making me flinch back as he lifts an arm so oddly shaped it looks almost mangled.

"Delantero," he says between notes from the guitar.

The shot of ice the name brings with it—a cold spark cracking through my veins—sends my thoughts flying to the newspapers back at the resort. One of them, a paper from the 1940s, had the headline *Delantero Strikes Again.* Two good hints that Delantero, whoever he was, is the murderer in this case. But I'm not sure the man in front of me was his victim.

"How did you…" I want to ask the ghost how he died, but this spirit doesn't seem aware of his own demise. The way he talks gives me the sense he's still planning something—still working towards the goal he never got to accomplish in life. "How does Delantero kill?" I ask instead.

The music flares with such intensity I cry out, gripping my ears through the pick of the bass.

"Their heads," the ghost hisses, his fury so great I'm glad Meander did not try to be stubborn and stay with me for this meeting. As much as I would love to have him with me, I already have proof that this ghost is angry. He's communicating fine without a boost to his senses. I can only imagine what an extra shot of fury would make him do.

I don't know what 'their heads' entails, but it's enough to answer my question. This ghost isn't a victim. He died because of his arm, either because he got sick, got buried in this house, or perhaps suffered an attack. The night of our initiation comes to mind, and I wonder how many pumas there are in these wilds. Or how many other prowling creatures can prove deadly. I don't know why this man was here. His death had something to do with a crime, but I don't know if this was his home, if he was exploring the area, if he was hiding here, or—or if he was investigating Delantero's case.

The idea comes suddenly, but as soon as I've had it I know it's correct. I'm not sure if this house is a crime scene. But I do think this ghost was an investigator. A cop, an agent, some kind of private eye. Someone trying to catch a killer—someone who died before his mission was complete.

I take a moment to sink into the pain of the music, hating the slow beats but working hard to try and understand how they might have a connection to this man's reason for sticking around. The music could have been played at a club, but there's a crackling sensation, a remnant of a different sort of static that makes me think this tune was heard on a radio. Whatever the song, it doesn't strike me as something with a strong emotional core. The rhythm is not chaotic or intense, nor do the slow beats resemble any grand romantic overtures. I can't grasp onto the truth of what this song once was. But a reverberating tremor in its strum shakes up my spine and plucks me with a familiar sort of irritation. It's the feeling I get when my mom has control of the radio, and an afternoon of errands results in the same annoying chart topper playing over and over again.

The same song. Annoying, grating, and heard on repeat because the radio keeps giving it more air play. The same song, played on a radio that never shuts off because this man was stuck in a house with nothing to do but wait for a bulletin to cut through the aggravating notes.

A bulletin about a murderer on the run.

"Were you looking for Delantero here?" I ask.

The ghost nods, and I glance around the empty hall of the house half-buried under the earth.

"Why?" I ask. "Why here?" I try to imagine what an investigator would be doing in a place like this, an unsafe harbor in the middle of nowhere. "Was Delantero heading this way?"

The ghost nods again, and I swallow hard through the bile that's trying to climb my throat. My arms are trembling now, the pain of the music so great it's exhausting my strength. I can't hold on for much longer. But I think I'm on the right track. I just need to answer our question before I wind up passing out from the pain.

"He was on the run," I say, even if I can't hear my own words. "So he… holed up in an abandoned building?" The ghost doesn't respond to my guess, and I let out a sickened breath as I keep thinking. The killer didn't kill this man. The man was here, but the killer might not have been. "You thought he'd be here," I say as I work the story out for myself. "So you came to wait. But… You were wrong?"

"He'll be here!"

I stagger back to the wall and roll towards the doorway, brain swelling with the force of his scream. Gasping and shaking, I wipe away tears and lower into a crouch, eyeing the door and promising myself I can leave as soon as I get the answer I need. From what little I've seen, I can make a guess that this ghost was as stubborn in life as he seems to be in death. He came here convinced Delantero would arrive. He kept the radio on, waiting for news to suggest the criminal was close. But the killer didn't show up, and something else did in his place.

It's the fastest I've ever gotten an understanding of a spirit. But it doesn't help right now. It doesn't answer the question I need.

"Where was he running from?" I ask. Struggling under the current of sound, I stand up and step away from the door, further into the corridor—diving deeper instead of rushing to the surface for clearer breath. "Where was the last place Delantero struck? Where was the scene of his latest crime?"

"*Concepción*," the ghost says, answering my question so easily I spend a moment in dumbfounded shock. A moment I quickly regret. Without my full, conscious effort to ward off the pain, I drift into the music's cutting notes, swirling with the horrendous melody until my vision blurs and I lose sense of my surroundings. Part of me knows that I should leave, that I should stagger back to the kitchen now that I have the answer I came for. But I feel a little unhinged, and as much as I want them to, my feet won't move of their own accord.

I stand in the hallway, staring at the ghost until I can no longer keep upright. Then I slump against the nearest wall, cold and sick and confused. I need to get out of here. The logical part of my brain knows this, but that part is being eaten alive with the dead man's song. And I hope to hell I'm not so stupid as to just give up and let a spirit knock me out when I'm capable— should be capable—of getting out of harm's way. But I can't make my legs move. I don't want to. Not yet.

The ghost hovers, his misty head tilted my way. "*Can't stomach it.*" His words burble through the music, and he takes a hovering step back. "*Leave him to me.*"

My eyes stay on him, watching the way he moves closer and back, like he's pacing the hall. Like he's impatient, waiting forever for a person who won't come.

"Delantero," I say. My syllables are slow and, if I could hear them, I suspect they'd be trembling. But I keep speaking, anyway, working through my own confused murk in the hope that what I'm saying makes some kind of sense. "Delantero's not coming. Didn't you hear?"

"*Hear what*?" the ghost asks.

I blink a few times, not sure what the hell I'm doing. Then I groan through a tumble of music and let my head drop back against the wall.

"Delantero," I say. "He's dead."

I have no clue if the killer is dead. But I've pulled something similar to this on a ghost before, and I guess I don't have the same qualms as Sabeena does about fooling spirits. I'm not sad to know I'm lying to a ghost. I'm just happy when my lie has the desired effect, and the floating mass gets riled up.

"*Dead*?" he wails in my head. A wail of frustration. A wail of knowing the man he wanted to catch has forever slipped from his grasp.

Unless I can convince him that's not the case.

"You're dead too," I struggle out. "Did you know that? You and Delantero both. But he's already gone. Bet you didn't… didn't guess. He left this place. That's why you can't catch him. You're waiting, but he's already gone. If you want him…"

"*I will have him*," the ghost cuts in. "*I will catch him. I will end him!*"

"Cal!"

I don't know who it is that calls my name, but soon more than one pair of arms is grabbing me as my sector mates come to retrieve me from the narrow corridor. So much for not looking like an idiot. I can't stop my spiel now, and I can't focus on anything but the dead man in front of me. Because the ghost is getting angrier by the second. And his music is starting an explosive crash of dissonance in my brain.

"You can't end him unless you find him!" I yell. I can feel the flinch of the people grabbing me, and I remember what Meander said about me not needing to be so loud. But I can't help that, either. It's the only way I can be sure I'm saying the right words. "You can't end him unless you leave this place for good!"

The ghost's anger flares, and I cry out, while the hands on my arms stop. They know as well as I do what's coming. They can't see this spirit. But they've done this enough to understand the shift in the energy around us.

"Go now and get him. If you stay, you lose!" I keep yelling, and the ghost begins to rage, rushing back and forth through the hall and sending sharp spikes of ice stabbing through my skull. I feel the pounding footsteps instead of hearing them as someone else rushes into the room, and I don't need to know who that someone else is—I can tell by the way the ghost's anger spikes so harshly my vision swims and the shapes in the room go hazy with the pain.

"Go!" I yell to the spirit, my throat aching and every point in my body cut through with burning ache. "Don't let him win! LEAVE!"

"Get him out of here!" Meander yells, his voice breaking through the music as the music itself finally starts to shift. I feel arms again, and I try to help my sector mates by getting to my feet. But I only manage to slump forward, lost to the humming sound and the bright light washing over the space. I blink, slow and dazed, as the others drag me from the room, and I cross the threshold at the same moment the spirit crosses out of our realm.

I DON'T KNOW IF THE ORACLE INTENDED US TO RELEASE SO MANY SPIRITS on this trip. But I'm glad there are at least several Senders to share in the burden of the crossing. The first time five of us released a ghost together, we were all unconscious afterward. Last year, my first post-sixteen release with Sefa had us out for five days straight. But typically speaking, as we've grown stronger, we've become more capable of dealing with spirit crossings. Still, that doesn't change the fact I'm mostly unconscious for an entire day after my release—and even then, I'm only awake long enough to hazily explain what happened and give the city name for the crime scene before I'm out of it again.

At some point, Meander helps me from my bed, half-carrying me to the van so I can load into the backseat and drop my head against the window. But the next thing I'm aware of is arriving somewhere else, another hotel, though this one more like the tall hotel buildings I'm used to at home. I manage to stay awake until we get into our room, where I promptly sprawl out on a bed and pass out again. The next time I wake, it's morning and, sleepy or not, I'm hungry enough to force myself up.

Making quick work of a shower, I fix my hair and put on fresh clothes before venturing out to the hotel room. Naasir is asleep in one of the beds, while Dylan is curled up on a sofa in the room's back half. Meander is awake by the time I'm cleaned and dressed, so I wait for him to get ready, while Dylan rolls off the sofa and offers me a groggy hello.

"Thanks for helping get me out of that house," I tell him.

"No sweat," Dylan says through a yawn. "It was an experience I'll never forget. And one I'll be happy never to repeat. I am most definitely glad I've got the talent I do. You are *weird* around ghosts."

I frown, though I can't deny I probably do look like a pure lunatic when a ghost is making me weak and streaming music in my brain.

"You don't know what it's like," I grumble, while Meander comes out of the bathroom, folding his pajamas before storing them neatly away with his toiletries bag.

"Nope," Dylan agrees. "And man am I glad for that. I'll take the gray skin over the crazy screaming any day. You two going for breakfast?"

I nod glumly, while Dylan grabs his bag and heads for the bathroom.

"I'll meet you downstairs," he says. "I need some food, then a good run."

Meander and I make our way to the mostly empty

third floor dining room. We grab trays and head for the buffet, my dour mood lightened a little by the host of breakfast options to choose from.

"Dylan texted the city name to our mysterious phone number," Meander explains once we've grabbed food and have found a table on a balcony overlooking the city of Concepción. He sips at his tea while I make my way through a bowl of cereal. "We haven't found the envelope yet, though, so I guess we've still got work to do."

"We haven't actually found the crime scene," I say. "The ghost only gave me the city. We don't know where *in* the city we have to go."

Meander picks at the pastry on his plate. "How long do you think we'll be running around here for?"

I finish my cereal and grab an orange, digging my nail in to start peeling the skin. "We haven't tried any old-fashioned research yet. We're in a city now. And we know the murderer. Maybe there are records?"

"We've got the date of that newspaper to go by," Meander agrees. "That will be useful in narrowing down our search."

"We'll look after breakfast," I say. "For now, I just want to eat."

Meander smiles, watching as I pop a slice of orange in my mouth. Then his expression falls. "I'm sorry I wasn't there," he says. "You were… You looked like you were in a lot of pain."

"I was," I say. I place the rest of the orange on the table and swallow the slice in my mouth as I look at him. "But that's not your fault. And you did come, at the end. I felt it—hard. If you'd been there the entire time, things would have gotten dangerous for everyone."

He nods, though I know my words are not exactly comforting. I let out a huff of breath and sit back in my seat.

"I'm still super tired, so you're not allowed to judge my consolation skills," I say. He breathes out a laugh, and I smile. "I wished you were with me. Considering the circumstances, it was better you weren't. But you came, even though you knew what it would do to you. You risked it because the others were taking too long to get me out."

I don't know that for certain. But I suspected Meander was the one who sent the others after me, and the way his cheeks pink as he considers me now confirms it.

"I could hear you yelling," he says. "I tried to stay outside, but…" He shrugs. "You're worth getting knocked out for."

A still sleepy and probably rather stupid smile spreads across my lips as I think of him pacing outside in the same way the ghost paced in the corridor, wishing he knew if I was okay and deciding to risk his own consciousness to make sure I was.

"Even when I'm falling over and screaming at ghosts?" I ask.

"Even then, you idiot," Meander laughs. He kicks my foot under the table, his stare growing surprisingly serious. "Don't listen to anyone. You're not crazy when you're near a spirit."

"Maybe not," I acquiesce. "But I am a bit of a mess."

Meander lets out another breath of laughter as he shakes his head. "You're not a mess, either," he says. "You're just… just a complete embodiment of *you*.

You could leave at any time. But instead, you rant at the ghost because you're trying to help it, even though helping it is horrid. You've never pretended pain is some worthwhile requirement for talking to the dead. You've never pretended that we deserve this, or that we should be grateful for it. Seeing ghosts is rubbish. You know it's rubbish. And you don't make shite excuses to pretend it isn't. But you'll still do it. You'll rant and scream and be utterly pissed off all the while. But you'll still deal with the pain. Because you know it's the right thing to do. Because you've got a good heart. And the ranting, the screaming, the falling over—the whole lot of it. It's... bloody magnificent. Because *you're* magnificent, Cal."

I stare at Meander, studying his face and replaying his words until I realize tears are dripping down my cheeks. Then I laugh, wiping my face as, through the open balcony doors, I see Dylan enter the dining room. I have a lot to say in response to what Meander just told me. Mostly about how I think the same things could be said about him. But I don't have time to start a sleep-deprived, sappy ramble. So, I dry my eyes and sum up my feelings in the most succinct—and honest—way I know how.

"I love you," I tell him.

He smiles, his cheeks going bright with pleasure as his leg rests against mine under the table. "I love you too."

We spend a few seconds with our gazes locked. Then Dylan steps out onto the balcony and we both awkwardly try to appear nonchalant as we return to our meals.

Once breakfast is finished and we're back in our

hotel room, we fill Naasir in on our plans before calling the girls to join us. Then Dylan pulls out his laptop so we can start our search.

It doesn't take long to find the killer. Delantero went on a murder spree in Concepción in the 1940s, killing and robbing eight people before he was caught in the act and was killed himself during his ninth attempt. Mim asks if we should go to the place the murderer was gunned down. But my ghost died before Delantero did, which means we're looking for one of the earlier crime scenes.

"Did you get any info on the detective?" Mim asks. "When he died? It would help us narrow down which crime scene we're looking for."

"No, I didn't," I say.

"Well, what was his name?" Sabeena asks. "We can look up his obituary."

I shrug. "I don't know."

Sabeena's brown eyes are wide and confused. "What do you mean, you don't know?"

"I… I never thought to ask," I admit.

Sabeena and Mim stare at me with something akin to horrified bewilderment, while to my right, Meander chuckles under his breath. I remember our conversation over breakfast, and my stomach swells knowing this is probably just what he meant by me being so… *me*. These two girls cherish the ghosts they see, and they would never be so uncaring as to forget to ask the spirit's name. I, on the other hand, am far more interested in getting rid of ghosts than of getting to know them.

"Look," I say, throwing my hands up in surrender before the girls attack my method of release. "Delantero only killed in this city, at least as far as the records show. The ghost wasn't in the city. He was waiting because he thought Delantero was going to make a run for it. That means that, whenever the investigator died, people already knew who the killer was. They had his name—they knew where he was likely to strike. If the investigator thought he was making a run for it, it means there's a good chance Delantero had a close call. And I'd wager that wouldn't have happened until near the end of his killing spree. There were eight killings before he was caught. Let's start with his final victim and work backwards from there."

It takes an hour to locate the crime scene of Delantero's eighth victim. Once we have an address, Dylan texts it to our mystery number. When his phone pings with a response, he stares at the screen, one hand scratching his head.

"What is it?" I ask. "Did we pick the wrong crime scene?"

Dylan shakes his head. "No. It says a van will be out front in thirty minutes." He glances up at me. "And it says to bring a pencil."

"A pencil?" I ask.

Dylan reads over the text again. Then he glances around with a shrug before getting Sabeena to fish a pencil from her bag.

WHEN THE VAN ARRIVES AND WE'RE TAXIED OFF TO OUR DESTINATION, Mim tries to get the driver to talk about the city, or to see if he knows anything of importance to our mission. But the man stays silent, his attention on the road as he takes us along busy streets until we reach a crowded plaza and a high-rise office building.

"This is it?" I ask with a frown. I stare through the window at the building, which must reach up at least thirty floors. "The address we have doesn't include an apartment number. And this doesn't look like an apartment, anyway."

"This doesn't look like it's from the forties, either," Dylan adds.

"They probably tore down whatever existed here before," Meander says. "Built something new overtop of it."

"Great," I say with a sigh. "How are we going to find the right spot?"

"Not to be an insensitive jerk or anything," Dylan says. "But we *do* have our very own bloodhound... so to speak."

"Phrased with the utmost respect," Meander mutters. "Good work."

"We need to get closer," Kornelía says, sounding unperturbed by Dylan's choice of words. "My vision doesn't extend forever. I can't see up that high."

"I thought you only saw white," Dylan says after we've exited the van. "And then, like, ghosts. You can't see the ghosts if they're too far away?"

Kornelía shakes her head. "If I could see all ghosts, I suppose I'd see every spirit in the world, at all times. Physical things don't obscure my view, so I can see spirits at a farther range than most. But it doesn't extend forever." She smiles. "I'm thankful for that."

"We'll start low," I say in regard to the building. "The original address didn't have units, so that suggests the person would likely have been close to the ground."

"Unless the ghost can roam," Meander says. "If there even *is* a ghost here."

"Yeah, well, if there is a roaming spirit, you're staying close to ground level," I say. "No exploring haunted high rises."

Meander sighs with a nod. "Let's hope it's on the first floor."

There's no lobby or security guard at the office's entrance, but there is a locked door to keep unwanted visitors out. While the rest of us talk about the best strategy for getting into the building, Kornelía stands near the door, chin tilted upwards. After a couple of minutes, she raises a hand and shoos us from sight while she and Draugur stay put. We leave, glancing confusedly between us, until we see a couple of people in business suits exiting the building. They take in the sight of Kornelía and her guide dog and immediately the open the door to let them through without asking if she's actually allowed inside. Kornelía smiles, thanking them and disappearing from view until the people have left. Then she returns, fumbling for the door until she pulls it open to let the rest of us inside.

Once we're in a dim, grey-carpeted hallway, Kornelía is quick to determine that there is, indeed, a ghost in the building. She guides us around a corner and along a dingy corridor until we stop before a closed elevator. Meander hesitates, not wanting to stay away but not wanting to brave the elevator in a building with known paranormal activity, either. When Kornelía explains that the ghost is only one floor above us, he says he's willing to risk a single story. Still, his fears are not unfounded, and the creaking elevator is not something I have any intention of seeing him inside of. The two of us leave the others to ride, while we find the nearest stairwell to take up instead.

We meet the rest of the sector in another hallway that's quiet—but not silent. We can hear office workers in the distance, murmuring voices and a phone ringing somewhere far off. We stick close and try to make our steps soundless as we creep down the hall, nervous about getting caught before we've found what we're looking for. At one point, we dive down a side hall as a woman bustles past on route to the elevator. Then, three-quarters of the way along the corridor, Kornelía stops before a closed door.

"Do we have to knock?" Dylan asks as we appraise

the door.

"Unless it's unlocked," Mim says.

He tries the door, but when it doesn't budge, he knocks instead. We wait, listening for sounds from within. After a long pause and a second attempt at rapping on the door, it's clear no one is going to answer. Dylan throws a questioning glance over his shoulder, while Meander appraises the area around the door before reaching up to the light fixture wired to the wall. He feels around the metal, then produces a key from where it's been wedged between the wall and the fixture's metal plate.

"Do you think it's standard office protocol to leave hidden keys lying around?" I ask.

"No," Meander replies with a smirk. "But it seemed like something the Oracle might do."

He hands the key to Dylan, and when the door's unlocked we take a few steps into what looks like an executive's office. I'm curious to know if the employee who usually occupies this space is gone for the day, or only on a break. I wonder, too, if they're the one who called in the Oracle's help—or if they have no idea we're trespassing in their space.

Whatever the case, I don't have long to dwell on the possibilities of whether our appearance has been anticipated. As soon as we're in the room, Meander's breath hitches. I try to make him wait out of the room again, but this time he refuses.

"You just saw a ghost," he says. "You don't have the energy to face another yet. Not by yourself."

"If you want to be able to drag me out again, you need to stay conscious," I say. "Everyone else is here to make sure I don't get too in over my head."

Meander hunches his shoulders. "Everyone else doesn't know you like I do," he mutters under his breath. He steps further into the office without waiting for my reply and, as much as I'm displeased he's continuing on, I can't help smiling as I trail behind him.

The executive's office comes complete with its own kitchenette and bathroom. We walk past these both, Meander's struggles to take in full breaths giving us as clear an indication as Kornelía could that someone dead is nearby. I brace myself outside of the final room in the office suite, then peek through the open door. On first sight, the boardroom appears to be void of people, living or dead. The ghost must be well-confined to this particular space, if it's not even noticeable from beyond the doorway.

I step forward to cross into the room, ready for the static to swell in my ears. But I don't hear any music, or any ghostly sound at all. The air is chilled, and there's a lingering dread in the room that tells me a ghost is inside. But as I make my way through the space, flicking on the light switch and circling the oval oak-veneer table positioned in the middle of the room—a pile of blank papers stacked neatly at one end—I don't sense anything more than the chilly inklings of death.

"I can't see it," I say to the others after I've completed my round.

"But this is the murder spot, isn't it?" Dylan asks.

"Yeah, but…"

"She's not a victim," Kornelía says. She steps into the room with me, her eyes moving as if she's checking over the ghost. "Her clothes… they're newer. Not old enough."

"So, she's not the murder victim ghost," Dylan says.

"Does that mean we got the location wrong, after all?"

"Not necessarily," I say. "It just means there aren't any ghosts here that I can see. Not all murder victims stick around. I guess a lot of them do, but… not all."

"You already s-saw one," Meander stammers from beyond the doorway.

"That's right," I muse. "I already saw a ghost. So, maybe this one's not for me."

"But… We've all seen one," Sabeena says. "All of us who can, anyway."

"Meander didn't release one," Mim says. "Could that be why?"

"He got the clue from the other ghost," I remind her. "Robbie said we didn't *have* to release the ghosts. Why should he be forced to face two?"

"Because no one else can see it?" Sabeena asks.

I sigh, annoyed by the truth of her statement. Crossing my arms over my chest, I slump against the wall near the boardroom door, while Meander eyes me from the hall.

"I'll do it," he says. I give him a look that is part pleading, part sympathy, and he takes as big of a breath as he can—which is not nearly big enough— before joining Kornelía and me inside the room.

The lights flicker as soon as he steps past the threshold, and he stays by the doorway, looking at the ghost and then closing his eyes as he tries to make sense of it. The overhead fluorescents continue to flash, and the papers on the table flutter and float all over the room while Meander shudders in pain. But nothing else happens. He stays put until he starts getting woozy. Then I help him stagger back to the office, where he drops heavily into the swivel chair behind the executive's desk.

When he gets his breath back, he shakes his head. "I can't get anything from her," he says. "Other than that she doesn't want anything to do with me."

"Well, what good is that?" Dylan asks. "If she won't talk to you, then we're screwed."

"Not necessarily," Mim says.

"What do you mean?" I ask. "Do you have a plan?"

"No," Mim says. Her eyes slide to the far end of the short hallway. "But we haven't tried everyone yet."

I follow her gaze until it lands on Kornelía. As if she can sense our eyes on her, the tall girl shakes her head.

"I can't communicate, you know that," she says.

"But we don't know that," I say. I think about last year, about the thing I wanted Kornelía to try—the thing she ultimately refused to attempt. Then I think about the pile of papers now strewn around the back room from Meander's unsuccessful attempt to talk to the ghost. With a smile, I turn to Dylan. "You have that pencil?"

Dylan scratches his head. "Yeah. In my pocket. Why?"

"No, Cal," Kornelía begins.

"Channeling," I say at the same time.

"Channeling?" Dylan looks at me, then Kornelía, then back at me. He grins and fishes out the pencil. "Korni, you never did try it last summer."

"Dylan, I can't channel," she says. Her voice has changed, the subdued calm growing frantic and mousy, and the break of her newfound state of constant peace makes me feel like I've suddenly gained back a piece of something I thought was lost. For a moment, the old Kornelía is with us, afraid of her own ability and uncomfortable with everyone's attention on her. I don't want her to be afraid of anything. But the familiarity of her uncertainty makes her feel a little closer, a little less distant than the wholly different being she's become since last year.

I grab the pencil from Dylan and walk back down the hall. Placing it in her hand, I close my fist around hers with a smile.

"You can do this," I say. "You can try. We don't always get it right, Kornelía. No one is going to care if you don't, either."

"She won't even talk to me," Meander calls from the office. "I've already failed, so it doesn't much matter if you do too."

"You're the only chance we've got," I add.

Kornelía's breath is unsteady as she stares straight ahead, one hand gripping Draugur's handle while the other holds the pencil tight. I look at the stick clenched between her fingers, remembering the times I've watched her sketch and wondering how often it is she relives similar moments, when she took her tool in hand and drew the spirits she could see in her mind.

I don't want to push Kornelía into something she's not ready for—or something she wants no part in. But I can't imagine never playing the violin again. Kornelía loved to sketch ghosts. If she can have the opportunity of using her pencil to interact with the dead once again, she should seize it.

Kornelía swallows several times as she contemplates what she will do. A single tear streaks down her cheek, curving over her chin and dropping into the air. But at last, she offers us a gentle nod.

"Okay," she whispers. "I'll try."

Dylan takes Draugur, and I walk with Kornelía to the oval table. She sits at the far end, and I gather the mess of papers before placing one piece in front of her. Kornelía spends a moment with her face tilted down toward her hand. Then she raises her eyes in the direction of the ghost.

"I don't know how to tell her what to do," she says. "I can't speak with her. She's watching me, but…"

The lights flicker, and I glance over to see Meander leaning against the doorway. His bloodshot eyes fix on the same place as Kornelía's, and his voice rasps as he begins to speak.

"You can talk to her, through her," he says. There's a pause, and he winces. "She won't hurt you. She knows."

He glances back at us with a nod before returning to the office. I smile as I watch him disappear. Then I look at Kornelía.

"Talk to her," I say. "Ask her questions. Let her know what you want to do."

Kornelía nods again. Reaching out, she finds my arm and gives it a squeeze. Then she sits straight, and I retreat to the doorway while she poises the pencil to write.

"I-I would like to talk with you," she says, her voice uncertain. "Communicate with you. But I can't hear what you say. So please, use my body as a vessel. Speak through me, by way of my hand."

Her head tilts, following the movement of the ghost. Then Kornelía gasps, head lowering to look at where I guess the ghost is probably touching her hand. More tears fall from her eyes, and she sniffs before speaking again.

"What is your name?" she asks. She waits, tense and

hopeful, while I stay by the door, feeling much the same. But as we continue to wait, nothing happens. Her hand stays still, and eventually, her shoulders slump. "I told you," she says. "I can't do this."

"You only asked one question," I say.

"Maybe you didn't ask the *right* question," Mim adds from behind me. "Ghosts can be fickle. You need to know what to ask."

"Keep trying, Kornelía," I urge.

She sighs, blinking several times before she gives us a little nod. Her shoulders rise, and she shifts in her seat. Then, moving her head in the spirit's direction, she begins again.

"How did you die?" She asks the question and waits, but still nothing happens. After a moment, she tries again. "What happened to you?" She waits, head shaking and frustration creasing her face. "What—" she pauses, breathing deep and steadying herself. "Why are you still here?"

Her hand twitches, and Mim grabs my arm in excitement as we watch the pencil slide across the paper.

"Korni?" Mim asks, but Kornelía doesn't say anything. Her head lifts, tilts, and rolls back on her neck until she is seemingly staring at the ceiling.

The pencil scratches against the paper, slowly at first and then gaining speed as either the ghost, Kornelía, or both of them get accustomed to the process. I watch the movement from afar, desperate to see what is going on at the table but not wanting to interrupt. Mim and I wait until the pencil ceases to move, and Kornelía's head lowers. Then she turns to us, her eyes wide.

"What does it say? Does it say anything?"

I walk into the room and approach the table, looking at the paper and putting a hand to my mouth to cover my surprise. I'd expected some scratchings that would hopefully look like rough words. But what's in front of me is something I wasn't expecting—though it seems foolish the idea hadn't already crossed my mind.

"It doesn't say anything," I say with a smile.

Kornelía looks crestfallen as she sits back in the chair. "It doesn't?"

"No." I laugh as I put a hand on her shoulder. "Kornelía, you didn't write anything. You *drew* something."

"I…" she sits forward, her free hand feeling for the paper. I slide it in front of her, and she roams her fingertips over the graphite marks. "What did I draw?"

"A person," I say. It's a person similar to the ones I saw Kornelía sketch last summer when her eyesight was failing her. The lines are rough, and the features are a bit off-kilter. But it's a person, I can tell that for sure. "A woman. Long, looks like frizzy hair? Thin lips?"

"That's the ghost," Kornelía says.

"Young?" I ask, but then Kornelía shakes her head.

"This woman is older. But it could be her—"

"Daughter?" I guess.

Kornelía nods. She turns her face to the side, in the direction of the ghost. Then she smiles. "Give me another piece of paper," she instructs.

I comply, placing the paper in front of her before stepping back to the door. I bring the first drawing with me, and we pass it between us as Kornelía begins questioning the spirit once more.

"Do you have a message for your daughter?" Kornelía asks. She doesn't get any response, and she frowns, concentrating until she thinks up another way to ask. "What do you need to say to her?" she tries, and when that doesn't work, "what do you need to *give* her?"

Kornelía gasps as the pencil starts scratching again, and I watch, entranced as it makes looping designs on the paper.

"What is it?" Kornelía asks when the ghost has finished.

I walk back into the room, crossing the space and lifting the paper again. This time, the drawing is rougher, and I have to pass it off because I can't quite make out what it's supposed to be. Mim isn't sure, either, nor is Sabeena. But when Meander gets a hold of it, he nods.

"It's numbers," he says, his voice still stilted from his shallow breath. "Look. That's a two, and, um… a six? Or an eight. An eight, I think. And a three. And a one or a seven. One, probably." He shows me the line, and as I follow the trace of his finger the shapes become clearer. The numbers adorn some kind of curved box and, sticking out of it, there's a jagged stick I think is likely a key.

"It wouldn't be a jewelry box, not with the numbers," I say. "Is it maybe a banking box?"

"Could be," Meander says with a nod. "Some money or deeds unknown to the daughter? That'd be a reason for a ghost to stick around."

"You need to get the numbers to your daughter?" Kornelía asks from the other room. I leave Meander with the second sketch and return to the doorway, where Kornelía's face is tilted up and to the side. She nods, slowly, and smiles. "Yes," she says. Then she faces me again, while at the same time reaching for the stack of paper.

Stepping into the room, I grab a third sheet and place it before Kornelía. This time, she doesn't hesitate at all.

"Where can we find your daughter?" she asks. Immediately, her hand twitches, and she begins scribbling furiously at the sheet. The pencil moves faster than I've ever seen it, wistful and somewhat careless as the ghost guides her hand. When the sketch is finished, Kornelía drops the pencil and slumps back against the chair. I walk over to the table and pick up the paper, staring at it for a long moment before I turn to show it to Mim.

"Am I crazy?" I ask, handing the paper over, "or is that—"

Mim lets out a disbelieving laugh. "You're not crazy," she says. "But the Oracle is certainly having its fun."

On the sheet of paper, Kornelía's sketched a familiar sight. One large dome surrounded by several smaller ones, all entwined with wooden paths and surrounded by grasses and plants.

It's the location we haven't been to in nearly two weeks. The soon to be eco-resort that is this summer's home for Camp Wanagi.

THE GHOST'S DAUGHTER, AS IT TURNS OUT, IS A CO-FOUNDER OF THE ECO-resort. It was while investigating reports of the spirit in Concepión that the Oracle first became aware of the resort's existence.

Once we've texted our final answer, we're driven back to the hotel to collect our things. Then we're at last able to return to camp. I'm exhausted by the time we make it back to our dome, but I'm so relieved to find my violin how I left it that I take it out and spend nearly an hour playing in the main room. The others filter off, some going for a walk, others looking for a meal, until only Meander and I remain. He lounges with a book and, despite the lack of a computer screen between us, the act is so familiar from our daily video chats that it makes me feel like I've returned home.

We're given the evening to relax from our trip. The next day, we go over the details of our hunt with Robbie and Alex.

"You were quite successful," Alex beams. "We knew you would be."

"Right up until the moment we sent a panicked SOS?" Dylan asks.

"Exactly," Robbie grins.

Dylan rolls his eyes, grabbing a slice of pizza and sitting back on the sofa.

"We're proud of what you accomplished," Alex says. "And we're glad you had the opportunity to explore the area and tackle some challenges for a final time as a team."

"Final time?" Dylan asks with his mouth full. "What does that mean?"

"That we'll be leaving here soon," Mim says in a quiet, surprisingly somber voice.

Alex nods. "If you haven't already chosen what you want to work on for your final assignment, this is the week for you to decide."

"Oh shit," Dylan says. "I forgot about that."

Mim gives Dylan a fond smile. "Of course you would forget. Too busy playing with the dog."

"I know not all of y'all are looking forward to this task," Robbie says. "But it's an important one. You can choose anything you'd like to do. Any ghost or paranormal situation, anywhere in the world. You can choose something you think will be a challenge, or something meaningful to you personally." He scans the group of us with a nod. "You can choose an intriguing case, or something to test your skills. Something to push your abilities, or a case to end your time at Wanagi with an easy finish." He laughs. "Although really, what's the fun in that?"

After more than three years, I know Robbie's

definition of *fun* is severely different from my own. I'm not looking forward to this task. In fact, I've hardly given it any consideration at all, and most of what I *have* considered has related more to the restrictions of this task, of how close—or how far apart—Meander and I will be when we choose our respective cases.

"What happens," I start, putting a voice to my nagging concerns, "if we pick the same area as someone else. Would that be allowed?" Better to know the answer early than to get false hopes up as we start making our plans. Better to know now if I need to be in my own city, region, or country for this last, awful encounter.

"Yeah, that'd be allowed," Robbie says with a knowing smile that would be thoroughly annoying, if he wasn't giving me the answer I hoped for. "But I'll do you one even better. Y'all know we're all about teamwork here. You can choose to pick a case of your own, if you wish. But this is your final task, and you get to make the rules. So, if you want to work *together* on something, you're welcome to it."

I sit up straighter, trying to hide my pleased surprise at this unexpected announcement. The beaming smile I can feel spreading across my cheeks suggests I'm doing a terrible job of it. But when I glance at Meander to find the expression mirrored on his face, I don't care.

"Theoretically speaking," Dylan says from around his pizza, while Meander shifts until his leg presses against mine, "if we wanted to skip the final task altogether, what would happen?"

Robbie shrugs. "You'd go home, probably. No point staying if you're not gonna even try, is there?"

He smiles. "But you wouldn't wimp out on me now, would you?"

"Nah," Dylan says. "Course not. I don't know what the hell I *am* going to do. But I'll do something."

"Does anyone know what they'll do?" Sabeena asks.

Silence is, for a moment, her only response, and I'm relieved to know no one else has been giving this task a lot of thought, either. But then Mim raises a hand, head bent as she stares at her lap.

"You know what you're going to do, Mim?" Sabeena asks.

"Yes," Mim replies. "I…" She sighs, hands braced on her knees before she raises her head. "I'm going home," she says. "I'm…" She falters again, and I'm surprised to see tears swimming in her eyes. "I'm going home to see Mama," she finishes after a long moment.

"What does your mother…" Dylan's words taper off as Mim looks at him. He stares, his yellow-tinted eyes incredulous as he takes in her meaning. "You can't… She's not…" "My mother is dead," Mim explains.

"When did she—" Dylan starts.

"She died when I was six years old," Mim cuts in.

Someone in the room makes a startled gasp, although I'm too stunned by Mim's declaration to even tell who it is. Mim's always talked about her mother as if the woman was still alive. It never occurred to me she might not be.

"You told me you were going home for your final task," Kornelía says. She reaches a hand across the gap between them. When she finds Mim's arm, her fingers snake down to grab her hand. "But I didn't—"

"She's a ghost," Mim says before her abrupt words

hitch, and she swallows back a sob. "She's… she was sick. It was a long time ago. But… the last time I saw her alive, I… I got mad at her. I… told her she wasn't allowed to leave us." Tears leak from her eyes, and she squeezes Kornelía's hand. "The day after she died, she appeared in my bedroom. She's been with me ever since."

"You've been living with a ghost?" Dylan asks.

My stomach churns with the thought. I can't stand being around ghosts for more than a few minutes—couldn't even before my talents developed to where they are now. I can't imagine ever *living* with a ghost. Let alone acting like that ghost was still alive.

"I believed, for a long time, that I performed a miracle in getting her to stay with me," Mim admits. She closes her eyes and shakes her head. "I've since learned that I was a foolish, selfish little girl so grieved over the impending loss of her mother that I forced that mother to be a prisoner in our home."

"You're not to blame for what happened, Mim," Kornelía says. "You were six. You didn't understand."

"No," Mim says. "I didn't. But I do now. And it's time for me to let her go. I've known it since last year. But I wanted to come here one more time before…" She takes a deep, unsteady breath. "I'm ready now. I'm ready to go home."

Her wet eyes alight on Alex, and the young woman nods with a sad smile.

"We'll make your arrangements, Mim," she says. "You have one last session with the new campers later this week. If you can stay until then, we'll book your flight to leave afterwards."

Mim nods, her hand still in Kornelía's. The two girls

stay like that while the room settles into a stiff silence, the rest of us stunned by the revelation so recently revealed.

"For the rest of you," Robbie says after a moment, "you have this week to figure out what you want to do. Let us know if you need help or…" he twirls his hand, *"inspiration*. We'll give you access to our database of records."

"There's a database?" I ask.

"Of course," Robbie says. "Where else would we store all the reports we get? Ancient tomes in the library?"

"That would be more appealing than a computer program," Meander says.

"Maybe," Robbie says. "But infinitely worse to maintain, don't you think?"

Meander shrugs, clearly not agreeing. I smirk, knowing he'd never choose a computer over a book if he had his way. Still, I can understand Robbie's argument. A database is much cleaner, and it doesn't need to be transported from country to country as the Oracle tries to go about its work.

Which is exactly what it feels like—work. Knowing a database exists makes all of this feel a bit more like a job, one we're definitely auditioning for. We've been training and prepping, and now, we're being sent out into the real world to find some ghost, help it, and get on our way. In theory, it should be easy—between the seven of us, we managed to release three ghosts in the past two weeks, with a fourth release probably coming soon for the spirit in Concepción. But not all ghosts are simple, nor are they hand-picked to align with our strengths. If we have to choose from a database of spirits no one in the Oracle has yet to figure out, it means we're probably in for a rough go. And what we choose—not to mention how we handle the case— might cement our worth in the Oracle's eyes.

The scavenger hunt was our final exam, and I think we all passed. We've finished our training. Now, it's time for our internship to begin.

"Can we see the database?" Sabeena asks. "I want to know how it works."

"Sure," Robbie says. "We can go over it in the library. If you're willing, you can hand over your personal devices and get it installed on there too. But you don't have to. You can access everything from the library, whenever you need to."

We follow our leads to the library and get an introduction to the database. Sabeena is the most invested in the topic, so when she sits down with Alex for a more comprehensive tutorial, the rest of us break off on our separate ways.

Meander and I go beyond the wooden boardwalks, out to a cleared area behind the resort where a few wide chairs have been positioned in a semi-circle around what I suspect will eventually be a fire pit. Together, we sit in one of the oversized chairs, my legs over his lap and my back against the arm rest.

"Where do you think we'll go?" Meander asks, and I smile again knowing this is now a joint decision for us to make. I thought the Oracle might force us to separate to prove our individual worth on this final outing. Knowing we can tackle the task together makes the prospect of picking a ghost far less daunting.

"I don't know," I say. "I don't really care. Neither of us need to impress anyone. We're not staying on with the Oracle after this is done."

"True," Meander says. He rubs absently at my leg. "So, I guess the question is more where do you *want* to go? Any sights you've been aching to see? Between us, we'll find a ghost anywhere."

There are many places in the world we could go, famous locations or scenic views we could experience. But no yearning thoughts burble at the back of my mind. I'm lucky to have the chance at traveling the world. But travel has never offered me a big thrill. Maybe it's because of my constant worry about seeing the dead. Or maybe I just find enjoyment in other ways. Whatever the case, the prospect of jet setting to some far-off locale doesn't strike in me any sort of excitement.

"I don't have any place in mind," I confess with a shrug. "You?"

Meander twists to face me, considering the question for a few beats before shaking his head. "I don't care where we end up," he says at last. His hand rests on my leg, and he leans his head back against the seat, face tilted to the sky as he closes his eyes with a smile. "It doesn't matter. We'll go together. And we'll finish our task. And that'll be worth everything. That'll be the last ghost either one of us ever has to release."

24

The first part of our week back at camp is spent making half-hearted attempts to find a subject for our final task. But on Wednesday night, a tense phone call with Liam leaves Meander in a solemn mood. For an hour after the call, he sits in the dome, brooding in silence. Then, quietly, he nudges my foot and asks if I can play my violin. I'm surprised by the request, though I'm more than happy to comply. I get my case, and we wander the campgrounds in search of somewhere private, ultimately settling in the empty library.

The familiar surroundings, a different building but with the same stacks of books where I first played him my violin in Tonga, eases his mood. He sits at a table, watching the pull and push of my bow as I play a few pieces by heart. When he stands up, I expect him to start wandering the shelves. But instead, he comes to my side, stopping my hand and drawing me into a grateful kiss before eventually telling me the details of his brother's call.

"She doesn't want me to come back," he says. He sits on the edge of a table, his arms loose around my hips. "She's already complaining. Telling Liam I'm on thin ice. Threatening what she'll do if I mess up."

"I don't understand why she's targeting you so bad," I say. My violin lies on the table, and my fingers splay through his curls as I brush back his hair. "You've never gotten along, but this is… different. It's gotten so much worse lately. And you haven't done anything."

Meander's teeth scrape over his lip as he looks up at me. "I've been happy," he says after a pause. "I've been working non-stop, saving money to see you. And I have—seen you. I've tried to stay out of her way. But she knows. Can't rightly hide it." He smiles a little, even while he sighs. "I'll deal with it, when I'm home. I have to deal with it, one way or another. But it's just… I'm envious of Liam. He got out the moment he turned eighteen. I will too. I just have to survive until then."

We talk a little longer, then I play more music and he does start to wander the library, combing the stacks and picking up a few books to bring back with him to our dome.

In addition to Wednesday's incident, another thing keeps us from spending too much time thinking about the details of our final task. Soon, we'll be separating from the rest of the sector. And that knowledge, constantly present like an undercurrent flowing beneath our every thought, means that Shade spends even more of its time together. No one says it out loud, but everyone is well-aware of the truth—that this is the last time we'll be at camp, and possibly the last time we'll see each other at all.

I can make peace with not seeing everyone from camp again. But knowing my closer friends might slip away is a surreal and bitter truth. I want to believe I'll stay in touch with my fellow Shades. But I'm not going to lie to myself about the reality of our lives outside of camp. I've never talked to Sabeena or Naasir between summers. And even the others are more distant now than perhaps they once were.

Mim has her own demons to face, and her own vision for the future that keeps her tethered to a life that does not involve any of us. Dylan and I have grown steadily apart over the years, our personalities not compatible for any real closeness—and his animosity with Meander driving a further wedge between any lasting friendship we may have once considered. Kornelía will stay in touch, and I'm glad for that. But she, too, has grown away from us. Her life has changed dramatically, and she's got a whole new existence separate from this camp and everyone in it.

Of course, I can't pretend I haven't drifted too. Every time I'm reminded of our upcoming departure, I inch a little closer to Meander, relieved he will be with me during the last half of this summer and sick with the inevitable fact of our separation after August.

The reality of our waning time here—of how close Camp Wanagi is to becoming part of our past—means that we focus more on the present moment than on planning our future conquests. Still, the ticking timeline cannot be erased, and by Friday, when we have our final mentoring session with the Revenants, the swift approach of our upcoming leave takes hold of my nerves. My foot taps an unrhythmic beat as the Revenants gather in their dome and my eyes scan the young faces of the campers who still have years of camp time left to them. When one of the kids says we have to retrieve Jonah from his room—which is apparently no longer located in the Revenant dome—I volunteer Meander and myself just so I can get away from the unexpected stab of jealously I feel for the kids who don't yet have to worry about life after the Oracle.

Mim looks troubled by the declaration about Jonah, and after I've volunteered our services, she decides to come along too. The three of us follow Trick's instructions to the leads' quarters on the right-hand side of the resort, where my old mentor turned Entity lead Daniel welcomes us inside.

"Yeah, he's here," Daniel says when he opens the door. He gives me a friendly pat on the shoulder and eyes my hair as we walk into the leads' dome.

"Why is Jonah staying here?" Mim asks before he can inquire about the white strands.

Daniel shrugs. "There's always a room for campers who need space here."

"Really?" I ask. It'd never occurred to me someone could stay in their own room. "Is it only for troublemakers?"

"No." Daniel shakes his head as he leads us across the dome that's almost identical to our own. "There are many reasons for its use. People who have certain medical conditions. People who need more time alone for their wellbeing. People who don't feel comfortable or appropriate staying with a gendered group. And sometimes, yes, people who have trouble with their roommates."

He knocks on the special room's door three separate times before Jonah finally makes his appearance. His hair is a mess, lanky and tangled as if he's just gotten out of bed. But he doesn't tell us to get lost. Instead, he hurries to find a pen and notebook, strangely eager as he grabs his Camp Wanagi sweater before following us back to the Revenant's dome.

"You're having trouble adjusting?" Mim asks once we're outside of the leads' quarters.

Jonah scoffs, his free hand balled into a fist at his side. "I'm probably going to be thrown out," he says. He wants to sound tough, but it's easy to detect the despair in his words.

"Why would you be thrown out?" Mim asks.

"People keep trying to get inside my head," Jonah says. "Like they understand what's going on. No one understands. No one gets it."

"You didn't answer her question," Meander says.

Jonah glares at him, then lowers his head in a sulk. "I've gotten in a few fights. I don't do well with people trying to boss me around."

"This place is here to help you," Mim says. "No one's trying to tell you what to do."

"People are always telling me what to do," Jonah says. "What to think."

"They always will," I say. Jonah raises his head to turn his glare on me, and I shrug. "I don't know you. I don't understand what it's like for you. But I had a doctor tell me I was making up the ghosts I see— which made me question my own sanity for years."

Jonah pauses his step, the glare shifting into a look of wary hope. "Really?" he asks, the word so quiet it's nearly a whisper.

"We all have," I say with a nod.

Jonah looks at Mim and Meander, who both nod as well.

"I've been prescribed more pills than I can count," Meander says.

Mim smiles. "I've got a resident demon in me, according to some."

To my surprise, Jonah laughs as he watches her. "That's great. In a shitty kind of way."

Mim smiles. But then she gives him a more serious look. "This place is full of people who understand what it's like to be strange. But they don't know what it's like to be *your* kind of strange. If you came here looking for an explanation, you won't find it. That's not what Camp Wanagi is for."

"Then why did you all come back?" he asks, his joyful tone snapping back to anger.

"Because we had things to learn," Mim says.

"Or we found what you're probably really after," Meander adds. "Someone who actually… *gets it*."

"If you keep getting in fights, you probably will be sent home eventually," Mim tells Jonah. "But you haven't been kicked out yet, and we can also tell you from experience that the Oracle is willing to go through a lot to make sure you have the chance to be here."

Jonah stares at her, his expression etched with confusion. "Why?" he asks. "What is this place, really? Why would they want to help someone like me?"

"Because they want people to work for their organization," Meander says. Then he sighs. "And they know what it's like to be us. Because they *are* us. They're all Senders too, and they know what the world is like when you don't fit into a preconceived mold. They could train us to hunt ghosts anywhere. They bring us together so we have the chance to know we're not alone."

"That was very well said," I say, raising one brow in curious consideration. "And distinctly lacking in irritation. Are you getting soft in your old age?"

Meander smirks. "Shut up. We haven't finished our summer yet. Still plenty of time to curse the Oracle. Hell, we've still got a chance to get ourselves kicked out too."

Mim rolls her eyes, turning to Jonah with a conspiratorial smile as she tells him to ignore us. The way Jonah looks back at her, his sour exterior giving way to an easiness that probably doesn't usually come easy at all, reminds me of our second summer of camp—when Mim and Reed did tutoring sessions together.

"Where did you all go, anyway?" Jonah asks as we pass out of the lobby. "You haven't been here."

"We were exploring our talents," Mim says. She explains the trip we did as a sector as she and Jonah walk across the grass to the far path. Meander and I let them get ahead, the two gravitating closer as they move towards the dome.

"It's too bad Mim's not coming back," Meander muses. "Looks like she might be just the kind of person that kid needs."

"Do you think he'll really go all summer without making a friend in his own sector?" I ask. "That didn't happen for us. For any of us."

"No," Meander says. "But to be fair, I did try rather hard not to make any friends. If it weren't for a certain annoyingly determined violinist…"

"You'd be lonely and miserable and probably living in a cave made of old books and used teabags," I finish.

Meander laughs. "I'm glad you have so much confidence in my survival skills. *Used teabags*?"

"I don't know." I shrug. "Insulation?"

"Okay. You get me a book on composers. I'm going to find you a podcast on basic construction techniques," he says. "Promise me you'll *never* use teabags for insulation in anything you build."

"I'll leave all our handyman work to you," I say. "You're probably better at following instructions than I am, anyway." The words are out before I can consider the connotation of them, and my heart skips while my cheeks warm at the uttered hint of a life that only exists in my head. But Meander doesn't give me an odd or awkward stare. He only steps closer, lacing his fingers with my own.

"I'll build whatever you want," he says with the casualty of simple fact. "So long as you do the cooking."

I swallow the breathless pause of imagining such a life, fearful of its seeming implausibility and aching for it with the added urgency that implausibility brings. With eyes trained ahead, I watch Mim and Jonah, thinking of what I've accomplished during my time at this camp and being suddenly granted with the clarity of understanding why it is I'm so bothered by Wanagi's looming end. It's never been about the ghosts. And it's not really about the development of my talent, either. It's about the life I've gained while being around the dead, and the possibility of a life that extends far beyond Wanagi's bounds.

"I'll cook," I say, allowing myself to imagine what I hope will someday be real. "I suppose I'll bake too."

Meander turns to me, his eyes bright with the joy I remember from the first time he tried one of my desserts. "Oh yes," he says, his enthusiasm making me want that *someday* all the more. "You *definitely* need to bake."

25

SOMEDAY STILL EXISTS IN THE MURKY FUTURE OF OUR THEORETICAL POST-Sender life. But baking is something I don't need to wait for.

The morning after our mentoring session, I get up early and sneak out of the dome. Crossing the dark, chilly boardwalk, I reach the lobby and make my way to the kitchen. Camp always runs late, which means breakfast won't start for another few hours. I plan on getting in and out before anyone is wise to my presence. But when I step through the swinging wooden doors, I'm startled to see I'm not the only camper with early morning baking on their mind.

"Oh." I stop in the kitchen doorway, halted by the sight of someone standing behind the steel prep counter that looks out of place in the otherwise wood-heavy design. "Isabis. Hi."

Isabis, the Entity camper who was a part of my ghost mission in our second year of camp, glances up in equal surprise. For a minute, she stares at my hair, looking like she might not recognize me. But then she smiles.

"Hello Cal," she says. "I was just doing some baking."

I stuff my hands into the front pocket of my sweatshirt. "I was actually going to do the same," I admit with a laugh.

Isabis smiles, leaning on her crutch as she makes her way to one of the big refrigerators. "Come in," she says in her halted breath. "Plenty of room. Plenty of food."

She carefully pulls the fridge door open, the smile still on her lips. But she doesn't actually look very happy. Or very well. Her gait is more off balanced than it ever used to be, and her once smooth skin looks worn and splotchy. Even the green and yellow head wrap she wears is crooked, like it was put on with very unsteady hands.

"Are you okay?" I ask as I step into the kitchen. I walk to the fridge and hold the door, while Isabis retrieves a carton of eggs. When she loses hold of the carton, I dive forward to grab it before it crashes to the floor. She stares at the carton, her eyes narrowed in annoyance. But when she sees my questioning look, her expression changes into one of exhaustion.

"Thanks," she says in her tired voice, and only when I recognize the weariness do I remember that this is Isabis's third summer with the Oracle—the summer her abilities are set to fully develop.

"How have things been?" I ask as I place the carton on the counter. "With your talent?"

She takes more care to pull out a container of cream

from the fridge before letting the door close and turning back towards the counter.

"Rough," she says after she's lowered the ingredient. "Things… changed."

The last time I saw Isabis's talent in action was two years ago, when she manipulated a spirit into picking up a hammer and helping us to knock out a wall.

"Can you still make ghosts move things?" I ask.

"Yes." Isabis spends a quiet moment arranging the ingredients and utensils. "But sometimes… I lose control."

My stomach squirms with her admission, and I remember the night in Tonga, when Meander saw what Isabis could do and worried that his ability and hers would result in a very dangerous ghost. Back then, everything turned out okay. But maybe he wasn't too far off the mark. If she loses control of her manipulation now, I'd hate to see her trying to deal with a ghost charged up from his presence.

"I don't try to work with them anymore," Isabis says while I'm still lost in my own contemplation. "The ghosts. I leave them alone. But sometimes… if they're close… my mind betrays me. I think of… commands. And it's enough to… start them off."

"Things get pretty out of hand for everyone in third year," I say.

"I didn't want to come back," she admits. "But I was… scared. By what is happening." She takes a few uneven breaths. Then she looks at me. "Can you help cut these peaches?"

Looking around the kitchen, I find a suitable knife and help Isabis cut peaches for the pudding cake she is making. Then I get to work on my own recipe.

Back in the winter, after Meander and I decided to pool our money and buy him a ticket to Canada so we could spend Christmas together, my giddiness at the prospect of his arrival led me to trying my hand at baking. I spent two weeks making apple crumble, badgering my mom to buy more apples and making my family eat it almost every night while I figured out what the hell I was doing. I'd never baked anything before that. But Meander was so pleased with the outcome I knew I wanted to do it again. So, for the last two months, I've been perfecting a new recipe.

I cut butter and blend it with salt, brown sugar, and flour to make pastry. Once it's chilling in the fridge, I help Isabis get her cake mixture into the oven. We talk about what we're making, but she doesn't mention anything else about her talent, nor does she ask me anything about my white hair. I'm happy not to press. I spent a good portion of last summer in pure misery. I can't blame her for wanting to avoid discussing whatever pain she's dealing with now.

When her cake is cooking, I start working on the filling for my butter tarts. I hedged my bets that the Wanagi kitchen would be well-stocked, and I'm pleased to find everything I need, including raisins. It's an oddity I never considered until now, but it makes me wonder if the Oracle stocks its kitchen on purpose for campers like Isabis. I don't know how important baking is to her. But I barely know her, and I've still seen—or tasted—the product of her baking three times now. With how comfortable she is navigating the kitchen, I imagine she does this a lot.

I get how this could be someone's passion. I don't think I'd ever want to run a bakery or cater someone's family functions, but I've discovered that I enjoy baking. The process of selecting a recipe and working it until it's just right is the type of problem-solving I can get behind. Of course, I'm not going to kid myself. If it weren't for the happy gleam I know I'll get when Meander sees the fruits of my labor, I probably wouldn't bother.

"You're almost done," Isabis says when I put the butter tarts in the oven for baking.

"Yeah, they'll be about fifteen minutes," I say.

She smiles. "I meant… here. This is your last summer."

"Oh." I start collecting my bowls and spatula to bring them to the sink. "Yeah. We'll be doing our final tasks soon. It's crazy. It's gone by really fast."

My first summer at Camp Wanagi feels like an absolute lifetime ago. But that lifetime has flown by in a blink. At the end of my first summer, I was happy to be going home. Now, the thought of camp ending— of my still so undefined non-Sender life beginning— makes the anxious ball in my stomach return.

"Good luck," Isabis says. She packs her cake into a sealed dome with a carrying handle.

"You too," I say with a nod. "And, uh… it gets better. I know that's not a comfort right now. I know what you're going through sucks in a way no one else could possibly understand. It doesn't really get any easier. But it does get a little better. You learn to anticipate it more. You learn how to handle it. You learn… You learn how to deal with it."

Isabis sets her trembling hands on the counter and stares at them. "I'm good at dealing," she says.

"Do you need any help carrying the cake?" I ask.

"No," she says. "I've got someone coming."

I turn on the sink and wash my bowls, and within a few minutes one of the Entity campers comes to help Isabis back to their dome. I vaguely recognize the girl as the same one who was with Isabis when I saw her last summer. She gives me a wary glance when she enters the kitchen. Then she focuses all her attention on Isabis, taking the dome and holding open the door. I watch her as she watches Isabis, her stern demeanor fading into a sad tenderness as the other girl struggles with her crutch. I'm sorry for what Isabis is going through. But I'm glad she's not going through it completely alone.

I remember the conversation we shared with Jonah yesterday, before the mentoring session we shared with his entire sector. The Revenants will face their own horrors as camp continues and they develop their talents as Senders. That can't be stopped, and it can't really be softened, either. But I hope that, if nothing else, they all find someone to share their pain with. The blows will land, one way or another. But having someone to help tend the wounds will make a big difference in how they heal.

WHEN I'M ALONE IN THE KITCHEN, I CLEAN UP THE REST OF MY SUPPLIES and wait for the tarts to finish baking. Once they've cooled enough to pack away, I take my tray and head back to the dome. I expect to find Meander lounging on one of the sofas with a book in hand, but he isn't in the main room when I return. I drop the tray of tarts on the coffee table before poking my head into the bedroom. But he's not there, either.

"Don't touch those," I tell Dylan as he reaches for one of the tarts. "They're for Meander."

"What?" Dylan asks with a scoff. "*All* of them?"

"Yes," I say. "Anyone know where he is?"

"I haven't seen him," Mim says.

"What did he do to earn an entire tray of tarts?" Dylan grumbles. Mim gives him a sideways look, and Dylan waves a hand in front of his face. "Don't answer that."

I roll my eyes, while trying to stop the prickle

of concern that's pinching the base of my spine. I disappeared to the kitchens this morning, so I can hardly be bothered that Meander's not around when I get back. Still, I'm uneasy as I pull out my phone and send him a text—and more than uneasy when I hear a buzz and follow it back to the bedroom where I see his phone plugged into the wall.

I sweep my gaze around the empty bathroom, then head back to the common area of the dome.

"Has anyone seen him this morning?" I ask.

"He was gone when I woke up for my run," Dylan says. "That was about an hour ago."

I sigh, swallowing back the panic I know I shouldn't feel. I don't need to stay tethered to Meander all of the time. But the fact he's without his phone worries me. Even when we're at home, I always have a means of contacting him. Being without it now makes my heart race.

"I'm sure he's fine, Cal," Kornelía says. She pats the empty seat on the sofa next to me, and with another sigh, I force myself to sit.

"Dylan's choosing his final task," Mim says with a smile, looping me into their morning.

"Got it down to two options," Dylan says with a nod. "A pack of menacing ghost dogs that roam the Jamaican beaches, or a dog suicide bridge in Scotland."

"Suicide bridge?" I ask.

"Yeah…" Dylan scratches his head as he stares at the computer. "It's weird. Dogs keep jumping off the bridge, seemingly at random. It's been happening for decades. There haven't specifically been reports of any ghosts, though. A lot of dogs die there. But I can't say for sure whether any of them hang around. I'm definitely interested. But honestly, I'll probably wind up in Jamaica. It's somewhere tropical, at least. Sun and sand, the perfect combination."

"Until you fall asleep on the beach and someone calls an ambulance because they think you're a corpse," I say.

"Ouch." Dylan holds a hand to his chest. "Thanks, Skunk."

"No problem, Sludge," I reply.

Mim gives us both strange looks before she shakes her head. "The beach is probably a better location for you," she says to Dylan. "Work with what you know, for now. You can tackle the other mystery later."

"Yeah, I think you're right," Dylan says.

He starts researching the area of Jamaica where the ghost reports have been found. I try to pretend I'm interested, but my foot won't stop tapping, and once thirty minutes have passed, I give up my weak pretense of being chill.

"I'm just going to look for Meander," I say. I stand up and round the back of the sofa before pointing a finger at Dylan. "Don't eat those. I'll be back."

After getting Dylan's promise that he won't touch the butter tarts, I head out along the path to the resort's main pavilion. Meander's not in the dining room or out on any of the boardwalks winding between domes. I check the library next, then zigzag past the unfinished fire pit and the far classrooms. I'm not shy about barging in where I'm not supposed to be. At one point, I even throw open the door to one of the makeshift instructor lounges, mumbling a quick apology to the four adults inside before ducking out again and keeping the location in mind should I need to ask someone for help.

The idea makes my panic worse, and I finish my loop of the camp buildings before I venture off the wooden paths and start scouring the land beyond the resort. We've gone off here together a couple of times, walking aimlessly until we're far enough away from camp we know we won't be bothered. But we've never followed a set path, so my walk now is directionless, a curving search of the grounds that lead me farther away from the resort than I've previously been.

I'm about to give up in despair when I see the distant shine of water. With a suck of breath, I follow the sight far out to a small meadow surrounding a shallow lagoon not unlike the one we went fly fishing in last week.

Meander sits near the lagoon's edge, his knees drawn into his chest as he stares off at the water. Relief floods through me, a relaxing wash that's soon chased by a more tense annoyance. I stalk into the meadow and drop beside him, my cheeks burning with exertion and worried frustration.

"What the hell are you doing out here?" I ask. I intend the question to sound only mildly annoyed, but my voice gives away the worry I've completely failed to hold back. I have my own anxieties about running into ghosts in the wild. But worse are the terrifying thoughts of what could happen if Meander encounters a ghost when he's by himself. I don't have any right to track his movements twenty-four seven, and I know full-well Meander has his own life to live. But that doesn't mean I can stop myself from wanting to know he's safe. Whenever he breaks from our usual routine, I'm twisted with fears about what he might be going through.

Now, my voice startles him. He jumps, lifting his chin from his knees as he turns towards me.

"Cal," he says. He looks me over, eyes slightly vacant until he finally reconnects with his surroundings. "I… I was looking for you."

"Out here?" I ask, incredulity tinging my words.

Meander shakes his head. "No." He takes in my frustrated gaze and offers me a more apologetic look. "I went to the library, but you weren't there. So I decided I'd try to find us a ghost while it was quiet. But… I made the mistake of checking my email first."

"Your email?" My brows furrow, then my eyes widen with concern, all the frustration sweeping away as I realize what it is that distracted him so badly he wandered away from camp. "What happened?"

"Mum," Meander says. He shrugs one shoulder, then licks his lips as he looks back at the water. "She's, um… She's kicking me out."

"She's what?" I reach out and grab his arm. When he looks back at me, his eyes are shining.

"Says she's not going to put up with me, now she has no income," he says. "I'm…" He pauses, struggling to keep his voice impassive. "I'm supposed to tell her when I'm back, and she'll leave my stuff on the front step."

"Meander." My mind reels, and my voice stutters as I try to make sense of what he's telling me. "That's not… She can't… She can't kick you out. You're not eighteen."

Meander shrugs again. "You can live on your own at sixteen in England," he says. "I could fight it until I'm eighteen. But by the time we're finished here, it'll only be eight months. No point, really. I'll just…"

"Just what, grab your stuff and live on the street?" I ask. Uncertainty floods his face, and I curse myself for sounding too harsh—for sounding like I'm admonishing him for making a stupid decision, when it's not his decision at all. "I'm sorry." Leaning over, I wrap my arm around his shoulder and pull him to me. "I'm just… You don't deserve this. *At all*. I can't believe…" Tears sting my eyes as Meander drops his head onto my shoulder, then twists his whole body to curl in against my side. I bring my other arm around and tighten my hold, resting my cheek on the top of his head. "Can you stay with Liam?"

"Maybe," Meanders mumbles against my neck. "For a bit. He shares a flat with four other blokes, though. I'd be on the floor. I… I'd be in the way." For a few seconds, he's completely silent. Then he breathes out a sob, a rough noise he tries to cut short by gritting his teeth. "I don't know what I'm going to do, Cal."

"We'll figure it out," I say. "You… You can come stay with me."

He lifts his head to meet my eyes. "I'm sure your parents would love that," he mutters.

"I don't care," I say. I reach forward to wipe a tear from his cheek. "They'll do it, if you don't have another choice."

"I couldn't stay forever," he says. "I'd need a job, eventually, yeah? A work permit?"

"We'll get you one," I say. "I don't care how. We'll figure it out, okay? You won't… You're not living on the street."

The fact I even have to make such a desperate promise brings my own tears falling, and he smiles, mimicking my earlier action to wipe them away.

"I can't believe she'd do that," I whisper.

"I can," Meander says. He sniffs and shifts so he can sit up straighter. "It's been shit. It's always been shit, but more so over the last six months. She's been telling me she can't wait until I'm eighteen for ages. Guess she just got impatient. Honestly, I'm surprised it took this long. After Liam moved out… I always thought she'd drop me off somewhere and forget about me."

"I'm serious," I say. "We'll look into visas or permits or whatever. I'll talk to my parents. I'll throw a huge tantrum, if I need to. I'll get Rose to throw a huge tantrum too." He smirks, and I brush curls from his face. "I'm not above being a total brat."

"And if they refuse?" he asks.

"Then… we'll run off and join some ghost-related freak show," I say. He laughs, and I smile despite the horrendous ache in my gut. My thumb strokes the scar on his jaw, and when the laugh fades I lean in and kiss him. He pulls back long enough to crawl into my lap, straddling my hips. Then we spend a few long minutes tangled together before he rests his forehead against mine.

"I didn't mean to worry you," he says.

"Disappearing and then telling me you're homeless isn't the best way to achieve that goal," I reply.

He groans. "I didn't disappear. After I got that message, I just needed a few minutes to think about what I was going to do."

"Meander, that was *hours* ago," I say.

"It was?" He looks so genuinely confused, I smile and reach my mouth up to kiss him again as I nod. "Sorry," he mumbles against my lips. Then he pulls back and fixes me with a glower. "Besides, you're the one who disappeared. Where were you this morning?"

"In the kitchen," I admit. "I made you butter tarts."

His eyes light up, the sun and his tears making the green of the hazel shine bright. "You baked?" he asks with a grin.

"Uh-huh. There's a whole tray waiting for you," I say. "So long as Dylan hasn't eaten them all while I've been gone."

Meander's glower returns, and I laugh as he climbs off my lap and gets to his feet.

"He'd better not have eaten them all," he grumbles. He reaches down his hand, waiting for me to grab it. I let him pull me up, and I hide my pain under another laugh as we go back in search of his dessert.

27

DYLAN ONLY MANAGED TO STEAL ONE BUTTER TART WHILE WE WERE GONE. Even so, Meander is livid as he hoards the remaining eleven until, with an amused glance from me, he begrudgingly hands the tray to the girls so they can pick a tart too.

"Ooh, what're we eating?" Robbie says as he wanders into the dome while the tray is being passed around. He doesn't wait for an answer before grabbing a tart and stuffing it into his mouth. Meander takes the tray back, his lips tight as he eyes the eight tarts still on the tray.

"I think you'll be okay," I say with a laugh.

"Yeah, I will," Meander replies. "So long as everyone else stops stealing them."

"You offered," Mim reminds him.

I put my hands up in surrender and sit down on the sofa, pleased by his grumpy determination not to share. He drops next to me and shoves a tart in my palm before finally taking one for himself.

"So, where'd you go?" Dylan asks after a moment. "Cal was flipping out."

"I was not *flipping out*," I say, although I can already feel my cheeks getting hot.

Meander's leg moves so it rests pressed against mine as he gives the others a shrug. "I just needed a moment," he says.

"Everything okay?" Robbie asks. The concern in his voice is surprising—not because it's present, but because his tone is so suddenly severe it makes me wonder if Robbie already knows some of what's been happening in Meander's life.

Meander eyes our lead, hesitating for a long moment before he swallows. "It's nothing," he says. "Just a problem at home."

Robbie's gaze flicks to me, and I can't help responding with a solemn stare. Meander might not want to talk about what happened in front of the others, and that's fine. But Robbie knows *something* is up, and I'm not going to pretend it's not. I don't think I could, even if I thought it would do any good.

Robbie gives me a nod, the movement so slight it's almost imperceptible. Then he takes out his phone and starts typing.

"Thanks for the… whatever it is I just ate," he says as he stuffs the phone back in his pocket a few seconds later. He rolls off the sofa and flashes us a grin. "It was good."

"You're welcome," I say.

Robbie's phone chimes, and he pulls it out while walking away. Meander watches his movement with suspicious eyes until I give his arm a gentle nudge.

"Are the tarts all right?" I ask, distracting him from thinking too hard about what Robbie may or may not be doing on his phone.

Meander pauses mid-bite to offer me a dubious look. "Do you really have to ask? I'm about to finish off my second one in… what, under a minute?"

I smirk. "Just don't eat them all in one go. You won't like them as much on the way up."

Meander breathes a laugh as he takes another bite.

In less than an hour, the remaining butter tarts have disappeared. Meander comes with me to return the empty tray to the kitchen, and we stop on the way back to make some tea. Then we help Dylan firmly settle on the details of what he's doing for his final task.

"I'll do the bridge someday," he says as he makes a fact sheet about the Jamaican ghost dogs. "I'm probably going to become the kind of weirdo that plans all his vacations around ghosts, aren't I?"

"There are worse ways to experience the world," Kornelía says. "I mean, at least you'll get a good sense of some of the local places."

"That is true," Dylan says. He reaches out a hand to absently stroke at Draugur's head. "Gives me an extra edge of intrigue. I like it. And hey, maybe it'll mean we can meet up, sometimes." He looks around the room. "I've seen it before—human and dog ghosts can exist in the same place. Maybe we'll have Sender vacations."

"Just as long as our hotel rooms aren't haunted too," Kornelía smiles.

We hang out in the dome for another hour or so before Meander suggests we do some ghost research of our own. We've been putting the search off for too long, and I'm—if not happy—content to finally dive in and pick a spirit. We leave Dylan and the girls as we set off to complete our own task. But when we're halfway to the library, Robbie flags us down.

"Before you get too far," he says with a stilted manner unbefitting his usual relaxed stance, "Mrs. Buxley needs to talk to you."

He doesn't say it to both of us. His eyes are firmly on Meander's as he speaks, and it doesn't take much for any of us to understand what the conversation is about. Meander hasn't had time to tell the Oracle what happened with his mother. But they know something. Which makes me again wonder if they've been keeping tabs on his homelife. If they keep tabs on us all.

Meander doesn't look like he wants to follow Robbie. But if Mrs. Buxley's trying to find him, there's not much he can do to hide.

"I'll go to the library and start looking for a ghost," I say with a gentle nudge to his back.

He steps forward before giving me a reluctant nod. "Wait for me there," he says. Then he follows Robbie in the opposite direction.

I do go to the library. But I don't end up looking for a ghost. Instead, I find myself researching what the requirements are for getting a work visa and how difficult it might be for Meander to actually come to Canada with me.

I read through resource pages for forty-five minutes, despairing more and more as I realize that Meander's too young to get a work permit. Visitors are only allowed for six months, and even then, he needs his legal guardian to permit him to come. I wonder if Liam could take his brother in and become his guardian for the sake of signing the permission forms. But by the time all of those pieces are in place, Meander will likely be eighteen anyway, making the whole effort pointless.

I slump in my seat, clicking page after useless page until I'm startled by a hand on my shoulder. When I look back, Meander looms behind me, his body rigid. My stomach drops, and I abandon the computer as I ask him what happened. He looks around the non-empty library, then motions for us to go outside before he's willing to talk.

My insides twist and pinch as we walk out of the library and exit the main dome. When we get a little ways off the wooden path, Meander grabs my hand and slows to a stop.

"They want me to work for them," he says in a quiet voice.

"Who?" I ask, my fingers gripping his tight. "The Oracle?"

Meander nods. He looks behind me, eyes trailing a bird as it swoops through the air. "They know. About Mum. About home." He sighs, dropping his gaze to mine. "They want me to do what we've always thought they would. Solve cases for them. Be a ghost hunter. Throw myself into the den with lion after bloody lion."

"You don't have to work for them," I say in a voice I wish sounded less pleading. "You have a choice. You have—"

"They'll give me somewhere to live," he says, cutting me off. "They have some kind of base in London. They'll find me a flat. They'll give me a wage." He takes a deep, ragged breath. "They'll pay my room and board until I'm old enough to do it myself."

My stomach does an entire acrobatic set, and I'm suddenly sorry I baked this morning because I suspect Meander must be feeling the ill-rot of this decision too.

"So you either live on the street, or live in comfort and owe the Oracle a debt," I say.

He nods. "There are no contracts. I don't have to sign my soul away, at least. And it's not all ghosts. They said something about records management, whatever that means. Information, I think. Organizing files, maybe even sourcing stuff for the library. And I'll... I'll have to stay on as long as I need them to pay my way, I guess. Once I can afford to live on my own, it's up to me what I do from there."

"Well, that's... that's not too bad," I stammer.

"No," he says. "Except it won't just be until then, will it?"

The truth of his statement hits me harder than I expected it to, and my eyes begin to sting as I step closer to him. "You still have a choice," I mumble.

"I don't, though," Meander says. "Not really. Mrs. Buxley... she had to phrase it just perfect, didn't she? She knew exactly what to say. Nothing we don't already know, but..."

"Phrase what?" I ask.

Meander stares down at the ground. "I'll never get away from it," he says. "Ghosts. Not with a talent like mine. Doesn't matter where I go. What I do. I can't make much of a living working in a cemetery. Can't totally get away from ghosts even there." He raises his head, his eyes red-rimmed as he catches my gaze. "How will I ever get a job, Cal? I can't pay for education. I can't work anywhere that's haunted. So, I can find some entry-level position in a safe building, and I can struggle to make my life passable. Or, I can say to hell with it and confront the damned spirits with the only organization that won't kick me out for causing destruction—and which will continue to pay me even if ghosts make it so I can't do things right on the first try."

I tilt my head back, my free hand rubbing over my face as I groan. "This is like the ultimate 'would you rather', isn't it?" I ask.

He lets out a cracked laugh. "Pretty much."

"You still have a choice," I say again. Then I sigh. "Maybe not right away. But eventually. You're good at saving money. If the work gets too bad, you can leave. You can always leave, and we'll find a new way to make it work. Just—don't sign any contracts with them. You know, to be on the safe side."

"I won't," he says. He gives me a sad smile that soon fades into wariness again. "I guess I won't be coming to Canada, then. Not for a while, anyway."

My stomach tries to crawl up my throat, but I swallow it down as I shake my head. "No, I guess not." I blink away a new sting of tears and force myself to laugh. "My parents will be happy."

Meander smiles. Then he steps closer to me and cups my chin in one hand. "I can visit," he says. "I *will*. If I'm working… I'll have money."

"I'll visit too," I say with a nod. "You're not getting rid of me."

He moves until we're nearly standing pressed together, his eyes fixed on mine. "I don't ever want to be rid of you," he whispers.

"Good," I whisper back, my arm circling around to draw him into a kiss.

We stay like that until the crest of pain retreats into the muddied waters of my ever-present anxiety. Then Meander's fingers graze my ear, his teeth scraping along his lip as he considers his new future.

"So," he says. "I guess I'm going to be a Sender, after all. Figures."

"You're great with your talent," I tell him. "Just… Be careful. Be *so* careful, okay?"

"I will," he says with a nod. Then he lets out a tired breath. "If I do something big this summer, do you think they'll let me off the hook for a while?"

"Maybe," I say. "But you could also take it easy this summer… More time before they start giving you cases."

"I'd rather do the big one first," he says. "Now."

"Why?" I ask.

He smiles, his hands sliding to my waist. "I don't want to do this without you," he admits. "So if we do it together now, maybe I'll get a break when you're… away."

I tighten my grip on him, hurting at the prospect of leaving him to do all of this on his own—but lifted indescribably by the fact he'd rather do it with me by his side.

"We'll do something big," I agree. "And the next time they want to put you on another case, well… I'll be there. One way or another. I'll be there, Meander."

He nods. Then he drops his head to my shoulder, and I hold him until we're ready to head back to camp.

28

"OKAY, SO HOW DO WE DO THIS?"

That night, after our other sector mates have gone to bed, Meander curls against my side, a blanket wrapped around us both while I prop my laptop on my knees and open the database I let the Oracle install on my computer.

"I have no idea," I admit. The interface of the database is pathetically plain, looking more like something from a made-for-tv movie than an actual virtual resource. There are search fields for names, dates, and geographic locations. But it takes a few clicks to figure out how to browse through the database without a specific spirit in mind.

"Any way to order your searches by talent?" he asks. "Or I don't know… level of violence?"

"I refuse to specifically search for violent ghosts," I tell him. "And I'd guess looking for talents is too complicated, since we're all so different."

"Suppose so," he mumbles.

I click around at random, looking at scanned newspaper reports and blurry photos of supposed hauntings. Some of the entries include notes from other Senders, ones that have confirmed sightings, declined witnessing any paranormal activity, or released the spirits altogether. After a few of these entries, I figure out how to filter results to only those spirits that might still exist.

"How many Senders do you think it takes before a haunting's debunked?" Meander asks as we click through entries. Most of the cases only contain one or two notes, if any. But occasionally, an entry will include multiple notes from Senders who have visited the sight and reported nothing of interest.

"Maybe they're never really debunked," I say. "Just in case *one* Sender can see them."

"Mmm," he hums in agreement. "But they probably get less visits once enough Senders have suggested a hoax." He shifts, sitting up a bit and looking more closely at the screen. "Some of these are ridiculous. Tourist traps, no doubt."

"Celebrity ghost sightings and grisly tales of old murder houses?" I click on a file that details a coastal inn in the States that's reported to have been the sight of cult magic and human sacrifices—but which has at least ten Sender accounts suggesting that nothing is lingering from beyond the grave. "Good fodder for bored sightseers."

"Can you filter out the ones that have been disproved?" he asks. "Or, likely disproved? There doesn't seem much point in planning to visit somewhere that's clearly not got a ghost in it."

"I don't think I can," I say as I return back to the top of the screen. "This database needs work. Someone in the Oracle's got to know how to design a better system."

Meander laughs. "I'll lodge a formal complaint once I'm an employee," he says.

My stomach squirms at the reminder of his new work prospects, and I sigh as I scroll down to keep searching.

The list of potential ghosts is endless, and at some point, my eyes glaze over until I'm not really paying attention to anything on the page. The sounds and chills from the wind outside our mesh roof mix with the quiet comfort of being huddled close under the warmth of the blanket, a relaxing mix that adds to the smooth, hypnotic motion of the scrolling. We search in easy silence until eventually Meander reaches out, stopping my hand before it can move any further down the page.

"Wait," he says, pulling himself up again. "Click on that one."

I go to the requested entry, blinking away my sleepiness so I can focus on the screen. The file is for a spirit in Wales, though the more I read through the entry, the less I'm sure it's really a spirit at all. The database classifies it as an entity, a spirit that's become too unfocused or narrow-minded to have clear motivations for remaining a ghost. Entities are known to be harder spirits to release, and this one is—apparently—exceptional. There are two photos, one an old, scanned polaroid that's discolored and streaky. The other is clearer, a more recent snapshot captured by someone who has the ability to make spirits seen through a camera lens. In both photos, the mass is totally unformed, a cloud of haze that looks more like someone set off a fog bomb than snapped any real spiritual being.

"What the hell is that?" I ask.

"That's not like any ghost I've ever seen," Meander says.

"It's got to be a hoax, right?" I scroll past the photos to the notes section, expecting Sender accounts showing no paranormal activity on site. But instead, I find over twenty notes from six different Senders confirming the entity's existence.

"How can so many people have seen it, and yet it's still around?" I ask.

"Maybe it needs a special touch," Meander mumbles. He eyes me, and I swallow, knowing full well he's caught the same notes I have. There is hardly any information about this supposed ghost—no mentions of who it is, or why it's likely hanging around. But there are plenty of notes detailing the same things. That this entity has a negative energy to it. That it's powerful. That it's angry.

"Okay, remember when we decided to tackle something big?" I ask. "I didn't think we meant, like, *colossal*. Meander, this is way too dangerous. We're not even there, and this case file alone is enough to tell me it's way too dangerous."

"Which is why it's a good choice," he argues. "We do it now, under full Oracle watch. If we can't manage anything with it, then we get off relatively light while still proving we're willing to make the risk. And if we do manage to release it—" He shrugs. "They'll lay off me for a while."

"Unless they think you've got superpowers and decide to send every violent ghost your way," I counter.

"I'll refuse if they do that," he says. "I'll be in a much better position for tantrum throwing myself, if I have such a successful release under my belt."

"This all feels really horrible and stupid," I grumble. I slump back against the sofa, while Meander shifts, pressing closer in against my side.

"It almost assuredly is," he says with a smile that does nothing to make me feel better. "But it shows I'm trying. Which means I can be a moody bugger later, and they won't be so quick to complain." He pokes me in the side. "What do you say? We'll be horrible and stupid together?"

I stare at the computer screen, my face set in a stony mask until he continues to poke me. Then my frown cracks into a laugh, and I swat his hand away before giving him a more serious look.

"We'll do it," I say with a heavy sigh. "But I won't be happy. And I'll be bringing a full first-aid kit with us." I took a first-aid course this spring and got my certification for providing CPR. The instructor of the course figured I wanted a lifeguarding job for the summer. I never told him why I really needed the skills.

Meander's smile grows soft as he nods. "Thank you," he says.

I sigh again, then pull him back against my side so we can look more thoroughly over the case file.

"I can't believe we're going to tackle this," I say as I read notes from some Sender's account in the nineteen eighties—notes that make me realize for the first time the place we're going to is a former prison. "What the hell is the Oracle going to say when we tell them? Will they let us go?"

"They didn't get all that mad when we fled the country last year," Meander says. "I doubt they'll stop us from tackling this."

He's right, though I wish he weren't. I miss our original plan, when we picked some easy spirit because neither one of us had anybody to impress. Him having a job and a proper place to live is better for his long-term future. But I miss our short-lived plan—realistic or not—for him coming to Canada too. I don't like the look of this entity. I don't like thinking of Meander facing something six Senders have failed to release. I know his assumptions are well-founded, that this will prove his worth and give him strength to fight back against anything the Oracle tries to push on him next. But how long will that bargaining chip last? If he does this, how long will it be until they want him to do it again? How long until they force him to do it when I'm not there?

I don't trust anyone else to watch out for Meander. Most of the time, he's capable of handling himself. But sometimes spirits get the better of him, and he needs help. I like being that help. I like being there for him, and I don't trust anyone else to be there for him like I can. Because no one else understands him like I do. No one loves him like I do. I fear for the day someone sends him into the lion's den while I'm on another continent, oblivious to his suffering.

This is the start of it. And I'll do it, for his sake. But damned if I'll be anything less than irate and terrified the entire time.

29

On Sunday night, the last night before we leave the eco-resort, Robbie and Alex sit with us in our dome. Beverages and snacks are shared between us as Robbie hands out travel packets, and we each check the contents to make sure we've got the right information for our specific tasks.

"What time do we leave?" Dylan asks as he opens his packet.

"Early," Alex says. "Your flight times are different, but everyone is leaving in the morning hours, so we'll go to the airport together. Most of you will meet with your mentor when you arrive at your destination."

I pull the tab on my own folder, rifling through the contents to find airline tickets to Amsterdam, Madrid, and Cardiff. There's also a map of the local area of Wales we'll be traveling to, a hotel confirmation, and some UK currency. The sight of the paper money is oddly comforting. Meander is not from Wales, but at least he knows how the currency works. That, combined with the fact Wales is a largely English speaking country, is the only decent thing about the trip we're soon going to make.

"We'll have mentors?" Dylan asks.

Robbie smiles. "You didn't think we'd leave you entirely alone, did you? Everyone completing their final task will have a team of Senders to assist them with research, equipment, and report writing. One person on that team will be your mentor, your best source of guidance—should you need it."

"You said most of us will have one," Sabeena says. "Not all of us?"

"*Everyone* gets a team and a mentor," Alex says. "But most of you won't meet them until you arrive at your destination. I, however, will be Mim's mentor. So I'll travel with her to Guatemala."

Mim's cheeks pale at the mention of her home. She nods at Alex and clutches her folder tight.

"And I get the Dynamic Duo over here," Robbie says, pointing a thumb at Meander and me.

My eyebrows raise, but I'm not actually that surprised by the news. Meander and I have been involved in some pretty severe mishaps. It's not a stretch to think the Oracle wants to put someone familiar with our exploits in charge of our final task. Although, if they're after a stern overlord to make sure we don't step out of line, I'm not sure Robbie's the best choice.

"Will I need… equipment?" Naasir asks.

"No," Alex says. "You're unique. We won't have equipment for your work, and your report won't require any private details of the people you visit."

Naasir is going to a hospice in Uganda, working with palliative care staff to put as many patients as he can at ease before the end of his time there. For him, this task isn't just another paranormal outing. He's stepping into what could easily become his career, a perfect way for him to combine his life outside the realm of spirits to the innate abilities he has within it.

The idea makes me envious. Naasir has always been assured of himself in a way I am not. And he—like so many of the campers here—value his talent and is eager to use it for the rest of his life. I wish I was so certain. I can't escape ghosts. But I don't want to make them my career. And yet, I'd be lying if I didn't admit that I'm scared to leave the Oracle for good. It's nice facing ghosts with a team of people ready to call an ambulance or negotiate terms to deal with breaking and entering. What will happen when I'm on my own, facing an unexpected spirit in a strange place? As much as I hate the idea of Meander working for the Oracle, it is a relief to know he won't ever be stranded without some sort of backup—although being pushed *into* dangerous situations instead isn't a hell of a lot better.

"So… this is it?" Dylan asks as he finishes looking at his packet. "This is our last night? Feels kind of lackluster. We should have thrown a party."

Alex looks at Robbie, then glances at the watch on her wrist. "We do have one thing planned. Give us about fifteen minutes."

We finish going over our documents. Then, while Robbie and Alex start setting up an oversized laptop on the coffee table, four of us venture to the main pavilion to top up our drinks. By the time we return to the dome, a video chat has been opened on the large computer screen.

"Who are we waiting for?" Sabeena asks. She draws her legs into a crossed position while she opens her journal and begins writing.

"You'll see in a minute," Robbie says.

I roll my eyes, tired of the ceaseless "surprises" the Oracle likes to pull for us—one thing I will unquestionably not miss when camp is over.

Meander runs a hand through his curls, then drapes his arm over the back of the sofa behind my head. "What, have you arranged some inspirational farewell message from a celebrity guest?" he mutters.

"Famous Senders?" Dylan asks. "That'd be cool."

"Or famous dead people," I offer.

Dylan frowns. "Well, that's less cool. I can't see dead people, famous or otherwise."

"It's not celebrity ghosts," Robbie laughs.

"Here we go," Alex says. She blocks the view for half a minute while she gets the guests connected. "Can you see me okay?" she asks.

"Yeah, we're good," a familiar voice answers.

"I can see you," another, slightly less familiar voice adds.

Alex glances at Robbie, then moves away and angles the screen so we can see it.

We may not have been graced with the presence of celebrities, but the screen is filled with Senders. Two Senders, in fact. Sefa Amasio. And Lu Tong.

Two of Shade's former members are sitting across from us, waving from their homes. Sefa looks more or less the same as he did last year, except that his dark hair is shorter and a new crop of piercings have been added to his left ear. But I haven't seen Lu in two years, and she looks so different I probably wouldn't even recognize her if her name wasn't logged into the chat. Her hair is in a messy bun, thin, black glasses adorn her face, and she's lost enough weight her jaw is now sharp and angled. But the biggest change is in her expression. Lu was always stern, vaguely annoyed by the rest of us and uninterested in the happenings of our sector. Now, her face is alight with a soft, warm glow as she takes in the sight of us.

"Sefa!" Sabeena says with a happy smile. She climbs off the sofa and leans in close to the screen. "Lu! What are you doing…" She gestures at the screen. "Here?"

"We thought they may want to say hello, before you leave," Alex says. "And share what they've been up to as well."

Sefa talks first, telling us all about the local work he's been doing, day trips he's made to explore haunted locales close to his home. He may be taking care of his grandmother, but he is just as dedicated to the Oracle as ever. Given what I know of Sefa and how he views his talents, I'm not surprised his work with ghosts hasn't ended just because he didn't make it to Chile.

Lu doesn't talk as much, and when she does, her English is rough, like she hasn't been keeping up with the extra language. But while I expected that her life as a Sender ceased when she didn't return to Wanagi after our second summer, I soon discover that she, too, has kept some ties with the Oracle. I don't know much about Lu's talent, except that it revolves around auras and knowing when people have some kind of spiritual energy clinging to them. I wonder how things have changed for her in the last two years. Going by the genuine smiles she offers as she says a few words about her latest spiritual endeavors, I'd guess it's going pretty well.

"I'll be traveling to the mountains next year," Lu says. "I'm going to stay there for a while. Learn more about spirits."

"That's wonderful, Lu," Sabeena says.

Lu nods, then shifts her eyes around the room. "Before I go, I wanted to ask…" Her searching gaze lands on Mim, and her eyes grow a little wide with expectation. "Maria?"

Mim's face shows the briefest flash of annoyance at the use of her birth name. But the look quickly fades as she gives Lu a nod of, if not friendliness, then respect.

"Yes," Mim says. "I'm going home tomorrow. Then… Yes."

The simple words, combined with the relieved look on Lu's face, brings with it a strange realization. In the brief time I knew her, Lu could apparently sense when the dead still clung to the living. Which means she must have known about Mim's mother, while the rest of us were clueless. No wonder the two girls never got along. If Lu sensed Mim's mother well before Mim herself was willing to accept what needed to be done, it makes sense that Mim pushed her so forcefully away.

Lu seems more than satisfied with Mim's response now, at least. She settles back in her chair, and for a few seconds, there is a pause as everyone takes in the sight of everyone else. Then Sefa folds his arms and nods.

"Good luck," he says. "With all of your tasks. I suspect you'll need it. Be safe everyone."

The statement drops into the room, and although he didn't mention it, I suspect everyone's thoughts turn to the one member of Shade who is still not with us now. Goosebumps rise on my flesh as I remember last year and think about the new dangers ahead of us.

"We will," Kornelía says from her spot on the sofa, reeling us in from our silence. She rests on hand on Draugur's head. "You two be safe as well."

"We will," Sefa says, while Lu bows her head in agreement.

We say goodbye to our former sector mates, then finish our drinks and clean up before bed. The mood in our room is stilted, everyone quiet as they go about making sure their bags are packed and ready for tomorrow's travels. Once I've crawled onto my mattress, I slip in my earbuds and put on Chopin's "Nocturne in C sharp Minor" as I try to fall asleep.

The night is restless, sleep coming in fits and nightmares plaguing me whenever I fall into more than a doze. I don't have night terrors as often as I did last year. But they still happen, and by the time the alarm on my phone rings in the morning, I'm more exhausted than if I had just stayed awake.

I lay in bed, staring at the top of my bunk for a long time before I struggle up to take a shower.

THE WHOLE SECTOR TRAVELS TO THE AIRPORT TOGETHER, CHECKING
our luggage and getting through security before we
have to separate for our flights. When it's time for our
group to split apart, we stand in an awkward circle, no
one quite knowing how to start their goodbyes. Then
Mim drops her bag and reaches for Kornelía, bringing
the other girl into a light embrace that sets the rest of
us in motion too.

"Have a good trip," I say to Mim when she makes
it to where I stand. "And uh… good luck, or… you
know. I hope everything goes…"

She cuts me off with a hug, nodding against my
shoulder. "Thank you," she says. "You too." Stepping
back, she eyes Meander where he stands a step behind
me, tense from the possibility of unexpected hugs
from over-sentimental Senders. She doesn't hug him
but gives him a nod and a smile. He does the same,
and she moves off down the line before leaving with

Alex for her flight.

Kornelía is coming part way with us to Amsterdam, so once Mim, Sabeena, and Naasir have left the group, she moves closer to where we stand while Dylan spends a moment petting Draugur. When he's said his farewell to the guide dog, he gives Kornelía a long hug.

"You're going to try channeling again?" He asks.

Kornelía nods. "There's an expert in the Netherlands. I'll get to visit my brother there too. I'm going to practice on a few spirits. See if the one here was a fluke."

"It wasn't," I say from beside her. Her head tilts in my direction, her expression dubious. But then she falls back into her private embrace with Dylan, the two holding each other for another minute before they finally let go.

Dylan takes a step back and stares at Kornelía with an expression that looks a little like fond regret. Then he blinks a few times, clearing his throat and looking at me.

"Well, I'm off to the beach," he says.

"Stay safe," I say. "And don't run off with the pack."

He grins. "I don't know, might not be too bad of a life."

I smile, and after a pause we both step in for a half-hug, half-pat. Then Dylan eyes Meander, hesitating for a few beats before he sighs.

"Good luck, Scarface," he says with the hint of a smile.

Meander breathes out a quiet laugh. "Yeah, you too."

Dylan gives the dog a last pat—and Kornelía a last, lingering glance—before heading to his gate. When he's out of sight, Robbie checks his watch.

"We leave in forty-five minutes," he says.

"That mean we have time to grab a drink?" Meander asks.

"Go ahead," Robbie says. "Might as well get some half-decent food while you're at it. Just don't lose track of time."

He offers Kornelía his arm, and she takes it as they move off in search of our gate while Meander and I venture to the nearest coffee counter. I grab a bottle of orange juice while Meander orders tea, then we sit in a vacant gate to enjoy a bit of peace before joining the crowd ten minutes before boarding.

I'm uneasy as we get on the plane, the way I'm always uneasy stepping onto an aircraft before I'm assured it's ghost-free. But once the four of us make certain the cabin is clear of spirits—a fairly easy thing to do with Kornelía in our midst—I sit in the middle seat of one row, Meander by the window and Robbie at the aisle while Kornelía and Draugur are given special accommodations closer to the front of the plane.

We spend a whole day in the air before arriving in Amsterdam. There, we see Kornelía off before switching planes to Madrid.

"You'll do great," I tell her as she gives me a wistfully gentle hug goodbye. "Have a good time visiting your brother."

"I will," she says, answering the latter part of my comment while still shyly avoiding the first. "You two be careful. I don't know anything about what you're facing. But I get an… *impression* that it's not going to be easy."

She doesn't let Meander off the hook, pulling him into a hug as well before walking a little ways with

Robbie so he can introduce her to whoever her mentor will be. When our lead returns, we continue on our own travel path, flying to Madrid before heading west and finally landing in Cardiff around the dinner hour. Knowing we're in Wales is a relief for my travel-weary bones. But our trip is not over, and we drive for several hours through a twilit countryside full of roads that are at times so narrow I'm half-convinced we're going to have a collision or veer straight into a stone wall.

When we reach our destination—a small country inn that's probably quaint during the bright hours of day, but which is stuffy and silent at night—the thought of a quiet room with a bed where I can pass out is magical enough by itself. But after we check in, I'm given an immense reward for the tedious day of travel by discovering that Robbie has his own room, while Meander and I will share.

"We'll be visiting the sight of the haunting early in the afternoon," Robbie says with a yawn as he hands us our key. "For now, rest. Breakfast will be sent to you around nine. Tomorrow—later today—will be busy."

I have no doubt that Robbie's telling the truth about the day ahead. But that doesn't make it any easier to sleep. Hours after we've shuffled into our room, Meander and I are still awake, eyes open in the dark as the reality of what's ahead keeps an active hold of our tired minds.

"Are you ready?" I ask. My head rests against his chest, fingers tracing the scars he got before I knew him, long streaks of white skin where the tines of a rake once slashed into his torso.

"No," Meander says. He sighs, one hand stroking

my shoulder and arm. "But I'm never ready."

"What do you think it'll be like?" I ask. "It doesn't seem like a normal ghost. Do you think it will feel the same?"

"The notes from the file suggest it will," he says. "At least sort of. But the six Senders who left the notes weren't consistent. Some of them said it felt like part of the spirit was missing. But not everyone said that. And even with all of the sightings, the file has almost no information in it. We don't know who the ghost was, nor do we have any inkling of what it's after. All I *do* know is that it's supposed to be aggressive and angry. And violent. So I'm guessing it's not going to be fun. I can only imagine what I'll bring out in it."

"Whenever you need to leave, we leave," I say. I push up so I can see his face in the shadows of the room. "And if we need to pick a different ghost, we will."

Meander swipes a drooping strand of hair away from my eye. "I don't think the Oracle will be too happy if we suddenly decide to tackle a ghost in Hawaii," he says.

I roll my eyes, then lean down to kiss him. "We could try for something closer to here," I say. "If we need to."

I start to pull back, but he rises up to keep me close.

"Thank you," he whispers against my lips. "For giving me the chance to leave. For not trying to tell me it's time I faced my fears or some shit."

"You've faced your fears enough," I say. "You can do it. I have no doubt of that. And if you want to release this entity, you will. But you don't *have* to. You never have to. It doesn't make you weak. It doesn't make you a failure. And I know you think you've got to prove something to the Oracle. And I know that you kind of *do*, since they're giving you a job and all. But if it goes to hell in there, I'm here to help you figure out another plan."

Meander studies my face, catching my gaze and holding it for a long time. Then he nods, smiling as he draws me back down against him and ending all further discussion for the remainder of the night.

I DON'T KNOW WHEN WE FALL ASLEEP. BUT ONCE WE DO, THE MORNING comes far too quickly. The knock on the door when our breakfast arrives at nine startles me out of a dark dream, and I wake drenched with sweat under the pile of blankets Meander heaped on us overnight. He mutters a curse while I crawl from the cocoon and stumble into clothes before answering the door. Once the tray of food has been delivered and the hotel staff is gone, I drop back onto the bed with a groan, and Meander throws an arm over my stomach so we can lay half-asleep for another twenty minutes before Robbie calls to ensure we've actually gotten up.

Eventually, we get ourselves ready, meeting Robbie in the inn's foyer before loading into a car to drive to the haunted location. Chile was unquestionably beautiful with its shallow pools and stunning mountains. But Wales is vibrant in its own right. Flat pastures give way to a town has been built along and in between hills, and when we crest them, the coast can be viewed far-off to the west. Although I've encountered enough spirits in my life to know the dead can haunt literally anywhere, when I think of dangerous ghosts like the entity, my mind still conjures gritty urban landscapes or creepy abandoned ruins tucked into the woods. The town we are in now is picturesque and bright. When the car stops at our destination, I find myself staring dubiously at an empty building that could easily have been used as a bed and breakfast similar to the inn where we're staying. Ornate gray stonework and lush, crawling vines cover the exterior of a wide building set in a rectangular block four stories high. Birds flit between the nearby trees, and in the distance, I can hear kids at a playground. The place feels remarkably alive, and I wouldn't even assume the building was empty, if it weren't for the boards over half of the windows—and the wildly overgrown gardens around the stone walkway leading to the large wooden doors.

"This is… almost quaint," I say as we climb out of the car.

Meander smirks, a relaxed look that nearly covers his nervousness as he surveys the building, his hands clenched into fists at his sides.

"Maybe we'll have a picnic when we're done," Robbie grins.

"You set out the sandwiches," Meander mutters. "I'm sure we'll be in and out in no time."

His eyes roam the covered windows, then drop to the street as another black car stops around the corner from us.

"That'll be our help," Robbie says.

The car's doors open, and three people climb out, all

of them Senders older than any of us. One girl looks like she's in her mid-to-late twenties, with curly black hair and skin that's dark in most places but splotched with lighter patches across her forehead and down her neck. The other two are older, one a man with ginger hair that's starting to turn white on his head but retains its full orange-red hue on his moustache, and the other a woman with platinum blonde hair I'm sure has been dyed.

"Robbie," the youngest of the three says as she nears us, her voice sing-songing with a lilting accent I can't place. Her happy expression and bouncy tone suggest a cheerful disposition, at least. Behind her, the blonde lady frowns at the sight of us, while the man fumbles with his bags of equipment, for the moment indifferent to our presence.

"This is Jess, Nattie, and Bark," Robbie says.

"That's Jessimine, Natalie, and Dr. Barkley," the happy girl replies. "Robbie likes to assume familiars whenever possible."

"You don't mind, do you Jess?" Robbie asks.

Jess laughs. "I don't, no. But *Nattie* and *Bark* certainly do."

Natalie considers us with a sigh. "Kids. Why would the Oracle send me to watch over some kids?" Her accent is hard to place as well, though I suspect it's because she's lived in more than one region. Her pronunciation makes me think she probably has some American ties. But there are elements to her speech that sound similar to Meander's dialect as well.

"Because they're going to attempt to release the entity," Jess says.

"They won't," Natalie replies. Her look is severe as

she surveys us. "No one will. It can't *be* released."

"Nattie's been here five times," Robbie says.

"And I've dragged two Senders to the hospital. Not to mention getting burned myself the last time a fire broke out."

Up close, I can see where the hair on her right temple veers back from her head and a scar covers the hairless portion of skin. My own skin crawls, and I swallow back the desire to grab Meander and haul him away to the inn where we can hide in bed, covered in blankets and pretending this place doesn't exist.

"Last time?" I ask in a small voice. "There's been more than one fire here?"

"Yes," Natalie snaps. "There have been three. And I don't fancy having to bandage up anymore foolish people who think they can handle what's inside."

"Don't worry," Meander cuts in, his voice hard. "Cal can do the bandaging, if you're too bothered. He brought a first-aid kit and everything."

"This isn't a joke," Natalie says.

"Am I laughing?" Meander asks.

"You're a child," Natalie replies. "And you have no idea what you're doing here."

"Natalie," Dr. Barkley says in a low voice.

"Don't discount them, Nattie," Robbie says. "They're not polished. But they've got a track record you'd be proud of."

"I highly doubt that," she replies.

"Well, yeah…" Robbie reflects. "It'd probably make you cringe."

"Why are you here, if you don't want to go in?" I ask. My throat is tight as I prod, worried what answer I might receive. "Is the Oracle forcing you here?"

Natalie eyes me with a displeasure I know from too many of the adults in my life. I don't like this woman. But I want to know if her job with the Oracle demanded she be here—if the Oracle regularly forces Senders to do things they don't want.

"No," she says at last. "I volunteered. As medic."

"Medic?" Meander asks. "For the Oracle?"

"Nattie's not a Sender," Robbie says. The revelation surprises me and Meander both, and we look at our lead as he shrugs.

"My mother was a Sender," Natalie explains in a terse voice. "I grew up among the Oracle. I'm a paramedic by trade. But I offer my assistance for particularly worrisome encounters around the UK."

"So… shouldn't you have an ambulance?" Meander asks, while I reel with the knowledge that the Oracle has specifically called in a favor from a medical professional for help with this case.

Natalie scowls. "There are medical supplies in the bags and in the car. This isn't an official outing. I'm off-duty." She turns away from us and stares squarely at Robbie. "And I'm not putting myself in danger on the foolish whim of some stupid kids."

Meander's cheeks turn pink, and he opens his mouth to retort. I place a hand on his back to soothe his irritation—and swoop in before he has a chance to make the situation worse.

"We know this is dangerous," I say in a calmer tone. "We've been in dangerous situations before. We're not ignorant."

"The Oracle knows what it's doing," Robbie says. He looks at Natalie, then cuts his gaze to us. "And so do they. We'll all get on much better if everyone understands that."

"Sure," Jess says. She hitches up her backpack as she smiles at us. "Natalie is here in case we need her. Dr. Barkley will run the equipment with my help."

"Why do we need so many people?" Meander asks.

"Because the more people involved, the less likely a disaster will occur," Natalie says.

"Shall we get on with it?" Dr. Barkley asks. "It's hot as blazes out here."

It is hot. After spending the first half of my summer in Chile, where the southern hemisphere's winter months meant mild days and cool nights, the heat of the Welsh summer is muggy and sweltering. I didn't think to bring shorts with me, and the anticipation of a dead cold made me dress in a long-sleeved tee. I'm glad Meander's kept his cardigan and his scarves folded in his backpack. I don't need him suffering heat exhaustion along with everything else.

"Yes, let's get on with it," Natalie says. She looks between us. "Which of you is going to try and make contact?" I look at Meander, who stares back at Natalie without speaking. She sets her face into a glower as she turns. "Of course," she mutters.

"Come on," Robbie says. He shares an amused glance with Jess as the two head for the doors. Dr. Barkley follows on their heels, equipment bags swinging awkwardly from his shoulders.

Meander stays rooted to the spot as the adults pass. As soon as they're out of the way, I peel open his fist and take his sweat-slicked palm.

"You say the word," I mumble close to his ear. "Anytime. Don't care about what they say. Don't care about what they think. If you want out, tell me.

We'll go."

Meander gives my hand a short squeeze before he drops it. He takes two steps forward. Then he pauses and spins on his heel, his hard look softening as his arm raises in wait. I cross the space between us, and he takes hold of my hand again, gripping tight as we make our way into the building.

THE INSIDE OF THE BUILDING IS IN WORSE SHAPE THAN ITS EXTERIOR. Jess props open the main doors, but even with the sun's light flooding the entryway, it feels properly deserted. This place was once a prison, but now it looks like a small apartment complex—complete with a cracked tile corridor and a row of half-broken mailboxes covered in a thick sheen of dust. The entryway is dank and cool, the change from outside so abrupt it'd be relieving, if it wasn't for the chill seeping up my spine as I watch Meander change into his warmer clothes. As it is, I shiver, trying to shake loose the sticky sense of foreboding while my nose stings with the lingering acridity of smoke from the last time this place was set ablaze.

"We'll start with the flat on the third floor," Jess says as she flicks on an oversized flashlight. "That's where the bulk of the paranormal activity has been reported."

I take stock of Meander's breathing and keep a firm grasp on his hand as my gaze flows around the rest of the corridor. When I see the stairwell at the end of the left-hand hall, I stare at the closed door, the steel block so apparently mesmerizing I'm startled out of a numbed fixation when Meander starts moving and I realize the whole group is heading in its direction.

Jess and Dr. Barkley reach the stairwell first. Together, they push the bar to unlatch the inner door, then work to prop it open.

"Make sure it *stays* open this time," Natalie says through clenched teeth.

"It has a tendency to get stuck," Dr. Barkley mumbles to us. He jabs the stopper at the top of the door, then shoves a doorstop underneath the bottom while Jess rips a length of duct tape to place over the latch. She covers the plate twice. Then she drops the roll next to the door to act as a final backup stop.

"That's one stubborn door," Robbie says, as if we don't all know these precautions are not needed because of a faulty hinge.

Dr. Barkley and Jess finish with the door, then Natalie leads the way up the stairs. As we walk into the stairwell, I glance over the main floor railing, sniffing the putrid smoke scent billowing up from below us. The ghostly activity is probably coming from downstairs, in the basement where the smoke smell emanates. If that was where the fire—one of the fires—began, it makes it likely the ghost would stay close.

I head to the right, on route to the first stair heading down, before my arm is stopped by Meander's pull.

"Cal," he says, while I continue to stare over the railing, watching the shadows as if I might be able to catch movement within them. He tugs my hand, then drops it in order to wave his palm in front of my face. "Cal?"

I blink, slowly, his voice taking a few beats to really register in my brain. When I turn to him, his expression is weird, his features creased with a confused sort of concern.

"Yeah," I say. I blink again, remembering what we are doing and checking over him to make sure his condition hasn't gotten worse. "Are you okay?"

"I'm fine," Meander says. He searches my face the same way I just searched his. "Are you?"

My eyes travel back down, over the railing to where the smoke scent is strongest. "Don't you think we should go to the basement?" I ask.

"They think it's on the third floor," he says. He takes my hand again. "Why do you want to go to the basement, Cal?"

"Are you two coming?" Robbie calls down from the second-floor landing.

I shake my head and look in the direction the others went. "Sorry," I mumble. "Let's go. We don't need to be in the building any longer than necessary."

Meander's eyes stay on me as we start up, and I try to keep my mind on what we've come to do instead of on the weirdly menacing sight of the stairs leading down to the building's lowest level. I can't help glancing over the railing as we climb to the second story. But once we make it around to start up to floor three, I focus more intently on watching the steady state of Meander's shortened breaths.

"Is he having an anxiety attack?" Natalie asks when she sees him. I want to be annoyed at her for not knowing anything about his talent. But I can see the professional concern in her face as she comes to his side, ready to dole out medical assistance should he need it. I appreciate that she's willing to treat anxiety with the care it deserves instead of writing it off as simple fear of the ghost.

"No, he's not," I answer for him, doing my best to keep my voice neutral. "He's near the spirit. This is what happens when the dead are close."

Meander's hand is still in mine as his eyes fix down the corridor of the third floor. I can't see anything in the hallway, and I'm not sure if he can, either. As raspy as his breaths are, he's still breathing at the same rate he was when we entered the apartment complex. And he hasn't done more than wince since we got inside. A spirit is unquestionably near. But I'm not sure if it's as close as I expected now that we're on the third floor.

"After the prison was torn down, this building was built into flats in the nineteen-fifties," Dr. Barkley says. "Four in total—second, third, and fourth floors, plus the basement. The main floor acted as the caretaker's home. This is the flat with the most activity. I'll start checking the rooms." He leaves the bags in a heap and retrieves an EMF meter from the pocket of the nearest one.

"Don't bother," Meander says. He steps into the hall, shoulders tense as he walks towards the rooms. I walk with him, noticing the annoyed look on the doctor's face as we pass. This mission isn't getting off to a great start. Apparently, these people know more about the spirit we're facing than we do. But for all they know about the dead, they seem to lack any understanding of how Meander sees ghosts. Then again, any Sender I've known who can see spirits has no need of equipment for their own paranormal encounters. The EMF meter is not for us—it's for everyone else, to ascertain what details they can for the Oracle's sake.

"You're not doing yourself any favors, you know," I whisper to Meander as we walk down the hall. He glances at me with narrowed eyes, and I laugh. "Just saying. Letting them set up their equipment doesn't hurt any. We could leave, go outside so you can get your breath back. Then they'll feel properly prepared, and they won't be so quick to write you off as a…"

My words trail off as we pass a wall vent, and a fresh bloom of rotten smoke twists under my nose.

"Cal?" I drop my gaze from the wall vent and look back to see Meander giving me the same concerned expression he did in the stairwell. "What's going on?" he asks.

"Nothing." I shake my head and step away from the air vent. "It's just the smell."

"You smell it too?" Meander asks.

We enter the first room, winding through a derelict kitchen and stepping on damp, soiled red carpet in the living room.

"It's pretty bad," I say. "Guess no one bothered to do a thorough cleaning."

We walk past the bathroom and stop in front of a little hallway where we can see into both of the two small bedrooms. Meander glances into the rooms. Then he looks back at me.

"It's not here," he says. He stares hard into my eyes before his teeth scrape along his bottom lip. "Where do you think we should look next?"

"The basement," I say without even thinking.

Meander frowns as he holds my hand a little tighter. "That's what I thought you'd say."

"I don't know why," I start. I glance up at the vent, confused by my own preoccupation. "It's just the smell of the smoke."

While I'm still staring at the vent, Meander leans in and plants a soft kiss to my cheek. Then he tugs my hand. "Show me where the smell is coming from, Cal."

We head out of the apartment, and I explain to the others why it is I want to go to the basement. Dr. Barkley complains because we haven't done any official recordings. But I don't fail to notice how quiet Natalie becomes when I start back towards the stairs.

As soon as we pass the main floor, the stench grows worse and Meander's breath begins to hitch in earnest. I pause on the stairs twice to make sure he's okay before we continue down. When we open the door to what was once the basement flat—but which is now only a rotted shell of a burned floor—my head starts to ache. Static burbles between my ears, but it short circuits, cutting in and out like something is blocking a clear signal to my brain. Meander leans heavily into my side, and I do my best to keep the pain out of my face so I can support him.

"Think we'll see a ghost today?" Robbie asks from the back of the group. He walks around to survey us both before he grins. "I'll take that as a yes. Bark, you'd better get that equipment rolling. I think the Oracle's just scored a two-in-one."

"A what?" Meander forces himself upright and glances at me, and while I try to keep my face impartial, he can obviously tell something is up. He doesn't look surprised, and I guess I'm not, either. The case file for this entity didn't mention anything about murder. But a violent, angry, convicted criminal isn't much of a stretch from someone who's got murder-related business to attend to.

Meander tries to move away to give me space, but I keep him close.

"I'm okay," I say. "It's not that bad." Which is true, as far as seeing ghosts go. The smell is terrible, and the static hurts, but there is no crashing music—and the cold is nothing more than it was when we first entered the complex.

"Where," he croaks, and I give him a pained look before my gaze slides to the two doors still standing on the floor's back half. Without hesitating, I point to the door on the left. I don't know why I do it, but Meander doesn't question my intuition. He only looks disturbed and ill as he nods and starts forward.

Robbie stays back to help Dr. Barkley set up some equipment, while Natalie and Jess follow us farther into the burned out room.

"I don't like this place," Jess mumbles. "Bad energy here."

Meander scoffs, which turns into a cough halfway through. I approach the door and, despite my usual preference for taking a moment to prepare myself, I don't hesitate to push it open.

WHICH PROVES TO BE A BIG MISTAKE.

The beam from Jess's flashlight flickers out immediately, and Dr. Barkley curses as the equipment he's setting up shuts off. Meander gasps, and I'm assaulted by roaring static as the room before us fills with a peculiarly unfocused splatter of bluish-white. The ghost's mass is not just unformed. It's totally gapped, appearing in some places and not in others, so convoluted and confused I can't make sense of what I'm looking at.

The wooden inner door rattles against its hinges as Meander steps into the room, but he doesn't get far before the force is too much. He swoons, staggering back and drooping against the edge of the doorframe. Holding a hand against his nose, he coughs from the smell, and I nod in vague agreement while I chance another step inside.

"Cal," he says, his voice already weak and broken. I

keep a hold of his hand, but I continue into the room, wanting a closer look at the spirit. The mass makes no sense. But it feels like if I just get a little closer, I can *make* it sensical in my brain.

"The temperature drop here is intense," Jess says from somewhere behind me. Her voice is so methodical, so void of pain, that I feel a bit like laughing. Then I feel a bit like flicking a match into the room to see if that warms things up.

I halt, my heart racing as the thought comes and goes from my head with a viciousness I've never felt before. Fear drips into my chest, and I step back, turning on my heel and taking in the sight of Meander. He's looking at the mass as well, hand to his mouth and sleeve pulled back far enough I can see the horrible dark bruising spreading at the edges of his scarf.

"Do you hear anything?" I ask. He shakes his head, eyes closing against the pain. "Do you feel anything?"

"I'm trying," he says. "There's something, but... it comes... and goes..."

I nod, moving close to him and wrapping my arm around his waist. Beside us, Jess's flashlight dies, and she leaves the room to find new batteries. Natalie hovers beyond the doorway, her arms crossed and her whole body stiff as she waits for us to finish.

"Do you..." Meander tries to ask, but I shake my head to stop his struggling words. I can't hear anything other than the in-and-out fading of static. No music. No voice. It would be a mild experience, if it weren't for the intensity of the smoke. And the presence of the fear.

"Angry," Meander whispers. "It's... I can't... It's just angry."

I turn back to the mass, wondering why the ghost is so quiet if it's anger is so intense. Staring hard at its top half, I search for a face and think about approaching it again to try and get a better view. But as soon as I entertain the idea, my head begins filling with other, darker thoughts, as if the ghost itself is pouring black smoke directly into my brain.

"What do you want?" I ask in a low voice.

Something rattles far off in the room, while my hands tremble with the clarity of the thought in my head.

Matches.

The urge to pull out a box of matches is strong, and if I had some on me now, I would strike them without hesitation. But that urge can't be what the mass wants. Because the mass doesn't talk. It just floats there, silent and—

Static flares in my head, like a communication working to break through. My hand drops from Meander's waist, and I shift, trying to better see into the room. Squinting my eyes, I stare at the cloud and inch closer, focusing on the blips of static and waiting for something else to sound in my ears.

"Cal, don't," Meander says. I step forward and he steps with me, tugging on my arm to try and get me back to the edge of the room.

"Stay by the door," I tell him.

"Cal!" His voice is wrecked, and he needs to get out of here. But I just want to try to wring a few words from the ghost. The faster we talk, the faster we understand what it wants.

And once we know what it wants, we can burn this place to the ground.

"Callum!" Meander half-shouts my name at the same moment the thought strikes. At the same moment the temperature in the room plummets further, and the door behind us slams closed. I gasp, staggering back and crashing into Meander. We fall together, and I twist so my arm takes the brunt of the impact against the concrete floor. Meander groans, rolling to his side and retching for air. I slide my arm out from under him and scramble over to the door.

"Help us out of here!" I yell.

"We're trying!" Jess calls from the other side. I grab the handle and twist at it uselessly, while Meander coughs and I turn back to see him clawing at the neck of his sweater. I rush back to him, undoing the top buttons while my eyes make a wild scan of the room, searching for another way out. The place is empty, a charred square with no fresh air or light. I can barely even see Meander now that the flashlight's beam is out of view. The only thing that emanates any sort of illumination is the mass of the spirit itself.

I refuse to look at the ghost, at the entity. Instead, I drag Meander up and pull him closer to the door.

"He's too angry," Meander hisses.

"Shh," I say, brushing his curls back with a shaking hand. "Don't talk."

Meander grabs my hand, his grip worryingly weak. "Don't—" he starts, but the words are soon cut off by the choke of a ragged swallow.

"We're going to break it down!" Robbie says from the other side of the door.

I change course, dragging us both away from where the splintering wood will crack. Propping Meander up farther along the wall, I hold his face in my hands and try to keep him making eye contact.

"We'll be out of here soon," I say. "I've got you. If you pass out, I'll do CPR. Okay?"

He smiles, while his eyes slip closed again and his breath diminishes to a series of short hiccups. I hold him, my ears trained on the sounds of something ramming the door from its far side. I can feel the entity watching us, and I close my eyes against its leer, willing it to go away while knowing all the while that it's drawing closer.

A dead mist drips against my pores, and with a shudder, I open my eyes to watch for the moment the door breaks. But my view is obscured, and instead of the door, I find myself looking directly at the mass. It's so close it's almost touching us, and I hold Meander tighter, afraid it's going to try and pull him away.

"What do you want?" I ask it through gritted teeth. But the only answer I get is another thought, another unnerving curiosity about how long it would take for our bodies to burn if this building was on fire.

Flames dance in my eyes, so real I can almost feel their heat. For a few seconds, I smile as the phantom warmth curls around my limbs. I smile, knowing full well that if I had a match, I would light it.

I would light it. I would light it, and then I would—

Something shifts, and I blink, swallowing smoke and clearing away all tempting thoughts until my eyes focus enough to know that the shift came from Meander. His body is limp against mine, and my heart slams against my chest as I position him on the ground and tilt his chin back so I can give him air.

The mass continues to hover over me, and my throat feels so clogged with smoke I'm terrified I'm going to do more harm than good if I have to push air into Meander's lungs. Tears sting my eyes, but I don't let panic stop me from lowering my face and listening for his breathing. Faint, gasping noises rattle from his throat, so I push his head further back and pinch his nose shut before lowering my mouth to his.

The door crashes open while I'm giving rescue breaths. Robbie curses, rushing in so he and Dr. Barkley can grab Meander to move him out of the room. I fall back and then climb to my feet, ignoring all pain and smell as I keep on his heels. They get him into the stairwell before Natalie ensures his breath has returned. When I see the steadier rise of his chest, my own chest feels like it might burst with relief. Robbie and Dr. Barkley grab him more gently and carry him up, through the main floor and back outside. The heat of the living day hits like a brick, and I gasp into it, thinking of fire and wondering if this is anything like stepping through a wall of flame.

The thought makes me sick, all of the sickness I didn't pay much attention to inside hurtling up my throat and making me gag. I cup my hands around my mouth, breathing deep and trying to hold back the tears that refuse to stay welled in my eyes.

"Is he okay?" I ask, getting myself under control so I can get back to Meander. I wipe my eyes, sniffing and swallowing down the smoke-tinted bile simmering at the back of my throat. Then I step past Robbie and kneel next to Meander as he comes to, squinting in the sun before shading his eyes with his arm.

"I'm fine," he says, though he doesn't look it. He's dreadfully white, and sweat glistens on his too-pale skin. I push damp hair from his eyes as Natalie takes his pulse and fishes a cooling pack out of her supply bag. Meander presses it against his forehead with a sigh, struggling to a seated position so I can help him out of his cardigan.

"You should never have gone in there," Natalie mutters. "What the hell is wrong with the Oracle? If ghosts make it so you can't breathe, you shouldn't be going near them. It's not that complicated a concept."

Meander lets out a harsh laugh. "Just stay away from ghosts? What an idea. Wonder why I've never thought of it."

Natalie tucks her platinum hair behind her ears and turns her attention to me.

"I thought you were the one meant to do the bandaging?" she asks. "You look nearly as bad as he does. And he was unconscious."

"It's not his fault," Meander says. But Natalie's look makes me feel sick all over again.

"Yes, it is," I say. "I was supposed to watch you. I knew you were fading. We should have left the room. I just… I couldn't stop…" I stare at the building, not knowing how to finish that sentence. But I don't need to find the impossible words. Meander's located them for me.

He grabs my hand, his expression full of gentle concern. "I think you were being guided," he says.

I blink. "I… What?"

"Guided?" Natalie asks, but Meander ignores her.

"You kept saying we should go to the basement," he explains. "You kept staring at nothing. You talked about smoke."

"The smell," I say. "It was all I could smell."

"Right," Meander says. "But the thing is, there was

no smoke smell. Not until we got to the basement. You said it was coming from the vents."

"It was!" I say. "You said you smelled it too."

"I smelled blood," Meander says.

"Blood?" I think back to the stench inside, wondering if there was any way I could have mistaken blood for smoke. But the scents are too different, and there is no doubt in my mind it was fire smoke I smelled.

No doubt in my mind of what I smelled. Or what I thought. About burning the building. About being inside it while we burned alive.

"Oh shit," I mutter. Tears well again, and Meander pulls me to him, hugging me close.

34

I'M SHAKY AND ILL THE ENTIRE WAY BACK TO THE INN. SITTING IN THE backseat of our car, I stare out the window while I try to regain composure, my mind reeling with the reality of being guided again after all this time. I need to break down the encounter and ask Meander questions about how he knew something was wrong. But I don't want to let myself dwell on what happened in the complex until everyone else is gone, and the two of us can figure it out in private.

We don't have any privacy yet. First, all six of us are brought to the inn so we can meet in Robbie's room. He calls the front desk and orders a tea service to be brought up. Then he sits cross-legged at the foot of his room's single bed.

"Did you get anything from the spirit?" he asks, looking first at Meander.

"It's a male," Meander says. "Angry. There's a smell of blood. And thoughts of the prison. He definitely feels caged."

I'm impressed at how much he managed to get, all while trying to remain conscious. I didn't hear a word from the entity. And the only feeling I wrangled from the mass was the desire to burn.

"Caged," Natalie echoes. "I've heard that before."

Jess pulls open a folder and reads from the contents. "The caginess—suspected to be related to his death."

"We didn't know that," I say. "It wasn't in the database."

"There's not much recorded in the database," Jess agrees.

"Well why not?" Meander asks. "Seems like pertinent information to be included in the bloody file."

"You didn't ask to see the actual file," Jess says with an all-too begrudging smirk.

"Rule one of being out in the field," Robbie says. "Ask around. Get as much information as you can before you see the spirit first-hand."

I balk. "You knew there was more information?"

Robbie nods. "And before you start yelling at me for it, it's a lesson you've got to learn for yourself. You've been researching for years. You shouldn't go jumping into a case without getting the info first."

"But we did get the info!" I remind him. "We read the entry in the stupid database at least five times. How were we supposed to know there was additional information just waiting?"

"Because we were supposed to play as a team and ask for help," Meander mutters in a sarcastic voice.

I roll my eyes. "Has it ever occurred to anyone that being a useful team member means stopping someone from doing something idiotic when you know they're missing key information?" I glower at the three older Senders. "Because it goes both ways. Are none of you pissed off that no one told you what our talents were? If you understand the rules so much better than we do, then how come no one asked Meander what happens when he sees a ghost?"

"Cal," Meander warns, though I can hear the smile in his voice even while he cautions me to stop.

I slump against my seat, frustrated and afraid of what happened in the building. I feel stupid that we didn't think to gain more information before trying to make contact. But at the same time, that's never been how it works here. Establishing contact is the first step. Finding out more about the ghost is the second. How can they expect us to learn anything, if they keep changing the rules?

Of course, I'm sure they would say that's the point. Because there are no rules when it comes to spirits, and every case is different. So, we should learn to be prepared in whatever ways we can.

I wonder if that lesson includes spirits unexpectedly guiding someone with thoughts of matches and flames.

"What else do you know about it?" Meander asks in a more controlled tone. "What information is that folder hiding that wasn't recorded in the database?"

Jess's eyes are watching me, contemplating the accusation I've made. When Meander speaks, she looks at him, smiling as she opens the folder.

"We think the entity was once a man named Gareth Davies," she says. "A major crime weasel in this area in the late eighteen hundreds. In nineteen oh one, a constable by the name of Rees infiltrated Davies's inner circle and befriended Davies himself. When the police busted a smuggling operation, Davies was locked up. But even after he was arrested, he had no idea Rees was on the force. Not until the constable visited his cell to reveal the truth. Then—and here's where it gets brutal—Davies reportedly grew so angry he began screaming, punching, and repeatedly smashing his head against the stone walls of his cell in a manic outburst. The final hit to his skull before he knocked himself unconscious did enough damage that he never woke up again."

Jess looks up from the file and stares at Meander, while I shake my head.

"You said you *think*... You haven't confirmed his identity?" I ask.

"No," Jess says. "Which is why none of the information was listed in the database. In total, there have been six Senders who have registered contact with the entity. But only one was ever able to communicate well enough to gain insight into his life. However, she wasn't convinced he was telling the truth. She said she felt like there was something else going on that she couldn't glean from him."

"Can we talk to her?" Meander asks. "See what she can tell us about her experience with it?"

"She's no longer with us," Jess says, and I don't fail to notice the way her head ducks when she says it.

"She's dead?" I ask. Cold fear washes down my spine for the second time this morning. "Was it the entity?"

"She got trapped in one of the fires," Jess says in a careful voice. Her eyes cut to Natalie, and the blonde scowls.

"She was my mother," Natalie says. My eyes widen, while she keeps her gaze firmly on the floral pattern of Robbie's bedspread. "I used to come with her on all her excursions, but she wouldn't let me accompany her trips to see that ghost. She visited the entity six times. On the sixth, she did not make it home."

"Natalie asked the Oracle to alert her anytime someone tried to contact the entity again," Robbie explains. "She's saved two others from harm in her time with us."

That explains her foul mood, and her fury at seeing two teenagers trying to tackle the spirit. But I still can't wrap my head around the lack of information being passed between parties in this organization. We've seen too many people get hurt because they kept things to themselves. Obviously, this crew knows something of that as well. So why did nobody tell Natalie what our talents are? And why the hell did nobody think to mention to us that a Sender has died trying to release this spirit?

"She believed there was something else going on?" Meander asks after a moment. He doesn't look at Jess, but at Natalie.

"Because of the fire," Natalie says with a nod. "There have been three fires since the nineteen eighties. Two when the building was a functioning set of flats. And once more since then. Mum always talked about the first fire. It was ruled as an accident, but she never believed it to be so. That fire killed two people, a father and his daughter. But it's never been proven that the entity was the cause of their deaths."

"If there's been two more fires since then, I'd think that's a good indicator," I say.

Natalie nods. "Mum always said there was something *wrong* about the fire."

"You smelled smoke," Meander says to me. "I smelled blood. That's not usual, is it? For us to smell different things."

"Could you see it?" I ask him. "I couldn't get a clear sense of anything."

"Me neither," Meander says.

"Then that settles it," Natalie says. Her manner becomes aggravated again as she looks between us. "We're done here."

"Done?" I ask. "You think this is over just because we saw it once?"

"No, I think it's over because you saw it once, got trapped in the building—and he almost died," she says.

My throat grows tight, her words sounding like an accusation to my ears.

"So we leave it until someone else makes a go and gets themselves killed instead, yeah?" Meander says. "Save ourselves to let someone else lose their life?"

"You don't have the stamina for dealing with a spirit like this," she says. "And you," she looks at me, "seemed to be off in your own head most of the time you were there."

"That's different," I mumble.

"He was under its influence," Meander says.

"Which means what, exactly?" Natalie says. "That he ignores everyone else and runs straight to the ghost? Because that's what I saw today. And that makes it even more vital that you don't go anywhere near the place."

I want to argue with her, but I can't. Being under that spirit's influence meant I was so busy thinking about lighting up the room, I didn't pay attention to how Meander was fairing. I almost didn't even notice when he lost consciousness.

"I think she's right," Jess says. She glances at Robbie. "It's too dangerous a situation. They can find something else to do for their project. This is beyond them."

Meander watches them, his face stony and his lips sealed. I rest my foot against his under the table as my gaze moves between the other four in the room.

"We'll talk," Robbie says, though I'm not sure if he's referring to us or them. Natalie stands, and he gets off the bed to follow her towards the door. "First, we need a report." She slips into the hall, and he goes after her, talking about the documentation the Oracle requires for our brief and disastrous attempt.

Once the two of them have left, Meander looks at me. "Let's go back to our room."

"That's a good idea," Jess says. "Have some downtime. It won't look so bad when you've recovered."

Meander doesn't respond, and neither do I. Silently, we leave Robbie's room and move next door to the solitude of our own. Once we're there, he sits propped up against the headboard of the nearest bed, looking tired and frustrated.

"They're writing us off," he says. He holds out his hand, and I kick off my sneakers before climbing onto the bed to sit next to him.

"Did you get anything from the spirit you didn't tell them?" I ask. "A book? A passage?"

He shakes his head. "Nothing concrete. I was vaguely reminded of Jekyll and Hyde. But not with enough precision to understand why. And the entity's simple existence might explain it. A man turning into a monster after death. I don't think it's really useful. Not with how little we saw of it."

"I know we're not as incapable as they seem to think," I say with a careful glance at him. "But do we really want to push it?"

He sighs, head tilting back against the bed frame. "I don't fancy joining the ranks of the dead," he says.

"But…" I prompt.

He smiles. "I also don't want to give up and let someone else get killed."

"Always virtuous," I say. "What makes someone else's life worth more than yours?"

He turns to me. "I don't want to get killed. And I'm not about to let *you* get killed." He frowns, while his finger begins trailing circles on my leg. "I don't know. Maybe we should leave it. It's just… We only had one shot. A shite shot, but only one. And, despite the general consensus that we're disaster-prone infants, I think we might have something to offer that no one else has."

"We do?" I ask.

"The smoke," he says. "You experienced something different than I did. Blood, that fits with the story of Davies. The anger and caginess I felt—that fits too. But the other Sender said there was something wrong with the fire. And you smelled smoke. I don't think that's a coincidence, but I do think it's unusual. Plus, there's the guiding thing."

"About that," I say. "There's more than just going to the basement." I tell him about the thoughts I had, the strange longings to set the place ablaze. He isn't disturbed by what I say. Instead, as I talk, his expression grows contemplative.

"Only a handful of people have ever seen this thing," he says once I've finished relating the way the thoughts seemed to seep into my brain. "As far as we know, there's never been two people to see it at the same time. And those two with differing experiences."

"Horrible and stupid," I mutter. "You want to go back."

Meander smirks. But then he gives me a more serious look. "Not if you don't. Or, not with you, if you don't feel safe. But if we can go in with more information—and more of a plan—we stand a chance of figuring out *something*."

I press my lips tight while I think about what we faced and what almost happened when we were locked in that room. Then I think about Natalie's mother, and the father and daughter who died in the first fire set by the ghost.

"Okay," I say at length. "We can go again. On three conditions."

"Three?" Meander smiles. "Getting demanding now. What conditions?"

"One, that we research the hell out of this guy before we go back in that building," I say.

"Reasonable," Meander agrees.

"Two, that we don't go alone," I continue. "I don't think that group will want to take us back. But until we know for sure what we're facing and how we're going to deal with it, I think it's best we have someone else there. Just in case…"

"I'm fine, Cal," Meander says. He shifts to look at me more fully. "You would have gotten me out."

"Not with the door locked," I say. "And not with my mind… I don't want to risk it. These conditions are about minimizing the risk of injury or, you know, *death*. I'm not going to chance something like that happening again."

"Okay," Meander says. "We won't go alone. Condition three?"

I sigh. "Before we arrive… check me over, okay? Make sure I haven't hidden any matches or lighters."

Meander takes my hand in his, and for a few seconds, he studies me, trying to ascertain the scope of my fear. When he nods, the movement slight and solemn, and it speaks to more than his simple agreement of my terms. He brings my hand up to his lips. Then, when he sees how my eyes are starting to shine, he clears his throat.

"Three conditions," he says. "I can do that."

"One more time," I say. I bring my free hand up to his neck, peeling under the collar of his shirt and feeling along his scar. "And if it goes bad, we're out. For good."

The first step in satisfying my conditions is to find out more about this spirit. But in order to keep the Oracle out of our hair while we work on our mission, condition one winds up going hand and hand with condition two—finding someone to return to the building with us.

"You two want to fly under the radar and work on a highly dangerous case in secret," Robbie says when he comes to debrief with us an hour later. "Why am I not surprised?"

"We have more to offer than they think," Meander says. "One of them isn't even a Sender. Whatever she's gone through—she still doesn't understand what it's really like. We can do this… We can at least try and get further along for someone else."

"The Oracle doesn't want trouble from you two," Robbie says. He laces his fingers together and raises them over and behind his mohawk to rest on the back of his head. "Jess is going to file a report stating that this mission is too dangerous to continue. Once that happens, my hands will be tied. Someone will be here to pack you two up and sweep you back to Chile to wait out the rest of camp."

"But you're not going to let that happen, right?" I ask with a hopeful smile.

Robbie considers me for a long time before his eyes slide to Meander. "I have to sign off on the report before it gets sent," he says. "I *could* delay submission for a while, *if* I thought there were grounds to do so."

"We've given you grounds," Meander says. "We can both see this entity, which is rare. Rarer still, we experienced different things in that basement. Things that don't fit together. Which means maybe we can figure out why they don't fit—what the missing piece is."

"You're also both prone to injuries," Robbie counters. "And *you* are prone to passing out. That's not a good start. You have a peaceful connection to ghosts? Sure, I can see letting this slip. But dangerous talents combined with dangerous spirits? That's asking for a whole different kind of trouble."

"That's why we want your help," I say.

"I thought you wanted my help to delay the Oracle?" Robbie asks.

"That's a necessary step," Meander says. "But it's not why we're talking to you. We want you to come with us to the flats. To assist. And to be backup. You know that Cal and I could have snuck out of here and gone back, just the two of us. We decided not to, for preservation's sake."

"Preservation of our reputations?" Robbie asks.

"Preservation of our lives," I reply.

Robbie lets a long breath whistle through his lips. Then he drops his hands to his knees and leans forward in his chair.

"The logical part of me knows this is a terrible plan," he says. "Even if we stay away from worst case scenarios, it could still well mean my ass and yours in trouble with the Oracle. And if we put those worst cases back into play, I could wind up letting you two die—while maybe also getting myself killed along the way."

He looks between us, and I bite down the inclination to plead for his assistance. What he's saying is true, and I won't try to talk over his thoughts as he considers the most rational course of action to take.

"But the forever reckless part of my brain thinks this is exactly why the Oracle let you two have this awful case," he continues after a pause. "And, if they do want to bitch about what happens, well… camp's almost over, for all of us. And my official time with the Oracle's over with it. Getting fired wouldn't be much of a problem."

"Does that mean you'll help us?" Meander asks.

"It means I'll think about it," Robbie says. "And I'll delay the report, at least while you get your research underway. Find out what you can, and I'll do the same. We'll discuss how—and if—we'll return to the old prison after we know what information we've got."

"Thanks, Robbie," I say. His mohawk slices through the air in a nod, and the room grows quiet as the relief of his temporary agreement settles over us. In the ensuing silence splintered only by the room's humming A/C, I rub my neck and consider what Robbie would be risking in order to help us. Then

I glance at him with a curious expression. "You're almost finished being a lead. Aren't you going to work for the Oracle when camp's done?"

"Nah," Robbie says with a smile. "Not full-time, at least. I'll probably do a few camp sessions here and there. But nothing on an ongoing basis."

"Do you know what you're going to do instead?" I ask.

"Sure," Robbie says. He leans back in his chair, a satisfied expression on his face. "I've been taking business courses for the last couple of years. Going to open my own shop."

"A shop?" The idea is certainly unexpected, though I suppose I don't know Robbie's life outside of the Oracle well enough to truly be surprised. "Selling what?"

"Antiques," Robbie says, and although I don't know his life outside the Oracle very well, his response still manages to make me eye Meander— before we both laugh.

"I'm sure the posh crowd will love getting appraisals from you," Meander says.

"I'm sure they will," Robbie agrees with a grin. "But they'll get over it once they know how good I am."

"Why antiques?" I ask. "That seems like the kind of career you fall into… Not something you set out to begin from scratch."

"I know it's insane," Robbie admits. "But I love old things. I always have. And I love tinkering. Besides, with my talent? I've got a knack for knowing when things have… ghostly connections. I'm not good enough to tell any specifics, mind you. But I get a sense. People love it when there's a sense about a thing, don't they? Anyway, that's what I'll do. And I'll work for the

Oracle on occasion—if they still want me after all this is over. Whenever they've got need of someone who can communicate with a nineteenth century ghost." He gives Meander a nod. "I'm planning on stationing in London or its outskirts, if I can get my permits in order. And manage to afford it. If I do, I'll be able to pester you once you're set-up."

"Wonderful," Meander mutters. Robbie chuckles at his unimpressed tone, while my own stomach pinches with jealousy—partly because Robbie, too, seems to have a full grasp on what his future holds for him, but mostly because he'll be close enough to visit Meander in person while I'm stuck on another continent.

"I'll intercept the ghost's file from Jess," Robbie says, bringing us back to the topic at hand. "You can use that to start your research. Oh—" He stands, fishing his wallet from his back pocket and pulling something from within it. "You can use these too."

He drops two cards on the table, and when I reach forward to pick one of them up I see they're cards for the local library system. The one I've grabbed has Meander's name on it. Given the way he looks at me, I suspect he's taken the one with mine.

"The Oracle made us fraudulent library cards?" I ask with a laugh.

Robbie shrugs. "Great way to do some research. And get a feel for the community culture. You know my favorite way to get information is by talking with the local crowds. Libraries can be a good way to do that."

Robbie pulls out his phone and sends a text to Jess. He arranges to meet her for dinner somewhere in town, then bids us farewell so he can get ready.

36

ROBBIE TALKS JESS INTO DELAYING THE REPORT FOR ANOTHER THREE days. It doesn't give us a lot of time. But it gives us some.

"What do you think the odds are you'll be all right at the library?" I ask the next morning when we prepare to head out for a day of research.

"At this point, we'll call it fifty-fifty," he sighs. During our first year of correspondence, I discovered Meander has a lifetime ban from his local library system, due to an incident involving a haunted branch and a lot of damaged books. "I'll give a better estimate when I see the place."

"Should we go now or wait until we get the file from Robbie?" I ask. Robbie got Jess's agreement to delay the report. But he said he had some more sweet-talking to do before he could secure us the file. I'm still annoyed the Oracle didn't give it to us outright, letting us have the information that could have prevented the disastrous first attempt with the entity. But I'm glad Robbie is on our side for this portion of our task. I don't know how well he is acquainted with Jess. But I'll bet anything he'll have better luck talking her into handing him the file than either of us would.

Meander runs a hand through his curls before he grabs the library cards from the side table.

"Let's go now," he says. "We know Davies's name and when he was alive. I'd rather find repeat information than miss our chance to find any if Robbie can't get the file—or the Oracle moves in before we have time to get back to that building."

"Okay," I say. "But tea first? Maybe the library's close enough we can get a drink and walk over."

"You do realize it's a bloody sauna out there," Meander says with a smile.

I walk into the bathroom to give my hair a quick once-over in the mirror. "Well yeah, but... it's tea. It's exempt from temperature considerations, right?"

He laughs. "To my way of thinking? Of course. But not everyone shares my way of thinking."

"What can I say?" I shrug as I step back into the room. "I like your way of thinking."

Meander watches me, his expression curiously pleased, until my quirked brow makes him cross the space between us.

"Then we're in agreement." His fingers trail down my back and around my side until they find my hand. "Tea first, then the library. Come on."

We find a coffee shop around the corner from the inn and order drinks before asking for directions to the nearest library branch. The day is overcast and muggy, and steam billows from our cups as we wander through town trying to follow the vague directions we received. We get lost twice, turning the wrong way and heading down side streets until we give up and backtrack to get us on the right course again. Meander grows grumpier the further along we go. I tease him for his gloomy mood until he begrudgingly starts to smile.

When we finally make it to the library, we relax in the blessed cool of the air-conditioned entrance for a few minutes before venturing in to start our research. The building is thankfully ghost-free, and we're not given any dubious stares as we wander around and then ask about the microfilm reader Meander spots tucked across from the circulation desk. We hand over our fraudulent cards and book out a time slot for the machine. Then we hunt through reels of old newspapers until we find the ones for the time period when Gareth Davies was alive.

"All of this checks out with what Jess told us," Meander says. "P.C. Rees made his career off of this case. He was a nobody beforehand, which is probably why Davies never saw him coming. He was young and new to the force. He put his neck out, risked his life to break up the smuggling circuit. Says here he worked in the group for two years, leaking information to the police to slowly crack Davies's armor. No wonder Davies was so pissed when he discovered the truth."

"When did they tear down the prison and build the apartment complex?" I ask. "Did Anyone mention it when we were there?"

"No." He takes his phone out of his pocket and connects to the building's Wi-Fi. "We might be able to find that out online, though."

We switch places, and he looks up the name of

the prison while I continue scrolling through the microfilm. When he finds a regional history page claiming the prison was torn down in October of 1963, we find the corresponding reels and load them into the reader.

"See if you can find out when the new apartments opened. Or when the fires happened," I say while I rewind the latest film. "There are reels here for papers up to the nineties. If we can figure out the dates, we should be able to find anything that was reported as local news."

"Right. And then we need to look up PC Rees," Meander says. "I want to make sure there was nothing odd about his death."

We spend the whole day hunting, focusing less on going through the information than on gathering snippets from the reels and printing off each article we think might be of use. It takes the longest to find mention of the first fire at the complex, and we give up without finding any account of the second two. Still, we collect a hefty stack of clippings by the time the dinner hour approaches and we're both starved from staying indoors all day. Eyes weary from staring at screens, we pay for our printing and leave the library. On our wandering way back, we order chicken burgers and fries from a take-out place. Then we lay out both the food and the papers once we're back at the inn.

"Rees died of heart failure," Meander says as we sort the papers and eat our burgers. He lies on his stomach, propped on his elbows next to me on the unused bed in our room. "Nothing unusual there."

"Do you think that could be your Jekyll and Hyde connection?" I ask. "Rees was the instigator. His betrayal made Davies so angry he killed himself in a fit of rage. Stands to reason he'd want something from Rees to see him to the other side. Or that he'd feel like Rees was a monster disguised as a friend."

"It's possible," Meander sighs. "But given that Rees has been dead for the better part of a century, we might be up the creek if Davies is sticking around hoping for a final confrontation."

He reaches over to grab a fry from the cardboard container open beside my pile of papers. I give him a dubious stare and swat his hand away.

"You have your own fries," I remind him.

"Yeah, but mine don't have any ketchup," he says.

"Because you didn't want any," I laugh. "You *disgustingly* decided to douse yours in vinegar, remember?"

He eyes me for a moment, then catches me off-guard by leaning in and pressing his mouth to mine. Rolling me back, he pushes me into the mattress, hand cupping my jaw as he languidly deepens the kiss. When a soft moan works its way up my throat, he pulls back, head tilted to one side and curls hanging in his eyes as he licks his lips.

"You don't seem to mind the vinegar," he says.

I blink, then glare, and he smirks as he plants a quicker kiss to my lips. Then he snatches a ketchup-drizzled fry from my container and moves back to his side of the bed.

Robbie finally brings us the file the next afternoon, after his second meal with Jess proves more successful than his first. Taking stock of the detailed reports the adult Senders kept from us, we compare notes and make a list of points we've gathered from the past two days of work.

"Everything Jess told us fits with what we've found," Meander says. "Davies was an angry man dealing with a betrayed friendship. But it doesn't explain how his energy has become so unfocused."

"It doesn't explain the fires, either," I add.

"Yeah, that part's always been strange," Robbie says.

"Davies died in nineteen oh one," Meander says. "The first fire wasn't until nineteen eighty-three. But then a second fire occurred in ninety-six, which is when the flats were evacuated for good. The third fire took place after the flats were empty, sixteen years ago."

"From nineteen oh one to nineteen eighty-three is a huge gap," I say. "Why wait so long, then repeat the event at closer intervals? Unless Davies didn't know he was capable of causing a fire." I swallow the memory of my thoughts back in the building, the scorched longing for matches and burning bodies. "Or, he never had the opportunity."

"The first fire was reported as an electrical fire," Meander says. "Accident. The next two were considered suspicious, but they never found a definitive cause or suspect."

"The first fire is when the other two died, right?" I ask. I search for the printed newsreel, a surprisingly small piece we found tucked deep into a Sunday issue of the '83 paper. "Malcolm Priddy and his daughter, Anne."

Meander nods. "And the second fire was the one that killed Natalie's mum."

"The third happened when Senders were inside the

building as well," Robbie says. "That's where Natalie got her burn. She pulled them out in time. No one able to make contact with the ghost has been back since."

"Could the first fire have been caused by a Sender's interaction with Davies?" I ask. "Given the long intervals between them, maybe that's why."

"Could be," Robbie shrugs. "But there were Sender visits before the first fire. No one ever had problems before that time."

"So, it's either total coincidence, or we haven't found the connection yet," Meander mutters. He reads over his notes with a frown. "I don't understand what the fire has to do with Davies. I didn't smell it. He was never involved in fires when he was alive. He didn't die in a fire. It was eighty-two years after his death that the first fire took place." He looks up and fixes his gaze on me. "It doesn't make sense."

"Are you sure you didn't smell the smoke from the building itself, Cal?" Robbie asks. "That you don't just have a sensitive nose?"

I shake my head, frustrated confusion pinching at the base of my neck. "I smelled smoke from the ghost. When we were there, I thought it was just the building, but... I also heard static. Some static. And my head hurt and it was cold—"

"You saw something," Meander cuts in, sounding surer than I am. "I know what you're like around ghosts. But that's what makes even less sense... you were guided because of the fire. And I don't understand how that fits with Davies's presence."

"Or what murder Davies is still preoccupied with," I add. I drop the newspaper article on the bedspread and let my hands drop to my knees. "We don't have enough information."

Meander nods again. "We have to go back to the building."

Robbie stares between us, then looks at the pile of papers we've amassed before he sighs. "We'll go," he says at last. "But first, we're getting prepared."

37

ROBBIE MAKES US WAIT ANOTHER TWO DAYS BEFORE WE RETURN TO THE complex—both to ensure we're prepared, and to be positive that Natalie and Dr. Barkley are well out of the way. I'm not sure if Jess is waiting around to submit her report. But we don't see any of the trio again, which is probably for the best.

Meander and I spend the first day indoors, alternating between bouts of productivity and hours of lazy comfort to settle our minds and ease the tension that creeps up whenever we contemplate our incomplete case. On the second day, we walk through the town, circling the complex from the outside and traveling along the nearby streets. I'm used to visiting haunted locales at night, when the spirits are easier to see and the outside world is less likely to interfere. But even when we return from the complex, ready to brave its interior again, Robbie insists we wait until the third day's approach. He doesn't want to go to the building when it's dark, and I'm not comfortable enough to push against his caution. If we need to get out of there in a hurry, it'll be easier to make sense of our surroundings and find assistance during the day.

I intend to get a good night's rest. But just like the nights before our first attempt at this final task, knowing that we'll soon be back in the building makes it impossible for me to fall asleep. For a while, I lie as still as I can, listening to Meander's rifling pages and trying to convince my body to relax. But when the memory of clogging smoke causes an anxious squeeze to clamp across my chest, I sit up and crawl out of bed to grab my violin case.

Sitting at the edge of the mattress, I take out my instrument and hope no other guests will be overly annoyed by the sound of my playing. Drawing the bow across the strings, my notes are random and uneven until muscle memory draws me into a more tuneful rendition. My fingers slide into position with fluid ease, but my shoulders remain taut as I focus too hard on keeping my posture firm. The music, as always, softens the edge of my panic. But it doesn't erase it, and no matter how hard I work through my song, I still can't shake the twisting fear.

Not until Meander shifts close.

The sound of the bed sheets rustling brings me out of my spiraling daze, while the smell of sandalwood and the feel of warmth against my back makes me sigh in time with the reverberation of the strings. When his finger trails over the side of my hip, the touch so soft and tickling it's hard not to laugh, the hard tension finally loosens. My breath slows, and after a final, soothing verse, I bring my short serenade to a close.

"Want me to move?" Meander mumbles against my shoulder when the music stops.

"No," I say, leaning back against him.

His arm curls around my waist. "We'll be okay tomorrow," he says after a pause.

"You don't know that," I reply.

"No, I don't," he agrees. "But I'll try my damnedest to make sure we are. I might as well channel good thoughts now, yeah?"

I laugh. "Manifesting positive outcomes?"

"Mmm." He rubs his hand over my skin, his touch warm and grounding. "This is my future now. It probably wouldn't hurt to start calling on whatever powers I can for help."

I turn to see his face better as I smile. "I'm not sure half-assed calls into the abyss will do you much good."

"Of course not," he says. "I wouldn't want to rely on mystical powers, anyway. The only one I can rely on is myself." His hand runs down my arm and over the hand that grips the violin. "And you."

I think of the awful thoughts I had during our first trip to the complex—the ones about us burning alive. "So long as I'm not under the influence of a menacing ghost," I mutter.

Meander smiles. "*Even* when you're under the influence of a menacing ghost. I'm not daft, Cal. I can tell when you're not acting normal. Don't worry about setting me on fire. I won't let you. And I won't blame you afterwards for trying."

His eyes lock on mine, and when he leans in to kiss me, the worry of what the morning will bring melts away. It used to be that my violin was the only thing that could soothe me on particularly anxious days.

But now—when he's not the one *causing* the stress—Meander's ability to calm me is a wondrous sliver of magic stirred into the reality of our troublesome lives.

Magic I can't afford to think about too hard because, if I do, I'll be forced to remember how temporary it is. We should be able to be like this always, without planning for plane tickets and figuring out when we'll have a few moments alone, and without the fears of the dead looming behind the rising sun. Meander is not only the boy I'm in love with—he's also my best friend. We should be able to spend anytime we want together, for no reason at all other than that we want to.

I don't want this magic to be temporary. And although I know we'll make whatever the future holds work for us, I wish there was a way we didn't have to wait—a way we could make the magic and the reality one and the same.

For now, we take what sprinklings we can get, putting aside my violin and making the most of the night's remainder until we're finally tired enough to sleep. In the morning, we laze in bed with my music and his open book, until Fauré's "Nocturne No. 1" is interrupted by a call from Robbie telling us to meet him downstairs in twenty minutes. Only then do I drag myself out of bed, my limbs heavy with the weight of what I know we're going to do.

When we meet Robbie in the inn's dining room, he's already ordered us breakfast. I'm not hungry, but I force down some toast and juice while Meander picks at his plate, and Robbie himself eats only half of his sausage and eggs.

We don't have the use of an Oracle-hired car for our under-the-radar outing, so after breakfast we return to our rooms to change before calling a local taxi driver to bring us to the complex. The man laughs at our outfits, thinking we're off to some kind of party, and I'm glad Robbie is amicable enough to do the chatting until we're dropped at a street corner so we can walk the final block in peace.

"You two ready for this?" Robbie asks. He's sweating, his trench coat and the thick leather glove he wears on one hand as unfitted for this heat as my suit. My palms are slick, and my heart is racing. But I nod anyway, while Meander makes no response except to stare at the building up ahead.

We make it to the complex's main door. Then Meander halts and turns to me.

"Condition three?" he asks.

I smile and hold out my arms so he can pat down my pockets. I certainly don't remember grabbing any matches. But I'm experienced enough not to trust myself to remember everything I do while potentially under the guidance of a ghost.

"All clear," he says after his check is complete. Then he straightens my suit jacket and smirks, his eyes lingering on mine in a way that makes me wish this were another of those small moments where we're alone.

We're not alone, though. And Robbie's not one to make himself an awkward third wheel.

"Then let's get this started," he says. He cracks his knuckles and his neck, looking full-on steampunk in his Sender getup. Apparently, Robbie missed out on seeing this ghost by a mere couple of years. But he's as prepared as we are for this mission. He grabs the handle of the complex doors, glancing furtively around to make sure we're not being watched. Then he fishes a key from his pocket and slides it into the lock.

I take a deep breath and sneak Meander a final, quick kiss. "You stay out here," I tell him. "Robbie and I will work inside. He'll keep an eye on me."

"Don't go into the basement alone," Meanders says in a quiet voice. He's not happy about being left outside, though I know it has nothing to do with him feeling like I'm stealing his task. He doesn't want me near the entity without him. But it's safer this way. Robbie and I have work to do to make sure we don't get trapped a second time. And if I can manage to talk with the entity on my own, Meander might not have to suffer it's wrath again.

"Okay, let's go over the rules one more time," Robbie says as the two of us enter the building. He walks down the hall to the stairwell door that's still taped from our previous visit. Dropping a bag at his feet, he unzips it and digs through its contents before pulling out a chisel and hammer. "Rule number one is that we don't go inside any room with a functioning door." He moves to the stairwell, and I brace against the weight of the steel door while Robbie works at taking out its hinge pins.

"Any other locked spaces you can think of?" I ask. "Aside from the doors?"

"The basement looked pretty empty," he says. "It might be a good idea to work at clearing the boards from the windows—and seeing if there's a second emergency exit." He grunts, hammering the topmost pin until it flies out of the hinge. "I'll get the windows opened first, then look for another exit while you two work on the ghosts. And you?"

"I'll repeat any unsettling thoughts I have," I say with a grimace. "Even if they're about any of us."

"And Meander won't push his luck," Robbie adds.

"I'll do my best not to let him pass out again," I sigh.

I know it was our choice to come back here today. And I know it was our choice to tackle this spirit in the first place. But I still hate that Meander has to do this—and that the Oracle thinks it's reasonable to ask him to do it for the rest of his life. Or, not ask. Bargain. They held his potential homelessness over his head because they knew it was the only way he wouldn't refuse their offer. But damn it if I don't want to find whoever made that decision and throw a lit match at their feet.

My cheeks burn and my stomach plunges as I stare at the ground.

"The thoughts are starting," I say.

"What did you think?" Robbie asks.

I keep my eyes on the floor, mortified by the ideas that skitter through my head while I'm here. "That there are people I would like to set on fire." I glance up. "Not either of you," I add.

"Well, that's a relief," Robbie says. He gets the second pin out. "One more to go, and we can pull the door free from the hinges. Then we can head downstairs."

"Are you sure you'll be all right down there?" I ask.

Robbie nods and speaks through gritted teeth as he works the hammer. "I didn't see or feel anything last time we were here. If I start getting bad thoughts, I'll come up. I don't have anything to prove, and I'm not of any real use. I'm not going to risk it for a ghost I can't even see."

"If you could see it, would you stay?" I ask.

Robbie pauses, then returns to his work with a final strike of the hammer that loosens the pin. "Can't say. Probably. At least for a while. There. Now, help me move this thing."

Robbie knows what he's doing with the door. He makes quick work of pulling it away from the wall hinges, and the two of us lower the steel to the hall floor. We might trip on it if we're in a real hurry when we leave. But tripping would be better than having it come crashing down from wherever it's been propped against a wall.

When the door is laid flat, we go to the basement to unhinge the other door. I'm nervous about venturing back into the burned-out room. But while the temperature is cooler down here—which isn't uncommon even for non-haunted basement dwellings—the smoke smell is minor, and there is only the faintest impression of static in my head. I stare around the basement while holding the door, and when we get it out and laid down, I walk a circle around the main, open space. I peek into the room we were in before, the one with the splintered wood from where the other Senders broke the door down. When nothing makes itself known, I carefully approach the one remaining entryway.

I scrunch my face as I push the final door back, ready for an onslaught of sound or thought. The room inside is nearly identical to the one we were in on our last visit, a small square that is dark and, in this case, empty. The ghost is having an effect on my thinking. But I can't see it or even hear it anywhere near as much as I could before. My insides squirm, battling between the relief of not experiencing the dead a second time—and the disappointing dread of knowing exactly why I can't.

"We need Meander," I say with a heavy breath. "It's not strong enough without him."

We give it another minute, wandering around the basement and removing the final door before walking up to the third floor where other reports of ghostly activity have been. But I don't come into contact with the entity. Robbie and I make a quick effort at looking at the other three floors as well. Then we go back down to meet Meander outside of the lobby—where the sorrowful look on my face makes him grab my arms in worry.

"I'm fine," I assure him. "I didn't see anything."

"Nothing?" he asks. He keeps searching my face, and I smile.

"I only had one disturbing thought, and I let Robbie know. But I couldn't see it. It…" I sigh. "It needs you."

Meander's smile is sad as he understands the reason for my mood. "I guess I get to play the hero then, yeah?"

"Don't go throwing yourself to the wolves just yet," Robbie says. "There are boards on the outside of the windows. I'll start removing them. You two can go inside where it's cooler. But stay upstairs until I'm done. And yell if you need me."

"Don't get overheated out here," I say. I'd like to go with him, but the heat is doing nothing for my anxiety, and Meander's already been scorching out here while we unhinged the doors.

"I won't," Robbie says. "You two behave yourself. Don't do anything I wouldn't."

"Is that referring to the ghost?" Meander asks. "Or each other?"

Robbie grins. "Just try to stay out of trouble," he says before heading along the front of the building.

"That didn't really answer the question," Meander mutters. He gives me a sideways glance, and I grab his hand as we venture back inside.

AS SOON AS WE'RE IN THE LOBBY, MY GAZE DRIFTS DOWN THE HALL. "WE took down three doors," I say. "That one. And the two in the basement."

Meander grabs my hand with more force than is probably necessary. "That's good," he says, his voice careful and measured. "That's what we planned."

"I know," I say. I force my eyes away from the stairwell. "How long do you think Robbie will take?"

"Not very," Meander says. He holds my gaze. "We'll stay here and wait for him."

I nod, but my head turns back to the hallway as something cracks beneath our feet. "Robbie?" I ask.

"Probably," Meander says.

"Maybe we should check it out," I suggest. "To be sure."

"Cal." Meander tugs my hand, but then the crack sounds again, and he gasps with an intake of painful breath. I look away from the hall and study his face, my nerves tingling.

"It knows you're here, doesn't it?" I ask. "Even from up here, you're making it stronger." Meander nods, and I glance at the building's main doors. "So, we go outside and get your breath back. Or we go downstairs and try to deal with this as soon as possible."

Meander squeezes his eyes against the pain, but he doesn't move. "If I take a break, it will only be worse when I get back in here," he says.

"Then we should go downstairs," I reply. "And deal with it now."

"We're supposed to wait for Robbie," Meander says as he opens his eyes.

"He's right outside the windows," I reason. "If we need him, we'll shout."

Even as I speak, I know my words are stupid. This isn't me—it's the ghost, trying to get me downstairs. But I can't fight it because right now, it makes too much sense. Of course we should wait for Robbie. But that only delays the inevitable. Robbie's presence is an extra precaution, but it does not serve any practical purpose for dealing with Davies. Whether our lead is outside the windows or inside with us doesn't make much of a difference. And Meander's right. The longer we tease ourselves with the pain and the thoughts, the worse they are going to become.

My feet start moving while I'm still thinking through the options, trying to convince myself not to give in to the entity's pull. But Meander doesn't stop me. Likely because he's in too much pain to reason clearly himself. Possibly because he also recognizes that there's no real reason for us to be putting this off any longer.

We head down the stairs, temperature plummeting as my stomach twists with knots of sparking pain. The static begins once we step over the door that's been laid on the ground, and I work hard to keep myself in the main basement room. The one door has been smashed from our last visit, and the other's been removed. But I can't see beyond the doorways, and I don't want to get lost in the darkness of the enclosed spaces.

"It's here," Meander rasps. I slide my arm around his waist so he can lean on me. "But it's hiding."

"It won't be for long," I say. "You're too incredible. It won't be able to resist."

Meander lets out a scraped breath of laughter. "That's one way to phrase it."

I smile, making myself look at him and not at the far doorway. The entity is not just hiding—it's trying to lure us deeper into the basement to get us under its control. But we're not so gullible as it seems to believe, and despite being under its influence, I have no intention of letting it trap us again. I focus my attention on Meander, determined not to give into any temptation to explore the basement. When I start to think it might be wise to look for the entity in the back room, I swallow the smoking inclination and bring Meander close to my side. And when my brain starts to slip again—when I begin to eagerly wonder what's beyond the doorways, waiting in the dark—I bring him in for a kiss. He doesn't have much breath. But he knows what I'm doing, and he grips my shirt, kissing me back until the ghost gets its revenge as it finally leaves the room to join us by the stairs.

We groan in unison, both of us flinching apart as the ghost closes in. Static flares in my head, but then it fades again, cutting in and out like it did on our last visit. Meander stumbles, and I catch him, helping him to the wall next to the stairwell. He leans against it, eyes closed as he tries to grab onto any new information the spirit might give.

"Gareth Davies." I say the entity's name out loud, hoping it will have some kind of effect. But it doesn't, at least not to me. My head does not cloud with more static or sound, and I can't get any sense of the stench of blood. But Meander gasps again, scarf-wrapped wrists pressed into his eyes as he tries to concentrate.

"What do you want?" I ask. I may not be getting anything from Davies, but Meander is, which at least confirms the ghost's identity. "Why are you still here?" I refuse to ask how we can help him, because I don't want to aid in his desires. This spirit has taken lives. I'm not going to pander to it just because it's dead.

"He's angry," Meander says.

"We already knew that," I reply.

"I know," Meander bites out. "There's nothing else. Just… anger." He winces and wheezes, while somewhere in the back of the basement, something clatters, bouncing against the concrete floor.

"You need to get out," I say, hoping whatever is making the noise isn't especially pointy or sharp. "I'll stay for a while."

"You can't stay alone," Meander says.

He's wrong, though. *He* can't stay alone, but I was fine when I was here without him. We haven't gotten any new information on this short visit. But if I stay a little longer, I might get somewhere with the entity before its strength totally disappears after Meander departs.

"Robbie will be back soon," I reason. Even now, I can hear our lead working on the boards. As soon as they're done, he'll be coming inside to join us.

And if we're lucky, he'll bring along some matches.

I groan. "Just make sure he doesn't have anything that could strike a flame," I say.

Meander opens his eyes, the whites so bloodshot they look fully red. He stares at the entity, eyes trained on a part of the mass I can't even make out. "What does the fire have to do with anything?" he asks it. "What the hell does that have to do with you?"

Static flares and, with it, I get my first tinny slice of music. A soft, hollow sound in a single, grotesquely soothing note. I grip my head, staring at the mass and seeing the briefest flash of features come into formation. A wide face, protruding forehead, crooked nose. Then it disappears, and I look back as Meander pushes off the wall.

"I have to go," he coughs. He tugs my arm, but I stay rooted.

"Go," I tell him. "Get Robbie and bring him back. I'm fine."

"Cal."

I turn to him, shoving his shoulder towards the stairwell. "I don't want you passing out," I say. "Go. I'll distract him so he can't follow you."

Meander hovers in the doorway until I press a kiss to his lips and shove him more forcefully towards the stairs. His expression is hurt as he stumbles into the hallway, and my stomach curdles with it. But it's not just the pull of guided curiosity keeping me here. The last time we tried to leave, Davies tried to stop us. I don't want Meander getting trapped again. If I keep the ghost busy, he can get outside where it's safe. And when he's gone, the ghost will lose its power—and its hold on my mind.

I hope.

Meander climbs the first couple of steps before he makes a dizzy sway to one side. I want to run after him, but if I do the ghost will follow with enough force to make Meander pass out. So instead of heading back to the stairs, I venture farther into the basement, trying to lure the ghost away from where Meander grips the railing.

"Gareth!" I call, waving my arms like an idiot as I act as live bait. "I know how much you like fire. Want to see what I've got in my pocket?"

I have nothing in my pocket, thankfully. But the ghost does not know that. I head into the basement, feeling a pinch of relief when the mass follows me. I back up as far as I can, listening to the sound of Robbie prying boards nearby and trying to get a glance behind the ghost to make sure Meander's out of harm's away.

The mass follows halfway into the basement before it stops. Static crackles, and the smoke stretches and pulls. The empty spots seem to break off of the mist, and soon the missing pieces of the ghost start to cloud and fill. Static streams steadily into my head, and I cry out at its intensity as Gareth's face appears clearly in my view.

I spend a few, painful seconds staring at the ghost. Then a sound from the stairs rings in my ears, and I pry my gaze from Davies to see that Meander has not made it outside. I've effectively distracted the spirit, but the intense way he stares at something close to him—while his face starts to change hues as it loses all air—makes it obvious that whatever I thought would happen hasn't worked.

"Shit," I mumble. Then I twist my head and cup my hands around my mouth. "Robbie!"

"You two are in the basement, aren't you?" Robbie says from somewhere not too far away. "I'm coming, hold on!"

I push off the wall and run across the room, veering around the mass but stumbling when something rolls under my foot. Crashing to the floor, I bite back a cry of pain and look at the hinge pin that's been pulled free of the door. The door itself is rattling, and the other pins are rolling around the concrete. I think about how easily one of them could impale someone. I think about how easy the wood door would be to burn. Then I gag and crawl the rest of the way to the stairwell.

Robbie runs in from the main floor, thudding down the steps to get Meander. We reach him at the same time, both of us grabbing hold as he clings to half-consciousness. I feel a twinge of desire to turn around and go back to the basement. But I push it away as we start up the stairs.

"It's following," Meander whispers as we round the main floor landing. I glance back over my shoulder and see nothing trailing us. Which means I'm unprepared for the sudden blast of cold and jerk of Meander's body, the force of it like something has hit him from behind. We all stumble forward, and Robbie staggers back before falling and landing hard on the edge of the dismantled steel door.

Our lead lets out a long string of curses, but he forces himself up and, pale-faced with pain, holds one arm against his chest while he helps me to drag Meander over the door. Once we're in the hall, Meander takes a slightly bigger, rasping breath, and he clings to me as we hurry back out into the morning heat.

The sun is beating down so hard I'm washed with dizziness as soon as we're outside. I lean against the stone wall, and Meander falls against my side until we slump together in a crumpled heap.

"Y'all were supposed to stay upstairs," Robbie says. His voice sounds weird, soft and vacant. I swallow hard and try to calm my raging heart, then look up at him—and find a new source of concern.

"Robbie, are you okay?" I ask.

Our lead nods, then presses his mouth tight and turns it into a shake of his head. He holds out the arm that landed against the door and smiles. "It's probably broken," he says. Then he staggers back onto a patch of overgrown weeds.

This time, he's the one who passes out.

39

WE GET ROBBIE TO THE NEAREST HOSPITAL, WHERE WE DISCOVER THAT the fracture in his arm is not bad. The doctor tells us the heat was as much to blame for him passing out as the pain, and we're given a long lecture on the many problems with filming amateur movies in abandoned buildings without permission—which must have been what Robbie gave as our excuse for being where we were, dressed as we are.

We suffer through the doctor's admonishment before we're allowed to see Robbie. As soon as we get in the room, he warns us that the Oracle will be alerted to what's been going on.

"Go back to the inn and pretend you weren't a part of anything," he says. "It probably won't work. But it might ease their anger."

"What about you?" I ask.

He waves his uninjured hand. "You know what it's like. Be a bystander, get a broken arm. Pretty typical stuff."

I let out a breath of laughter, rubbing my arm where it was broken two summers ago.

"They're going to make us leave here, aren't they?" Meander asks.

Robbie nods. "We'll all be heading back to Chile in a day or two. You tried. No one's gonna fault you because it didn't work out."

Meander's not satisfied with Robbie's response. His mood is stony as I talk with Robbie for a few more minutes before our lead urges us to get on our way. We're silent as we head back outside to wait for the car that's been called to drive us to the inn. Once we're beyond the sliding entrance doors, however, Meander crosses his arms with a huff.

"I can't believe they're going to make us give up," he mutters. He paces back and forth between two bricked planters, while I sit on the edge of one.

"Did you get anything new?" I ask, my voice weary with resignation. We didn't have time to discuss our second failed attempt while we were rushing Robbie to the hospital. Now, it looks like debriefing won't matter, anyway. We didn't release the spirit. And there's no way the Oracle's going to sit idly by while we make yet another go.

Meander shakes his head. "No, nothing. Just anger. Rage that he was betrayed by someone he thought was a friend."

"What happened on the stairs?" I ask. I think over the event again, trying to pick up on anything I missed. "It felt like you got hit or something."

"I did," he says. "Davies was following us, remember?"

My foot taps against the side of the planter. "That's what you said. But I didn't see anything."

Meander pauses in his pacing to look at me. "But you saw something downstairs."

"Yes," I say. "I was starting to get a clear look at the end. I almost heard music too. But then…" I throw up my arms, my irritation at the heat, the ghost, and this whole miserable day making my words come out grouchier than I intend. "You didn't go upstairs like you were supposed to."

"Like *I* was supposed to?" Meander steps closer to me, his eyes flashing. "You weren't supposed to stay in the basement by yourself."

"I was trying to help you," I say. "You needed to get out. I was distracting the spirit so you could."

"It was a stupid plan," he mutters.

"At least I was trying!" I stand up, annoyed by his brooding and fed up with everything else. "I thought it was the best thing to do. I'm sorry it didn't work, but maybe it would have if you'd listened to me the first time and left before I had to call Robbie for help!"

"Abandoned you in the basement while that thing followed me upstairs?" he asks. "Brilliant plan, that."

"It wasn't following you upstairs," I say. "It was with me in the basement. I told you. I was finally starting to get a clearer look at Davies before he decided to cling to you."

Meander pauses again, the anger fading from his voice as his expression shifts into one of contemplation. "I was getting a clearer look too, at the end." He shakes curls from his eyes as he takes another step towards me. "What'd he look like, Cal?"

"Wide face. Big forehead," I start. "Uh, his nose

was… crooked, and—what?"

Meander stares at me, his brows furrowed and a perplexed expression in his eyes. "That's not what he looks like," he says after a pause.

My eyes narrow, and I point a finger accusingly in his direction. "I *saw* him, Meander. Don't you think—"

"I know you saw him," he says, cutting me off. He puts a hand on my arm and fishes his phone from his pocket. Turning it on, he waits for it to load before pulling up his saved web searches. Most of the articles we found at the library were about the prison. But he has one bookmarked newspaper clipping about Gareth Davies himself.

He opens the article and scrolls to a point midway down the page. Then he holds his phone up for me to see.

"This is what he looks like," he says.

I stare at the grainy photo I hadn't paid much attention to before. The man in the photo has a skinny face, long neck, beady eyes and a pointed nose. It's a man I immediately know is not the one I saw in the basement.

"So… it's not Gareth Davies at the complex?" I ask.

"It *is*," Meander says. I blink away from the phone to meet his widened eyes as he clutches the phone tighter. "The man I saw. The man who attacked us on the stairs. This is him, Cal."

"But then…" I trail off, remembering the way the entity stretched and pulled when Meander and I were in different parts of the basement. One of us smelled blood, the other smoke, and neither of us could get a clear view of the spirit—not until we were on opposite sides of the room.

Not until the entity began to separate.

"Jekyll and Hyde," I breathe. "Two personalities."

"It's two ghosts." Meander nods. "That must be why it was so hard to understand. Two ghosts, muddled together until neither of them could be comprehended by outsiders—so entwined they appear as something no one can explain."

"So Gareth Davies is one of the ghosts, for sure," I say.

"Yes," Meander says. "I finally got a look at him. He's there, all right. But that leaves the question of who the other ghost is."

I look at the picture of Davies on Meander's phone, and I think about what I smelled in the building. What I *thought* in the building.

"Fire," I say, my mouth dry as the understanding comes. "The first fire in nineteen eighty-three. That created the second ghost."

"Two people died in that fire," Meander says. "It's not the daughter who's still around, so that must mean—"

"Malcolm Priddy," I finish. I look away from the phone and focus on Meander's eyes as both of us reel with the revelation we've just uncovered. For a long moment, neither of us speaks. Then I smile and shove his shoulder. "And you thought my plan didn't work."

Meander laughs. "I'm sorry I doubted your genius." He kicks my foot, his expression softening. "I'm sorry I snapped at you too."

"It's fine," I say. "I snapped too. And I *did* leave you to get attacked by a ghost." I shrug my shoulder and eye him suggestively. "I suppose we can make it up to each other later."

He smirks, while behind us the taxi arrives to take us back to the inn.

"We will *definitely* make it up to each other later," he says with a sigh. "But first, we've got a lot of work to do before the Oracle shuts us down."

WE MAKE IT BACK TO THE INN AND DASH AROUND OUR ROOM, STUFFING whatever can fit into our backpacks before sneaking out a side exit and returning to the library. The destination is a gamble—if the Oracle comes to pick us up and finds we're missing, the library might well make the list of possible locations to find us. But there's a decent chance they'll stake out in front of the complex in case we venture back there instead. I don't know what we're going to do once we figure out this entity's secret. But before we can even discuss our next steps, we need access to information we can't easily get anywhere else.

When we're back in the library, we each take a topic to research. Meander looks for more articles about the fire, while I search for records on Malcolm Priddy. For a long time, I don't come across anything worthwhile. The name is not unique enough for the area we're in to warrant an easy discovery. But after a lot of random search strings, I manage to find an old photo someone has uploaded from nineteen seventy-nine. The picture is of a group of teens eating fries out of paper cones on a stone wall before a school. Scanning the photo, it doesn't take long to recognize the facial features I saw impressions of at the complex. When I read the caption posted along with the picture, I notice Malcolm's been referred to as "Priddy Boy".

The new name helps my search efforts, and after printing a copy of the photo to keep in front of me, I find a few old article snippets about a local gang—probably the guys from the photo—which included Malcolm "Priddy Boy" Priddy. I write down the names of the papers and the dates of the articles. Then I kick Meander out of his seat so I can take over using the microfilm reader to find the original text.

"Have you found anything more about the fire?" I ask as I load my first reel.

Meander shakes his head. "Only two mentions that I can find. One the article we already read. The other's an interview with WPC Gable, one of the first responders at the scene."

"What does WPC stand for?" I ask.

"Woman Police Constable," Meander explains. "Used to be what they called female officers."

"Well, maybe we can find more about Gable," I say with a shrug. "I don't know what else to look for."

Meander nods, watching as I scroll through the first pages of a reel before taking my place at the table where I've set up my laptop. We spend another two hours combing through reels and online searches in an effort to track down WPC Gable or get more information on "Priddy Boy". My eyes hurt from staring at screens, and the chair in front of the microfilm reader is uncomfortably hard. At least I changed into jeans and a t-shirt while we were back at the inn, although I wish I'd been smarter and planned ahead for the possibility of a warmer climate for this summer's final task. Better clothing aside, who knows how much further Meander and I could have gotten in our research if we'd taken the time to properly plan this venture out. Then again, we haven't found anything new on Gareth Davies, which means weeks of research may not have amounted to much. Even with two spirits instead of one, we still have no idea what the ghosts need to move on.

I've started going through random newspaper reels, cheek in hand as I scroll mindlessly through the pages, when a short article catches my eye. Written in nineteen eighty-one—two years before the fire at the complex—the article details an arson attempt at a local school. The text doesn't mention any names connected with the case. But the building pictured is the same one from the '79 photograph with Malcolm Priddy.

"Meander," I call, rousing him from his own vacant searching. He looks up from his book—one I never even saw him retrieve—and closes it before he comes back to the microfilm reader.

"You find something?" he asks. He sounds tired, and I know how he feels. I'd love to go back to the inn and nap away the rest of the afternoon.

"Not really," I admit. I find the picture of Malcolm and his friends sitting outside of the school. "Just this. I'm pretty sure Malcolm Priddy attended this school at, or around, the time there was an arson attempt on it. They could be totally unconnected, but…"

"If you think it's important enough to call me over, I'm guessing this isn't a coincidence," Meander says with a glance at me. "We wondered how the ghost managed to set the fire. What if Davies *didn't* set it?"

I nod. "Whoever attempted to burn down the school may have attempted to burn down the complex," I say as I shift to face him. "And it wouldn't have been an accident. Malcolm was involved in some sort of gang, just like Davies. Malcolm and his daughter died in that fire. Since I'm the one who sees him, it means he wasn't just killed by the flames. He was murdered."

"Maybe he was betrayed by a friend too," Meander says as he studies the picture. "Someone from the gang. Whatever the case, if we find the arsonist, we find the killer." He crosses his arms over his chest and tucks a fist under his chin. "Do you think we need to find out who set the fire, though? If his daughter died, maybe that's got something to do with Priddy's sticking around."

"Could be," I say. "But…" I think about being in the building, the press I felt to go to the basement and the thoughts I had to accompany it. "He wants revenge," I say. "Or something like it. He… I kept thinking of burning the place down. He doesn't want to see his daughter again. He wants to do what was done to him."

I lean back in the chair, staring at the photograph and wondering which one of the long-ago, smiling faces belongs to a murderer. I can't imagine being betrayed in such a horrific way by someone I considered a friend. But then I *do* imagine it, playing through horrendous scenarios until the impression of being engulfed by flame is so intense I clench my fists and roll my shoulders, glancing at our study table as I force my mind to leave the burning thoughts behind.

"Did you find anything?" I ask, blinking away the brightness of the fire as I nod to the book laid out next to my laptop.

Meander walks back to the table and grabs the book. "Local history," he says. "Found WPC Gable. Evidently, she was quite the controversial constable. She had radical beliefs—that by sweeping all crimes under the rug, it would eliminate significant portions of future crimes of the same sort."

"How did she figure that?" I ask.

"Her ideas made sense, sort of," Meander says as he flips through the pages. "She thought that a big part of the problem with crime was the "celebrity status" criminals would get. You know, serial killers who get *more* famous when they're caught and on trial. She thought that, instead of drawing attention to the crimes, the criminal activity should be left out of the news and away from public knowledge. That way, aspiring criminals wouldn't see the appeal of committing a crime just to gain fame and glory."

"That sounds reasonable," I say. "So where does the controversy come in?"

"Eventually she was investigated for falsifying incident reports," he says. "This book doesn't detail much. From what I can gather, she lied about some crimes, stating that they weren't crimes at all. Trying to downplay them to the point of calling them accidents, instead of putting the community on high alert for suspicious activity."

"Huh." I turn back to the newsreel, my finger hovering over the mouse. "Do you think that downplaying might have included an *accidental* fire?"

Meander lets out a long breath. "That would make sense, wouldn't it? Intentional fire, two murders, and she plays it off like the wiring's to blame."

"Do you think she knew who did it?" I ask.

"Now that's a good question." He taps his fingers against the book. "She was fairly young at the time. Could be she's still alive."

I raise an eyebrow. "Living here?"

"Why not?" He shrugs. "Might be worth a look."

We do look, finding her profile online and searching a directory to figure out her phone number. Meander uses his cell phone to call it, but when there's no answer, I search in vain for an address that isn't listed.

"The number is local," Meander says. "She's here. And we need to talk to her."

"She might not want to talk to us," I say. "In fact, I'm almost positive she won't. But if we can't find her address, we're out of luck either way."

Meander doesn't respond. Instead, he stares at something across the library. For a moment, I think he's just lost in thought. But when he continues to stare, I follow his gaze to the library's circulation desk. A middle-aged woman is helping someone to pay a fine on their account. I watch him watching her and suspect he's going to suggest asking if she knows who Gable is. But as it turns out, he has a much riskier plan.

"Library systems store patron information," he says when he finally turns away from the desk. "Names, phone numbers, emails—addresses."

"You cannot look her up in the library's directory," I say. "That is almost assuredly illegal." He opens his mouth, and I stand to clap a hand over it. "And if you say the words 'horrible and stupid' as a means to convince me, I'm going to steal all your books and blast Rose's club mixes every time you're trying to sleep from now until… ever."

He smirks under my hand, and I drop it to give him a menacing stare.

"Good to know where your moral line rests," he says. "Trespassing and destroying private property? No bother. Looking up someone's library record? That's too far."

I sigh, shoulders slumping in exaggerated despondency. "How long will we be using that treehouse as a gauge for our criminal acts?"

Meander considers it. "Until we do something more illegal?"

I groan and look again at the circulation desk. "Fine. Let's engage in further criminal activity so we can get back to investigating someone *else's* criminal activity. How are we going to distract her?"

"*You'll* distract her," Meander clarifies. "I'll look up Gable."

"All right," I say, "how am *I* going to distract her?"

"Just be your attractive, charming self," he says with a shrug. "And maybe play up your idiot side a bit."

I tilt my head to one side and stare at him. "Did you just compliment *and* insult me in one go?"

Meander laughs, then leans into my side. "You're perfect," he whispers. He plants a soft kiss to the edge of my ear. Then he gives my back a push. "Now go be perfect over there."

His smile is all too sweet as he watches me off, and despite my intention to be indignant, by the time I reach the circulation desk, I'm smiling too.

I wait my turn, then ask the lady behind the desk

if she can help me find something in the book stacks. She stays seated while she asks what I'm looking for, so I start babbling on about a non-existent school project on the architectural history of the area. The lady looks at me like I am, in fact, a bit of an idiot, probably because I don't actually know how the school system works in Wales and I have no idea what kind of architectural history might be required learning for its students. But eventually she gets up to help me, and we venture far enough into the stacks I can successfully angle her away from the desk while I ask after information on the prison that once stood where the abandoned complex is now.

The lady doesn't know anything about the prison or the apartments. But we rifle through a few books, and by the time she offers to do some computer searching instead, Meander has already slipped away from the desk. He gives me a subtle wave, and I thank the lady for her time after declining any more assistance. Then we gather our things and leave the library before any stray patrons inform her of what Meander did while she was away from the desk.

"I can't believe that worked," I say as we casually cross the street then speed our walk until we've disappeared around a corner. "How did you even know how to do that?"

Meander gives me an embarrassed shrug. "Years ago, I nicked a user manual from a library desk," he mumbles. "I used to spend my days in the safe branches reading. But after I got banned, they started watching for me. One time, they told me I had to leave and warned me that the next time they saw me they'd call the police. I was pissed they weren't going to let me stay, and when

I saw the user manual I knew it wouldn't set the gates off. So, I took it. Which was stupid, but..." He smirks. "Came in useful, at least. I think most systems probably function more or less the same—at least when you're trying to look up patron info."

"I guess that's one good thing about you moving to London," I say, trying not to sound mopey. "New library system. You won't be banned there."

Meander smiles. "I suppose not. So long as I don't have any *incidents*."

My heart aches for the *incidents* he's been blamed for in the past, and I'm weirdly glad to know that over the years he's found small ways to get his revenge. The thought of him moving to London makes me unhappy. But I'm sure the city has a lot of library branches. Hopefully he'll be able to find one to safely visit, without getting banned from all the others.

Meander gives me a sideways glance as he holds up the paper. "Now all we need to do is convince this woman to confess to withholding criminal activity, while divulging the truth about who set the fire in eighty-three," he says.

I try to push away my worrisome thoughts with a laugh. "Shouldn't be a problem. How do we get there?"

I use my phone to figure out that the address is about a twenty-minute walk from our current location. It's not a pleasant stroll in the muggy heat, but it's a necessary discomfort if we want to stay inconspicuous. We follow the map on my phone, stopping once at a corner shop to grab bottles of water and bags of chips. Then we wind through side streets, passing rows of narrow houses and climbing a hill so steep I'm panting by the time we crest it. At the top, we stop under the shade of a tree for a few minutes' reprieve from the sun. Then we force ourselves to continue on.

By the time we reach Gable's house, my face is slick with sweat, and I can feel my hair starting to droop. Meander's not faring any better, his cheeks flushed bright pink and his curls plastered to his face, and I'm sure together we make a rather sorry sight. I don't want this lady's first impression of us to be a bad one. So, since our looks are not currently going to be a strong point in our favor, I do my best to channel all the natural charm and innocent idiocy I can before pressing the bell.

"We shouldn't have eaten those crisps," Meander complains as he rests against the bricked alcove next to the door.

"If you're going to puke, do it in the bushes," I say. "She might not be too happy if you vomit all over her doorstep."

He starts to laugh but cuts the noise short when the door swings open. Pushing off our respective walls, we face the house as an elderly woman surveys us from inside.

"Can I help you?" she asks. She doesn't look wary, which is good. But she holds herself half-way protected by the door, ready to shut it at any moment should she decide we're a threat—or a waste of her time.

"We're looking for Sian Gable," Meander says.

"You've found her," the woman replies. "What can I do for you?"

"This is going to sound ridiculous," Meander says. "But we need to know who set fire to the complex off Station Road. The fire in nineteen eighty-three."

My eyes go wide, but I quickly try to reel the

panicked look back into a more neutral expression. I expected we'd take a slow approach to wheedling information out of this lady. But Meander's apparently not as patient as I am.

"That fire was an accident," Sian says, but the slow drawl of her words—and the fact she seems to know exactly what we're referring to—gives her away.

"No, it wasn't," I say, a note of earnest pleading in my tone. "And it's incredibly important you tell us the truth."

"I'm retired from the force," she says. "If you want to look into old records—"

"We want you to tell us who killed Malcolm Priddy and his daughter," Meander cuts in. The woman's sharp gaze turns on him, and he gives her a defiant stare in return. "Because someone is still killing people at that building. And we need it to stop."

I'm hot, sick, and exhausted from the efforts of today. But I beam at the fierce way Meander delivers his message. He's pissed off and as tired as I am. But he's not giving up on this case, and I'm proud of his stubborn determination to end the entity's deadly reign.

Sian stares at Meander for a long moment before she sighs. Then she steps back and sweeps her arm out.

"I think you'd better come inside."

41

I'M NOT EXACTLY COMFORTABLE GOING INTO A STRANGER'S HOME WHEN no one even knows where the hell we are. But the lady is old, and she doesn't look particularly menacing. Plus, the house is blessedly cool. Once we're inside, she offers us water to gulp down while sitting at her kitchen table, and I appease myself with the knowledge that she's the one taking the greater risk.

We finish our water. Then former WPC Gable flicks on her kettle and plops a few tea bags in a brown porcelain pot. The movement is so automatic, and so unnecessary given our intrusion and the sweltering mugginess outside, that I can't help the laugh I try to keep hidden behind my cup. Meander smirks at my amusement, but he keeps a furtive eye on the lady while she sets out cups and pours the boiling water—probably trying to ensure she doesn't slip something into our drinks.

"You want to know who set fire to that complex,"

Sian says once she's left the pot to steep. She sits at the kitchen table and studies us each in turn. "Who are you? You're not from the area."

"No," Meander says. "We're not."

He doesn't elaborate further, so I pick up the subject in his place. "We're studying the complex," I say. "We're part of a… team. That looks into, uh, unsolved mysteries. Sort of."

"Paranormal mysteries?" she asks, so suddenly it catches us both off guard. My eyes snap to her, and I'm guessing Meander's do as well. She smiles, nodding to herself before she stands. "I've seen folks like you before. A long time ago, mind you."

"What do you mean, 'folks like us'?" Meander asks.

"Strange looking people," Sian says. I frown at the implication that we're inherently strange looking, but when I catch sight of the scar on Meander's jaw, I'm reminded that we are. Perhaps individually we're not all that unusual. But put two of us together, and the oddities that mark us become more apparent.

"Strange," Meander echoes, while Sian nods.

"And nosy," the old woman adds. She brings the teapot to the table, then fetches the mugs and a tin of cookies. I'm torn between gratefulness at her cozy show of friendship, and wariness for why it is she's being so kindly when she's clearly put-off by our appearance here. But Meander doesn't share my qualms. He grabs the mugs and pours out three cups without waiting for an invitation, and since I know he's been keeping a careful eye, I trust his judgement that nothing here is amiss.

"Do you know what those people wanted?" I ask as I watch him pour.

"They had questions," Sian says. "Similar to yours. Wanting to know about any odd sightings or experiences people claimed to have noticed in the flats. After the fire, they bothered me to no end, wondering if there was anything unusual about the way the blaze began."

"And was there?" Meander asks.

Sian sits, placing a little milk jug and a sugar pot on the table. She takes one of the mugs and drops in two sugar cubes for herself.

"Nothing paranormal," she says in a careful voice. "The fire was caused by human hands."

"And it was set intentionally," I say.

"Yes," Sian agrees. I'm surprised she doesn't try to deny it, although I suppose that would be pointless now.

Meander prepares my tea and slides it over. I'm still too hot to drink a full cup of steaming liquid, so I let it sit on the table in front of me.

"Who set it?" I ask. "That's all we want to know."

"Unless you're aching to tell us everything about the case," Meander adds.

Sian smiles. Then she blows on her tea and takes a small sip before setting it on the table. "You already know who the culprit is," she says.

My brows knit together. "I'm fairly sure we don't," I say. "We wouldn't be pestering you if we did."

"You have his name, at any rate," she amends.

"You said it wasn't paranormal," I say. "So, it can't have been Gareth Davies."

Sian looks confused by the name for a moment, before something registers, and she shakes her head. "No. The fire was not set by a dead man. It was set by a young one." She lets out a long breath. "With a daughter."

Meander pauses with his mug halfway to his mouth. "Priddy?" he asks.

Sian nods. "Malcolm Priddy was a thorn in my side for years," she admits. "He had a fondness for arson. He tried to burn down his school. He tried to burn down the police headquarters. He successfully burned two abandoned houses and one shop with the shopkeeper still inside."

"But… if he'd done all that, why wasn't he in jail?" I ask.

"We couldn't prove anything," she says. "Not until the shop. We kept it out of the papers and arrested him quietly. But he slipped from us on a technicality. He was thrilled that he got free, but he was unhappy when he realized that no one knew what he'd done. He wanted to be infamous. He'd been playing up his crimes to his friends, but no one believed he'd killed the shopkeeper. The papers said it was an accident, you see. Everyone thought Priddy was making it up."

"But why would he set his own home on fire?" I ask. "His daughter was there."

Sian grips her mug of tea so tight I'm sure it must burn her fingers. "His girlfriend left him. I don't know the full story, but I suspect she got tired of his lies. Thought he'd been away with some other girl or getting into some other kind of trouble while he was under arrest. She left the little girl with him, which was a mistake. I don't think Mr. Priddy was ever very fatherly. And he was in a dark place after the shop fire. No girlfriend. No fame. No one to believe him. He must have got it into his head that if he killed the whole building, everyone would have to know the truth."

"But how do you actually know it was him?" Meander asks. "Not someone else?"

"He told us," Sian says. She smiles bitterly. "He rang up the station and told us what he'd done. He was so calm. Even while we could hear…" She pauses, closing her eyes and swallowing before she continues. "We could hear his daughter screaming. We got over as fast as we could. But it was too late for them. Everyone else got out in time. But Priddy barricaded his flat. We couldn't—it took too long to break in."

"So, he wanted fame, but in the end you still didn't give it to him," I say. My throat is thick, and the very sight of the hot tea makes it feel raw, like it's been… like it's been burned. I never questioned that Priddy was the victim of the crime. I'm used to seeing murder victims. I've seen a murder witness and an investigator as well. But I've never interacted with an actual murderer before.

Under the table, Meander rubs my knee. I slide a hand down and grip his fingers as Sian continues her story.

"I would not give him the satisfaction," she says. "Not after what he did to that little girl. He deserved to be forgotten. Which is exactly what has happened. I know there are some who disagreed with my actions while in the force. But I stand by what I did. Malcolm Priddy should not be remembered."

"Tell that to Malcolm Priddy," Meander says.

"Malcolm Priddy is dead," Sian replies.

"Again—tell that to him."

The woman looks Meander over, then slides her eyes to me. I have no idea how much Sian knows about the Oracle, if she knows anything at all. But after a long moment, she nods.

"Finish your tea," she says. "Then I'll ask you to leave. You have the information you came for. Do with it what you—what you can, to set things right. But I ask you not to betray what legacy I tried to create. Don't let Priddy become a household name."

"We won't," I tell her. "You can be assured of that."

I force down half the tea out of politeness, then Meander and I thank Sian for her help. She sees us to the hallway, talking to Meander about the best way to get back to the complex from where we are. While they're talking, my eyes alight on the sideboard table in the narrow hall. In the middle of the table is a bowl. And in the bowl is a set of matches.

While Sian opens the door, my hand drops into the bowl and grabs hold of the matches. Guilt rushes through me as I slide the packet into my pocket, then let my arm hang loose at my side. I'm not under the spirit's guidance right now, and I know resisting the sticks will be hard once I am. But while Meander sees the spirit of Gareth Davies, for some reason Malcolm Priddy has been left to me. The entity has to be separated if we're ever going to get anywhere with either ghost, but Priddy is too weak without Meander—without Davies—to bolster him. The murderer and I have some sort of connection. But if I want to get him alone, away from Davies while retaining enough strength to entertain my presence, I'll need to entice him.

And this is just the way to do it.

42

"OKAY, SO HOW DO WE TACKLE THIS?"

As we walk back down the hill, the scorching sun giving way to an evening sky that's quickly filling in with dark, heavy clouds, I wipe my forehead and regret every sip of tea I took in Sian Gable's kitchen. My stomach is full, my nerves are shot, and my body is ready to collapse from heat, tension—and fear for what I suspect is coming next.

"The Oracle may or may not be on our trail," Meander relates. "Robbie's in the hospital, and we made an agreement not to go to the complex by ourselves."

"Do you think the Oracle will be waiting?" I ask. "At the apartments?"

"If they know we've gone rogue again, then yes," Meander says. "They'll expect us to make another attempt."

"Right." I hitch my backpack further up one

shoulder. "So, what are we going to do?"

"We have new information," Meander says. "We know the entity is two spirits."

I nod. "Gareth Davies who is angry about being betrayed. And Malcolm Priddy, who killed…" I pause, gathering the nerve to think about the crime. "Who killed his daughter and himself in an effort to be famous."

"What we don't have," Meander says, "is a reasonable idea of what the spirits need to be released."

"We can tell the Oracle what we've found, and they'll put new resources into finding the right Senders to work on the case," I offer.

"Putting more people in danger and giving Malcolm Priddy the extra attention he's always wanted," Meander adds.

"Do you think it would make him stronger?" I ask. "If people started calling for him, knowing who he is and asking after his ghost—do you think he'd gain more power from it?"

"He might." Meander shrugs. "Ghosts seem to have more power when they feel more strongly about something. Could be his smug pleasure at the recognition would give him a boost."

"I don't think that boost would be enough to release him, though," I say. I remember the thoughts I've had in the complex, the dark desires to add more destruction to the building's already abysmal history. "I think he'd feed on it."

"I haven't seen him," Meander says. "But I think so too. And if he gets stronger…"

"It might make their combined energies stronger as well." I swipe away a strand of hair that's fallen out of place as we reach the base of the hill and follow Sian's directions back towards the complex. "Telling the Oracle is sensible and safe. But it doesn't solve any of the problems—and potentially makes everything worse."

"Precisely," Meander says. He glances at me. "Doing something about it ourselves is horrible and stupid. We know that already. But it could solve all the problems."

"Tell me again why we decided not to laze about and pick an easy spirit to work with this summer?" I ask.

Meander smirks. "Because it's the right thing to do." He pulls one hand from his pocket and reaches over to lace his fingers with mine. "And because as much as we both hate being a part of this world, it's penance. For all the things we've gotten from it."

My heart skips a beat, and I step closer to his side. "All right," I mumble. "We've already ascertained that the Oracle will probably be watching the complex. And condition number two of this escapade is that we don't go into the building by ourselves. So how do you propose we continue with this terrible plan?"

"Let's get back to the flats first," Meander says. "And make sure our suspicions are correct."

The light is growing dimmer when we close in on the complex. We move cautiously the nearer we get, hugging close to neighboring structures and circling far around to approach the building from its back. When we get near enough to see the place, we find one person idling around the entrance. Meander notices two black cars parked further away too, suggesting at least one more lurker, if not more.

"Suspicions officially confirmed," I say from where we stand shaded in a grove of trees. "Now what?"

Meander sighs. "We wait until it's dark. Then we find a way inside without them being aware."

"You don't think they're going to notice once we're in there with the ghosts?" I ask.

"We don't have to keep it a secret then," Meander says. "Condition number two, remember? We don't want to be in there alone. We just need to *get* in there alone. We can't release both halves of the entity, anyway. I can't stay sensible long enough for that. So, we go in, get Priddy riled up, and then I lure Davies away. Once the ghosts are apart, I'll leave via the front door and let whoever's standing watch know you're still inside." His jaw hardens, the plan logical but requiring him to let me do the brunt of the work while he stays outside. It's not an ideal situation for the project he intended to tackle front and center. But Priddy's the dangerous one. If we can get him to leave, Davies will be a regular ghost. And if we bring the total from two spirits down to one, the Oracle might let us continue on the case. Even if they don't, at least the murdering arsonist will be truly dead—and gone.

"Do you think they'll stop me?" I ask. "Escort me from the premises before I can finish with Priddy?"

Meander shrugs. "If they see you're doing something, they might operate on standby."

"And if they don't notice?" I ask. "What if we get in there and the ghosts knock us both unconscious without anyone realizing where we are?"

Meander looks at me, his expression uncertain. "I'm kind of hoping that's not a scenario we have to play out."

With a frown, I look around us, then retreat with him farther back into a nearby alcove of bushes. Pulling out my phone, I check my signal and start a video chat, calling up three people I'm not sure will even be able to answer. Luckily, it doesn't take long until the chat's picked up and Kornelía appears on the screen, followed by Dylan. A few seconds later, Mim arrives as well.

I smile at the familiar faces of my friends.

"This a party line?" Dylan asks. He looks rough, his skin grayer than normal and his eyes bloodshot and yellow. His cheek is covered with scratches.

"How are you?" I ask to no one in particular. "How are your projects going?"

"I've had better experiences," Dylan says. "But I'm hopeful."

"What happened to your face?" Mim asks. "Attacked by a cat?"

"No pumas in Jamaica," Dylan says. "Thank goodness. I fell over a stump of driftwood."

"You should stick to saying you got attacked by a cat," Meander says over my shoulder. "Sounds more impressive."

Dylan flips him off, while Kornelía stares unnervingly at the screen, her unseeing gaze so intense it's off-putting.

"Mim, how are you?" she asks.

Mim looks down, black bangs shining under the lights of wherever she is. "I've been better as well," she says. "But it will be okay. Tomorrow is... the event."

"Good luck," Kornelía says. The rest of us murmur our agreement, and Mim nods.

"How's channeling going, Korni?" Dylan asks.

Kornelía smiles, though her expression is solemn. "I had to leave the city. There were… too many people. I mean, too many ghosts. I'd never thought about it. At home, I'm only ever in close enough range to see one at a time. But the city—in Santiago and Concepción, there were many ghosts. But I was so focused on camp and our hunt, I didn't pay attention. In Amsterdam, I noticed. They're everywhere. It was… overwhelming."

"I'm sorry," Dylan says. "Where are you now?"

"Home," Kornelía says. "Just for a bit. I got to visit my brother while I was in the city, and the channeling expert followed me to Iceland. We're going over exercises. It's fascinating, actually. We tried it on one spirit in Amsterdam before it got to be too much. It worked." She laughs. "I didn't think it would."

I open my mouth, but despite being in separate countries, Kornelía is quick to hold up a finger. "Don't you dare say 'I told you so', Cal," she says with a grin. "I know. Thank you."

"I'm glad it worked," I say instead. "Hey, maybe you can start that blind artist business of yours, after all. You know, if our movie making scheme doesn't pan out."

"Movie making scheme?" Dylan asks. "What'd I miss?"

"Our brilliant plan to become millionaires," Kornelía says. "You're in charge of directing."

"I have no idea what you are talking about," Dylan says. "But I'm in."

"Cal," Mim interrupts. "Why'd you call? How is your project going?"

"Right." I lean back a little into Meander, and he wraps his arms around my waist as I tell the others what we've discovered. "We need to get in there tonight," I explain. "Oracle personnel are standing guard. But in case they don't notice when we sneak in, it's important someone else realizes where we've gone."

"You're going to get yourselves killed," Mim says. She 'tsks'. "I thought I was the risk-taker."

"You are," Meander says. "We're just too daft to learn our lesson. Keep believing we might be able to do some good."

On the screen, Kornelía smiles. "How long do we wait, Cal?" she asks. "Before we send out the alert?"

"Not long," I say. "We'll stay here until the light's gone, then we'll try to get inside. If you don't hear back from me within an hour and a half, try to get in touch. If we don't answer, call Robbie, just in case we've made it out okay. If he doesn't know where we are, tell him."

"We will," Dylan says. "But do your best not to get yourselves killed, okay? I've had enough trauma in my life. I don't need any more."

"We'll do everything we can to keep this a trauma-free night." My stomach twists as I say the words, the matches feeling like they're burning a hole in my pocket. "Thank you all. And good luck with your projects. You stay safe too."

We say goodbye to the others, then rest for a short while in the bushes while we wait for it to get darker. When clouds roll in to bring about an early night, we pull our outfits from our bags and change.

"How pathetic would it be if, after all this, we never make it into the building because we get picked up on a public indecency charge?" I ask while swapping my jeans for the pants of my suit.

Meander smirks. "I think we'd need to be doing something far more *indecent* to warrant an arrest."

"Well, when you put it like that, it sounds a hell of a lot more tempting than what we're about to face," I say.

I finish putting on my pants and shirt before Meander helps me with the suit jacket. Just as the first drops of rain begin to fall, he cups my jaw and studies me in the darkness.

"This is the part where I say you don't have to do this," he murmurs, his other hand holding lightly to the lapel of my jacket. "This was supposed to be my case. And you were not supposed to be putting yourself at any risk. The reality of you being in danger still makes every part of me hurt, Cal."

My arms circle his waist, leaning closer. "I know this isn't how things were supposed to play out," I say. "But we're in this together. Sometimes helping means stepping up and taking on a role you didn't intend."

For a moment, he studies me in silence as he considers what I've said—and perhaps thinks about what we're both about to do. Then he nods and draws me into a kiss.

I melt into the touch of his lips, the taste of his mouth. The muggy night is pricked with cool drops of rain, and I hold Meander tighter, fear, hope, and longing clouding around us in a haze of heat until we break apart to breathe in tandem, our hands gripped tight as our gazes lock.

"I love you," Meander says.

I smile, pressing my forehead to his as the rain hardens into a steady drizzle. "I love you too," I whisper. Then I force myself to step back.

Twisting around, I bend low and snatch my jeans from the ground. When I straighten to face him again, my expression is hard. "When we get inside, I want you to stay far away from me," I tell him. "Do your best to keep the entity's focus off of you. I'll attract it and try to pull Priddy out."

"How are you going to separate them?" Meander asks. "Do you think identifying Priddy will be enough?"

I shake my head and push my hand into the pocket of my discarded jeans. "You're not going to like this," I warn. I pull out the matches and lay them on my palm. "But I think it's what will do the trick."

 plan. But we don't have another option. If I can't get the entity to separate, we have no chance of releasing either ghost. And since Meander can't be in Davies's presence long, this is a job I have to do alone.

"You stay on the main floor," I say. "I'll go the basement. We know that's where Priddy likes to be."

We leave the bushes and survey the exterior of the building, taking in the open basement windows from Robbie's earlier efforts at prying away the boards, as well as the cracked panes of a still intact window on the building's second floor. But there's nothing on ground level that offers us a way in.

"We can't go up a story," Meander says. "The doors are still standing up there. We could get trapped." He glowers at the dark windows. "Not to mention the fact those doors are made of wood. *Flammable* wood."

"I'll go in through the basement, then," I say. "See

what I can do with the matches by myself. You stay outside where you can breathe."

"You know that's not likely to work without me inside," Meander says. "And on the off chance it does, I'm not leaving you alone with two mad ghosts and a fire starter. This is our project, and my case, remember? You can take the lead. But there's no way you're getting killed before I've even stepped in the building."

I sigh, patting the packet of matches now stored in my suit pocket. "Okay, so we're agreed. Neither of us wants to do this because we don't want the other one to get hurt. But since both of us are determined to do it one way or the other, I think we're going to have to stop trying to protect each other out here—and just focus on protecting each other in there."

Meander lets out a huff of breath. He swallows, then turns to me.

"Okay," he says. "In the basement. But we'll go together. I'll run for the stairs. You stay down and try to get Priddy out." He looks me up and down and takes a deep, unsettled breath. Then he grabs my hand and heads for the window.

I don't let him climb down first, lest he be hit hard on the way inside and wind up falling to the concrete floor. After another short argument, he relents and lets me enter the building ahead of him. I ease myself through the window's small opening, glad my arms don't give out as soon as they bear the weight of my whole body. When I'm hanging from the window, I mentally count down until I drop into a crouch. My feet tingle from the impact, but I stand upright and look around as Meander starts in.

He doesn't even get to the ground before the cold

makes us both shiver. I grab his waist to help him drop, then hold his hand as we cross to the stairs. I didn't realize how light the basement was during the day. Now that the setting sun is obscured from view, the rooms are all pitch black, and we stumble twice on the ground we can't see without a flashlight.

We make it to the door Robbie unhinged, tripping over its edge and stumbling into a fall before the static starts in my head.

"It's coming," I say as I struggle to stand.

"I know," Meander groans. He gets up and walks across the unsteady door to reach the stairwell. He takes the stairs halfway up—to the same place he got this morning—before the entity's mass materializes between us.

The static flares and the sickness I'm already feeling doubles as the ghosts come into view, but I don't waste any time reacting to my own pain. Retreating into the black basement, I try to keep from coughing in the stench of the smoke as I pull the matches out of my pocket.

"Malcolm Priddy!" I call, and I'm rewarded with a flare of pain and a flash of dark desire as my eyes fall to the matches in my grip. "That's right," I say in a quieter voice. "Look what I've got. You want them, don't you?"

I backstep, shuffling my feet to hopefully keep from toppling over something I can't see in the dark. Meander's footsteps ring on the stairs, which is good. But he doesn't retreat as far as I want him to. So, I keep moving, getting as much distance between him and the entity as I can.

The mass follows me, its misty blue-white the only

thing I can make out. It's still unformed, pockets of black air poking through the fog, but now I understand that the parts I can't see are the parts belonging to Gareth Davies. I wave the matches before my face, searching for Priddy's expression in the twists of disturbed energy.

"Come on, Priddy," I say. "I know about you. What you did. What you did to *her*."

The static kicks up and the low note I heard this morning slices through my head. But Priddy does not peel away from the mass. Instead, the mass as a whole crowds in, floating closer as the entity keeps on my trail.

It moves closer. And then it moves closer still. *Too close*. Panicking at the approaching, blue-white menace, I step back and try to keep my distance. But the entity doesn't give up. It advances on me, both of the ghosts swirled together, slinking as one. Closer and closer—until I'm backed up against the wall with nowhere else to go. Then the entity pauses, hovering achingly close until I instinctively hold my arm out to protect myself—and the mist descends over my skin.

I gasp in pain and tug my arm back, prickling with the sharp, electric jolt of being touched by a ghost. The sensation is awful, an ache so frigid and hollow it's like being groped by the grim reaper. Death runs from my elbow to my wrist, and the hand holding the matches quivers. I stare at the packet, wondering how much warmer the fire would be than this ghastly cold. How much lighter it would be than this unending dark. How much nicer a hot death would be compared to one as frozen as what I've just felt.

I jerk to the side, taking a rough step before I stumble

and clatter to the ground with a hiss of pain. The entity descends again, lancing across the skin of my cheek like a fist made out of ice, and my breath halts with a hiccupping stutter. I've never been assaulted by one ghost, let alone two. I didn't expect Davies to want any part in dragging me down, but apparently that assumption was wrong. I cough and work to swallow more air, but when the entity hits my face again, the cold clenches my jaw and makes it too hard to breathe.

I grab my neck, clutching my skin and begging my body to keep working the way it's supposed to, to stop freezing up and start allowing me the air it needs. Then the entity draws closer again—and my hand drops hard to my side as the mass clouds over my body like a billow of frozen steam.

"Hey!" The voice at the far end of the room is both beautiful and terrifying as it stops the entity from making a third strike to my face. My eyes slide to the far stairwell, but it's too dark to make out the shape of Meander as he stands somewhere near the stairs. I try to call to him, to warn him away from the basement, but I can't make any noise with the death-touch so close. "Gareth Davies!" Meander continues, and the entity retreats, its attention shifting. The freeze melts from my skin, and I retch, cough, and swallow, my arms shaking as I watch the entity sliding away from me.

And towards Meander.

I don't want Meander to be doing this, even if I understand why he is. The entity pivots in his direction, and the thought that these spirits will do to him what they just did to me makes me finally find my voice again.

"Priddy Boy!" I call as I hold the matches up in one,

trembling hand. "I'm not done with you yet!"

"Davies!" Meander yells from the other side of the room. "You want anger? I'll give you anger."

The taunts, the temptations—they're too much for the entity. It splits, faster than this morning now that its intentions are clear. I see the separation, and as soon as I do Meander's feet ring up the stairwell again as he works to pull one spirit away. I can't see how fast Davies moves. But I hear a choked cry from the stairwell too soon to be of any comfort.

My thoughts are whiplashed, the cry swallowed as Priddy closes in on me, the mass filling into the appearance of a more normal ghost as the static in my head finally gives way to a clear song. The smooth, low sounds are painful, but I am positive that once they were meant to soothe. They are dark. Menacing. But soothing all the same. The music sways like a black tide, washing me in agony with a low hum of sound that rattles inside my head. The instrumentation is strange and grotesque, until I realize it's not an instrument at all. It's man himself, a human voice singing words I can't decipher—in a tone meant to hush someone to sleep.

I don't need to think about what the song might be, or why it might connect with the ghost. As I look up at the almost-clear face of Malcolm Priddy, I know with absolute certainty that this song is a lullaby, one sung to a little girl right before her father set their home ablaze.

My stomach clenches. I gag, double-over, and—for the first time ever in the presence of a ghost—I vomit.

WIPING A SHAKING HAND OVER MY MOUTH, I CRINGE AGAINST THE thick smoke and acidic vomit flooding my nostrils. Struggling to stand, I move back, forcing my eyes away from the shadowed pool of sick as I look up at the ghost. He's disturbingly close to me, hovering so near it would seem like he was whispering his song, if it wasn't so sickeningly loud in my head.

"You didn't get what you wanted," I mutter. My voice is so weak I stand no chance of hearing my words over his disgusting lullaby. But I know he hears me, even if he doesn't want to. "No one knows what you did. No one will ever know. You died thirty-five years ago, Malcolm. And no one remembers who you are."

I don't want to be nice to this spirit. I don't want to be nice to either of them. Some Senders revere the dead and are dedicated to helping lost souls find their way home. But not all souls are good, and this half of the entity has taken more than one life already. I can't let Malcolm Priddy take any more.

Which means I really should burn this place to the ground.

The idea is sharp and painful, rushing in my head almost like lyrics to the sadistic melody in my brain. I hold up the matches and flick open the pack, staring at the sticks that are barely visible in the misted glow seeping from the ghost. Malcolm Priddy floats near me, the fogged energy that makes up his dead being flowing from him like icy breath on my neck.

"I won't do what you want," I say in a voice I wish sounded more convincing. With a conviction I wish felt more real. The words come from my lips, but all the while different thoughts echo in my head with a brightness that's hard to turn away from. Echoes telling me to burn the complex down. Impressions convincing me that all my problems will be over if I listen—that with just a flick of the match, everything will be done.

The idea is horrible. But it makes a horrible sort of sense. If I burn the complex to a crisp, no one will ever come here again.

"Until they build another place," I whisper, the argument terse and grating against the back of my teeth. I force myself to look away from the matches, blinking slow as I drag my gaze back up to the ghost. "Until you find another means to take someone's life."

As Malcolm Priddy stares at me, I get the distinct impression the fog of his spirit curves in a twisted smile. He reaches out and again touches my arm, while I flinch back from the shock of pain.

"You're not going to get what you want from me,"

I say.

"Then I'll wait for someone else."

The first words he's spoken roll into my head like tendrils of choking smoke. The voice is dark and harsh. And honest. The realization of the honesty is another blow, engulfing me with the quiet agony of understanding his way of thought. Priddy wants to be remembered. He wants to be famous. And if I can't make that happen, he'll wait for someone else.

There's nothing I can do to convince him otherwise. No threats or bargains or pleas will make him willing to move on. Priddy Boy's not going to give up his chance at fame. He's never going to leave the living world behind.

No wonder Meander can't see this half of the entity. Because Priddy is nothing, if not a patient man. He was calm when he burnt the building the first time. He was calm when he died in the blaze. He needs Meander's presence—and Davies's anger—to make him more substantial. But even without those, his influence still exists. He's set fires before, even in this cold, deathly form. He knows what he is capable of, and he's willing to play the long game when it comes to claiming his glory.

He'll set as many fires as necessary to claim his place in history.

I stare at the ghost, gaping in astonished horror until the ebbing lullaby is punctured by the soft vibrations of the steel door lying on the basement floor. With a gasp of breath, I listen to the shaking doors—the steel one as well as the wood door somewhere to my right. Two loud thuds sound above my head, then something cracks like the peeling groan of splintering plaster. A noise caught somewhere between a shout and a cry fills in the lowest points of the lullaby, and my nerves twist as I realize Meander hasn't left the building.

Bolting forward, I rush so fast I brush against the side of the ghost. But Malcolm Priddy's not ready to let me go. As I try to pass him, he latches onto my arm, and the pain is so vicious I careen forward onto the floor.

Splaying my hands to cushion my head, I brace against the impact of the concrete before scrambling onto my knees. Crawling forward, my eyes stay trained on the rattling door next to the stairwell, until my gaze slides unbidden to where the other door lies in the farthest corner of the room.

The wooden door. The door worth burning.

I try to push the thought away, turning my head and focusing on the stairs. But when an image of those stairs alight with flame ignites behind my eyes, I don't cast it off.

I can't.

Malcolm Priddy approaches me from behind. I feel the ice draping across my back, and when I twist around I find him looming over me. Hurrying to my feet, I try to run as the ghost circles round to my front. The mist begins to stretch again, this time not to separate but to block my escape. My heart races, and my eyes veer up to the ceiling as the entire floor above me creaks with vibrations that run like a shudder through the basement walls. The very building is shaking, and my limbs are shaking along with it. But then my limbs, my heart, even my panic slows with an aching chill. My eyes drop from the ceiling, and

I realize that—doors or no—I've still managed to get myself trapped.

The ghost's mass has encased my body, locking me within his hold.

My jaw clenches, and fiery ice trails down my cheeks as tears roll from my eyes to freeze on my skin. My mind rages, fighting against the pain that makes my brain feel like it's spreading into frozen webs that will soon begin to crack. I've never been attacked by a spirit. Not like this. I've had things hurled at me on more than one occasion. But never before has the blue-white mass itself overcome me. Perhaps this is the full horror of what it means to be guided by a ghost. Because this is not how the dead are supposed to be. This is not… This is not…

I gasp as the arm holding up the matches rises, while my other hand reaches in to pull one from the pack. With a too-expert flick of my wrist, I strike the match and set it aflame. I study the small spot of heat, watching the fire's dance as it twirls and flickers in the dark. And then my face spreads into a smile, and I know what to do. How to set the door on fire. How to stand by and watch it burn. How to make the world know exactly who I am.

And I know that this… *this is not me*. But it doesn't matter. Because I no longer have any control. I am *not* me. Not anymore.

I cross the room to face the dismantled door. Raising the match, I prepare to flick it onto the old, dry wood.

A horrendous crash sounds from above me, and the whole of the building shudders more violently than before. A flash of something—something bright, something light—blinds me, before Priddy's force bears down, gripping me in a vise so tight it feels like I am going to snap in two. I lose all manner of footing and all concept of balance, yet the ghost's grip keeps me upright, holding me still as I sob through the pain. A noise, nearly imperceptible in the chaos of the complex's shuddering cacophony, echoes in the clanging stairwell. Then the light fades, the shuddering halts and, as all other sight and sound swiftly dies, something tumbles into view.

Falling over itself, it twists into odd shapes, rolling and crashing before it lands in a crumpled heap at the bottom of the stairs.

I tilt my head, holding the flame until I can make out the shadowy curls of hair.

"Meander."

All at once, my body floods with slicing heat as my stomach bucks and my brain wakes up. The spirit of Malcolm Priddy is gripping me on all sides, prying into my mind and forcing up my hand. I close my fist over the match, fingers stinging as the flame burns and extinguishes. I drop the match book and crush it under my foot, retching as I see the unmoving lump by the bottom of the stairs. I try to move forward, but the ghost keeps me pinned, locking me in place with it. *Trapping* me with it.

I stare at Meander, and my horror at being trapped while he is lying unmoving on the floor floods into panic so intense I start to scream.

Priddy's lullaby courses through me, gushing through my veins until it drops to my feet and seeps out of my shoes like liquid fire. The ice starts to melt, and I keep screaming, pushing forward against the trap of the dead. My knees tremble and strain, and my arms struggle against the blue-white barrier. Throat burning, I kick my voice louder and louder, screaming with every ounce of strength I have until the sound breaks through the lullaby and light rips through my head— filling me and blinding me until the agonizing scream stops as I hurtle forward into a room as black as death.

As I fall close to Meander, I try to call his name but can't make more than a feeble whine. My eyes blur with tears, and I stretch out my hand, desperate to touch him—failing to reach him, failing to keep him safe—before the blackness wins and all hope fades as my consciousness gives way.

THREE DAYS LATER, I WAKE IN A HOSPITAL ROOM.

Unlike the blurry, uncomprehending moments I usually feel post-release, this waking is frantic. With a single breath, I sit up fast, panic seizing every inch of my flesh. My face is wet by the time I realize there are tubes attached to my body, and I look around in wild terror until I find the button to call for a nurse.

A young woman comes in two minutes later, her scrubs blue and her smile bright as she looks at me.

"Nice to see you awake," she says with an English accent.

"Meander," I croak, my throat so raw I wince at the pain of speaking.

The nurse doesn't respond to my word. She starts checking the machine by my bed, asking if I remember what happened to me.

"Meander," I say again. I cough, and she smiles, turning as if she still hasn't heard me speak.

"I'll bring you some water," she says. "It'll help your throat. You'll have to rest your voice for a few days."

I glare at her, my insides twisted so hard it's like I'm still back in the basement with Priddy.

"Where is Meander?" I bite out, my throat as raw as if I've been swallowing thorns.

This time, the nurse gives me a perplexed look. "I'm sorry, I don't know who that is." She glances me over, studying my face, the way tears continue to leak from my eyes. Then her face draws tight. "I'll go and check, okay?"

I give her a feeble nod, all my desperate hope dwindling as she walks away. To go and check. Or to find someone else to deliver the bad news. I try to keep my mind clear of any thought while she is gone, but the exercise is futile. By the time the door swings open again, I'm openly sobbing as I wait for a doctor with a solemn face to approach my bed. When Robbie appears instead, his blue hair hanging limp over the side of his head and his left arm in a sling and cast, I feel even worse knowing they're letting him talk to me first.

"I'm starting to think you don't like me very much," Robbie says as he walks into the room. "Seems the only explanation for why you insist on getting me into so much trouble all the time."

"Meander," I say. It feels practically like the only word I *can* say right now. There's no point in any other speech. There's no point in trying to talk about any other subject. I remember the heap at the bottom of the basement stairs, and my throat clogs with bile. I need to know what happened.

Fresh tears drip down my cheeks as Robbie

approaches my bed. He sits by my foot, patting my leg through the blankets as he gives me a smile softer than any I've ever seen on him.

"Meander's alive," he says.

My heart stills for a breathless second as my stomach plunges and my hands begin to shake. When my body remembers it needs to keep pumping blood, I let out a shuddering gasp of surprise.

"He's okay?" I wipe my eyes, although they refill so quickly my vision remains blurred.

"He's unconscious," Robbie says. "Broke his leg pretty damn bad. They're keeping him under tight surveillance because they're worried about a coma. But between you and me, I think he's just sleeping off the release."

"Release?" I ask. I wipe my eyes again. "He released Gareth Davies?"

I remember the white light, the brightness that flashed right before the building finally stopped shaking. I remember too the pain of Priddy's grasp when the light overcame us. He must have been clinging to me to make sure he wasn't swept away by Davies's release and Meander's unconsciousness. He must have been keeping me imprisoned to ensure he didn't lose his hold over my mind if I lost consciousness too.

Robbie nods. Then he frowns. "When'd you decide there were two ghosts?" he asks. "You never mentioned that to me. I only found out when my phone blew up with texts and calls from half of Shade, telling me you two had decided to test your luck with the Fates again. It's a good thing there were people outside that building. Apparently, one of the remaining windows shattered, and then they heard you screaming. If they hadn't…"

"We were counting on them hearing us," I explain. "But we called the others as a backup. As for the two ghosts… After we left you, we talked about what we saw and realized that we experienced different things because we saw different spirits. That's why the entity was so unclear. We, uh, figured out who the second spirit was, and how to separate them. I was supposed to work on one of them. Meander was supposed to stay out of the way. But I think—the entity started attacking me. He distracted Davies so I wouldn't get hurt. And then he got hurt instead." I shake my head. "Idiot."

Robbie laughs. "You're both idiots, as far as I can tell. But you're idiotically good when you're together. He released one half. You released the other. At least, seems like that's the case, right? No sign of activity there anymore."

"I didn't release Priddy," I say. But then I remember the white-hot heat battling the icy cold—the white light and the burst of rage before I crawled to Meander and passed out. "He was unlike any spirit I've ever encountered. He didn't just talk to me—he came at me. He surrounded me, and for a minute there, I… I shared his thoughts completely. I did what he wanted me to do. I lost myself."

Robbie studies me, a curious expression sweeping over his face. "Sounds like you were possessed," he says slowly.

My eyes snap to his. "Possessed?" As soon as I say it, I know it's true. I've always been worried about possession. Now I know those fears were not totally unfounded. "How did I get away?" I ask.

"I wasn't there," Robbie says with a shrug. "But you did. And there doesn't seem to be any presence left over. Something must have happened."

"There… There was a light, at the end," I say. I explain what happened as best as I can, my throat burning and my voice weak as I recall the details of the event. I can't remember everything, and a lot of what I tell Robbie amounts to a confused babbling about pain and fear and fury. But Robbie doesn't look bewildered or annoyed by my attempts at relating what occurred. Instead, he grows more contemplative as I continue to talk.

"I can't say for certain," he says when I've finished my fragmented story. "But it sounds like an exorcism to me."

I remember well Mim's failed exorcism in Tonga. The one Meander finished last summer. Could this have been the same? That was something planned, with ornaments and prayers—with a set plan and a very specific end goal. But Mim once said that exorcism was less about the props than about what the Sender believed in. I didn't think I could ever exorcise a spirit, because I didn't believe in anything strongly enough to manifest that sort of power.

But maybe that's not right. Because I can still see Meander falling down the stairs, can still picture the unnatural way his body crumbled at its base. I remember the horrific realization that it was him, that he was unmoving—that I was stuck with the ghost while he needed my help.

Another, unexpected sob escapes my throat as I recall what happened in the basement. I bring a hand to my mouth to stifle it and try to smile at Robbie. But I'm too exhausted and overwhelmed to make a real show at being okay. Not that I have to pretend. Robbie understands. He pats my leg again, then gets up from the bed.

"Meander's all right," he says. "And you are too. You got a cut on your arm from that door in the basement. A few stitches, but nothing major. Now that you're awake, I'll get the doctor in to give you the once over and get you discharged. Then we'll go and see him."

I nod, swallowing through my rough throat. "Thanks Robbie," I say. "And… sorry. For all the trouble."

Robbie grins. "No sweat. Only real trouble is this damn arm. I can't even do my hair properly. I'm going to be wearing it down for weeks, and it's already driving me insane."

I smile for real as he waves me off and leaves the hospital room. Not long after he's disappeared, the nurse returns to fiddle with my equipment and offer me water while we wait for the doctor to make an appearance.

It takes a couple of hours to be confirmed healthy enough to leave. I shower while I wait for the discharge papers to come through, then sit impatiently in the visitor's chair until the nurse arrives with my paperwork in hand.

As soon as I get the okay, I walk on still unsteady feet into the hall. Robbie meets me outside the ward, and he forces me to go at an easier pace as we travel up the two floors to reach Meander's room.

I push into the hospital room, and my heart lodges in my sore throat as Meander comes into view. His left leg is propped on a pillow, a white cast encasing him from toe to thigh. The rest of his set-up is similar to my own, IV and catheter along with machines that read his vitals and alert the nurses every time his fluids need refilling. But it's his face that makes my chest ache. The right side is covered with bruises from where he fell, black, purple, and green marks trailing from his forehead to his jaw. I try to be relieved that he's okay, and in the grand scheme of things, I am because I know he will be. But he's not really okay right now, and I can't stop from crying as I make my way to him.

I round to the left side of the bed and take his hand carefully in mine. Robbie pulls a chair over for me, and I sit down hard, my legs wobbling.

"I'll give you a few minutes," Robbie says. "I'll be back with some food."

I wait until he leaves. Then I lean forward and press my lips to Meander's hand.

"Hey," I say. "It's Cal. I'm here. I'm okay. You're going to be okay too. We did it. It was stupid and horrible and if we weren't already finished with camp we'd probably be kicked out for good this time. But we did it. I'm not really sure how, but..."

I stop, my throat aching and my eyes stinging. I study Meander's face, then push myself up so I can whisper in his ear.

"I'm so proud of you," I say. "You need to wake up so I can tell you that in person, but... don't rush it. Rest, Meander. You've earned it. Wake up when you're ready. I'll be here when you do. I love you."

I kiss his ear, his scar, his lips. Then I sit back in the chair, holding his hand and closing my eyes as I wait for Robbie's return.

46

FOR THE NEXT SEVERAL DAYS, I LIVE IN MEANDER'S HOSPITAL ROOM. I'M
not sure what official visiting hours are. But his room
is private, and no one urges me to pack up my stuff
and go. Robbie brings the rest of our things from the
inn, and I claim the visitor's chair that folds out into a
makeshift bed. Our lead comes and goes, bringing me
food and channel surfing on the room's tv. Whenever
he leaves, I sleep, listen to music, or talk to Meander to
fill in the room's sterile silence.

On the first day after my discharge, I call my
friends to thank them for helping us out. Mim is
unavailable. But Dylan and Kornelía join me for a
short conversation about what happened, and we
talk a little about what their past few days have
looked like as well. Kornelía is happier now she's had
another successful channeling. Dylan's scratches are
healing, but he looks positively wild as he relates how
he's been spending his nights with the pack of ghost

dogs, trying to figure out why they're all sticking around together. They're both relieved to know that Meander and I are still on the side of the living. But they're also too invested in their own projects to talk for long, and I'm content to end our call so they can get back to their own ghosts.

Two days after taking residence in Meander's room, I'm surprised when an unexpected visitor arrives in the form of Natalie, the woman who was so set against us continuing our mission at the complex.

"I read the report," she says by way of greeting. She hovers by the door, a rain-splashed coat hung over one arm. "I wanted to see how you are."

"We're fine," I say. My eyes slide to Meander, and I shrug. "We'll be fine, eventually."

Natalie nods. She purses her lips as she takes another step into the room. "You shouldn't have gone back in there," she says. Her words are a reprimand, but her voice is much gentler than the other times she's talked to us. "I won't pretend I wasn't furious when I found out you went back without our permission."

"We didn't need your—" I start, but she holds a hand up to stop me.

"I know you don't care about what I think," she says. "You Senders never do. I'm not happy about what happened. And I don't particularly like the two of you." My eyes narrow into a glower, but she doesn't flinch away from my dark look. "I only came by to say that, while I disagree with everything about this case and how it was handled, I'm happy you were successful. I'm happy no more lives were lost because of that... that *thing*. My mother tried so hard to release it. And I feel immensely... grateful that it's finally been done."

I open my mouth, trying to form a suitable response. But I can't think of anything good to say, so I only nod. Natalie spends a long moment looking at Meander. Then she nods too before turning on her heel and leaving the room.

On the third day after waking, I sit by Meander's bed, my hand laid lightly overtop his as I talk about Rose's latest email from home.

"She had a brawl with Mom about quitting ballet camp," I say. My throat is still a little sore, so I keep my voice quiet as I ramble. "Which is good. It means Mom and Dad will be more preoccupied with her than with me. I haven't told them what happened. Don't really plan to, honestly. I wonder what it must be like to go to a normal summer camp. I don't even know how the Oracle gets away with it. No full incident reports. No meetings with social services. Just a quick phone call to say your kid's in the hospital *again*, and then it all goes back to normal. Last year, Rose sprained her ankle during a rehearsal, and Mom drove all the way to camp to bring her medicine because they couldn't even administer it without her written consent."

I lean back and close my eyes with a scoff. "Can you imagine the shit we'd be in if the Oracle was like that? I suppose it wouldn't count for hospital visits. Like, if she'd *broken* her ankle, they'd have had to fix it. But you know Mom and Dad would have been in the waiting room the whole time. Mom finished her workday early just to bring Rose some pain meds and a heat pack. It's not fair, really. No one's ever brought *me* a heat pack."

"Remind me when I get paid by the Oracle. It'll be

the first thing I buy."

My eyes fly open, and I sit forward to lean over the bed. "Meander?"

His eyes open more slowly than mine, and he blinks a few times before his gaze focuses on me. "Hey, Callum." His hand turns over, and his fingers lace with mine as he searches my face. "Are you okay?"

I give his hand a squeeze as I nod. "I'm fine."

He nods too, then gives me a confused look. "Am *I* okay?"

I laugh. "I think so. You broke your leg. But… it could have been worse. A lot worse. Do you need anything? Water? A nurse?"

He closes his eyes with a smile. "Are you going anywhere?"

"No, I'm staying right here," I say.

"Then I'm good," he murmurs.

My stomach drops and my chest swells in a dance of relief and joy. I settle back in my chair, holding his hand tighter. "Do you remember anything?" I ask.

"Not much," he says. "Just that bloody ghost attacking me."

"You were supposed to stay out of the way," I chide.

"So you could get killed?" he asks. "Not ever. I went upstairs and headed for the door, like we'd planned. But when he realized I was leaving, Davies turned back towards the basement. I couldn't let the two halves combine so they could go after you again. So, I blocked his way. He could have gone around me, or right through the floor, if he'd wanted. But as it turns out, I don't think Davies had any unfinished business. Not really. He was just angry. I'm a good target for the angry ones."

"You gave him a power boost," I say. "The place went crazy. You fell down the stairs."

Meander flinches. "Did I? I tried to keep away from the stairwell. But everything got hazy near the end." His eyes open and he tilts his head towards me. "Was it the end? What happened after I fell down the stairs? We must have gotten out somehow."

"We released them, apparently," I say. "I don't know what you did, but—"

"I absorbed his anger," Meander says.

I stare at him, astonished at the explanation while understanding its simple truth. "It really does come full circle, doesn't it?" I ask. "Just like our first summer. You absorbed a ghost's anger. I was guided." I smirk. "You fell down the stairs back then too, if I recall." Meander groans through a laugh, and I squeeze his hand. "Of course, this is considerably worse than the first time. No wonder we were told not to go seeking trouble."

"How'd you get Priddy?" he asks.

I squirm in my seat, the memory still uncomfortable. "I almost didn't," I admit. "I think I was… well, Robbie thinks maybe I was possessed."

"What?" Meander shifts to look at me, but the movement is too much. He flinches in pain, and I help him settle, ensuring he doesn't need a nurse's attention before I continue.

"I'm not sure if I was. I've always heard that possession happens inside. Like, the spirit's inside of you and you have to try and get it out. That's what it seemed like with Mim. But that's not what happened. If anything, it was the opposite. Priddy surrounded me. He trapped me inside of his energy. I had to break my way out. But I almost didn't. He had the matches. He took control of my head. And my body. He got me to light one."

"What happened?" Meander asks.

I smile. "You fell down the damned stairs. I knew I had to get to you. So, I got away from him. And, I don't know, that was enough to break him. Robbie said it might have been an exorcism, of sorts. I'm not sure. But they said the building's clear. We did it— haphazardly and almost fatally—but… We did it."

His eyes catch mine, and we stare at each other with mirrored expressions of disbelief and pride. He is bruised, his cheek swollen and his face lined with ill exhaustion. But he is beautiful, and I cannot imagine having gone through what I did without him. I couldn't have—if Meander hadn't been there, I would never have gotten Priddy to separate from Davies. And, even if I had, I would never have broken free from the ghost's hold.

If I hadn't been there, screaming my head off as I ripped away from the spirit, Meander would have been left at the bottom of the stairs alone.

I hate seeing ghosts. Meander does too. I wish both of us could be rid of our talents forever. But I have to admit that this part—knowing we've done what we set out to, knowing we've made a place safer and potentially saved lives in the process—is great. Releasing ghosts has its purpose. Sometimes it helps spirits that need to be freed. Sometimes it stops spirits that need to be banished. It's not the life I would have chosen for myself. But in these moments, it's hard to imagine accomplishing something so wonderful any other way. Or with any other person by my side.

My eyes brim with tears again, and I blink them back as I look at Meander's leg.

"I think you've achieved your goal, at any rate," I say with a nod at his cast. "The Oracle won't be after you to take up any new cases for a while."

"Good," Meander says. He grips my hand, and when I look back at him, he gives me a sad smile. "Gives us more time to start saving for plane tickets."

The statement makes me feel a little ill. Not because I won't fly to meet him—I'll fly anywhere in the world, anytime to see this boy—but because I don't want to have to. Maybe Meander will be assigned some Oracle-hired partner to keep him safe on his cases. But I hate that idea. Because most Senders don't understand how much he wishes his talent could go away. Because no one else can read his moods like I can to know when he's not really okay, even if he says he is. Because it's always been us, and I can't stand the thought that suddenly I'll be going to school and avoiding my own ghosts while he's sent around the globe to face spirits that will keep dragging him down.

"Speaking of," I say, trying to clear my head and instead only succeeding in shifting my focus, "I was thinking... They're not going to make you finish the summer in Chile. So, I'm not going back, either. I've got a bit of money saved from when I was helping my dad fix up my grandma's new place. I can buy my own ticket home for the end of the summer and spend the next couple of weeks helping you get settled in wherever they send you."

Meander's expression is strange, his mouth frowning while his eyes shine with what I think is hope. "What about your parents?" he asks.

I shrug. "School doesn't start until September. If I can convince someone from the Oracle to tell them it's okay, they won't fight. And anyway, you need help. If they try to tell me I can't stay, I'll resort back to tantrum-mode." I smile. "I can't let you… I don't want to let you…" I pause, then sigh. "I'm not ready to say goodbye yet. Not again. Not so soon."

Meander smiles, while a tear streaks down his swollen cheek. I wipe it away as gingerly as I can, and he smiles more.

"I want you to stay," he says. The words are cracked and quiet, and they fill me with more pained happiness than I can comprehend. I nod, and he sniffs before curving his lips into a smirk. "But I'm paying for the ticket. At least half of it. I have a career now, of sorts. I'm not letting you take the brunt of the cost."

"Yeah, but you owe me a heat pack, remember?" I tease. "That's going to break the bank."

Meander laughs, then shifts in discomfort.

"Should I get the nurse?" I ask. "They'll want to know you're awake."

He settles back into place with a nod. "Yeah, okay. But can I ask a favor first?"

"Always," I say. "What is it?"

He lifts his arm to touch my jaw. "Kiss me."

I smile, more than happy to oblige.

I'M CONTENT TO STAY IN THE QUIET BUBBLE OF MEANDER'S HOSPITAL room until he's ready to leave. But the day after he wakes up, Robbie arrives with lunch for the three of us—and a plane ticket just for me.

"I'm not going anywhere," I say, angry and panicked that they're trying to separate us so soon after Meander's regained consciousness. I'd intended to talk to our lead about my options, about who in the Oracle I could beg to let me skip the final two weeks of camp. But now that chance has slipped away and, although Robbie's expression is sympathetic, I'm aggravated he didn't mention anything about this sooner.

"Sorry, Cal," he says. "Orders from above."

"Orders from above," Meander scoffs from the bed. "It's bollocks, is what it is. Don't we get a say in anything? We released the entity for you. Can't you have the bloody decency to let us heal in peace? I don't want him to go."

"I'm *not* going," I add, irritated at the Oracle's rules and Robbie's continually perky attitude. "I'm not leaving him to go back to Chile. I'm sorry, but I don't care about the rest of camp. I'm done. I'm staying."

"You're not going to Chile," Robbie says. He nods at the ticket. Confused, I open the paper flap to see the destination printed in black.

"Athens?" I ask as I glance back at Robbie. "Why the hell are they sending me to Athens?"

Robbie's lips tug in a small smile, as if he wants to grin but knows I won't be amused if he does. "Your last stop at Camp Wanagi," he says.

"What for?" I press. "And *don't* say it's a surprise. Tell me."

Robbie crosses one arm under his sling. "Way to take the fun out of it," he says. "But fine. The truth is, you're going to Athens for your exit interview. The Oracle wants to talk to you, to discuss your time at camp and figure out where you want to go from here."

"Don't bother," Meander says. He settles back against his pillows, a painful glint flashing through his eyes before he covers it with a smile. "Cal's not working for the Oracle. He's going to study music."

My stomach pinches, pleased by the assurance in his tone—and sickened by the implication that our paths will so soon diverge.

Robbie eyes me carefully before he shrugs again. "Be that as it may, you've got an appointment. Doesn't matter if you want to. You have to go."

"But... I..." I wave in the direction of the bed. "I can't leave him," I say with a pathetic whimper.

Robbie sighs. "Sorry," he says to Meander. "You

were supposed to come too, but alas—" he nods his chin in the direction of Meander's casted leg, then turns back to me. "He's not going anywhere for a while, Cal. And you won't be gone long. A couple of days, and you can come back."

I give him a suspicious stare. "I can?" I ask.

"Yes, you can," he says. "You're supposed to finish out the year in Chile. But when I talked to Buxley, we both agreed you'd be pretty damn annoying if we tried to make you do that."

My face falls into a frown, while Meander lets out a little laugh.

"Shut up, you," I say to him, which makes him laugh more.

"I didn't say anything," he insists, while his lips settle into a smirk. "But you know he's right."

My glare is indignant, even if I *do* know he's right. Still, at least I can take solace in the fact that if our situations were switched, Meander would probably be worse.

"We leave for the airport in an hour," Robbie says. "We'll finish lunch. Then you can get ready."

The three of us eat together. When Robbie leaves to meet the car out front, I start sulkily stuffing clothes back in my bag.

"How you've managed to make such a mess in *my* hospital room, I have no idea," Meander says with a smile. "You're lucky they haven't kicked you out."

I stop trying to shove a pair of jeans into my duffel bag as I turn to him with a sigh. "Am I really that annoying?" I ask.

He laughs. "To some people? Probably."

"And to you?" I press.

"I told you at the library," he says. "You're perfect. You can make as much mess and be as stubbornly annoyed as you want. I don't mind. I won't ever mind."

I smile, momentarily abandoning my packing to come to his bedside. "I don't want to go," I tell him.

"I don't want you to go," he says. "But if you comply, maybe it'll make it easier to convince them to let you stay here a little longer afterwards." His teeth scrape across his lip. "Unless they're lying about you getting to come back."

My stomach lurches at the thought, but I refuse to let paranoia overtake me. I lean over the bed, capturing Meander's lips and kissing him for a long moment before I pull back enough to speak against his mouth.

"I'm coming back," I murmur. "One way or another."

"You'd better," he says. Then he kisses me again, tempering the disappointment of leaving with the promise of what will happen when I return.

Ultimately, I do leave his room, after further promises and me deciding to leave him with my violin so I'll have another source of ammo if they try to prevent my return. On the way out of the hospital, I stop at the gift shop to buy a bag of chocolates and a few random paperbacks to be delivered to his room. Then I shuffle to meet Robbie near the main entrance so we can venture out into the gray, drizzly day.

We get into the waiting car and head for the airport. As soon as the hospital is out of sight, I realize my surroundings are more familiar than I expected.

"Where are we?" I ask in confusion. "Are we in London?"

As if in answer, the car makes a wide right turn, and

we pass a double decker. Robbie laughs at my puzzled expression as he looks out the window on my far side.

"Sure are," he says. "Thought it best to transport you to an Oracle hospital."

"The Oracle has its own hospitals?" I ask.

Robbie smiles. "No. But they have agreements with a few around the globe. Senders keep a close eye for any paranormal patients that might check-in. They keep the floors clear, to keep it safe. That's a lot of what Buxley does, actually. When she's not doing, you know, *everything* else. At any rate, it makes it easier for Meander to come here. Easier to get care in his home country. And less travel once he leaves."

The last part of that sentence dampens my curiosity. I slump in my seat and don't say anything else as we drive to the airport.

OUR FLIGHT IS SHORT, NO STOPOVERS AND ONLY A COUPLE OF HOURS IN THE
air before we arrive in Athens late in the afternoon. I'm
grateful for the straightforward travel. But it doesn't
change my foul mood as we collect our luggage and
make our way out into the hot day.

We drive to a hotel. And although I know why I've
been summoned, I'm still vaguely surprised to find
Alex and other members of Shade lounging in the
hotel's lobby upon our arrival. Naasir looks the same
as when I last saw him, as does Kornelía. But Sabeena
is asleep in one of the lobby chairs, Dylan is sporting a
black eye, and Mim—Mim is nowhere to be seen.

"Is she on her way?" I ask when I meet with the
others.

Kornelía shakes her head. "She's with her father,"
she explains.

"The Oracle will talk with her when she's ready,"
Alex adds.

I nod, then look at Dylan. "Driftwood?" I ask as I take in his swollen eye.

"Something like that," he grumbles.

Naasir stands a step back from the rest of us, quietly watching our conversation until he catches my gaze.

"Is Meander coming?" he asks, and I can hear a note of genuine concern in his tone that warms a little of my grouchy coldness.

"No," I say with a small smile. "He's in the hospital. He's fine, just... broken leg. Makes it hard to travel."

Relief washes over Naasir's usually stoic features, and it gladdens my heart to see that—close or not— he cares about what happens to us too. "I'm glad he's well," he says.

"I am too," I reply. I glance at Sabeena. "Is she okay?"

"She's fine," Naasir says. "Tired."

I nod, dropping my duffel bag at my feet as I think about how tired I am as well, weary from ghosts and fears and travelling all summer long. "When do we meet with the Oracle?" I ask, ready for this particular trip to reach its end as soon as possible.

It's nice seeing some of my friends again. But we all said our goodbyes in Chile, and seeing them now feels like a weird afterthought that no one is totally prepared for. I'm glad we're all alive and intact. But we're not all together, and more than anything right now, I want to get on with this interview so I can get back to London.

"Tomorrow," Alex says, and I stifle a groan as she comes to my side and pats me on the shoulder. "After you check into your rooms, we'll do a tiny bit of sightseeing. Then we'll have dinner, and in the morning, your interviews will begin." She looks at Robbie. "I'll meet you in an hour, yes?"

"Meet us?" Dylan asks. "Where are you going?"

Alex smiles. "I'm staying with my cousins. My home is a couple of hours from here, but my cousins live in town."

"It must be strange for you, being home," Dylan says.

"It's always strange to arrive someplace different," Alex says. "Even if that place is familiar. I guess because we change, even if the place does not. But I enjoy being with my cousins. And there are plenty of ghosts in a city like this."

She says it like it's a comfort, but I don't fail to notice how Kornelía's expression droops with her words. If what Kornelía said about Amsterdam holds true here as well, she'll be seeing as many people as the rest of us. I suppose there's something innately uncomfortable— even for her—about all those people being dead.

After Alex bids us goodbye, we check into our rooms, and I send Meander a note to let him know what the plan is. He's quick to respond, and we text back and forth until Robbie knocks on the hotel room door telling us it's time to go.

It takes two hours to reach our destination, a long time in the van for us to share stories of what we encountered on our final tasks. Sabeena is still too sleepy to recount her project. But the rest of us talk as we drive through the Greek countryside.

"Three people were going to suffer because they were worried about the same girl," Naasir says, relating his efforts at the care facility. "She was a volunteer, with an unsteady home life. She stopped coming, and they worried. I tracked her down. She had left home and found a new, better life. She was studying to become a caregiver. When I told the patients, they smiled. All three of them died within the week. None of them remained. I'm going back there after this. See if I can help some more."

"That's incredible, Naasir," Kornelía says. She tucks hair behind her ear and continues scribbling random shapes on the notepad on her lap. I watch her aimless doodling, happy to know she's found some method of drawing again.

"Come on," I say to Dylan after an hour on the road, "how'd you really get the black eye?"

Dylan grimaces. "Told a fisherman his brother was scum. He didn't take it too well."

I eye him in surprise. "You really said that? Why?"

"He was!" Dylan exclaims. His raises his arms, swinging them somewhat wildly in the cramped space of the van's backseat. "He owned five dogs. Then one day, he got a job offer on the other side of the island. Instead of bringing his dogs with him, he left them to starve. They were still waiting. All five of them. Hanging around in the afterlife for their scumbag master to return with some food."

He slumps back against the seat with a petulant huff, while Kornelía's hand stills against the paper.

"Did you help them?" she asks, head tilting back as she waits for his reply.

"Yeah, I did," Dylan says. He smiles, the morose look melting into a proud one. "Got them to understand that they'd be forever hungry if they stayed, and full-bellied if they left."

"So, you tricked them," I say.

He waves me off. "No. Probably not. I think they'd be full-bellied, don't you? It's got to be better, anyway. It feels better, doesn't it? Seeing them off. Feels… right. Feels… full-bellied."

He sits back, hand resting on his own stomach as he considers what he did. I don't ply him with any more philosophical questions about what we do and do not know about life after, well… life.

When we finally pull to a stop, I climb out of the van and survey a vast set of ruins set among a landscape of rocky hills. It doesn't take any real knowledge to know we've arrived somewhere incredibly old, an ancient relic in an impressive location. The sun is hot, but the early evening hour means its glow streams from between the far valleys, washing the ruins in soft light. Sloped up the sides of the nearer hills, stone and grass grow together, and on a level of flat ground, a long rectangle of old stonework is accented by round columns stretching up at one end.

"Where are we?" I ask.

Alex comes to my side, pulling her sunglasses down as she studies the ruins before us. "The Temple of Apollo," she beams.

"Okay." I look around and shake my head. "Any particular reason why? We drove two hours to be here—aren't there sights to be seen closer in Athens?"

"Apollo was the god of many things," Alex says. She tilts her head in my direction. "Music. And oracles."

"Oracles?" Sabeena asks from where she leans heavily into Naasir's side.

Alex nods. "This is where the most famous oracles did their work. The Oracle of Delphi."

The reason for this visit doesn't change the sight.

The ruins are still ruins, a bunch of stone and grass and craggy hills. But knowing that this is where Senders started—that this is where the concept of oracles began, no matter how wrong the interpretation of them once was—gives this place a wholly different meaning. I'm awed by the grandness of the landscape from another time, and the reality that even in that faraway era, people like us still existed.

We make our way along the ruins, our pace slow as we take in the sights and wander near other tourists who look at our collective strangeness and give us space. I expect Kornelía to be a bit morose, the location only hot and uneven without vision to make the grandeur of the place come alive. But as we step over the crumbling terrain, her eyes are wide—and her smile is bright.

"There are ghosts," she says to me in a soft voice when we reach the temple's far end. I look away from the sunset to see her pointing towards the columns. "There," she says. "Ghosts. *Old* ghosts. Older than I've ever seen. As old as…"

"These ruins?" I ask.

Kornelía nods, then lets out a squeak of a laugh. She gives Draugur's head a quick scratch and grips the guiding handle so she can explore more on her own.

I'm not a wanderer by heart, and after four years jet-setting with the Oracle, for the next while my travels will be restricted to ones made out of necessity. But the ruins are undeniably astonishing, and as I return to admiring how the setting sun soaks the scenery in a deep, golden glow, I make a mental note to put this place on my list for the future so that someday I can return here with Meander. This temple, as strange as it is, feels somehow connected to us. It's a little bit like discovering an old family heirloom. He deserves to see it for himself.

For a while, I continue to watch the lowering sun. Then, with the rest of the group, I cross the paths around the temple and head up to the base of an open-aired amphitheater before Robbie claps his hands.

"What do you think," he says as we study the old rows of seats stretching up the hillside. "Is it time for us to reveal the hidden underground lair of the Oracle's most elusive headquarters?"

"Headquarters?" Dylan asks. "You're not suggesting the Oracle operates from *here*."

"Got to have a headquarters somewhere," Robbie says. "Why not under an ancient landmark?"

Dylan and I exchange confused glances while Alex rolls her eyes.

"The Oracle's headquarters are in an office building in Athens," she says. Dylan's face crumples while Robbie starts to laugh, and Alex shakes her head with fond exasperation. "We came here so you could see where our organization began," she says to the rest of us. "So you can connect with the past and understand something of how many Senders there have been over the history of mankind."

Disappointing fake-out aside, Alex's words strike a chord in my chest. I face away from the amphitheater and look back down over the massive ruins of the temple, feeling appropriately small and insignificant amidst the ancient buildings of the long-gone civilization where this organization started. Feeling somehow found and lost all at once—feeling completely twisted in every way. Seeing this history makes me kind of want to be a part of it. I suppose I'm a Sender, whether I work for the Oracle or not. But there's a difference between actively contributing and staying firmly out of the way.

I've never been entirely certain where I fit on that spectrum. And now, I've run out of time to figure it out.

49

THE NEXT MORNING, WE CHECK OUT OF THE HOTEL AND MAKE OUR WAY to the much less impressive office building that apparently houses the Oracle headquarters. The place is so undefined—its white waiting room without blue accents or even black furniture—that I'm not convinced this is really where the Oracle does the bulk of its work. But that isn't much of a surprise. This has always been a society of secrets, and there is a lot about Sender life I'm still clueless about. I've never been interested in uncovering conspiracies or solving the mysteries at the heart of the Oracle, and my years at Camp Wanagi have taught me that usually, the answer is simpler—and more chaotic—than any organized explanation my imagination could conjure. Still, there are a few things I'd like to figure out. A few motives I don't want to be left in the dark.

The office building may not be the Oracle's real headquarters. But it *is* where our exit interviews take place, one after another, before we're sent on our way.

Dylan and Sabeena are going back to Chile to see out the final weeks of camp and meet one last time with the new Revenants. Naasir is traveling back to Uganda, while Kornelía is returning to Iceland. And I, thankfully, am given a plane ticket back to London. The slip of paper calms my nerves as I wait for my turn in the interview room, although my stomach stays knotted as I think of saying my firm goodbye to the Oracle. Still, if I make it through this meeting, I can get back where I belong. Whatever transpires inside the room, returning to London is all that really matters right now.

Dylan is the first to have his interview, followed by Naasir.

"Not a big deal," Dylan says when he gets out. "Basically just saying goodbye. We talked about the future and decided on what I already knew. I'm not going to work for the Oracle. But, I'll be around if they ever have need of someone with my spectacular talents."

Dylan leaves while Naasir is in the room. Ten minutes into the second interview, Kornelía sits down beside me.

"I'll be next," she says. She lifts her bag and places it on my lap. "If you open the main pouch, there's something for you."

"For me?" I give her a sideways glance, then unzip the backpack and see a framed picture inside. "The frame?" I ask.

Kornelía nods. "While I was at home, I had my little brother go through my old sketches with me. I… hope this one is right." She smiles. "I described it as best I could."

I pull out the frame and am stunned to see one of Kornelía's sketches inside. It's an old one, before her eyesight failed her. It's of a ghost, one I think I recognize.

"Is… Is this Isabelle?" I ask.

Kornelía nods, her hand rising to glide over the side of the frame. "He got it right, then," she says.

The sketch of Isabelle Levasseur, the ghost we released during our first summer at Camp Wanagi, is one I've never seen before. Kornelía wouldn't let me see, in those days. But I recognize the spirit. The sketch is, years later, still an incredible rendition of the ghost.

"The first spirit I was ever involved in releasing," she says. "The spirit we released together. All five of us."

"It's… Why are you giving it to me?" I ask in bewilderment.

Kornelía's hand moves over the frame and up onto my arm. "You were the one who kept telling me to explore my talent's connection to drawing. You were the one who kept urging me to try channeling too. I didn't want to hear it, then. I was too afraid. But I appreciate what you were trying to do, Cal. I got there, eventually. But even if I didn't always listen to you… I've always appreciated how much you believed in me."

I place the frame on my lap and lean over to wrap my arms around Kornelía. She hugs me back until the door on the side of the lobby opens, and Naasir steps back outside.

Kornelía goes into the room next, and I study the sketch while Naasir talks about his interview and says his goodbyes to Sabeena and me. When he leaves, Kornelía and Draugur come out of the room, and she tells me my turn is next. I say a final goodbye to Kornelía before I place the frame in my bag. Then I collect my things and take a deep breath as I walk into the room.

My earlier assumption of this building being a fake location for the Oracle may not have been entirely accurate. Beyond the boring office-front, I step into a long room decorated in a more grandeur style. High, vaulted ceilings with ornate crown moldings are met by three walls draped in black velvet, and the fourth covered with an elaborate, almost graffiti-style mural of ghosts that resemble the sketch in my backpack. I study the blue, silver, and white figures, paintings of spirits that curve and overlap, stretching the length of the long room. Then my eyes drift to the room's far end, where a simple table stands—and three Senders sit behind it. Before the table, a single chair has been placed for me on the middle of the otherwise empty, dark wood floor.

I drop my bags by the door and make my way over, while the three Senders smile at me from behind the table. One is a man I've never met, who looks somewhere in his forties and has more facial piercings than I can count. The second person is Ms. Kappel, one of my first year camp instructors and the person who hauled Meander and me back to Greenland at the end of last summer. And in the middle, unsurprisingly and welcoming all the same, is Mrs. Buxley.

"Take a seat, Mr. Silver," my instructor says. I do, wiping my sweaty palms on my jeans as I wait to hear what they're going to say.

"You've had an eventful summer," Ms. Kappel

begins. She eyes me with something like tired impatience. "But that is hardly surprising, given what we know of your past behavior."

I resist the temptation to argue or even look sullen at the rebuke. I'm not here to be reprimanded. I'm here, like Dylan said, to say goodbye.

"You always have an eventful summer with us," Mrs. Buxley says in a more even tone while I try to ignore my coiling stomach. "For better or for worse. But today, we're not here to talk about the past. Not with you. Today, we're here to discuss the future."

I swallow, my throat tight with displeasure.

"Do you have any plans?" the man asks before he laughs at his own words. "I hate asking that. Like you're supposed to have it all figured out at the age of—what are you, seventeen?" I nod, and the man shakes his head.

"No one ever has everything figured out," Mrs. Buxley cuts in. I'd assume this was all a practiced conversation, if it weren't for the fact she looks both amused and annoyed by his going off-script. "But in my experience, having something of a plan is a good thing. Even if the direction changes along the way, it's better than being totally aimless."

"*Do* you have any plans?" Ms. Kappel asks me, reeling the discussion back. "You're still in school, yes? Are you going to pursue further education when you're done?"

"Yes," I say. "I'm going to study music." The statement is true, yet the words sound hollow in my ears. I want to study music. But I have no idea what I want to do after that. Because as much as I love playing the violin, the only reason I've become so dedicated to music studies over the last year is because of how it relates to my talent. Because I can't help ghosts if I don't know anything about the songs they play in my head. Because the dead make music for me, and that's not a skillset any normal job is going to require.

The three adult Senders nod at my response. Then Mrs. Buxley steeples her fingers together and gives me a more serious look.

"Have you given any thought to how ghosts might play into your future?" she asks.

I take another deep breath, willing my anxiety to keep to a low simmer. "I…" I falter, insides pinching, palms sweating, and my foot tapping a rough rhythm on the floor. "W-Why do you care?" I fix my gaze on Mrs. Buxley. "Why do you care what I do? What any of us do? Why does the Oracle want us at all?"

I keep my eyes on Mrs. Buxley, because I know she will not dismiss the accusation in my tone. The Oracle has done a lot for me over the years. But I've never really known why.

"The world is crowded with ghosts, which is problematic for the living *and* the dead," Mrs. Buxley says.

"That answer's not good enough," I reply, my nervous words quiet.

My instructor tilts her head to one side, her lips pressed as she considers me.

"Okay," she says after a pause. "Well, I could tell you that we need recruits. That unique talents makes it necessary for us to employ as many Senders as possible to cover as wide a breadth of cases as we can. I could tell you that we are a workplace, like any other, with special qualifications that the majority of people do not possess. I could tell you we specialize in studying Senders as much as we specialize in studying ghosts. I could tell you all of this, and it would, of course, be true. But if you are looking for the simplest answer, Mr. Silver, as to why we do what we do, then I will tell you this—everyone deserves a place in the world. Many people find that place away from all of this, and that is fine. But there are many others who don't feel like their place in the world is adequate, if it exists as well. We can't be that place for everyone. But we can be it for some. For Senders who need somewhere to be supported. To be understood. To be needed. To be normal. That is why we are here. To rid the living world of dead energy. To study our talents and the people who possess them. And to be a place for those who need one." She gives me a steady look. "Is that answer sufficient?"

I nod, and she mimics the movement. Then Mrs. Buxley picks up her pen and studies it as she continues to speak.

"Then shall we resume our discussion?" she asks. "I believe we were just ascertaining your plans for the future."

"I don't want to work for..." I pause, opening and closing my mouth until my lips lie flat and I swallow back the remainder of my mentally practiced speech. I can't make myself say the words. No matter how easy they seemed in my head, I can't bring myself to utter them out loud.

Mrs. Buxley's eyes rise from the pen to me. Then she stands and rounds the table. Her high heels click slowly against the wood floor until she stands directly across from my chair. Then she leans her hands back against the table, looking just as she did whenever she taught one of my courses.

"Your talent is strong and useful," she says. "The Oracle would be happy to have you in our ranks working on cases." I look down at the ground, still hating the idea of doing cases, of being assigned ghost after ghost for the rest of my life. "However," she adds, waiting until I look back up at her before she continues. "Not everyone wants to take the lead in releasing spirits." I nod again, and she gives me a soft smile. "There are *other* options."

"W-What sort of options?" I ask.

"Some Senders choose to stay more or less behind the scenes, as it were," Mrs. Buxley says. "Working as educators, administrators, location scouts…" My curious expression falls at the list of positions that sound even worse than doing my own releases, until Mrs. Buxley speaks again. "Supporters."

The simple word rings in my ears. "What does that mean?"

"It means that being a Sender is hard, and Senders need support." She stops, her look significant as she stares at me. "Some Senders more than others."

My breath hitches, and I sit up straighter in my chair. "What does a supporter do?"

"Support comes in many forms," my instructor says. "In our organization, we have psychiatrists and psychologists. Therapists and counsellors. Mediators. Aides. All number of support staff, many of whom live non-Sender lives and simply help us when needed." She crosses her arms over her chest. "And occasionally, some Senders choose to offer support on a more… *personal* basis. As I said, being a Sender is hard. Physically. Emotionally. Mentally. Some individuals—particularly those with harsher talents—can benefit from a personal support network to help them prepare, tackle, and debrief from spiritual encounters. An assistant, of sorts. Or, rather—a partner."

My heart is racing, and my lips are dry as I stare wide-eyed at Mrs. Buxley. She's not talking in vague terms anymore, and we both know it.

"I'm interested," I say, my words rushed in my excitement of a prospect I didn't think was possible. "What... What would that entail?"

Mrs. Buxley shrugs one shoulder. "We could send you case files to review and grant you access to databases for your own research. We can setup virtual check-ins and help cover travel costs if in-person meetings are required. On the occasion your talents overlap, you could work in a partnership for a particular case. Everything can be done in conjunction with your life in Canada. Or," she continues, "we can help you get set up in a more central location. Say—London, perhaps?"

London. My breath hitches again, this time so forcefully I make a noticeable gasp for air. The thought of leaving Canada had never actually occurred to me. For months I've been collecting university brochures, planning which school I'll attend in Ontario. But this...

"What about school?" I ask.

Mrs. Buxley spares me the knowing smirk I probably deserve. "If I'm not mistaken, there are several schools in London. Some might even have decent music programs. You could attend school and engage with the Oracle in your off time. Or we could work on developing an educational path that combines your musical studies with a program that would benefit you in a Sender-specific support role."

"I have a friend who's a music therapist," the man suddenly cuts in.

I look at him in stunned silence. I had no idea that "music therapist" was a career that even existed, but I feel overwhelmed by the possibility of what such a profession might offer. I don't always know what to say or how to help people. But I *have* helped in the past, occasionally. And helping feels good. It feels better than taking charge and barreling into the paranormal simply because I can. I don't want to be an action hero or some super-powered ghost detective. But I could learn how to be better at helping the ones who are. Apparently, I could even learn to help them with music.

"Nothing has to be set in stone," Mrs. Buxley says. "But there are options. Options that could benefit you. And others."

I glance up at Mrs. Buxley and try not to look like an overeager idiot as I nod.

"Yes," I say. "Yes, I'll do it."

Her smile is fond as she circles back to her seat. "I'm very happy to hear that, Callum. We'll draw up a plan and start our conversations." She picks something up from the desk and holds it out to me. I stand up and cross to the table to take what turns out to be a pin— its design that of the letter S entwined with the wavy form of a ghost. "Welcome, officially, to the Oracle of Senders, Mr. Silver," she says. She smiles, then hands me a second, identical pin. "Perhaps you can deliver this to your partner when you get back."

I nod, my smile tugging into a grin. Grabbing the second pin, I hold them both tight in my fist as I turn from the table and head back towards the door.

50

I grip the handles on the back of Meander's wheelchair, surveying the hospital room to make sure we've collected all of our belongings.

"Yeah," he says. "Did you text Liam the address?"

"Mhmm." Meander's brother visited him while I was in Greece. He's going to collect Meander's things from their mom's place to drop off at the new apartment. "He'll be by tomorrow."

"Do you think this place will have any food?" Meander asks.

"No idea," I say. "Robbie said it's furnished. Maybe they provided food too. If not, I'll go to the shop after we get settled."

Meander wasn't happy when I first told him what happened in Greece. But once I assured him I hadn't been tricked into the position and that I was, indeed, still going to study music, he let our new reality sink in. I stood by his bed as he stared at the Oracle pin. Then his eyes began to shine, his smile brightened, and he grabbed me so fiercely I fell half on top of him and nearly ripped out his IV as he pulled me into a kiss.

Now, I unstop the break and push the wheelchair forward, overestimating the force I'll need and moving too fast.

"You're going to run my foot into at least five walls before we get there, aren't you?" Meander asks.

"I will not," I say. "I'm an excellent driver."

"You've never driven," he says.

"Shut up. I go grocery shopping with my parents sometimes. I'm an expert at steering the cart."

Meander groans, clutching my violin case tighter on his lap. "At least six walls."

I give his head a push, and he laughs before leaning back to look at me. "Let's just hope the elevator works when we get to this flat. I can't believe they've picked a place on the thirteenth floor."

"Let's just hope the place isn't haunted," I amend. "With our luck, we'll pick up a ghost on floor twelve."

"We'd better get a move on then. The haunted, cursed, probably rat-infested flat awaits our arrival."

I smirk. "Rat-infested? You really have no faith in the Oracle, do you?"

"I don't have faith in anyone," Meander says with a smile. "Except myself. And you."

My smirk turns into a grin as his eyes catch mine, and I lean over the back of the wheelchair to give him an upside-down kiss.

Four years. Six countries. Ten releases. Exorcism, death, wounded bodies and minds. Wounded hearts as well. It's all combined, good and bad, extraordinary and every day, until it's boiled down to this. Four years ago, I joined the Oracle of Senders with no idea how they were going to shape my life. Four years ago, I came to Camp Wanagi alone. Now, I'm leaving camp for the last time, knowing that the Oracle will probably always be a part of my life. And now, I'm not alone. Not anymore.

Meander reaches a hand up to my neck, pulling me closer. I kiss him as deeply as our awkward angle allows, mindful of his bruises but reveling all the same in his smell, his taste, the feel of his always warm touch on my skin. I kiss him as my stomach swoops and my head fills with the magnitude of what we've done together. And of what we'll be able to accomplish next.

I kiss him until I lean too far forward and send the wheelchair rolling so his foot bumps into the doorframe.

"Sorry," I mumble, while Meander chuckles.

"One down, five more to go," he teases. I stand up straight, and he closes his eyes, head tilted back with a smile. "Onto the rat-infested, cursed, haunted flat?"

I ruffle the top of his head and back the wheelchair up so we can exit the room. "Maybe we could give it a different name?" I suggest.

"What were you thinking?" Meander asks.

I study his content expression as I straighten the chair's wheels. "How about… home?"

Meander opens his eyes, the green and brown hazel bright as he reaches up to grab my hand. "Okay, Cal," he says. He places a soft kiss to my fingers before releasing me so I can push the chair forward. "Let's go home."

ABOUT THE AUTHOR

MERE JOYCE is a Canadian author of books for young adults. Her writing includes contemporary tales, high-action mysteries, fairy-tale fantasies, and her personal favorite–ghost stories. When she's not writing, Mere can be found teaching library studies, or spending time at home with her family in Nova Scotia. She's also been known to be a selective, yet highly enthusiastic fangirl.

Find her online at:

MEREJOYCE.COM